Wilhelmine von Hillern, Mary Joanna Safford

On the cross

A romance of the passion play at Oberammergau

Wilhelmine von Hillern, Mary Joanna Safford

On the cross
A romance of the passion play at Oberammergau

ISBN/EAN: 9783742877024

Manufactured in Europe, USA, Canada, Australia, Japa

Cover: Foto ©Andreas Hilbeck / pixelio.de

Manufactured and distributed by brebook publishing software
(www.brebook.com)

Wilhelmine von Hillern, Mary Joanna Safford

On the cross

ON THE CROSS

A ROMANCE

OF THE

PASSION PLAY AT OBERAMMERGAU

BY

WILHELMINE VON HILLERN

AUTHOR OF " ERNESTINE," " THE HOUR WILL COME," ETC., ETC.

FROM THE GERMAN

BY

MARY J. SAFFORD

NEW YORK
GEO. GOTTSBERGER PECK, Publisher
11 MURRAY STREET
—
1893

TO

HERR JOHANNES DIEMER,

THE RENOWNED DELIVERER OF THE PROLOGUE IN THE PASSION PLAYS
OF THE LAST DECADE, A TRUE SON OF AMMERGAU, IN WHOSE
UNASSUMING PERSON DWELLS THE CALM, DEEP SOUL OF
THE ARTIST, THE LOYAL SYMPATHIZING FRIEND, IN
WHOSE PEACEFUL HOME I FOUND THE QUIET
AND THE MOOD I NEEDED TO COMPLETE
THIS WORK, IT IS NOW DEDICATED,
WITH GRATEFUL ESTEEM, BY

THE AUTHORESS.

OBERAMMERGAU, MAY, 1890.

CONTENTS.

INTRODUCTION.

It was in the Garden of Gethsemane that the risen Son of God showed Himself, as a simple gardener, to the penitent sinner. The miracle has become a pious tradition. It happened long, long ago, and no eye has ever beheld Him since. Even when the risen Lord walked among the men and women of His own day, only those saw Him who wished to do so.

But those who wish to see Him, see Him now; and those who wish to seek Him, find Him now.

The Garden of Gethsemane has disappeared—the hot sun of the East has withered it. All things are subject to change. The surface of the earth alters and where the olive tree once grew green and the cedar stretched its leafy roof above the head of the Redeemer and the Penitent, there is nothing now save dead, withered leafage.

But the Garden blooms once more in a cool, shady valley among the German mountains. Modern Gethsemane bears the name of Oberammergau. As the sun pursues its course from East to West, so the salvation which came from the East has made its way across the earth to the West. There, in the veins of young and vigorous nations, still flow the living streams that water the seeds of faith on which the miracle is nourished, and the stunted mountain pine which has sprung from the hard rocks of the Ettal Mountain is transformed to a palm tree, the poor habitant of the little mountain village to a God. It is change, and yet constancy amid the change.

The world and its history also change in the passage of the centuries. The event before which the human race sank prostrate, as the guards once did when the risen Christ burst the gates of the tomb, gradually passed into partial oblivion. The thunder with which the veil of the temple was rent in twain died away in the misty distance; heaven closed forever behind the ascended Lord, the stars pursued their old courses in undisturbed regularity; revelations were silent. Men rubbed their eyes as though waking from a dream and began to discuss what portion was truth and what illusion. The strife lasted for centuries. One tradition overthrew another, one creed crowded out another. With sword in hand and the trumpet of the Judgment Day the *Ecclesia Militans* established the dogma, enforced unity in faith. But peace did not last long under the rule of the church. The Reformation again divided the Christian world, the Thirty Years War, the most terrible religious conflict the earth has ever witnessed began, and in the fury of the battle the combatants forgot the *cause* of the warfare. Amid the streams of blood, the clouds of smoke rising from burning cities and villages, the ruins of shattered altars, the cross, the holy emblem for which the battle raged, vanished, and when it was raised again, it was still but an emblem of warfare, no longer a symbol of peace.

There is a single spot of earth where, untouched by the tumult of the world, sheltered behind the lofty, inhospitable wall of a high mountain, the idea of Christianity has been preserved in all its simplicity and purity—Oberammergau. As God once suffered the Saviour of the World to be born in a manger, among poor shepherds, He seems to have extended His protecting hand over this secluded nook and reserved the poor mountaineers to repeat the miracle. Concealed behind the steep Ettal mountain was a monastery where, from ancient times, the beautiful arts had been sedulously fostered.

One of the monks was deeply grieved because, in the outside world, iconoclasm was rudely shaking the old forms and, in blind fear, even rejecting religious art as "Romish." As no holy image would be tolerated; the Saviour and His Saints must disappear entirely from the eyes of men. Then, in his distress, the inspiration came that a sacred drama, performed by living beings, could produce a more powerful effect than word or symbol. So it was determined in the monastery that one should be enacted.

The young people in the neighborhood, who had long been schooled by the influence of the learned monks to appreciate beauty, were soon trained to act legends and biblical poems. With increasing skill they gained more and more confidence, till at last their holy zeal led them to show mankind the Redeemer Himself, the Master of the world, in His own bodily form, saying to erring humanity : " Lo, thus He was and thus He will be forever."

And while in the churches paintings and relics were torn from the walls and crucifixes destroyed, the first Passion play was performed, A. D. 1634, under the open sky in the churchyard of Oberammergau—for this spot, on account of its solemn associations, was deemed the fitting place for the holy work. The disgraced image of love, defiled by blood and flames, once more rose in its pure beauty! Living, breathing! The wounds inflicted more than a thousand years before again opened, fresh drops of blood trickled from the brow torn by its diadem of thorns, again the " Continue ye in My love " fell from the pallid lips of the Lamb of God, and what Puritanism had destroyed in its *dead* form was born anew in a *living* one. But, amid the confusion and roar of battle, the furious yells of hate, no one heard the gentle voice in the distant nook beyond the mountains.

The message of peace died away, the Crucified One shed His blood unseen.

Years passed, the misery ot the people constantly increased, lands were ravaged, the ranks of the combatants thinned.

At last the warriors began to be paralyzed, the raging storm subsided and pallid fear stared blankly at the foes who had at last gained their senses—the plague, that terrible Egyptian Sphinx, lured by the odor of corruption emanating from the long war, stole over the earth, and those at whom she gazed with the black fiery eyes of her torrid zone, sank beneath it like the scorched grass when the simoom sweeps over the desert.

Silence fell, the silence of the grave, for wherever this spectre stalks, death follows.

Fear reconciled enemies and made them forget their rancor in union against the common foe, the cruel, invincible plague. They gazed around them for some helping hand, and once more turned to that over which they had so long quarrelled. Then amid the deathlike stillness of the barren fields, the empty houses, the denuded churches, and the desolated land, they at last heard the little bell behind the Ettal mountain, which every decade summoned the Christian world to the Passion Play, for this was the vow taken by the Ammergau peasants to avert the plague and the divine wrath. Again the ever patient Saviour extended His arms, crying: " Come unto Me, all ye who are weary and heavy laden !" And they did come. They threw themselves at His feet, the wearied, hunted earthlings, stained with dust and blood, and He comforted and refreshed them, while they again recognized Him and learned to understand the meaning of His sacrifice.

Those who thus saw Him and received the revelation announced it to others, who flocked thither from far and near till the little church-yard of Oberammergau became too narrow, and could no longer contain the throngs; the open fields became a sacred theatre to receive the pilgrims, who longed to behold the Redeemer's face.

And, strangely enough, all who took part in the sacred play seemed consecrated, the plague passed them by, Ammergau alone was spared.

So the pious seed grew slowly, often with periods when it stood still, but the watchful eye can follow it in history.

Peace at last came to the world. Purer airs blew. The Egyptian hyena, satiated, left the ravaged fields, new life bloomed from the graves, and this new life knew naught of the pangs and sufferings of the old. From the brutality and corruption of the long war, the new generation longed for more refined manners, culture, and the pleasures of life. But, as usual after such periods of deprivation and calamity, one extreme followed another. The desire for more refined manners and education led to hyperculture, the love of pleasure into epicureanism and luxury, grace into coquetry, mirth into frivolity. Then came the so-called age of gallantry. The foil took the place of the sword, the lace jabot of the leather jerkin, the smoke of battle gave way to the clouds of powder scattered by heads nodding in every direction.

Masked shepherds and shepherdesses danced upon the graves of a former generation, a new Arcadia was created in apish imitation and peopled with grimacing creatures who tripped about on tiptoe in their high-heeled shoes. Instead of the mediæval representations of martyrs and emaciated saints appeared the nude gods and cupids of a Watteau and his school. Grace took the place of majesty. Instead of moral law, men followed the easy code of convenience and everything was allowable which did not transgress its rules. Thus arose a generation of thoughtless pleasure seekers, which bore within itself a moral pestilence that, in contrast with the "Black Death," might be termed the "Rosy Death" for it breathed upon the cheeks of all whom it attacked the rosy flush of a fever which wasted more slowly, but none the less surely.

And through this rouged, dancing, skipping age, with the click of its high-heeled shoes, its rustling hooped petticoats, its amorous glances and heaving bosoms, the chaste figure of the Man of Sorrows, with a terrible solemnity upon his pallid brow, again and again trod the stage of Ammergau, and whoever beheld Him dropped the flowing bowl of pleasure, while the laugh died on his lips.

Again history and the judgment of the world moved forward. The "Rosy Death" had decomposed and poisoned all the healthful juices of society and corrupted the very heart of the human race—morality, faith, and philosophy, everything which makes men manly, had gradually perished unobserved in the thoughtless whirl. The tinsel and apish civilization no longer sufficed to conceal the brute in human nature. It shook off every veil and stood forth in all its nakedness. The modern deluge, the French Revolution burst forth. Murder, anarchy, the delirium of fever swept over the earth in every form of horror.

Again came a change, a transformation to the lowest depths of corruption. Grace now yielded to brutality, beauty to ugliness, the divine to the cynical. Altars were overthrown, religion was abjured, the earth trembled under the mass of destroyed traditions.

But from the turmoil of the throng, fiercely rending one another, from the smoke and exhalations of this conflagration of the world, yonder in the German Garden of Gethsemane again rose victoriously, like a Phœnix from its ashes, the denied, rejected God, and the undefiled sun of Ammergau wove a halo of glory around the sublime figure which hung high on the cross.

It was a quiet victory, of which the frantic mob were ignorant; for they saw only the foe confronting them, not the one battling above. The latter was vanquished long ago,

He was deposed, and that settled the matter. The people in their sovereignty can depose and set up gods at pleasure, and when once dethroned, they no longer exist; they are hurled into Tartarus. And as men can not do without a god, they create an idol.

The country groaned beneath the iron stride of the Emperor and, without wishing or knowing it, he became the avenger of the God in whose place he stood. For, as the Thirty Years War ended under the scourge of the pestilence, and the age of mirth and gallantry under the lash of the Revolution, the Revolution yielded to the third scourge, the self-created idol!

He, the man with compressed lips and brow sombre with thought, ruled the unchained elements, became lord of the anarchy, and dictated laws to a universe. But with iron finger he tore open the veins of humanity to mark upon the race the brand of slavery. The world bled from a thousand wounds, and upon each he marked the name "Napoleon."

Then, wan as the moon floats in the sky when the glow of the setting sun is blazing in the horizon, the sovereign of the world in his bloody splendor confronted the pallid shadow of the Crucified One, also robed in a royal mantle, still wet with the blood He had voluntarily shed. They gazed silently at each other—but the usurper turned pale.

At last, at the moment he imagined himself most like Him, God hurled the rival god into the deepest misery and disgrace. The enemy of the world was conquered, and popular hatred, so long repressed, at last freed from the unbearable restraint, poured forth upon the lonely grave at St. Helena its foam of execration and curses. Then the conqueror in Oberammergau extended His arms in pardon, saying to him also: "Verily I say unto thee, To-day shalt thou be with me in paradise."

A time of peace now dawned, the century of *thought*. After the great exertions of the war of liberation, a truce in political life followed, and the nations used it to make up for what they had lost in the development of civilization during the period of political strife. A flood of ideas inundated the world. All talent, rejoicing in the mental activity which had so long lain dormant, was astir. There was rivalry and conflict for the prize in every department. The rising generation, conscious of newly awakening powers, dared enterprise after enterprise and with each waxed greater. With increasing production, the power of assimilation also increased. Everything grand created in other centuries was drawn into the circle of their own nation as if just discovered. That for which the enlightened minds of earlier days had vainly toiled, striven, bled, now bloomed in luxuriant harvests, and the century erected monuments to those who had been misjudged and adorned them with the harvest garland garnered from the seeds which they had sowed in tears.

What Galvani and Salomon de Cäus, misunderstood and unheard, had planned, now made their triumphal passage across the earth as a panting steam engine or a flashing messenger of light, borne by and bearing ideas.

The century which produced a Schiller and a Goethe first understood a Shakespeare, Sophocles and Euripides rose from the graves where they had lain more than a thousand years, archæology brought the buried world of Homer from beneath the earth, a Canova, a Thorwaldsen, a Cornelius, Kaulbach, and all the great masters of the Renaissance of our time, took up the brushes and chisels of Phidias, Michael Angelo, Raphael, and Rubens, which had so long lain idle. What Aristotle had taught a thousand, and Winckelmann and Lessing a hundred years before, the knowledge of the laws of art, the appreciation of the beautiful, was no longer mere dead capital in the hands of learned men, but circulated in the throbbing veins of a vigorously developing civilization; it demanded and obtained the highest goal.

The circle between the old and the new civilization has closed, every chasm has been bridged. There is an alternate action of old and new forces, a common labor of all the nations and the ages, as if there was no longer any division of time and space, as if there was but one eternal art, one eternal science. Ascending humanity has trodden matter under foot, conquered science, made manufactures useful, and transfigured art.

But this light which has so suddenly flamed through the world also casts its shadows. Progress in art and science matures the judgment, but judgment becomes criticism and criticism negation. The dualism which permeates all creation, the creative and the destructive power, the principle of affirmation and of denial, cannot be shut out even now, but must continue the old contest which has never yet been decided. Critical analysis opposes faith, materialism wars against idealism, pessimism contends with optimism. The human race has reached the outermost limit of knowledge, but this does not content it in its victorious career, it wishes to break through and discover *the God* concealed behind. Even the heart of a God must not escape the scalpel which nothing withstood. But the barrier is impenetrable. And one party, weary of the fruitless toil, pulls back the aspiring ones. "Down to matter, whence you came. What are you seeking? Science has attained the highest goal, she has discovered the protoplasm whence all organism proceeded. What is the Creator of modern times? A physiological—chemical, vital function within the substance of a cell. Will ye pray to this, suffer for this, ye fools?"

Others turn in loathing from this cynical interpretation of scientific results and throw themselves into the arms of beauty, seeking in it the divinity, and others still wait, battling between earth and heaven, in the dim belief of being nearest to the goal.

It is a tremendous struggle, as though the earth must burst under the enormous pressure of power demanding room, irreconcilable contrasts.

Then amid the heat of the lecture rooms, the throng of students of art and science, comes a long-forgotten voice from the days of our childhood! And the straining eyes suddenly turn from the teachers and the dissecting tables, from the glittering visions of art and the material world to the stage of Oberammergau and the Passion Play.

There stands the unassuming figure with the crown of thorns and the sorrowful, questioning gaze. And with one accord their hearts rush to meet Him and, as the son who has grown rich in foreign lands, after having eaten and enjoyed everything, longs to return to the poverty of his home and falls repentantly at the feet of his forsaken father, the human race, in the midst of this intoxication of knowledge and please ure, sinks sobbing before the pale flower of Christianity and longingly extends its arms toward the rude wooden cross on which it blooms!

That powerful thinker, Max Müller, says in his comparative study of religions:* "When do we feel the blessings of our country more warmly and truly than when we return from abroad? It is the same with regard to religion." That fact is apparent here! It is an indisputable verity that, at the precise period when art and science have attained their highest stages of development, the Oberammergau Passion Play enjoys a degree of appreciation never bestowed before, that during this critical age, from decade to decade, people flock to the Passion Play in ever increasing throngs. Not only the uncultivated and ignorant, nay, the most cultured—artists and scholars, statesmen and monarchs. The poor village no longer has room to shelter all its guests; it is positively startling to see the flood of human beings pour in on the evening before the commencement of the play, stifling, inundating everything. And then it is marvellous to notice how quiet it is on the morning of the play, as it flows into the bare room called the theatre, how it seems as it were to grow calm, as if every storm within or without was subdued under the influence of those simple words, now more than two thousand years old. How wonderful it is to watch the people fairly holding their breath to listen to the simple drama for seven long hours without heeding the time which is far beyond the limit our easily wearied nerves are accustomed to bear.

What is it, for whose sake the highest as well as the lowest, the richest and the poorest, prince and peasant, would sleep on a layer of straw, without a murmur, if no bed could be had? Why will the most pampered endure hunger and thirst, the most delicate heat and cold, the most timid fearlessly undertake the hard journey across the Ettal mountain? Is it mere curiosity to hear a number of poor wood-carvers, peasants, and wood-cutters repeat under the open sky, exposed to sun and rain, in worse German than is heard at school the same old story which has already been told a thousand times, as the enemies of the Passion Play say? Would this bring people every ten years from half the inhabited world, from far and

---

* "Chips from a German Workshop." Vol. I. ",Essays on the Science of Religion."

near, from South and North, from the mountains and the valleys, from palaces and huts, across sea and land ? Certainly not ? What is it then ? A miracle ?

Whoever has seen the Passion Play understands it, but it is difficult to explain the mystery to those who have not.

The deity remains concealed from our earthly vision and unattainable, like the veiled statue of Sais. Every attempt to raise this veil by force is terribly avenged.

What is gained by those modern Socinians and Adorantes who, with ill-feigned piety, seek to drag the mystery to light and make the God a *human being*, in order to worship in the wretched puppet *themselves ?* Even if they beheld Him face to face, they would still see themselves only, and He would cry : " You are like the spirit which you understand, not me."

And what do the Pantheists gain who make man *God*, in order to embrace in Him the unattainable ? Sooner or later they will perceive that they have mistaken the *effects* for the *cause*, and the form for the essence. Loathing and disappointment will be their lot, as it is the lot of all who have nothing but—human beings.

But those to whom the visible is only the *symbol* of the *invisible* which teaches them from the effect to learn the cause, will, with unerring logical correctness, pass from the form to the essence, from the *illusion* to the *truth*.

That is the marvel of the modern Gethsemane, which this book will narrate.

CHAPTER I.

SOLEMN and lofty against the evening sky towers the Kofel, the land-mark and protecting rock-bulwark of Oberammergau, bearing aloft its solitary cross, like a threatening hand uplifted in menace to confront an advancing foe with the symbol of victory.

Twilight is gathering, and the dark shadow of the mighty protector stretches far across the quiet valley. The fading glow of sunset casts a pallid light upon the simple cross which has stood on the mountain peak for centuries, frequently renewed but always of the same size, so that it can be seen a long distance off by the throngs who journey upward from the valley, gazing longingly across the steep, inhospitable mountains toward the goal of the toilsome pilgrimage.

It is Friday. A long line of carriages is winding like a huge serpent up the Ettal mountain. Amid the throng, two very handsome landaus are especially conspicuous. The first is drawn by four horses in costly harnesses adorned with a coronet, which prance gaily in the slow progress, as if the ascent of the Ettal mountain was but pastime for animals of their breed. In the equipage, which is open, sit a lady and a gentleman, pale, listless, uninterested in their surroundings and apparently in each other; the second one contains a maid, a man servant, and on the box the courier, with the pompous, official manner, which proclaims to the world that the family he has the honor of serving and in whose behalf he pays the highest prices, is an aristocratic one. The mistress of this elegant establishment, spite of her downcast eyes and almost lifeless air, is a woman of such remarkable beauty that it is apparent even amidst the confusion of veils and wraps. Blonde hair, as soft as silk, clusters in rings around her brow and diffuses a warm glow over a face white as a tea rose, intellectual, yet withal wonderfully tender and sensuous in its outlines. Suddenly, as though curious to penetrate the drooping lids and see the eyes they concealed, the sun bursts through a rift in the clouds, throwing a golden bridge of rays from mountain to mountain. Now the lashes are raised to return the greeting, revealing sparkling dark eyes of a mysterious color, varying every instant as they follow the shimmering rays that glide along the cliff. Then something flashes from a half-concealed cave and the beams linger a moment on a pale face. It is an image of Christ carved in wood which, with uplifted hand, bids the new comers welcome. But those who are now arriving do not understand its language, the greeting remains unanswered.

The sunbeams glide farther on as if saying, "If this is not the Christ you are seeking, perhaps it is he?" And now —they stop. On a rugged peak, illumined by a halo of light, stands a figure, half concealed by the green branches, gazing with calm superiority at the motley, anxious crowd below. He has removed his hat and, heated by the rapid walk, is wiping the perspiration from his brow. Long black locks parted in the middle, float back from a grave, majestic face with a black beard and strangely mournful black, far-seeing eyes. The hair, tossed by the wind, is caught by a thorny branch which sways above the prematurely furrowed brow. The sharp points glow redly in the brilliant sunset light, as if crimsoned with blood from the head which rests dreamily against the trunk. A tremor runs through the form of the woman below; she suddenly sits erect, as though roused from sleep. The wandering rays which sought her eyes also lead her gaze to those of the solitary man above, and on this golden bridge two sparkling glances meet. Like two pedestrians who cannot avoid each other on a narrow path, they look and pause. They grasp and hold each other—one must yield, for neither will let the other pass.

Then the sunbeam pales, the bridge has fallen, and the apparition vanishes in the forest shadows.

"Did you see that?" the lady asked her companion, who had also glanced up at the cliff.

"What should I have seen?"

"Why—that—that—" she paused, uncertain what words to choose. She was going to say, "that man up there," but the sentence is too prosaic, yet she can find no other and

says merely, " him up there !" Her companion, glancing sky-
ward, shakes his head.

" *Him* up there ! I really believe, Countess, that the air
of Ammergau is beginning to affect you. Apparently you
already have religious hallucinations—or we will say, in the
language of this hallowed soil, heavenly visions !"

The countess leans silently back in her corner—the cold,
indifferent expression returns to the lips which just parted in
so lovely a smile. " But what did you see ? At least tell me,
since I am not fortunate enough to be granted such visions,"
her companion adds with kindly irony. " Or was it too
sublime to be communicated to such a base worldling as I ?"

" Yes," she says curtly, covering her eyes with her hand,
as if to shut out the fading sunset glow in order to recall the
vision more distinctly. Then she remains silent.

Night gradually closes in, the panting train of horses has
reached the village. Now the animals are urged into a trot
and the drivers turn the solemn occasion into a noisy tumult.
The vehicles jolt terribly in the ruts, the cracking of whips, the
rattle of wheels, the screams of frightened children and poul-
try, the barking of dogs, blend in a confused din, and that
nothing may be wanting to complete it, a howling gust of
wind sweeps through the village, driving the drifting clouds
into threatening masses.

" This is all we lacked—rain too !" grumbled the gentleman. "Shall I have the carriage closed ?"

" No," replied the Countess, opening her umbrella.
" Who would have thought it; the sun was shining ten minutes ago !"

" Yes, the weather changes rapidly in the mountains. I
saw the shower rising. While you were admiring some
worthy wood-cutter up yonder as a heavenly apparition, I
was watching the approaching tempest." He draws the
travelling rug, which has slipped down, closer around the
lady and himself. " Come what may, I am resigned; when
we are in Rome, we must follow the Roman customs. Who
would not go through fire and water for you, Countess ?"
He tries to take her hand, but cannot find it among the
shawls and wraps. He bites his lips angrily; he had expected that the hand he sought would gratefully meet his in

return for so graceful an expression of loyalty! Large drops
of rain beat into his face.

"Not even a clasp of the hand in return for the infernal
journey to this peasant hole," he mutters.

The carriages thunder past the church, the flowers and
crosses on the graves in the quiet church-yard tremble with
the shaking of the ground. The lamps in the parsonage are
already lighted, the priest comes to the window and gazes
quietly at the familiar spectacle. "Poor travellers! Out in
such a storm!"

One carriage after another turns down a street or stops before a house. The Countess and her companion alone have
not yet reached their destination. Meantime it has grown
perfectly dark. The driver is obliged to stop to shut up the
carriage and light the lantern, for the rain and darkness have
become so dense and the travellers are drenched. An icy
wind, which always accompanies a thunderstorm in the
mountain, blows into their faces till they can scarcely keep
their eyes open. The servant, unable to see in the gloom,
is clumsy in closing the carriage, the hand-bags fall down
upon the occupants; the driver can scarcely hold the horses,
which are frightened by the crowds in pursuit of lodgings.
He is not familiar with the place and, struggling to restrain the
plunging four-in-hand, enquires the way in broken sentences
from the box, and only half catches the answers, which are
indistinct in the tumult. Meantime the other servants have
arrived. The Countess orders the courier to drive on with
the second carriage and take possession of the rooms which
have been engaged. The man, supposing it is an easy matter
to find the way in so small a place, moves forward. The
Countess can scarcely control her ill humor.

"An abominable journey—the horses overheated by the
ascent of the mountain and now this storm. And the lamps
won't burn, the wind constantly blows them out. You were
right, Prince, we ought to have taken a hired—" She does not
finish the sentence, for the ray from one of the carriage lamps,
which has just been lighted with much difficulty, falls upon a
swiftly passing figure, which looks almost supernaturally tall
in the uncertain glimmer. Long, black locks, dripping with
moisture, are blown by the wind from under his broad-brimmed

hat. He has evidently been surprised by the storm without an umbrella and is hurrying home—not timidly and hastily, like a person to whom a few drops of rain, more or less, is of serious importance, but rather like one who does not wish to be accosted. The countess cannot see his face, he has already passed, but she distinguishes the outlines of the slender, commanding figure in the dark dress, noticing with a rapid glance the remarkably elastic gait, and an involuntary: "There he goes again!" escapes her lips aloud. Obeying a sudden impulse, she calls to the servant: "Quick, ask the gentleman yonder the way to the house of Andreas Gross, where we are going."

The servant follows the retreating figure a few steps and shouts, "Here, you—" The stranger pauses a moment, half turns his head, then, as if the abrupt summons could not possibly be meant for *him*, moves proudly on without glancing back a second time.

The servant timidly returns. A feeling of shame overwhelms the countess, as though she had committed the blunder of ordering him to address a person of high rank travelling incognito.

"The gentleman wouldn't hear me," says the lackey apologetically, much abashed. "Very well," his mistress answers, glad that the darkness conceals her blushes. A flash of lightning darts from the sky and a sudden peal of thunder frightens the horses. "Drive on," the countess commands; the lackey springs on the box, the carriage rolls forward—a few yards further and the dark figure once more appears beside the vehicle, walking calmly on amid the thunder and lightning, and merely turns his head slightly toward the prancing horses.

The equipage dashes by—the countess leans silently back on the cushions, and shows no further desire to look out.

"Tell me, Countess Madeleine," asks the gentleman whom she has just addressed as "Prince," "what troubles you to-day?"

The countess laughs. "Dear me, how solemnly you put the question! What should trouble me?"

"I cannot understand you," the prince continued. "You treat me coldly and grow enthusiastic over a vision of the imagination which already draws from you the exclamation:

'There he is *again!*' I cannot help thinking what an uncertain possession is the favor of a lady whose imagination kindles so easily."

"This is charming," the countess tried to jest. "My prince jealous—of a phantom?"

"That is just it. If a *phantom* can produce such variations in the temperature of your heart toward me, how must my hopes stand?"

"Dear Prince, you know that whether with or without a phantom, I could never yet answer this question which Your Highness frequently condescends to ask me."

"I believe, Countess, that one always stands between us! You pursue some unknown ideal which you do not find in me, the realist, who has nothing to offer you save prosaic facts— his hand, his principality, and an affection for which unhappily he lacks poetic phrases."

"You exaggerate, Prince, and are growing severe. There is a touch of truth—I am always honest—yet, as you know, you are the most favored of all my suitors. Still it is true that an unknown disputes precedence with you. This rival is but the man of my imagination—but the world contains no one like my ideal, so you have nothing to fear."

"What ideal do you demand, Countess, that no one can attain it?"

"Ah! a very simple one, yet you conventional natures will never understand it. It is the simplicity of the lost Paradise to which you can never return. I am by nature a lover of the ideal—I am enthusiastic and need enthusiasm; but you call me a visionary when I am in the most sacred earnest. I yearn for a husband who believes in my ideal, I want no one from whom I must conceal it in order to avoid ridicule, and thus be unable to be true to my highest self. He whom my soul seeks must be at once a man and a child—a man in character and a child in heart. But where in our modern life is such a person to be found? Where is gentleness without feeble sentimentality? Where is there enthusiasm without fantastic vagueness, where simplicity of heart without narrowness of mind? Whoever possesses a manly character and a strong intellect cannot escape the demands which science and politics impose, and this detracts from the emotional life, gives prominent development to concrete thought, makes men realistic and critical. But of all who suffer from these defects of our time, you are the best, Prince!" she adds, smilingly.

"That is sorry comfort," murmurs the prince. "It is a peculiar thing to have an invisible rival; who will guarantee that some person may not appear who answers to the description?"

"That is the reason I have not yet given you my consent," replies the countess, gravely.

Her companion sighs heavily, makes no reply, but gazes steadfastly into the raging storm. After a time he says, softly, "If I did not love you so deeply, Countess Madeleine—"

"You would not bear with me so long, would you?" asks the countess, holding out her hand as if beseeching pardon.

This one half unconscious expression of friendship disarms the irritated man.—He bends over the slender little hand and raises it tenderly to his lips.

"She must yet be mine!" he says under his breath, by way of consolation, like all men whose hopes are doubtful. "I will even dare the battle with a phantom."

CHAPTER II.

OLD AMMERGAU.

AT last, after a long circuit and many enquiries, the goal was gained. The dripping, sorely shaken equipage stopped with two wheels in a ditch filled with rain water, whose overflow flooded the path to the house. The courier and maid seemed to have missed their way, too, for the second carriage was not there. People hurried out of the low doorway shading small flickering candles with their hands. The countess shrank back. What strange faces these peasants had! An old man with a terribly hang-dog countenance, long grey hair, a pointed Jewish beard, sharp hooked nose, and sparkling eyes! And two elderly women, one short and fat, with prominent eyes and black curling hair, the other a tall, thin, odd-looking person with tangled coal-black hair, hooked nose, and glittering black eyes.

In the mysterious shadows cast by the wavering lights upon the sharply cut faces, the whole group looked startlingly like a band of gypsies.

"Oh! are these Ammergau people?" whispered the countess in a disappointed tone.

"Does Gross, the wood-carver, live here?" the prince enquired.

"Yes," was the reply. "Gross, the stone-cutter. Have you engaged rooms here?"

"We wrote from Tegernsee for lodgings. The Countess von Wildenau," answered the prince.

"Oh yes, yes! Everything is ready! The lady will lodge with us; the carriage and servants can go to the old post-house. I have the honor to bid you good evening," said the old man. "I am sorry you have had such bad weather. But we have a great deal of rain here."

The prince alighted—the water splashed high under his feet.

"Oh Sephi, bring a board, quick; the countess cannot get out here!" cried the old man with eager deprecation of the discomfort threatening the lady. Sephi, the tall, thin woman, dragged a plank from the garden, while a one-eyed dog began to bark furiously.

The plank was laid down, but instantly sunk under the water, and the countess was obliged to wade through the flood. As she alighted, she felt as if she should strike her head against the edge of the overhanging roof—the house was so low. Fresco paintings, dark with age, appeared to stretch and writhe in distorted shapes in the flickering light. The place seemed more and more dismal to the countess.

"Shall I carry you across?" asked the prince.

"Oh no!" she answered reprovingly, while her little foot sought the bottom of the pool. The ice-cold water covered her delicate boot to the ankle. She had been so full of eager anticipation, in such a poetic mood, and prosaic reality dealt her a blow in the face. She shivered as she walked silently through the water.

"Come in, your rooms are ready," said the old man cheeringly.

They passed through a kitchen black with myriads of flies,

into an apartment formerly used as the workshop, now converted into a parlor. Two children were asleep on an old torn sofa. In one corner lay sacks of straw, prepared for couches, the owners of the house considered it a matter of course that they should have no beds during the Passion. A smoking kerosene lamp hung from the dark worm-eaten wooden ceiling, diffusing more smoke than light. The room was so low that the countess could scarcely stand erect, and besides the ceiling had sunk—in the dim, smoke-laden atmosphere the beams threatened to fall at any moment.

A sense of suffocation oppressed the new-comer. She was utterly exhausted, chilled, nervous to the verge of weeping. Her white teeth chattered. She shivered with cold and discomfort. Her host opened a low door into a small room containing two beds, a table, an old-fashioned dark cupboard, and two chairs.

"There," he cried in a tone of great satisfaction, "that is your chamber. Now you can rest, and if you want anything, you need only call and one of my daughters will come in and wait upon you."

"Yes, my good fellow, but where am *I* to lodge?" asked the prince.

"Oh—then you don't belong together? In that case the countess must sleep with another lady, and the gentleman up here."

He pointed to a little stair-case in the corner which, according to the custom in old peasant houses, led from one room through a trap-door into another directly above it.

"But I can't sleep *there*, it would inconvenience the lady," said the prince. "Have you no other rooms?"

"Why yes; but they are engaged for to-morrow," replied Andreas Gross, while the two sisters stood staring helplessly.

"Then give me the rooms and send the other people away."

"Oh! I can't do that, sir.—They are promised."

"Good Heavens! I'll pay you twice, ten times as much."

"Why, sir, if you paid me twenty times the price, I could not do it; I must not break my promise!" said the old man with gentle firmness.

"Ah," thought the prince, "he wants to screw me—but I'll manage that. Countess, excuse me a few minutes while I look for another lodging."

"For Heaven's sake, try to find one for me, too. I would rather spend the night in the carriage than stay here!" replied the countess in French.

"Yes, it is horrible! but it will not be difficult to find something better. Good-bye!" he answered in the same language.

"Don't leave me alone with these people too long. Come back soon; I am afraid," she added, still using the French tongue.

"Really?" the prince answered, laughing; but a ray of pleasure sparkled in his eyes.

Meanwhile, the little girl who was asleep on the sofa had waked and now came into the room.

The countess requested every one to retire that she might rest, and the peasants modestly withdrew. But when she tried to fasten the door, it had neither lock nor bolt, only a little wire hook which slipped into a loose ring.

"Oh!" she exclaimed, startled. "I cannot lock it."

"You need have no anxiety," replied the old man soothingly, "we sleep in the next room." But the vicinity of those strange people, when she could not lock the door, was exactly what the countess feared.

She slipped the miserable wire hook into its fastening and sat down on one of the beds, which had no mattresses — nothing but sacking.

Covering her face with her hands, she gave free course to indignant tears. She still wore her hat and cloak, which she had not ventured to take off, from a vague feeling of being encompassed by perils whence she might need to fly at any moment. In such a situation, surely it was safer not to lay aside one's wraps. If the worst came, she would remain so all night. To go to bed in a house where the roof might fall and such strange figures were stealing about, was too great a risk. Beside the bed on which the countess sat was a door, which, amid all the terrors, she had not noticed. Now it seemed as though she heard a scraping noise like the filing of iron. Then came hollow blows and a peculiar rattling. Horrible, incomprehensible sounds! Now a blow fell upon the door, whose fastening was little better than the other. And now another.

"The very powers of hell are let loose here," cried the countess, starting up. Her cold, wet feet seemed paralyzed, her senses were on the verge of failing. And she was alone in this terrible strait. Where were the servants? Perhaps they had been led astray, robbed and murdered—and meanwhile the storm outside was raging in all its fury.

There came another attempt to burst the door which, under two crashing blows, began to yield. The countess, as if in a dream, rushed to the workshop and, almost fainting, called to her aid the uncanny people there—one terror against another. With blanched lips she told them that some one had entered the house, that some madman or fugitive from justice was trying to get in.

"Oh! that is nothing," said Andreas, with what seemed to the terrified woman a fiendish smile, and walking straight to the door, while the countess shrieked aloud, opened it, and— a head was thrust in. A mild, big, stupid face stared at the light with wondering eyes and snorted from wide pink nostrils at the strange surroundings. A bay horse—a good-natured cart horse occupied the next room to the Countess Wildenau!

"You see the criminal. He is a cribber, that is the cause of the horrible noises you heard."

The trembling woman stared at the mild, stupid equine face as though it was a heavenly vision—yet spite of her relief and much as she loved horses, she could not have gone to bed comfortably, since as the door was already half broken down by the elephantine hoofs of the worthy brute, there was a chance that during the night, lured by the aromatic odor of the sea-weed, which formed the stuffing of the bed, the bay might mistake the countess' couch for a manger and rouse her somewhat rudely with his snuffing muzzle.

"Oh, we'll make that all right at once," said Andreas. "We'll fasten him so that he can't get free again, and the carter comes at four in the morning, then you will not be disturbed any more."

"After not having closed my eyes all night," murmured the countess, following the old man to see that he fastened the horse securely. Yes, the room which opened from here by a door with neither lock nor threshold was a stable. Several frightened hens flew from the straw—this, too. " When the horse has left the stable the cocks will begin to crow. What a night after the fatigues of the day!" The old man smiled with irritating superiority, and said:

" Yes, that is the way in the country."

" No, I won't stay here—I would rather spend the night in the carriage. How can people exist in this place, even for a day," thought the countess.

"Won't you have something to eat? Shall my daughter make a schmarren?" *

" A schmarren! In that kitchen, with those flies." The countess felt a sense of loathing.

" No, thank you." Even if she was starving, she could not eat a mouthful in this place.

The bay was at last tied and, for want of other occupation, continued to gnaw his crib and to suck the air, a proceeding terribly trying to the nerves of his fair neighbor in the next room. At last—oh joy, deliverance—the second carriage rattled up to the house, bringing the maid and the courier.

"Come in, come in!" called the countess from the window. " Don't have any of the luggage taken off. I shall not stay here."

The two servants entered with flushed faces.

" Where in the world have you been so long?" asked their mistress, imperiously, glad to be able, at last, to vent her ill-humor on some one.

" The driver missed the way," stammered the courier, casting a side glance at the blushing maid. The countess perceived the situation at a glance and was herself again. Fear and timidity, all her nervous weakness vanished before the pride of the offended mistress, who had been kept waiting an hour, at whose close the tardy servants entered with faces whose confusion plainly betrayed that so long a delay was needless.

She drew herself up to her full height, feminine fears forgotten in the pride of the lady of rank.

---

* A dish made of flour and water fried in hot lard, but so soft that it is necessary to serve and eat it with a spoon.   TRANSLATOR.

"Courier, you are dismissed—not another word!"

"Then I beg Your Highness to discharge me, too," said the excited maid, thus betraying herself. A contemptuous glance from the countess rested upon the culprit, but without hesitation, she said, quietly:

"Very well. You can both go to the steward for your wages. Good evening."

Both left the room pale and silent. They had not expected this dismissal, but they knew their mistress' temper and were aware that not another word would be allowed, that no excuse or entreaty would avail. The countess, too, was in no pleasant mood. She was left here — without a maid. For the first time in her life she would be obliged to wait upon herself, unpack all those huge trunks and bags. How could she do it? She was so cold and so weary, too, and she did not even know which of the numerous bags contained dry shoes and stockings. Was she to pull out everything, when she must do the repacking herself? For now she must certainly go to another house, among civilized people, where she could have servants and not be so utterly alone. Oh, if only she had not come to this Ammergau—it was a horrible place! One would hardly purchase the salvation of the world at the cost of such an evening. It was terrible to be in this situation—and without a maid!

And, as trivial things find even the loftiest women faint-hearted because they are matters of nerve, and not of character, the lady who had just confronted her servants so haughtily sank down on the bed again and wept like a child.

Some one tapped lightly on the door of the workshop. The countess opened it, and the short, stout sister timidly entered.

"Pardon me, Your Highness, we have just heard that you have discharged your maid and courier, so I wanted to ask whether my sister or I could be of any service? Perhaps we might unpack a little?"

"Thank you—I don't wish to spend the night here and hope that my companion will bring news that he has found other accommodations. I will pay whatever you ask, but I can't possibly stay. Ask your father what he charges, I'll give whatever you wish—only let me go."

The old man was summoned.

" Why certainly, Countess, you can be entirely at ease on that score; if you don't like staying with us, that need not trouble you. You will have nothing to pay—only you must be quick or you will find no lodgings, they are very hard to get now."

" Yes, but you must have some compensation. Just tell me what I am to give."

" Nothing, Countess. We do not receive payment for what is not eaten !" replied Andreas Gross with such impressive firmness that the lady looked at him in astonishment. " The Ammergau people do not make a business of renting lodgings, Countess; that is done only by the foreign speculators who wish to make a great deal of money at this time, and alas ! bring upon Ammergau the reputation of extortion ! We natives of the village do it for the sake of having as many guests witness the play as possible, ard are glad if we meet our expenses. We expect nothing more."

The countess suddenly saw the " hang-dog " face in a very different light ! It must have been the dusk which had deceived her. She now thought it an intellectual and noble one, nay the wrinkled countenance, the long grey locks, and clear, penetrating eyes and an aspect of patriarchal dignity. She suddenly realized that these people must have had the masks which their characters require bestowed by nature, not painted with rouge, and thus the traits of the past unconsciously became impressed upon the features. In the same way, among professional actors, the performer who takes character rôles can easily be distinguished from the lover.

" Do you act too ?" she asked with interest.

" I act Dathan, the Jewish trader," he said proudly. " I have been in the Play sixty years, for when I was a child three years old I sat in Eve's lap in the tableaux." The countess could not repress a smile and old Andreas' face also brightened.

The little girl, a daughter of the short, plump woman, peeped through the half open door, gazing with sparkling eyes at the lovely lady.

" Whose child is the little one ?" asked the countess, noticing her soft curls and beaming eyes.

"She is my grand-daughter, the child of my daughter, Anna. Her father was a foreigner. He ran away, leaving his wife and two children in poverty. So I took them all three into my house again."

The countess looked at the old man's thin, worn figure, and then at the plump mother and child.

"Who supports them?"

"Oh, we help one another," replied Andreas evasively. "We all work together. My son, the drawing teacher, does a great deal for us, too. We could not manage without him." Then interrupting himself with a startled look, as if he might have been overheard, he added, "but I ought not to have said that—he would be very angry if he knew."

"You appear to be a little afraid of your son," said the countess.

"Yes, yes—he is strict, very strict and proud, but a good son."

The old man's eyes sparkled with love and pride.

"Where is he?" asked the countess eagerly.

"Oh, he never allows strangers to see him if he can avoid it."

"Does he act, too?"

"No; he arranges the tableaux, and it needs the ability of a field marshal, for he is obliged to command two or three hundred people, and he keeps them together and they obey him as though he was a general."

"He must be a very interesting person."

At that moment the prince's step was heard in the sitting-room.

"May I come in?"

"Yes, Prince."

He entered, dripping with rain.

"I found nothing except one little room for myself, in a hut even worse than this. All the large houses are filled to overflowing. Satan himself brought us among these confounded peasants!" he said angrily in French.

"Don't speak so," replied the countess earnestly in the same language. "They are saints." The little girl whispered to her mother.

"Please excuse me, Sir; but my child understands French

and has just told me that you could get no room for the lady,"
said Andreas' daughter timidly.   "I know where there is one
in a very pretty house near by.   I will run over as quickly as
I can and see if it is still vacant.   If you could secure it you
would find it much better than ours."   She hurried towards
the door.

"Stop, woman," called the prince, "you cannot possibly
go out; the rain is pouring in torrents, and another shower is
rising."

"Yes, stay," cried the countess, "wait till the storm is
over."

"Oh, no! lodgings are being taken every minute, we must
not lose an instant."   The next moment she threw a shawl over
her head and left the house.   She was just running past the
low window – a vivid flash of lightning illumined the room,
making the little bent figure stand forth like a silhouette.   A
peal of thunder quickly followed.

"The storm is just over us," said the prince with kindly
anxiety.   "We ought not to have let her go."

"Oh, it is of no consequence," said the old man smiling,
"she is glad to do it."

"Tell me about these strange people," the prince began,
but the countess motioned to him that the child understood
French.   He looked at her with a comical expression as if he
wanted to say: "These are queer 'natives' who give their
children so good an education."

The countess went to the window, gazing uneasily at the
raging storm.   A feeling of self-reproach stole into her heart
for having let the kind creature go out amid this uproar of the
elements.   Especially when these people would take no compensation and therefore lost a profit, if another lodging was
found.

It was her loss, and yet she showed this cheerful alacrity.

The little party had now entered the living room.   The
countess sat on the window sill, while flash after flash of lightning blazed, and peal after peal crashed from the sky.   She no
longer thought of herself, only of the poor woman outside.
The little girl wept softly over her poor mother's exposure to
the storm, and slipped to the door to wait for her.   The prince,
shivering, sat on the bench by the stove.   Gross, noticing it,

put on more fuel "that the gentleman might dry himself." A bright fire was soon crackling in the huge green stove, the main support of the sunken ceiling.

"Pray charge the fuel to me," said the prince, ashamed.

The old man smiled.

"How you gentle-folks want to pay for everything. We should have needed a fire ourselves." With these words he left the room. The thin sister now thought it desirable not to disturb the strangers and also went out.

"Tell me, Countess," the prince began, leaning comfortably against the warm stove, "may I perfume this, by no means agreeable, atmosphere with a cigarette?"

"Certainly, I had forgotten that there were such things as cigarettes in the world."

"So it seems to me," said the prince, coolly. "Tell me, *chère amie*, now that you have duly enjoyed all the tremors of this romantic situation, how should you like a cup of tea?"

"Tea?" said the countess, looking at him as if just roused from a dream, "tea!"

"Yes, tea," persisted the prince. "My poor friend, you must have lived an eternity in this one hour among these 'savages' to have already lost the memory of one of the best products of civilization."

"Tea," repeated the countess, who now realized her exhaustion, "that would be refreshing, but I don't know how to get it, I sent the maid away."

"Yes, I met the dismissed couple in a state of utter despair. And I can imagine that my worshipped Countess Madeleine—the most pampered and spoiled of all the children of fortune and the fashionable world—does not know how to help herself. I am by no means sorry, for I shall profit by it. I can now pose as a kind Providence. What good luck for a lover! is it not? So permit me to supply the maid's place—so far as this is *practicable*. I have tea with me and my valet whom, thank Heaven, I was not obliged to send away, is waiting your order to serve it."

"How kind you are, Prince. But consider that kitchen filled with flies."

"Oh, you need not feel uncomfortable on that score. You are evidently unused to the mountains. I know these flies,

2

they are different from our city ones and possess a peculiar skill in keeping out of food. Try it for once."

"Yes, but we must first ascertain whether I can get the other room," said the countess, again lapsing into despondency.

"My dearest Countess, does that prevent our taking any refreshment? Don't be so spiritless," said the prince laughing.

"Oh, it's all very well to laugh. The situation is tragical enough, I assure you."   .

"Tragical enough to pay for the trouble of developing a certain grandeur of soul, but not, in true womanly fashion, to lose all composure."

The prince shook the ashes from his cigarette and went to the door to order the valet to serve the tea. When he returned, the countess suddenly came to meet him, held out her hand, and said with a bewitching smile :

"Prince, you are charming to-day, and I am unbearable. I thank you for the patience you have shown."

"Madeleine," he replied, controlling his emotion, "if I did not know your kind heart, I should believe you a Circe, who delighted in driving men mad. Were it not for my cold, sober reason, which you always emphasize, I should now mistake for love the feeling which makes you meet me so graciously, and thus expose myself to disappointment. But reason plainly shows that it is merely the gratitude of a kind heart for a trivial service rendered in an unpleasant situation, and I am too proud to do, in earnest, what I just said in jest—profit by the opportunity."

The countess, chilled and ashamed, drew her hand back. There spoke the dry, prosaic, commonplace man. Had he *now* understood how to profit by her mood when, in her helpless condition, he appeared as a deliverer in the hour of need, who knows what might have happened! But this was precisely what he disdained. The experienced man of the world knew women well enough to be perfectly aware how easily one may be won in a moment of nervous depression, desperate perplexity and helplessness, yet though ever ready to enjoy every piquant situation, nevertheless or perhaps for that very reason he was too proud to owe to an accident of this kind the woman whom he had chosen for the companion of his life. The countess felt this and was secretly glad that he had spared her and himself a disappointment.

"That is the way with women," he said softly, gazing at her with an almost compassionate expression. "For the mess of pottage of an agreeable situation, they will sell the birthright of their most sacred feelings."

"That is a solemn, bitter truth, such as I am not accustomed to hear from your lips, Prince. But however deep may be the gulf of realism whence you have drawn this experience, you shall not find it confirmed in me."

"That is, you will punish me henceforth by your coldness, while you know perfectly well that it was the sincerity of my regard for you which prompted my act. Countess, that vengeance would be unworthy; a woman like you ought not to sink to the petty sensitiveness of ordinary feminine vanity."

"Oh, Prince, you are always right, and, believe me, if I carried my heart in my *head* instead of in my breast, that is, if we could love with the *intellect*, I should have been yours long ago, but alas, my friend, it is so *far* from the head to the heart."

The Prince lighted another cigarette. No one could detect what was passing in his mind. "So much the worse for me!" he said coldly, shrugging his shoulders.

At that moment a sheet of flame filled the room, and the crashing thunder which followed sounded as if the ceiling had fallen and buried everything under it. The countess seemed bewildered.

"Mother, mother!" shrieked a voice outside. People gathered in the street, voices were heard, shouts, hurrying footsteps and the weeping of the little girl. The prince sprang out of the window, the countess regained her consciousness—of what?

"Some one has been struck by lightning." She hastened out.

A senseless figure was brought in and laid on the bench in the entry. It was the kind-hearted little creature whom her caprice had sent into the storm—perhaps to her death. There she lay silent and pale, with closed lids; her hands were cold her features sharp and rigid like those of a corpse, but her

heart still throbbed under her drenched gown. The countess asked the prince to bring cologne and smelling salts from
her satchel and skillfully applied the remedies; the prince
helped her rub the arteries while she strove to restore consciousness with the sharp essences. Meanwhile the other sister
soothed the weeping child. Andreas Gross poured a few drops
of some liquid from a dusty flask into the sufferer's mouth, saying quietly, "You must not be so much frightened, I am something of a doctor; it is only a severe fainting fit. The other is
worse."

"Were two persons struck?" asked the countess in horror.

"Yes, one of the musicians, the first violin."

A sudden thought darted through the countess' brain, and
a feeling of dread stole over her as if there was in Ammergau
a beloved life for which she must tremble. Yet she knew no
one.

"Please bring a shawl from my room," she said to the
prince, and when he had gone, she asked quickly: "Tell me,
is the musician tall?"

"Oh, yes."

"Has he long black hair?"

"No, he is fair," replied the old man.

The countess, with a feeling of relief, remained silent, the
prince returned. The sick woman opened her eyes and a faint
moan escaped her lips.

"Here will be a fine scene," thought the prince. "Plenty
of capital can be made out of such a situation. My lovely
friend will outweigh every tear with a gold coin."

After a short time the woman regained sufficient consciousness to realize her surroundings and tried to lift her feet from
the bench. "Oh, Countess, you will tax yourself too much.
Please go in, there is a strong draught here."

"Yes, but you must come with me," said the countess, "try
whether you can use your feet."

It was vain, she tried to take a step, but her feet refused to
obey her will.

"Alas!" cried the countess deeply moved. "She is paralyzed—and it is my fault."

Anna gently took her hand and raised it to her lips. "Pray
don't distress yourself, Countess, it will pass away. I am only

sorry that I have caused you such a fright." She tried to smile, the ugly face looked actually beautiful at that moment, and the tones of her voice, whose tremor she strove to conceal, was so touching as she tried to comfort and soothe the self-reproach of the woman who had caused the misfortune that tears filled the countess' eyes.

"How wise she is," said the prince, marvelling at such delicacy and feeling.

"Come," said the countess, "we must get her into the warm rooms."

Andreas Gross, and at a sign from the prince, the valet, carried the sick woman in and laid her on the bench by the stove. The countess held her icy hand, while tears streamed steadily down the sufferer's cheeks.

"Do you feel any pain?" asked the lady anxiously.

"No, oh no—but I can't help weeping because the Countess is so kind to me—I am in no pain—no indeed!" She smiled again, the touching smile which seeks to console others.

"Yes, yes," said the old man, "you need not be troubled, she will be well to-morrow."

The child laid her head lovingly on her mother's breast, a singularly peaceful atmosphere pervaded the room, a modest dignity marked the bearing of the poor peasants. The prince and the countess also sat in thoughtful silence. Suddenly the sick woman started up, "Oh dear, I almost forget the main thing. The lady can have the lodgings. Two very handsome rooms and excellent attendance, but the countess must go at once as soon as the shower is over. They will be kept only an hour. More people will arrive at ten."

"I thank you," said the countess with a strange expression."

"Oh, there is no need. I am only glad I secured the rooms, and that the countess can have attendance," replied the sick woman joyously. "I shall soon be better. then I'll show the way."

"I thank you," repeated the countess earnestly. "I do not want the rooms, I shall *stay here*."

"What are you going to do?" asked the prince in amazement.

"Yes, I am ashamed that I was so foolish this evening.

Will you keep me, you kind people, after I have done you so much injustice, and caused you such harm."

"Oh! you must consult your own pleasure. We shall be glad to have you stay with us, but we shall take no offence, if it would be more pleasant for you elsewhere," said the old man with unruffled kindness.

"Then I will stay."

"That is a good decision, Countess," said the prince. "You always do what is right." He beckoned to Sephi, the thin sister, and whispered a few words. She vanished in the countess' room, returning in a short time with dry shoes and stockings, which she had found in one of the travelling satchels. The prince went to the window and stood there with his back turned to the room. "We must do the best that opportunity permits," he said energetically. "I beg your highness to let this lady change your shoes and stockings. I am answerable for your health, not only to myself, but to society."

The countess submitted to the prince's arrangement, and the little ice-cold feet slid comfortably into the dry coverings, which Sephi had warmed at the stove. She now felt as if she was among human beings and gradually became more at ease. After Sephi had left the room she walked proudly up to the prince in her dry slippers, and said: "Come, Prince, let us pace to and fro, that our chilled blood may circulate once more."

The prince gracefully offered his arm and led her up and down the long work-shop. Madeleine was bewitching at that moment, and the grateful expression of her animated face suited her to a charm.

"I must go," he thought, "or I shall be led into committing some folly which will spoil all my chances with her."

CHAPTER III. ·

YOUNG AMMERGAU.

THE valet served the tea. The prince had provided for everything, remembered everything. He had even brought English biscuits.

The little repast exerted a very cheering influence upon the depressed spirits of the countess. But she took the first cup to the invalid who, revived by the unaccustomed stimulant, rose at once, imagining that a miracle had been wrought, for she could walk again. The Gross family now left the room. The prince and the countess sipped their tea in silence. What were they to say when the valet, who always accompanied his master on his journeys, understood all the languages which the countess spoke fluently ?

The prince was grave and thoughtful. After they had drank the tea, he kissed her hand. " Let me go now—we must both have rest, you for your nerves and I for my feelings. I wish you a good night's sleep."

" Prince, I can say that you have been infinitely charming to-day, and have risen much in my esteem."

" I am glad to hear it, Countess, though a trifle depressed by the consciousness that I owe this favor to a cup of tea and a pair of dry slippers," replied the prince with apparent composure. Then he took his hat and left the room.

And this is love ? thought the countess, shrugging her shoulders. What was she to do ? She did not feel at all inclined to sleep. People are never more disposed to chat than after hardships successfully endured. She had had her tea, had been warmed, served, and tended. For the first time since her arrival she was comfortable, and now she must go to bed. At ten o'clock in the evening, the hour when she usually drove from the theatre to some evening entertainment.

The prince had gone and the Gross family came in to ask if she wanted anything more.

"No, but you are ready to go to bed, and I ought to return to my room, should I not ? " replied the countess.

Just at that moment the door was flung open and a head like the bronze cast of the bust of a Roman emperor appeared. A face which in truth seemed as if carved from bronze, keen eagle eyes, a nose slightly hooked, an imperious, delicately moulded brow, short hair combed upward, and an expression of bitter, sad, but irresistible energy on the compressed lips. As the quick eyes perceived the countess, the head was drawn back with the speed of lightning. But old Gross, proud of his son, called him back.

" Come in, come in and be presented to this lady, people don't run away so."

The young man, somewhat annoyed, returned.

" My son, Ludwig, principal of the drawing school," said old Gross. Ludwig's artist eyes glided over the countess; she felt the glance of the connoisseur, knew that he could appreciate her beauty. What a delight to see herself, among these simple folk, suddenly reflected in an artist's eyes and find that the picture came back beautiful. How happened so exquisite a crystal, which can be polished only in the workshops of the highest education and art, to be in such surroudings? The countess noted with ever increasing amazement the striking face and the proud poise of the head on the small, compact, yet classically formed figure. She knew at the first moment that this was a man in the true sense of the word, and she gave him her hand as though greeting an old acquaintance from the kingdom of the ideal. It seemed as if she must ask: " How do you come here?"

Ludwig Gross read the question on her lips. He possessed the vision from which even the thoughts must be guarded, or he would guess them.

" I must ask your pardon for disturbing you. I have just come from the meeting and only wanted to see my sister. I heard she was ill."

"Oh, I feel quite well again," the latter answered.

" Yes," said the countess in a somewhat embarrassed tone, " you will be vexed with the intruder who has brought so much anxiety and alarm into your house? I reproach myself for being so foolish as to have wanted another lodging, but at first I thought that the ceiling would fall upon me, and I was afraid."

" Oh, I understand that perfectly when persons are not accustomed to low rooms. It was difficult for me to become used to them again when I returned from Munich."

" You were at the Academy?"

" Yes, Countess."

" Will you not take off your wet coat and sit down?"

" I should not like to disturb you, Countess."

"But you won't disturb me at all; come, let us have a little chat."

Ludwig Gross laid his hat and overcoat aside, took a chair, and sat down opposite to the lady. Just at that moment a carriage drove up. The strangers who had engaged the rooms refused to the prince had arrived, and the family hastened out to receive and help them. The countess and Ludwig were left alone.

"What were you discussing at so late an hour?" asked the countess.

"Doré sent us this evening two engravings of his two Passion pictures; he is interested in our play, so we were obliged to discuss the best way of expressing our gratitude and to decide upon the place where they shall be hung. There is no time for such consultations during the day."

"Are you familiar with all of Doré's pictures?"

"Certainly, Countess."

"And do you like him?"

"I admire him. I do not agree with him in every particular, but he is a genius, and genius has a right to forgiveness for faults which mediocrity should never venture to commit, and indeed never will."

"Very true," replied the lady.

"I think," Ludwig Gross continued, "that he resembles Hamerling. There is kinship between the two men. Hamerling, too, repels us here and there, but with him, as with Doré, every line and every stroke flashes with that electric spark which belongs only to the genuine work of art."

His companion gazed at him in amazement.

"You have read Hamerling?"

"Certainly. Who is not familiar with his 'Ahasuerus?'" *

"I, for instance," she replied with a faint blush.

"Oh, Countess, you must read it. There is a vigor, an acerbity, the repressed anguish and wrath of a noble nature against the pitifulness of mankind, which must impress every one upon whose soul the questions of life have ever cast their shadows, though I know not whether this is the case with you."

"More than is perhaps supposed," she answered, drawing a long breath. "We are all pessimists, but Hamerling must be a stronger one than is well for a poet."

"That is not quite correct," replied Ludwig. "He is a pes-

---

* A drama. Hamerling is better known in America as the author of his famous novel "Aspasia." TRANSLATOR.

simist just so far as accords with the poesy of our age. Did not Auerbach once say: 'Pessimism is the grief of the world, which has no more tears!' This applies to Hamerling, also. His poetry has that bitter flavor, which is required by a generation that has passed the stage when sweets please the palate and tears relieve the heart."

"Your words are very true. But how do you explain—it would be interesting to hear from you—how do you explain, in this mood of the times, the attraction which draws such throngs to the Passion Play?"

Ludwig Gross leaned back in his chair, and his stern brow relaxed under the bright influence of a beautiful thought.

"One extreme, as is well known, follows another. The human heart will always long for tears, and the world's tearless anguish will therefore yield to a gentler mood. I think that the rush to our simple play is a symptom of this change. People come here to learn to weep once more."

The countess rested her clasped hands on the table and gazed long and earnestly at Ludwig Gross. Her whole nature was kindled, her eyes lingered admiringly upon the modest little man, who did not seem at all conscious of his own su·periority. "To learn to *weep!*" she repeated, nodding gently. "Yes, we might all need that. But do you believe we shall learn it here?"

Ludwig Gross gazed at her smiling. "You will not ask that question at this hour on the evening of the day after to-morrow."

He seemed to her a physician who possessed a remedy which he knows *cannot* fail. And she began to trust him like a physician.

"May I be perfectly frank?" she asked in a winning tone.

"I beg that you will be so, Countess."

"I am surprised to find a man like you here. I had not supposed there were such people in the village. But you were away a long time, you are probably no longer a representative citizen of Ammergau?"

Ludwig Gross raised his head proudly. "Certainly I am, Countess. If there was ever a true citizen of Ammergau, I am one. Learn to know us better, and you will soon be convinced that we are all of one mind. Though one has perhaps learned more than another, that is a mere accident; the same purpose, the same idea, unites us all."

" But what binds men of such talent to this remote village ? Are you married?"

The bitter expression around the artist's mouth deepened as though cut by some invisible instrument. " No, Countess, my circumstances do not permit it; I have renounced this happiness."

The lady perceived that she had touched a sensitive spot, but she desired to probe the wound to learn whether it might be healed. " Is your salary so small that you could not support a family ?"

" If I wish to aid my own family, and that is certainly my first duty, I cannot found a home."

" How is that possible. Does so rich a community pay its teacher so poorly ?"

" It does as well as it can, Countess. It has fixed a salary of twelve hundred marks for my position; that is all that can be expected."

" For this place, yes. But if you were in Munich, you would easily obtain twice or three times as much."

" Even five times," answered Ludwig, smiling. "I had offers from two art-industrial institutes, one of which promised a salary of four thousand, the other of six thousand marks per annum. But that did not matter when the most sacred duties to my home were concerned."

" But these are superhuman sacrifices. Who can expect you to banish yourself here and resign everything which the world outside would lavish upon you in the richest measure ? Everyone must consider himself first."

" Why, Countess, Ammergau would die out if everybody was of that opinion."

" Oh ! let those remain who are suited to the place, who have learned and can do nothing more. But men of talent and education, like you, who can claim something better, belong outside."

" On the contrary, Countess, they belong here," Ludwig eagerly answered. " What would become of the Passion Play if all who have learned and can do something should go away, and only the uneducated and the ignorant remain ? Do you

suppose that there are not a number of people here, who, according to your ideas, would have deserved ' a better fate ?'
We have enough of them, but go among us and learn whether
any one complains.   If he should, he would be unworthy the
name of a son of Ammergau!" He paused a moment, his
bronzed face grew darker. " Do you imagine," he added,
" that we could perform such a work, perform it in a manner
which, in some degree, fulfills the æsthetic demand of modern
taste, without possessing, in our midst, men of intellect and
culture ? It is bad enough that necessity compels many a
talented native of Ammergau to seek his fortune outside, but
the man to whom his home still gives even a bit of *bread*
must be content with it, and without thinking of what he
might have gained outside, devote his powers to the ideal interests of his fellow citizens."

" That is a grand and noble thought, but I don't understand
why you speak as if the people of Ammergau were so poor.
What becomes of the vast sums gained by the Passion Play ?"

Ludwig Gross smiled bitterly. " I expected that question,
it comes from all sides. The Passion Play does not enrich individuals, for the few hundred marks, more or less, which each
of the six hundred actors receives, do not cover the deficit of
all the work which the people must neglect. The revenue is
partly consumed by the expenses, partly used for the common
benefit, for schools and teachers. The principal sums are swal-
lowed by the Leine and the Ammer! The ravages of these malicious mountain streams require means which our community
could never raise, save for the receipts of the Passion Play, and
even these are barely sufficient for the most needful outlay."

" Is it possible? Those little streams!" cried the countess.

"Would flood all Ammergau," Gross answered, "if we did
not constantly labor to prevent it. We should be a poor, stunted
people, worn down by fever, our whole mountain valley would
be a desolate swamp. The Passion Play alone saves us from
destruction—the Christ who once ruled the waves actually
holds back from us the destroying element which would gradually devour land and people. But, for that very reason, the
individual has learned here, as perhaps nowhere else in the
world, to live and sacrifice himself for the community ! The
community is comprised to us in the idea of the Passion Play.

We know that our existence depends upon it, even our intellectual life, for it protects us from the savagery into which a people continually struggling with want and need so easily lapses. It raises us above the common herd, gives even the poorest man an innate dignity and self-respect, which never suffer him to sink to base excesses."

" I understand that," the countess answered.

" Then can you wonder that not one of us hesitates to devote property, life, and every power of his soul to this work of saving our home, our poor, oppressed home, ever forced to struggle for its very existence ?"

" What a man!" the countess involuntarily exclaimed aloud. Ludwig Gross had folded his arms across his breast, as if to restrain the pulsations of his throbbing heart. His whole being thrilled with the deepest, noblest emotions. He rose and took his hat, like a person whose principle it is to shut every emotion within his own bosom, and when a mighty one overpowers him, to hide himself that he may also hide the feeling.

" No," cried the countess, " you must not leave me so, you rare, noble-hearted man. You have just done me the greatest service which can be rendered. You have made my heart leap with joy at the discovery of a *genuine* human being. Ah! it is a cordial in this world of conventional masks! Give me your hand! I am beginning to understand why Providence sent me here. That must indeed be a great cause which rears such men and binds such powers in its service."

Ludwig Gross once more stood calm and quiet before her. " I thank you, Countess, in the name of the cause for which I live and die."

" And, in the name of that cause, which I do not understand, yet dimly apprehend, I beg you, let us be friends. Will you? Clasp hands upon it."

A kindly expression flitted over the grave man's iron countenance, and he warmly grasped the little hand.

" With all my heart, Countess."

She held the small, slender artist-hand in a close clasp, mournfully reading in the calm features of the stern, noble face the story of bitter suffering and sacrifice graven upon it.

CHAPTER IV.

EXPELLED FROM THE PLAY.

THE storm had spent its fury, the winds sung themselves softly to sleep, a friendly face looked down between the dispersing clouds and cast its mild light upon the water, now gradually flowing away. The swollen brooks rolled like molten silver—cold, glittering veins of the giant mountain body, whose crown of snow bestowed by the tempest glimmered with argent lustre in the pallid moonbeams. A breeze, chill and strengthening as the icy breath of eternity, sweeping from the white glaciers, entered the little window against which the countess was dreamily leaning.

Higher and higher rose the moon, more and more transfigured and transparent became the mountains, as if they were no longer compact masses, only the spiritual image of themselves as it may have hovered before the divine creative mind, ere He gave them material form.

The village lay silent before her, and silence pervaded all nature. Yet to the countess it seemed as if it were the stillness which precedes a great, decisive word.

"What hast Thou to say to me, Viewless One? Sacred stillness, what dost thou promise? Will the moment come when I shall understand Thy language, infinite Spirit? Or wilt Thou only half do Thy work in me—only awake the feeling that Thou art near me, speaking to me, merely to let me die of longing for the word I have failed to comprehend.

"Woe betide me, if it is so! And yet—wherefore hast Thou implanted in my heart this longing, this inexplicable yearning, which *nothing* stills, no earthly advantage, neither the splendor and grandeur Thou hast given me, nor the art and science which Thou didst endow me with capacity to appreciate. On, on, strives my thirsting soul toward the germ of all existence, toward *Thee*. Fain would I behold Thy face, though the fiery vision should consume me!

"Source of wisdom, no knowledge gives Thee to me; source of love, no love can supply Thy place. I have sought Thee in the temples of beauty, but found Thee not; in the shining spheres of thought, but in vain; in the love of human beings, but no matter how many hearts opened to me, I flung them aside as worthless rubbish, for Thou wert not in them! When will the moment come that Thou wilt appear before me in some noble form suited to Thy Majesty, and tell the sinner that her dim longing, into whatever errors it may have led her, yet obtained for her the boon of beholding Thy face?"

Burning tears glittered in the moonlight in the countess' large, beseeching eyes and, mastered by an inexplicable feeling, she sank on her knees at the little window, stretching her clasped hands fervently towards the shining orb, floating in her mild beauty and effulgence above the conquered, flying clouds. The mountain opposite towered like a spectral form in the moonlit atmosphere, the peak over which she had driven that day, where she had seen that wondrous apparition, that man with the grief of the universe in his gaze! What manner of man must he have been whose glance, in a single moment, awed the person upon whom it fell as if some higher power had given a look of admiration? Why had it rested upon her with such strange reproach, as if saying: "You, too, are a child of the world, like many who come here, unworthy of salvation." Or was he angry with her because she had disturbed him in his reveries? Yet why did he fix his eyes so intently upon hers, that neither could avert them from the other? And all this happened in a single moment—but a moment worthy of being held in remembrance throughout an eternity. Who could he be? Would she see him again? Yes, for in that meeting there was something far beyond mere accident.

An incomprehensible restlessness seized upon her, a longing to solve the enigma, once more behold that face, that wonderful face whose like she had never seen before!

The horse was stamping in its stall, but she did not heed it, the thin candles had burned down and gone out long ago, the worm was gnawing the ancient wainscoting, the clock in the church-steeple struck twelve. A dog howled in the distance, one of the children in the workshop was disturbed by the nightmare, it cried out in its sleep. Usually such nocturnal sounds would have greatly irritated the countess' nerves. Now she had no ears for them, before her lay the whole grand expanse of mountain scenery, bathed in the moonlight, naked as a beautiful body just risen from a glittering flood! And she was seized with an eager longing to throw herself upon the bosom of this noble body, that she, too, might be irradiated with light, steeped in its moist glow and cool in the pure, icy atmosphere emanating from it, her fevered blood, the vague yearning which thrilled her pulses. She hurriedly seized her hat and cloak and stepped noiselessly into the workshop. What a picture of poverty! The sisters and the little girl were lying on the floor upon sacks of straw, the boy was asleep on the " couch," and the old man dozed sitting erect in an antique arm-chair, with his feet on a stool.

" How relative everything is," thought the countess. " To these people even so poor a bed as mine in yonder room is a forbidden luxury, which it would be sinful extravagance to desire. And we, amid our rustling curtains, on our silken cushions, resting on soft down, in rooms illuminated with the magical glow of lamps which pour a flood of roseate light on limbs stretched in comfortable repose, while the bronze angels which support the mirror seem to laugh gaily at each other, and from the toilet table intoxicating perfumes send forth their sweet poison, to conjure up a tropical world of blossom before the drowsy senses ! While these sleeping-places here ! On the bare floor and straw, lighted by the cold glimmer of the moon, shining through uncurtained windows and making the slumberers' lids quiver restlessly. Not even undressed, cramped by their coarse, tight garments, their weary limbs move uneasily on the hard beds ! And this atmosphere ! Five human beings in the low room and the soot from the lamp which has been smoking all the evening still filling the air. What lives ! What contrasts ! Yet these people are content and do not complain of their hard fate ! Nay, they even disdain a favorable opportunity of improving it by legitimate gains. Not one desires more than is customary and usual. What pride, what grandeur of self-sacrifice this requires ! *What gives them this power ?"*

Old Andreas woke and gazed with an almost terrified expression at the beautiful figure of the countess, standing thoughtfully among the sleepers. Starting up, he asked what she desired.

" Will you go to walk with me, Herr Gross ? "

The old man rubbed his eyes to convince himself that he

had slept so long that the sun was shining into his room. But no. " It is the moon which is so bright," he said to the countess.

"Why, of course, that is why I want to go out!" she repeated. The old man quickly seized his hat from the chamois horn and stood ready to attend her. " Are you not tired ? " she said hesitatingly. " You have not been in bed."

" Oh, that is of no consequence!" was his ready answer. " During the Passion it is always so."

The countess shook her head ; she knew that the people here said simply " the Passion," but she could not understand why, during "the Passion," they should neither expect a bed nor the most trivial comfort or why, for the sake of " the Passion," they should endure without a murmur, and without succumbing, every exertion and deprivation. She saw in the broad light which filled the room the old man's bright, keen eyes. " No, these Ammergau people know no fatigue, their task supports them!"

The countess left the room with him. " Ah!" an involuntary exclamation of delight escaped her lips as she emerged into the splendor of the brilliant moonlight, and eagerly inhaled the air which blew cold and strong, yet closed softly around her, strengthening and supporting her like the waves of the sea. And, amid these shimmering, floating mists, this "phosphorescence " of the earth, these waves of melting outlines, softly dissolving shapes—the Kofel towered solitary in sharp relief, like a vast reef of rocks, and on its summit glittered the metal-bound cross, the symbol of Ammergau, sending its beams far and wide in the light of the full moon like the lantern of a lighthouse.

Madeleine von Wildenau stretched out her arms, throwing back her cloak, that her whole form might bathe in the pure element.

" Oh, wash away all earthly dust and earthly ballast, ye surging billows: steal, purify me in thy chaste majesty, queen of the world, heaven-born air of the heights!" Was it possible that hitherto she had been able to live without this bliss, *had* she lived ? No, no, she had not! " Ammer-

3

gau, thou art the soil I have sought! Thy miracles are
beginning!" cried an exultant voice in the soul of the
woman so suddenly released from the toils of weary desolation.

Without exchanging many words—for the old man was
full of delicacy, and perceived what was passing in the
countess' soul—they involuntarily walked in the direction of
the Kofel; only when they were passing the house of a
prominent actor in the Passion Play, he often thought it his
duty to call his companion's attention to it.

Their way now lead them past a small dilapidated tavern
which had but two windows in the front. Here the Roman
Procurator lay on his bed of straw, enjoying his well-earned
night's rest. It was the house of Pilate! Nowhere was any
window closed with shutters—there were no thieves in Ammergau! The moon was reflected from every window-pane.
They turned into the main street of the village, where the
Ammer flowed in its broad, deep channel like a Venetian
lagoon. The stately, picturesquely situated houses threw
sharp shadows on the water. Here the ancient, venerable
"star," whose landlord was one of the musicians, thrust its
capacious bow-window into the street; yonder a foot-bridge
led to the house of Caiaphas, a handsome building, richly
adorned with frescoes representing scenes from ancient history; farther on Judas was sleeping the sleep of the just, rejoicing in the consciousness of having betrayed his master so often!
On the other side Mary rested under the richly carved gable
with the ancient design of the clover leaf, the symbol of the
Trinity, and directly opposite, the milk-wart nodded and
swayed on the wall of the churchyard!

A strange feeling stole over the countess as she stood
among these consecrated sleepers. As the fragrance of the
sleeping flowers floats over a garden at night, the sorrowful
spirit of the story of the Passion seemed to rise from these
humble resting places, and the pilgrim through the silent village was stirred as though she was walking through the streets
of Jerusalem. A street turned to the left between gardens
surrounded by fences and shaded by tall, ancient trees. The
shadows of the branches, tossed by the wind, flickered and
danced with magical grace. "That is the way to the dwell-

ing of the Christ, " said old Gross, in a subdued, reverential tone.

The countess involuntarily started. " The Christ," she repeated thoughtfully, pausing. " Can the house be seen ?"

" No, not from here. The house is like himself, not very easy to find."

" Is he so inaccessible?" asked the countess, glancing down the mysterious street again as they passed.

" Oh yes," replied Andreas. " He is a peculiar man. It is difficult to approach him. He is a friend of my son, but has little to do with the rest of us."

" But you associate with him ?"

" Very little in daily life; he goes nowhere, not even to the ale-house. But in the Passion I am associated with him. I always nail him to the cross," added the old man proudly. " No one is permitted to do that except myself."

The countess listened with eager interest. The brief description had roused her curiosity to the utmost. "How do you do it ?" she asked, to keep him to the same subject.

" I cannot explain that to you, but a great deal depends upon having everything exactly right, for, you know, the least mistake might cost him his life."

" How ? "

" Why, surely you can understand. Just think, the man is obliged to hang on the cross for twenty minutes. During this time the blood cannot circulate, and he always risks an attack of palpitation of the heart. *One* incautious movement in the descent from the cross, which should cause the blood to flow back too quickly to the heart, might cause his death."

" That is terrible !" cried the countess in horror. " And does he know it ?"

" Why, certainly."

" And *still* does it !"

Here Andreas gazed at the great lady with a compassionate smile, as if he wanted to say : "How little you understand, that you can ask such a question !"

They walked on silently. The countess was thinking : "What kind of man must this Christ be?" and while thus pondering and striving to form some idea of him, it suddenly flashed upon her that there was but *one* face which could belong to this man, the face she had seen gazing down upon her from the mountain, as if from some other world. Like a blaze of lightning the thought flamed through her soul. " *That* must have been he!"

At that moment Gross made a circuit around a gloomy house that had a neglected, tangled garden.

" Who lives there ?" asked the countess in surprise, following the old man, who was now walking much faster.

" Oh," he answered sorrowfully, " that is a sad place! There is an unhappy girl there, who sobs and moans all night long so that people hear her outside. I wanted to spare you, Countess."

They had now reached the end of the village and were walking, still along the bank of the Ammer, toward a large dam over which the mountain stream, swollen by the rain, plunged in mad, foaming waves. The spray gleamed dazzlingly white in the moon-rays, the massive beams trembled under the pressure of the unchained volume of water, groaning and creaking with a sinister noise amid the thundering roar until it sounded like the wails of the dying amid the din of battle. The countess shuddered at the demoniac power of this spectacle. High above the steep fall a narrow plank led from one bank of the stream to the other, vibrating constantly with the shock of the falling water. Madeleine's brain whirled at the thought of being compelled to cross it. " The timbers are groaning," she said, pausing. " Does not it sound like a human voice ?"

The old man listened. " By heaven! one would suppose so."

" It *is* a human voice—there—hark—some one is weeping —moaning."

The dam was in the full radiance of the moonlight, the countess and her companion stood concealed by a dense clump of willows, so that they could see without being seen.

Suddenly—what was that ? The old man made the sign of the cross. " Heavenly Father, it is she !"

A female figure was gliding across the plank. Like the ruddy glow of flame, mingled with the bluish hue of the moonlight, a mass of red-gold hair gleamed around her head and fluttered in the wind. The beautiful face was ghost-like in its pallor, the eyes were fixed, the very embodiment of despair. Her upper garment hung in tatters about her softly-moulded shoulders, and she held her clasped hands uplifted, not like one who prays, but one who fain would pray, yet cannot. Then with the firm poise of a person seeking death, she walked to the middle of the swaying plank, where the water was deepest, the fall most steep. There she prepared to take the fatal plunge. The countess shrieked aloud and Gross shouted :

"Josepha! Josepha! May God forgive you. Remember your old mother!"

The girl uttered a piercing cry, covered her face with both hands, and flung herself prone on the narrow plank.

But, with the speed of a youth, the old man was already on the bridge, raising the girl. "Shame on you to wish to do such a thing! We must submit to our fate! Now take care that you don't make a mis-step or I, an old man, must leap into the cold water to drag you out again, and you know how much I suffer from the rheumatism." He spoke in low, kindly tones, and the countess secretly admired his shrewdness and tenderness. She watched them breathlessly as the girl, at these words, tried not to slip in order to spare him. But now, as she did not *wish* to fall, she moved with uncertain, stumbling feet, where she had just seemed to fly. But Andreas Gross led her firmly and kindly. The countess' heart throbbed heavily till they reached the end and, in the utmost anxiety she stretched out her arms to them from the distance. Thank Heaven, there they are! The lady caught the girl by the hand and dragged her on the shore, where she sank silently, like a stricken animal, at her feet. The countess covered the trembling form with her cloak and said a few comforting words.

"Do you know her?" she asked the old man.

"Of course, it is Josepha Freyer, from the gloomy house yonder."

"Freyer? A relative of the Freyer who played the Christ."

"A cousin; yes."

The old man was about to go to the girl's house to bring her mother.

"No, no," said the countess. "I will care for her. What induced the unfortunate girl to take such a step?"

"She was the Mary Magdalene in the last Passion!" whispered the old man. At the words the girl raised her head and burst into violent sobs.

"My child, what has happened!" asked the countess, gazing admiringly at the charming creature, who was as perfect a picture of the penitent Magdalene as any artist could create.

"Why don't you play the Magdalene *this time ?*"

"Don't you know ?" asked the girl, amazed that there was any human being still ignorant of her disgrace. "I am not *permitted* to play now—I am—I have"—she again burst with convulsive sobs and, clasping the countess' knees, cried: "Oh, let me die, I cannot bear it."

"She fell into error," said Gross, in reply to the lady's questioning glance. "A little boy was born last winter. Now she can no longer act, for only those who are pure and without reproach are permitted to take part in the Passion."

"Oh, how harsh!" cried the countess; "And in a land where human beings are so near to nature, and in circumstances where the poor girls are so little guarded."

"Yes, we are aware of that—and Josepha is a heavy loss to us in the play—but these rules have come down to us from our ancestors and must be rigidly maintained. Yet the girl takes it too much to heart, she weeps day and night, so that people never pass the house to avoid hearing her lamentations, and now she wants to kill herself, the foolish lass."

"Oh, it's very well for you to talk, it's very well for you to talk," now burst from the girls lips in accents tremulous with passion. "First, try once what it is to have the whole world point at you. When the Englishmen, and the strangers from all the foreign countries in the world, come and want to see the famous Josepha Freyer, who played in the last Passion, and fairly drag the soul out of your body with their questions about the reason that you no longer act in it. Wait till you have to tell each person the story of your own disgrace, that it may be carried through the whole earth and know that your name is branded wherever men speak of the Passion Play. First try what it is to hide in a corner like a criminal, while they are acting in the Passion, and bragging and giving themselves airs as if they were saints, while thousands upon thousands listen devoutly. Ah, I alone am shut out, and yet I know that *no one* can act as I do." She drew herself up proudly, and flung the magnificient traditional locks of the Magdalene back on her shoulders. "Just seek such a Magdalene as I was—you will find none. And then to be forced to hear people who are passing ask: 'Why doesn't Josepha Freyer play the Magdalene this year ?' And then there are whispers, shrugs, and laughter, some one says, 'then she would suit the character exactly.' And when people pass the house they point at it—it seems as if I could feel it through the walls—and mutter: 'That's where the Penitent lives!' No, I won't bear it. I only waited till there was a heavy storm to make the water deep enough for me to drown myself. And I've been prevented even in this."

"Josepha!" said the countess, deeply moved, "will you go with me—away from Ammergau, to another, a very different world, where you and your disgrace are unknown ?"

Josepha gazed at the stranger as if in a dream.

"I believe," the lady added, "that my losing my maid to-day was an act of Providence in your behalf. Will you take her place ?"

"Thank heaven!" said old Gross. "Brighter days will dawn for you, Josepha!"

Josepha stood still with her hands clasped, tears were streaming down her cheeks.

"Why, do you hesitate to accept my offer ?" asked the countess, greatly perplexed.

"Oh, don't be angry with me—I am sincerely grateful; but what do I care for all these things, if I am no longer permitted to act the Magdalene ?" burst in unutterable anguish from the very depths of the girl's soul.

"What an ambition!" said the countess to Andreas in astonishment.

"Yes, that is the way with them all here—they would rather lose their lives than a part in the Passion!" he answered in a low tone. "But, child, you could not always play the Magdalene—in ten years you would be too old for it," he said soothingly to the despairing Josepha.

"Oh that's a very different thing—when we have grown grey with honors, we know that we must give it up—but so—" and again she gazed longingly at the beautiful, deep, rushing water, where it would be so cool, so pleasant to rest—which she had vowed to seek, and now could not keep her word.

"Do you love your child, Josepha?" asked Countess Wildenau.

"It died directly after it was born."

"Do you love your mother?"

"No, she was always unkind and harsh to me, and now she has lost her mind."

"Do you love your lover?" the lady persisted.

"Yes—but he is dead! A poacher shot him—he was a forester."

"Then you have no one for whom you care to live?"

"No one!"

"Then come with me and try whether you cannot love me well enough to make it worth while to live for me! Will you?"

"Yes, your Highness, I will try!" replied the girl, fixing her large eyes with an expression of mingled inquiry and admiration upon the countess. A beautiful glow of gratitude and confidence gradually transfigured the grief-worn face: "I think I could do anything for you."

"Come with me then—at once, poor child—I will save you! Your relatives will not object."

"Oh, no! They will be glad to have me go away."

"And your cousin, the—the—" she does not know herself why she hesitates to pronounce the name.

"The Christ-Freyer?" said Josepha finishing the sentence. "Oh! he has not spoken to me for a year, except to say what was absolutely necessary, he cannot get over my having brought disgrace upon his unsullied name. It has made him disgusted with life here and, if it were not for the Christ, he would not stay in Ammergau. He is so severe in such things."

"So *severe!*" the countess repeated, thoughtfully.

The clock in the steeple of the Ammergau church struck two.

"It is late," said the countess, "the poor thing needs rest." She wrapped her own cloak around the girl.

"Come, lonely heart, I will warm you."

She turned once more to drink in the loveliness of the exquisite scene.

"Night of miracle, I thank thee."

CHAPTER V.

MODERN PILGRIMS.

"WHAT do you think. The Countess von Wildenau is founding an Orphan's Home!" said the prince, as, leaving the Gross house, he joined a group of gentlemen who were waiting just outside the door in the little garden.

The news created a sensation; the gentlemen, laughing and jesting, plied him with questions.

"Oh, *Mon Dieu*, who can understand a woman? Our goddess is sitting in the peasants' living room, with the elderly daughters of the house, indescribable creatures, occupying herself with feminine work."

"Her Highness! Countess Wildenau! Oh, that's a bad joke."

"No, upon my honor! If she had not hung a veil over the window, we could see her sitting there. She has borrowed a calico apron from one of the 'ladies of the house,' and as, for want of a maid, she was obliged to arrange her hair herself, she wears it to-day in a remarkably simple style and looks,"—he kissed his hand to the empty air—"more bewitching than ever, like a girl of sixteen, a regular Gretchen! Whoever has not gone crazy over her when she has been in full dress, will surely do so if he sees her *thus*."

"Aha! We must see her, too; we'll assail the window!" cried his companions enthusiastically.

"No, no! For Heaven's sake don't do that, on pain of her anger! Prince Hohenheim, I beg you! Count Cossigny, don't knock! St. Génois, *au nom de Dieu*, she will never forgive you."

"Why not—friends so intimate as we are?"

"I have already said, who can depend upon a woman's whims? Let me explain. I entered, rejoicing in the thought of bringing her such pleasant news. I said: 'Guess whom I met just now at the ticket office, Countess?' The goddess sat sewing."

There was a general cry of astonishment. "Sewing!" the prince went on, "of course, without a thimble, for those in the house did not fit, and there was none among Her Highness' trinkets. So I repeated my question. An icy 'How can I tell?' was the depressing answer, as if at that moment nothing in the world could possibly interest her more than her work! So, unasked and with no display of attention, I was forced to go on with my news. 'Just think, Countess, Prince Hohenheim, the Counts Cossigny, Wengenrode, St. Génois, all Austria, France, and Bavaria have arrived!' I joyously exclaimed. I expected that she would utter a sigh of relief at the thought of meeting men of her world again, but no—she greeted my tidings with a frown."

"Hear, hear!" cried the group.

"A frown! I was forced to persist. 'They are outside, waiting to throw themselves at your feet,' I added. A still darker frown. 'Please keep the gentlemen away, I can see no one, I will see no one.' So she positively announced. I timidly ventured to ask why. She was tired, she could receive no one, she had no time. At last it came out. What do you suppose the countess did yesterday?"

"I dare not guess," replied St. Génois with a malicious glance at the prince, which the latter loftily ignored.

"She sent me away at eleven o'clock and then went wandering about, rhapsodizing over the moonlight with her host, old Gross."

A universal peal of laughter greeted these words. "Countess Wildenau, for lack of an escort, obliged to wander about with an old stone-cutter!"

"Yes, and she availed herself of this virtuous ramble to save the life of a despairing girl, who very opportunely attempted to commit suicide, just at the time the countess was passing to rescue this precious prize. Now she is sitting yonder remodeling one of her charming tailor costumes for this last toy of her caprice. She declares that she loves the wench most tenderly, will never be separated from her; in short, she is playing the novel character of Lady Bountiful, and does not want to be disturbed."

"Did you see the fair orphan?"

"No; she protested that it would be unpleasant for the girl to expose herself to curious glances, so she conceals this very sensitive young lady from profane eyes in her sleeping room. What do you say to all this, Prince?"

"I say," replied Prince Hohenheim, an elderly gentleman with a clearly cut, sarcastic face, a bald forehead, and a low, but distinct enunciation, "that a vivacious, imaginative woman is always influenced by the environment in which she happens to find herself. When the countess is in the society of scholarly people, she becomes extremely learned, if she is in a somewhat frivolous circle, like ours, she grows—not exactly frivolous, but full of sparkling wit, and here, among these devout enthusiasts, Her Highness wishes to play the part of a Stylite. Let us indulge her, it won't last long, a lady's whim must never be thwarted. *Ce que femme veut, Dieu le veut !*"

"Has the countess also made a vow to fast?" asked Count Cossigny of the Austrian Embassy, and therefore briefly called "Austria," "could we not dine together?"

"No, she told me that she would not leave the beloved suicide alone a moment at present, and therefore she intended to dine at home. Yesterday she shuddered at the bare thought of drinking a cup of tea made in that witch's kitchen, and only the fact that my valet prepared it and I drank it first in her presence finally induced her, at ten o'clock last evening, to accept the refreshment. And to-day she will eat a dinner prepared by the ladies of the house. There must really be something dangerous in the air of Ammergau!"

"To persons of the countess' temperament, yes!" replied Prince Hohenheim in his calm manner, then slipping his arm through the prince's a moment, whispered confidentially, as they walked on: "I advise you, Prince Emil, to get her away as soon as possible."

"Certainly, all the arrangements are made. We shall start directly after the performance."

"That is fortunate. To-morrow, then! You have tickets?"

"Oh yes, and what is still better, whole bones."

"That's true," cried Austria, "what a crowd! One might think Sarah Bernhardt was going to play the Virgin Mary."

"It's ridiculous! I haven't seen such a spectacle since the Paris Exposition!" remarked St. Génois.

"It's worse than Baden-Baden at the time o he races," muttered Wengenrode, angrily. "Absurd, what brings the people here?"

"Why, *we* are here, too," said Hohenheim, smiling.

"*Mon Dieu*, it must be seen once, if people are in the neighborhood," observed Cossigny.

"Are you going directly after the performance, too?" asked Prince Emil.

"Of course, what is there to do here? No gaming—no ladies' society, and just think, the burgomaster of Ammergau will allow neither a circus nor any other ordinary performance. He was offered *forty thousand marks* by the proprietor of the Circus Rouannet, if he would permit him to give performances during the Passion Play! Mademoiselle Rouannet told me so herself. Do you suppose that obstinate, stiff-necked Philistine could be persuaded? No, it was not in harmony with the dignity of the Passion Play. He preferred to refuse the 40,000 marks. The Salon Klüber wanted to put up an elegant merry-go-round and offered 12,000 marks for the privilege. Heaven forbid!"

"I believe these people have the mania of ambition," said Wengenrode.

"Say rather of *saintship*," corrected Prince Hohenheim.

"Aye, they all consider themselves the holy personages whom they represent. We need only look at this arrogant burgomaster, and the gentleman who personates Christ, to understand what these people imagine themselves."

All joined in the laugh which followed.

"Yes," said Wengenrode, "and the Roman procurator, Pilate, who is a porter or a messenger and so drags various loads about, carried up my luggage to-day and dropped my dressing case containing a number of breakable jars and boxes. 'Stupid blockhead!' I exclaimed, angrily. He straightened himself and looked at me with an expression which actually embarrassed me. 'My name is *Thomas Rendner*, sir! I beg your pardon for my awkwardness, and am ready to make your loss good, so far as my means shall allow.'"

"Now tell me, isn't that sheer hallucination of grandeur?"

Some of the gentlemen laughed, but Prince Emil and Hohenheim were silent.

"Where shall we go to-morrow evening in Munich to recompense ourselves for this boredom?" asked Cossigny.

"To the Casino, I think!" said the prince.

"Well, then we'll all meet there, shall we?"

The party assented.

"Provided that the countess has no commands for us," observed St. Génois.

"She will not have any," said the prince, "for either the Play will produce an absurd impression which is not to be expected, and then she will feel ashamed and unwilling to grant us our triumph because we predicted it, or her sentimental mood will draw from this farce a sweet poison of emotion, and in that case we shall be too frivolous for her! This must first be allowed to exhale."

"Very true," Hohenheim assented. "You are just the man to cope with this capricious beauty, Prince Emil. Adieu! May you prosper!"

The gentlemen raised their hats.

"Farewell!" said Cossigny, "by the way, I'll make a suggestion. We shall best impress the countess while in this mood, by our generosity; let us heap coals of fire on her head by sending a telegram to the court-gardner to convert the whole palace into a floral temple to welcome her return. It will touch a mysterious chord of sympathy if she meets only these mute messengers of our adoration. When on entering she finds this surprise and remembers how basely she treated us this morning, her heart will be touched and she will invite us to dine the day after to-morrow."

"A capital plan," cried Wengenrode and St. Génois, gaily. "Do your Highnesses agree?"

"Certainly," replied Hohenheim, with formal courtesy, "when the point in question is a matter of gallantry, a Hohenheim is never backward."

"I beg to be allowed to contribute also, but *incognito.* She would regard such an attention from me as a piece of sentimentality, and it would produce just the contrary effect," Prince Emil answered.

"As you please."

"Let us go to the telegraph office!" cried Wengenrode, eagerly.

"Farewell, gentlemen."

"*Au revoir,* Prince Emil! Are you going to return to the lionesses' den?"

" Can you ask ?" questioned Hohenheim with a significant smile.

" Then early to-morrow morning at the Play, and at night the Casino, don't forget!" Cossigny called back.

The gentlemen, laughing and chatting, strolled down the street to their lodgings. The prince watched them a moment, turned, and went back to the countess.

" I cannot really be vexed with her, if these associates do not satisfy her," he thought.

" Should I desire her to become my wife, if they did ? Certainly not. Yet if women only would not rush from one extreme to another ? Hohenheim is perfectly right, she ought not to stay here too long, she must go to-morrow."

He had reached the house and entered the neglected old garden where huge gnarled fruit trees, bearing small, stunted fruit, interlaced their branches above a crooked bench. There, in the midst of the rank grass and weeds, sat the countess, her beautiful head resting against the mouldy bark of the old trunk, gazing thoughtfully at the luminous mountains gleaming in the distance through the tangled boughs and shrubbery.

From the adjoining garden of the sculptor Zwink, whose site was somewhat higher, a Diana carved in white stone gazed curiously across, seeming as if she wished to say to the pensive lady who at that moment herself resembled a statue: " Art will create gods for you *everywhere!*" But the temptation had no effect, the countess seemed to have had no luck with these gods, she no longer believed in them!

" Well, Countess Madeleine, did the light and air lure you out of doors ?" asked the prince, joyfully approaching her.

" Oh, I could not bear to stay there any longer. Herr Gross' daughters are finishing the dress. We will dine here, Prince; the meal can be served on a table near the house, under a wild-grape vine arbor. We can wait on ourselves for one day."

" For *one* day!" repeated the prince with great relief; " oh yes, it can be managed for one day." Thank Heaven, she had no intention of staying here.

" Oh, Prince, see how beautiful, how glorious it is !"

" Beautiful, glorious ? Pardon me, but I see nothing to

call forth words you so rarely use! You must have narrowed your demands if, after the view of the wondrous garden of the Isola Bella and all the Italian villas, you suddenly take delight in cabbage-stalks, wild-pears, broom, and colt's foot."

"Now see how you talk again!" replied the countess, unpleasantly affected by his words. "Does not Spinoza say: 'Everything is beautiful, and as I lose myself in the observation of its beauty, my pleasure in life is increased.' "

"That has not been your motto hitherto. You have usually found something to criticise in every object. It seems to me that you have wearied of the beautiful and now, by way of a change, find even *ugliness* fair."

"Very true, my friend. I am satisfied, nothing charms me, nothing satisfies me, not even the loveliest scene, because I always apply to everything the standard of perfection, and nothing attains it." She shook herself suddenly as if throwing off a burden. "This must not continue, the æsthetic intolerance which poisoned every pleasure must end, I will cast aside the whole load of critical analysis and academic ideas of beauty, and snap my fingers at the ghosts of Winckelmann and Lessing. Here in the kitchen-garden, among cabbage-stalks and colt's foot, wild-pear and plum-trees, fanned by the fresh, crystal-clear air of the lofty mountains, whose glaciers shimmer with a bluish light through the branches, in the silence and solitude, I suddenly find it beautiful; beautiful because I am happy, because I am only a human being, free from every restraint, thinking nothing, feeling nothing save the peace of nature, the delight of this repose."

She rested her feet comfortably on the bench and, with her head thrown back, gazed with a joyous expression into the blue air which, after the rain, arched above the earth like a crystal bell.

This mood did not quite please the prince. He was exclusively a man of the world. His thoughts were ruled by the laws of the most rigid logic, whatever was not logically attainable had no existence for him; his enthusiasm reached the highest pitch only in the enjoyment of the noblest products of art and science. He did not comprehend how any one could weary of them, even for a moment, on the

one side because his calm temperament did not, like the
countess' passionate one, exhaust everything by following it
to its inmost core, and he was thus guarded from satiety; on
the other because he wholly lacked appreciation of nature
and her unconscious grandeur.   He was the trained vassal
of custom in the conventional, as well as in every other province.   The countess, however, possessed some touch of that
doctrine of divine right which is ready, at any moment, to
cast off the bonds of tradition and artificial models and obey
the impulse of kinship with sovereign nature.   This was the
boundary across which he could not follow her, and he was
perfectly aware of it, for he had one of those proud characters
which disdain to deceive themselves concerning their own
powers.   Yet it filled him with grave anxiety.

"What are you thinking of now, Prince?" asked his companion, noticing his gloomy mood.

"That I have not seen you so contented for months, and
yet I am unable to understand the cause of this satisfaction.
Especially when I remember what it usually requires to bring
a smile of pleasure to your lips."

"Dear me, must everything be understood?" cried the
beautiful woman, laughing; "there is the pedant again! Must
we be perpetually under the curb of self-control and give ourselves an account whether what we feel in a moment of happiness is sensible and authorized? Must we continually see
ourselves reflected in the mirror of our self-consciousness, and
never draw a veil over our souls and permit God to have one
undiscovered secret in them?"

The prince silently kissed her hand.   His eyes now expressed deep, earnest feeling, and stirred by emotion, she laid
her other hand upon his head:

"You are a noble-hearted man, Prince; though some un-
spoken, uncomprehended idea stands between us, I know
your feelings."

Again the rose and the thorn! It was always so! At the
very moment her soft, sweet hand touched him caressingly,
she thrust a dagger into his heart.   Aye, that was the continual "misunderstanding" which existed between them, the
thorn in the every rose she proffered.

Women like these are only tolerable when they really love;

when a powerful feeling makes them surrender themselves completely. Where this is not the case, they are, unconsciously and involuntarily, malicious, dangerous creatures, caressing and slaying at the same moment.

First, woe betide the man whom *they believe* they love. For how often such beings are mistaken in their feelings! Such delusions do not destroy the woman, she often experiences them, but the man who has shared them with her! Alas for him who has not kept a cool head.

The prince was standing with his back turned to the street, gazing thoughtfully at the beautiful woman with the fathomless, sparkling eyes. Suddenly he saw her start and flush. Turning with the speed of lightning, he followed the direction of her glance, but saw nothing except the figure of a man of unusual height, with long black hair, pass swiftly around the corner and disappear.

"Do you know that gentleman?"

"No," replied the countess frankly, "he is the person whom I saw yesterday as we drove up the mountain."

"Pardon the indescretion, but you blushed."

"Yes, I felt it, but I don't know why," she answered with an almost artless innocence in her gaze. The prince could not help smiling.

"Countess, Countess!" he said, shaking his finger at her as if she were a child. "Guard your imagination; it will prove a traitor some day."

The countess, as if with a sweet consciousness of guilt, drew down the uplifted hand with a movement of such indescribable grace that no one could have remained angry with her. The prince knelt at her feet an instant, not longer than a blade of grass requires to bend before the breeze and rise again, then he stood erect, somewhat paler than before, but perfectly calm.

"I'll go in and tell my valet to serve our dinner here."

"If you please, Prince," replied the lady, gazing absently down the street.

Andreas Gross entered the garden. "Everything is settled, Your Highness. I have talked with Josepha's relatives and guardian and they will be very glad to have you take her."

"All, even the Christ-Freyer?"

4

"Certainly, there is no objection."

She had expected something more and looked at the old man as if for the rest of the message, but he added nothing.

"Ought not Freyer to come here, in order to discuss the particulars with me?" she asked at last, almost timidly.

"Why, he goes to see no one, as I told you, and he surely would not come to speak of Josepha, for he is ashamed of her. He says that whatever you do will be satisfactory to him."

"Very well," replied the countess, in a somewhat disappointed tone.

"What a comical tête-à-tête!" a laughing voice suddenly exclaimed behind the fence. The countess started up, but it was too late for escape; she was caught.

A lady, young and elegantly dressed, accompanied by two older ones, eagerly rushed up to her.

"Dear Countess, why have you hidden yourself here at the farthest corner of the village? We have searched all Ammergau for you. Your coat-of-arms on the carriage and your liveries at the old post-house betrayed you. Yes, yes, when people want to travel *incognito*, they must not journey with genuine Wildenau elegance. We were more cautious. We came in a modest hired conveyance. But what a life this is! I was obliged to sleep on straw last night. Hear and shudder! On *straw!* Did you have a bed? You have been here since yesterday?"

"Why, Your Highness, pray take breath! Good morning, Baroness! Good morning, Your Excellency!"

The Countess von Wildenau greeted all the ladies somewhat absently, yet very cordially. "Will you condescend to sit on this bench?"

"Oh, you must sit here, too."

"No, it is not large enough, I am already seated."

She had taken her seat on the root of a tree, with her face turned toward the street, in which she seemed to be deeply interested. The ladies were accommodated on the bench, and then followed a conversation which no pen could describe. This, that, and the other thing, matters to which the countess had not given a single thought, an account of everything the new comers had heard about the Ammergau people, the appearance of the Christ, whom they had already met, a handsome man, very handsome, with magnificent hair, and mysterious eyes—not the head of Christ, but rather as one would imagine Faust or Odin; but there was no approaching him, he was so unsociable. Such a pity, it would have been so interesting to talk with him. Rumor asserted that he was in love with a noble lady; it was very possible, there was no other way of explaining his distant manner.

Countess von Wildenau had become very quiet, the eyes bent upon the street had an expression of actual suffering in their depths.

Prince Emil stood in the doorway, mischievously enjoying the situation. It was a just punishment for her capricious whims that now, after having so insolently refused to see her friends, she should be compelled to listen to this senseless chatter.

At last, however, he took pity on her and sent out his valet with the table-cloth and plates.

" Oh, it is your dinner hour !" The ladies started up and Her Highness raised her lorgnette.

" Ah, Prince Emil's valet ! So the faithful Toggenburg is with you."

" Certainly, ladies !" said a voice from the door, as the prince came forward. " Only I was too timid to venture into such a dangerous circle."

Peals of laughter greeted him.

" Yes, yes; the Prince of Metten-Barnheim timid !"

" At present I am merely the representative of Countess Wildenau's discharged courier, whose office, with my usual devotion, I am trying to fill, and doing everything in my power to escape the fate of my predecessor."

" That of being sent away ?" asked the baroness somewhat maliciously.

Countess Madeleine cast a glance of friendly reproach at him. " How can you say such things, Prince ?"

" Your soup is growing cold !" cried the duchess.

" Where does Your Highness dine ?"

" At the house of one of the chorus singers, where we are lodging. A man with the bearing of an apostle, and a black-smith by trade. It is strange, all these people have a touch of ideality about them, and all this beautiful long hair ! Haven't

you walked through the village yet? Oh, you must, it's very
odd; the people who throng around the actors in the Passion
Play are types we shall not soon see again. I'm waiting
eagerly for to-morrow. I hope our seats will be near. Farewell, dear Countess!" The duchess took the arm of the
prince, who escorted her to the garden gate. "I hope you
will take care that the countess, under the influence of the
Passion, doesn't enter a convent the day after to morrow."

"Your Highness forgets that I am an incorrigible heretic,"
laughed Madeleine Wildenau, kissing the two ladies in waiting, in her absence of mind, with a tenderness which they
were at a loss to understand.

The prince accompanied the ladies a short distance away
from the house, while Madeleine returned to Josepha, as if
seeking in the society of the sorrowful, quiet creature, rest
from the noisy conversation.

"Really, Countess von Wildenau has an over-supply of
blessings. This magnificent widow's dower, the almost boundless revenue from the Wildenau estates, and a host of
suitors!" said the baroness, after the prince had taken leave
to return to "his idol."

"Yes, but she will lose the revenue if she marries again,"
replied the duchess. "The will was made in that way by
Count Wildenau because his jealousy extended beyond the
grave. I know all the particulars. She must either remain a
widow or make a *very* brilliant match; for a woman of her
temperament could *never* accommodate herself to more
modest circumstances."

"So she is not a good match?" asked Her Excellency.

"Certainly not, for the will is so worded that on the day
she exchanges the name of Wildenau for another, the estates,
with the whole income, go to a side branch of the Wildenau
family as there are no direct heirs. It is enough to make one
hate him, for the Wildenau cousins are extravagant and avaricious men who have already squandered one fortune. The
poor countess will then have nothing except her personal
property, her few diamonds, and whatever gifts she received
from her husband."

"Has she no private fortune?" asked the baroness, curiously.

"You know that she was a Princess Prankenburg, and the

financial affairs of the Prankenburg family are very much embarrassed. That is why the beautiful young girl was sacrificed at seventeen to that horrible old Wildenau, who in return was forced to pay her father's debts," the duchess explained.

"Oh, so *that's* the way the matter stands!" said Her Excellency, drawing a long breath. "Do her various admirers know it? All the gentlemen undoubtedly believe her to be immensely rich."

"Oh, she makes no secret of these facts," replied the duchess kindly. "She is sincere, that must be acknowledged, and she endured a great deal with her nervous old husband. We all know what he was; every one feared him and he tyrannized over his wife. What was all her wealth and splendor to her? One ought not to grudge her a taste of happiness."

"She laid aside her widow's weeds as soon as possible. People thought that very suspicious," observed the baroness in no friendly tone.

"That is exactly why I say: she is better than her reputation, because she scorns falsehood and hypocrisy," replied the duchess, leading the way across a narrow bridge. The two ladies in waiting, lingering a little behind, whispered: "*She* scorn falsehood and deception! Why, Your Excellency, her whole nature is treachery. She cannot exist a moment without acting some farce! With the pious she is pious, with the Liberals she plays the Liberal, she coquets with every party to maintain her influence as ex-ambassadress. She cannot cease intriguing and plotting. Now she is once more assum·ing the part of youthful artlessness to bewitch this Prince Emil. Did you see that look of embarrassment just now, like a young girl? It is enough to make one ill!"

"Yes, just see how she has duped that handsome, clever prince, the heir of a reigning family, too," lamented Her Excellency, who had daughters. "It is a shocking affair, he is seen everywhere with her; and yet there is no report of a betrothal! What do the men find in her? She captivates them all, young and old, there is no difference."

"And she is no longer even *beautiful*. She has faded, lost all her freshness, it is nothing but coquetry!" answered the baroness hastily, for the duchess had stopped and was waiting for the ladies to overtake her. So they walked on in the

direction of the Passion Theatre where, on the morrow, they
were to behold the God of Love, for whose sake they made
this pious pilgrimage.

"You were rightly served, Countess Madeleine," said the
prince laughing, as they took their seats at the table. "You
sent away your true friends and fell into the hands of these
false ones."

"The duchess is not false," answered the countess with a
weary look, "she is noble in thought and act."

"Like all who are in a position where they need envy no
one," said the prince, pushing aside with his spoon certain
little islands of doubtful composition which were floating in the
soup. "But believe me, with these few exceptions, no one
save men, deals sincerely with an admired woman. Women
of the ordinary stamp cannot repress their envy. I should
not like to hear what is being said of us by these friends on
their way home."

"What does it matter?" answered his companion, leaving
her soup untasted.

"Our poor diplomatic corps, which had anticipated so
much pleasure in seeing you," the prince began again. "I
would almost like to ask you a favor, Countess!"

"What is it?"

"That you will invite us to dine day after to-morrow. The
gentlemen have resolved to avenge themselves nobly by
offering you an ovation on your return to Munich to-morrow
evening."

"Indeed, what is it?"

"I ought not to betray the secret, but I know that you do
not like surprises. The Wildenau palace will be transformed
into a temple of flowers. Everything is already ordered, it is
to be matchless, fairylike!"

The speaker was secretly watching the impression made by
his words; he must get her away from this place at any cost!
The mysterious figure which had just called to her cheeks a
flush for whose sake he would have sacrificed years of his life,
then he had noticed—nothing escaped his keen eye and ear—
her annoyed, almost jealous expression when the ladies spoke
of the "raven-locked" Christ and his love for some high-born
dame. She must leave this place ere the whim gained a firm

hold. The worthy peasant-performer might not object to the admiration of noble ladies, a pinchback theatre-saint would hardly resist a Countess Wildenau, if she should choose to make him the object of an eccentric caprice.

"It is very touching in the gentlemen," said the countess; "let us anticipate them and invite them to dine the day after to-morrow."

"Ah, there spoke my charming friend, now I am content with you. Will you permit me, at the close of this luxurious meal, to carry the joyous tidings to the gentlemen?"

"Do so," she answered carelessly. "And when you have delivered the invitation, would you do me the favor to telegraph to my steward?"

"Certainly." He pushed back the plate containing an unpalatable cutlet and drew out his note-book to make a memorandum.

"What shall I write?"

"STEWARD GERES, Wildenau Palace, Munich.—Day after to-morrow, Monday, Dinner at 6 o'clock, 12 plates, 15 courses," dictated the countess.

"There, that is settled. But, Countess, twelve persons! Whom do you intend to invite?"

"When I return the duchess' visit I will ask the three ladies, then Prince Hohenheim and Her Excellency's two daughters will make twelve."

"But that will be terribly wearisome to the neighbors of Her Excellency's daughters."

"Yes, still it can't be helped, I must give the poor girls a chance to make their fortune! With the exception of Prince Hohenheim, you are all in the market!" she said smiling.

"No one could speak so proudly save a Countess Wildenau, who knows that every other woman only serves as a foil," replied the prince, kissing her hand with a significant smile. She was remarkably gracious that day; she permitted her hand to rest in his, there was a shade of apology in her manner. Apology for what? He had no occasion to ponder long— she was ashamed of having neglected a trusted friend for a chimera, a nightmare, which had assumed the form of a man with mysterious black eyes and floating locks. The ladies' stories of the love affairs of the presumptive owner of these locks had destroyed the dream and broken the spell of the nightmare.

" Admirable, it had happened very opportunely."

" But, Countess, the gentlemen will be disappointed, if the ladies, also, come.   Would it not be much pleasanter without them ? You are far more charming and entertaining when you are the only lady present at our little smoking parties."

" We can have one later.   The ladies will leave at ten. Then you others can remain."

" And who will be sent away *next*, when you are wearied by this *après soirée ?* Who will be allowed to linger on a few minutes and smoke the last cigarette with you ? " he added, coaxingly.   He looked very handsome at that moment.

" We shall see," replied the countess, and for the first time her voice thrilled with a warmer emotion.   Her hand still rested in his, she had forgotten to withdraw it.   Suddenly its warmth roused her, and his blue eyes flashed upon her a light as brilliant as the indiscreet glare which sometimes rouses a sleeper.

She released it, and as the dinner was over, rose from the little table.

" Will you go with me to call on the duchess later ? " she asked.   " If so, I will dress now, while you give the invitation to the gentlemen, and you can return afterward."

" As you choose ! " replied the prince in an altered tone, for the slight variation in the lady's mood had not escaped his notice.   " In half an hour, then.   Farewell ! "

CHAPTER VI.

THE EVENING BEFORE THE PLAY.

JOSEPHA sat in the countess' room at work on her new dress.   She was calm and quiet ; the delight in finery which never abandons a woman to her latest hour—the poorest peasant, if still conscious, asks for a nicer cap when the priest comes to bring the last sacrament—had asserted its power in her.   The countess noticed it with pleasure.

" Shall you finish it soon, Josepha ? "

" In an hour, Your Highness ! "

" Very well, I shall return about that time, and then we'll try the dress on."

" Oh, your ladyship, it's a sin for me to put on such a handsome gown, nobody will see me."

" Not here, if you don't wish them to do so, but to-morrow evening we shall go to Munich, where you will begin a new life, with no brand upon your brow."

Josepha kissed the countess' hand; a few large tears rolled down on the dress which was to clothe a new creature. Then she helped her mistress to put on a walking toilette, performing her task skillfully and quickly. The latter fixed a long, thoughtful look upon her. " You are somewhat like your cousin, the Christ, are you not ? "

"So people say ! "

" I suppose he sees a great many ladies ? "

" They all run after him, the high as well as the low. And it isn't the strangers only, the village girls are crazy over him, too. He might have *any* one he wanted, it seems as if he fairly bewitched the women."

" I heard that the reason for his secluded life was that he had a love affair with some noble lady."

" Indeed ? " said Josepha carelessly, " I don't know anything about it. I don't believe it, though he would not tell me, even if it were true. Oh, people talk about him so much, that's one reason for the envy. But his secluded life isn't on account of any noble lady! He has had nothing to say to anybody here since they refused to let me take part in the Play and gossiped so much about me. Though he doesn't speak of it, it cuts him to the heart. Alas, I am to blame, and no one else."

Countess Wildenau, obeying a sudden impulse, kissed the girl on the forehead : "Farewell, keep up courage, don't weep, rejoice in your new life ; I will soon return."

As she passed out, she spoke to the Gross sisters commending Josepha to their special care.

" The gentlemen are delighted, and send you their most grateful homage," called the prince.

" Then they are all coming ?" said Countess Wildenau, taking his arm.

"All, there was no hesitation!" he answered, again noticing in his companion's manner the restlessness which had
formerly awakened his anxiety. As they passed down the
street together, her eyes were wandering everywhere.

"She is seeking some one," thought the prince.

"Let me tell you that I am charmed with this Ammergau
Christ," cried the duchess, as they approached the blacksmith's house. She was sitting in the garden, which contained a tolerably large manure heap, a "Saletl," the name
given to an open summer-house, and three fruit-trees, amid
which the clothes lines were stretched. On the house was a
rudely painted Madonna, life-size, with the usual bunch of
flowers, gazing with a peculiar expression at the homage
offered to her son, or at least, so it seemed to the countess.

"Have you seen him, Duchess? I am beginning to be
jealous!" said the countess with a laugh intended to be natural, but which sounded a little forced.

The visitors entered the arbor; after an exchange of greetings, the duchess told her guests that she had been with the
ladies to the drawing-school, where they had met Freyer.
The head-master (the son of Countess von Wildeau's host)
had presented him to the ladies, and he had been obliged to
exchange a few words with them, then he made his escape.
They were "fairly *wild*." His bearing, his dignity, the
blended courtesy and reserve of his manner, so modest and
yet so proud, and those eyes!

The prince was on coals of fire.

The blacksmith was hammering outside, shoeing a horse
whose hoof was so crooked that the iron would not fit. The
man's face was dripping with sooty perspiration, yet when he
turned it toward the ladies, they saw a classic profile and soft,
dreamy eyes.

"Beautiful hair and eyes appear to be a specialty among
the Ammergau peasants," said the prince somewhat abruptly,
interrupting the duchess. "Look at yonder smith, wash off
the soot and we shall have a superb head of Antinous."

"Yes, isn't that true? He is a splendid fellow, too,"
replied the duchess. "Let us call him here."

The smith was summoned and, wiping the grime from his
face with his shirt sleeves, modestly approached. The prince

watched with honest admiration the man's gait and bearing, clear-cut, intelligent features, and slender, lithe figure, which betrayed no sign of his hard labor save in the tense sinews and muscles of the arms.

"I must apologize," he said in excellent German—the Ammergau people use dialect only when speaking to one another—"I am in my working clothes and scarcely fit to be seen."

"You have a charming voice. Do you sing baritone?"

"Yes, Your Highness, but I rarely sing at all. My voice unfortunately is much injured by my hard toil, and my fingers are growing too stiff to play on the piano, so I cannot accompany myself."

"Do you play on the piano?"

"Certainly, Your Highness."

"Good Heavens, where did you learn?"

"Here in the village, Your Highness. Each one of us learns to use some instrument, else where should we obtain an orchestra for the Passion?"

"Think of it!" said the duchess in French, "A blacksmith who plays on the piano; peasants who form an orchestra!" Then addressing her host in German, she added, "I suppose you have a church choir!"

"Certainly, Your Highness."

"And what masses do you perform?"

"Oh, nearly all the beautiful ones, some dating from the ancient Cecilian Church music, others from the later masters, Händel, Bach, down to the most modern times. A short time ago I sung Gounod's Ave Maria in the church, and this winter we shall give a Gethsemane by Kempter."

"Is it possible!" said the duchess, "*c'est unique!* Then you are really all artists and ought not to follow such hard trades."

"Yes, Duchess, but we must *live*. Our wives and children must be supported. *All* cannot be wood-carvers, smiths are needed, too. If the artisan is not rough, the trade is no disgrace."

"But have you time, with your business, for such artistic work?"

"Oh, yes, we do it in the evenings, after supper. We meet

at half past seven and often practise our music till twelve or even one o'clock."

" Oh, how tired you must be to study far into the night after the labor of the day."

" Oh, that doesn't harm us, it is our recreation and pleasure. Art is the only thing which lifts men above their daily cares! I would not wish to live, if I did not possess it, and we all have the same feeling."

The ladies exchanged glances.

" But, when do you sleep? You must be obliged to rise early in the morning."

" Oh, we Ammergau people are excitable, we need little sleep. To bed at one and up at five gives us rest enough."

" Well, then, you must live well, or you could not bear it."

" Yes, we live very well, we have meat every Sunday," said the smith with much satisfaction.

" *C'est touchant!* " cried the duchess. " Meat *once* a week? And the rest of the time? "

" Oh, we eat something made of flour. My wife is an excellent cook, she was the cook in Count P.'s household! " he added with great pride, casting an affectionate glance at the plump little woman, holding a child in her arms, standing at the door of the house. He would gladly have presented this admirable wife to the strangers, but the ladies seemed less interested in her.

" What do you eat in the evening? "

" We have coffee at six o'clock, and drink a few glasses of beer when we meet at the tavern."

" And do all the Ammergau people live so? "

" All. No one wants anything different."

" Even your Christ? "

" Oh, he fares worse than we, he is unmarried and has no one to care for him."

" What a life, dear Countess, what a life! " the duchess, murmured in French.

" But you have a piano in your house. If you are able to get such an instrument, you ought to afford better food," said Her Excellency.

The blacksmith smiled, " If we had had better food, we

should not have been able to buy the piano. We saved it
from our stomachs."

"That is the true Ammergau spirit," said the countess
earnestly. "They will starve to secure a piano. Every endeavor is toward the ideal and the intellectual, for which they
are willing to make any personal sacrifice. I have never seen
such people."

"Nor have I. It seems as if the Passion Play gave them
all a special consecration," answered the duchess.

Countess von Wildenau rose. Her thoughts were so far
away that she was about to take leave without remembering
her invitation. But Prince Emil said impressively:

"Countess, surely you are forgetting that you intended to
invite the ladies—."

"Yes, yes," she interrupted, "it had almost escaped my
mind." The smith modestly went back to his work, for the
horse was growing restless, and the odor of burnt horn and
hair soon pervaded the atmosphere.

Meanwhile the countess delivered her invitation, which
was accepted with great enthusiasm.

A stately, athletic man in a blouse, carring a chest on his
shoulder, passed the ladies. The burden was terribly heavy,
for even his powerful, well-knit frame staggered under it,
and his handsome kingly head was bowed almost to the
earth.

"Look, Countess, that is Thomas Rendner the Roman
procurator. We shall soon make the acquaintance of the
whole company. We sit here in the summer-house like a
spider in its web, not a fly can pass unseen."

"Good Heavens, that Pilate!" exclaimed the countess,
watching him with sympathizing eyes, "Poor man, to-day
panting under an oppressive burden, to-morrow robed in
purple and crowned with a diadem, only to exchange them
again on the third day, for the porter's dusty blouse, and take
the yoke upon himself once more. What a contrast, and yet
he loses neither his balance nor his temper! Indeed I think
that we can learn as much here outside of the Passion Play,
as from the spectacle itself."

"Yes, if we watch with your deep, thoughtful eyes, my
dear Countess!" said the duchess, kissing the speaker's brow.

"We will discuss this subject farther when we drive with you the day after to-morrow."

The ladies parted. Madeleine von Wildenau, leaning on the prince's arm, walked silently through the crowd which now, on the eve of the play, thronged the narrow streets. The din and tumult were enough to deprive one of sight and hearing. Dazed by the confusion, she clung closely to her companion's arm.

"Good Heavens, is it possible that Christianity still possesses such a power of attraction!" she murmured, involuntarily, while struggling through the throng.

The ground in the Ettal road trembled under the roll of carriage wheels. The last evening train had arrived, and a flood of people and vehicles poured into the village already almost crushed beneath the tide of human beings. Horses half driven to death, dragging at a gallop heavy landaus crowded with six or eight persons. Lumbering wagons containing twenty or thirty travellers just as they had climbed in, sometimes half clinging to the steps or the boxes of the wheels, swayed to and fro; intoxicated, excited by the mad rush and the fear of being left behind—raging and shrieking like a horde of unchained fiends come to disturb the sacred drama rather than pious pilgrims who wished to witness it, the frantic mob poured in. "*Sauve qui peut*" was the motto, the prince lifted the countess on a small post by the roadside. Just at that moment the fire-brigade marched by to watch the theatre. It was said that several of the neighboring parishes, envious of Ammergau, had threatened to ruin the Play by setting the theatre on fire. Fire engines and strangers' carriages passed pell-mell. The people of Ammergau themselves, alarmed and enraged by the cruel threat, were completely disconcerted; passionate discussions, vehement commands, and urgent entreaties were heard on all sides. Prompt and energetic action was requisite, the fate of all Ammergau was at stake.

The bells now began to ring and at the same moment the first of the twenty-five cannon shots which were to consecrate the morrow's festival was discharged, and the musicians passed through the streets.

The air fairly quivered with the deafening uproar of all these mingling waves of sound. Darkness was gathering, the countess grew giddy, she felt as if she were stifling in the tumult. A pair of horses fell just below them, causing a break in the line of carriages, which the prince used to get his companion across, and she at last reached home, almost fainting. Her soul was stirred to its inmost depths. What was the power which produced such effects?

Was this the calm, petty doctrine, which had been inculcated so theoretically and coldly at the school-room desk and from the pulpit, and with which, when a child, she has been disgusted by an incomprehensible school-catechism? Was this the doctrine which, from earliest childhood, had been nothing more than a wearisome dead letter, to which, as it had become the religion of the state, an official visit to church was due from time to time, just as, on certain days, cards were left on ambassadors and government officials?

The wind still bore from the village the noise of the throngs of people, the ringing of the bells, and the thunder of the cannon, blended with occasional bursts of music. The countess had had similar experiences when tidings of great victories had been received during the last war, but those were *facts*. For the first time in her life she asked herself if Christianity was a fact? And if not, if it was only an idea, what inherent power, after the lapse of nearly two thousand years, produced such an effect?

Why did all these people come—why did she *herself?* The human race is homesick, it no longer knows for what; it is only a vague impulse, but one which instinctively draws it in the direction where it perceives a sign, a vestige of what it has lost and forever seeks. Such, she knows it now, such is the feeling of all the throngs that have flocked hither to-day, she realized that at this moment she was a microcosm of weary, wandering mankind seeking for salvation.

And as when, deceived and disappointed in everything, we seek the picture of some dead friend, long since forgotten, and press it weeping to our lips, she clung to the image of the Redeemer. Now that everything had deluded her, no system which had boastfully promised a victory over calamity and death had stood the test, after one makeshift had supplanted another without supplying what was lacking, after all the vaunted remedies of philosophy and materialism proved mere palliatives which make the evil endurable for the moment but do not heal it, suffering, cheated humanity was suddenly seeking the image of the lost friend so long forgotten. But a dead friend cannot come forth from a picture, a painted heart can no longer beat. Could *Christ* rise again in His image? Could *His* word live once more on the lips of a stranger? And would the drops of artificial blood, trickling from the brow of the personified Messiah, possess redeeming power?

That was the miracle which attracted the throngs from far and near, *that* must be the marvel, and to-morrow it would be revealed.

" Of what are you dreaming, Countess Madeleine?" asked the prince after a pause which she had spent in the wild-grape arbor near the house gazing into vacancy, with her head resting on her hand. She looked up, glancing at him as if she had entirely forgotten his presence. " I don't know what is the cause of my emotion, the tumult in the village has stirred me deeply! I feel that only potent things could send such a storm before them, and it seems as if it was the portent of some wonderful event!"

" Good Heavens! What extravagant fancies, my dear Countess! I believe you add to all your rich gifts the dangerous one of poesy! I admire and honor you for it—but I can perceive in this storm nothing save a proof that curiosity is the greatest and most universal trait in human character, and that these throngs desire nothing more than the satisfaction of their curiosity. The affair is fashionable just now, and that explains the whole."

" Prince, I pity you for what you have just said," replied the countess, rising. Her face wore the same cold, lifeless expression as on the day of her arrival.

" But, my dearest friend, for Heavens's sake tell me, did *you* and *I* come from any other motive than curiosity?"

" You, no! I, yes!"

" Don't say that, *chère amie*. You, the scholar, superior to us all in learning; you, the disciple of Schopenhauer, the proud philosopher, the believer in Nirvâna."

" Yes, I, Prince!" cried the countess, " The philosopher who was not happy for an hour, not content for a moment. What is this Nirvâna? A stone idol, which the fruitless speculation of our times has conjured from the rubbish of archæological excavations, and which stares at us with its vacant eyes until we fall into an intellectual hypnotism which we mistake for peace." An expression of bitter sarcasm rested on her lips. "I came here to bring pessimism and Christianity face to face. I thought it would be very novel to see the stone idol Nirvâna, with his hands on his lap and the silence of eternal death on his lips, watch the martyr, dripping with sweat and blood, bear His own cross to the place of execution and cheerfully take up the work where Buddha faltered; on the boundary of non-exsistence. I wanted to see how the two would treat each other, if for nothing more than a comparative study of religion."

"You are irresistible in your charming mockery, dearest Countess, yet logically I cannot confess myself conquered!" replied the prince. The countess smiled: "Of course, when did a man ever acknowledge that to a woman, where intellectual matters were concerned? A sunny curl, the seductive arch of an upper lip, a pair of blue eyes sparkling with tears will make you lords of creation the dupes of the most ordinary coquette or even the yielding toy of the dullest ignorance. We women all know it! But, if we assail your dry logic, you are as unconquerable as Antæus so long as he stood upon the earth! You, too, could only be vanquished by whoever had the power to lift you from the ground where *you* stand."

"You might have that power, Countess. Not by your arguments, but by your eyes. You know that *one* loving glance would not only lift me from the earth but into heaven, and then you could do with me what you would."

"You have forfeited the loving glance! Perhaps it might have *rewarded* your assent, but it would never *purchase* it, I scorn bribed judges, for I am sure of my cause!"

"Countess, pardon my frankness: it is a pity that you have so much intellect."

"Why?"

"Because it leads you into sophistical by-ways; your tendency to mysticism gives an apparently logical foundation and thereby strengthens you the more in this dangerous course. A more simple, temperate judgment would *guard* you from it."

"Well, Prince—" she looked at him pityingly, contemptuously—"may Heaven perserve me from *such* a judgment as

5

well as from all who may seek to supply its place to me.
Excuse me for this evening. I should like to devote an hour
to these worthy people and soothe my nerves—I have been
too much excited by the scenes we have witnessed. Good-
night, Prince!"

Prince Emil turned pale. "Good-night, Countess. Perhaps to-morrow you will be somewhat more humane in this
cat and mouse game; to-day I am sent home with a bleeding
wound." With lips firmly compressed, he bowed his farewell
and left the garden. Madeleine looked after him: "He is
angry. I cannot help him, he deserved it. Oh, foolish man,
who deemed yourself so clever! Do you suppose this glowing heart desires no other revelations than those of pure
reason? Do you imagine that the arguments of all the phil-
osophical systems of humanity could offer it that for which it
longs? Shall I find it? Heaven knows! But one thing is
certain, I shall no longer seek it in *you*."

The sound of moans and low sobs came from the chamber
above the countess' room. It was Josepha. Countess Wildenau passed through the little trap-door and entered it. The
girl was kneeling beside the bed, with her face buried in the
pillows, to shut out the thunder of the cannon and the sound
of the bells, which summoned the actors in the sacred Play
from which she alone, the sinner, the outcast, was shut out.

Mary Magdalene, too, had sinned and erred, yet she had
been suffered to remain near the Lord. She was permitted to
touch His divine body and to wipe His feet with her hair!
But *she* was not allowed to render this service to His *image!*
She grasped the mass of wonderful silken locks which fell in
loosened masses over her shoulders. What did she care for
this beautiful hair now? She would fain cut it off and throw
it into the Ammer or, better still, bury it in the earth, the
earth on which the Passion Theatre stood. With a hasty
movement, she snatched a pair of shears which lay beside the
bed, and just as the countess' foot touched the threshold, a
sharp, cutting sound was heard and the most beautiful red
hair that ever adorned a girl's head fell like a dying flame at
her feet. "Josepha, what are you doing?" cried the countess,
"Oh, what a pity to lose that magnificent hair!"

"What do I care for it?" sobbed Josepha. "It can never

be seen in the Play! When the performance is over, I will slip into the theatre before we leave and bury it under the stage, where the cross stands. There I will leave it, there it shall stay, since I am no longer able to make it serve Him." She threw herself into the countess' arms and hid her tear-stained face upon her bosom. Alas, she was not even allowed to appear among the populace, she alone was banished from the cross, yet she knew that the *real* Saviour would have suffered her to be at His feet as well as Mary Magdalene.

"Console yourself, Josepha, your belief does not deceive you. The real Christ would not have punished you so cruelly. Men are always more severe than God. Whence should they obtain divine magnanimity, they are so petty. They are like a servant who is arrogant and avaricious for his master because he does not understand his wishes and turns from the door the poor whom his master would gladly have welcomed and refreshed." She kissed the young girl's brow. "Be calm, Josepha, gather up your hair, you shall bury it to-morrow in the earth which is so dear to you. I promise that I will think of you when the other Magdalene appears; your shadow shall stand between her and me, so that I shall see you alone! Will this be a slight consolation to you?"

Josepha, for the first time, looked up into the countess' eyes with a smile. "Yes, it is a comfort. Ah, you are so kind, you take pity on me while all reproach and condemn me."

"Oh, Josepha! If people judged thus, which of us would be warranted in casting the first stone at you?" The countess uttered the words with deep earnestness, and thoughtfully left the room.

CHAPTER VII.

THE PASSION PLAY.

DAY was dawning. The first rays of the morning sun, ever broader and brighter, were darting through the air, whose blue waves surged and quivered under the flaming coursers of the ascending god of day. Aphrodite seemed to have bathed and left her veil in the foam of the wild mountain stream into which the penitent Magdalene had tried to throw

herself. Apollo in graceful sport, had gathered the little white
clouds to conceal the goddess and they waved and fluttered
merrily in the morning breeze around the rushing chariot.
Then, as if the thundering hoof-beats of the fiery chargers had
echoed from the vaulted arch of the firmament, the solemn
roar of cannon announced the approach of the *other* god, the
poor, unassuming, scourged divinity in His beggar-garb. The
radiant charioteer above curbed his impatient steeds and gazed
down from his serene height upon the conflict, the torturing,
silent conflict of suffering upon the bloody battlefield of the
timorous earth. Smiling, he shook his divine head, for he
could not understand the cause of all this. Why should a
god impose upon Himself such misery and humiliation! But
he knows that He was a more powerful god, for *he* was forced
to fly from the zenith when the former rose from His grave.—
So thought Helios, glancing over at the gentle goddess Selene,
whose wan face, paling in his presence, was turned full toward
the earth. She could not bear to behold the harrowing spectacle, she was the divinity of peace and slumber, so, averting
her mild countenance, she bade Helios farewell and floated
away to happier realms

Blest gods, ye who sit throned in eternal beauty, eternal
peace; ye who are untouched by the grief and suffering of
the human race, who descend to earth merely to taste the joys
of mortals when it pleases ye to add them to your divine delights, look down upon the gods whom sorrowing humanity,
laden with the primeval curse, summoned from his heaven to
aid, where none of ye aided, to give what none of ye gave, *the
heart's blood of love!* Gaze from your selfish pleasures, ye gay
Hellenic deities, behold from your Valhalla, grim divinities of
the Norsemen, look hither, ye dull, stupid idols of ancient
India, hither where, from love for the human race, a god bleeds
upon the martyr's cross—behold and turn pale! For when the
monstrous deed is done, and the night has passed, He will cast
aside His humble garb and shine in His divine glory. Ye will
then be nothing but the rainbow which shimmers in changeful
hues above His head! " Excelsior!" echoes a voice through
the pure morning-sky and: " Gloria in excelsis, Deo!" peals
from the church, as the priests chant the early mass.

An hour later the prince stopped before the door in a

carriage to convey the countess to the Passion Theatre, for the way was long and rough.

He gave the Gross sisters strict orders to have everything ready for Countess Wildenau's departure at the close of the performance.

"The carriages must stand packed with the luggage before the theatre when we come out. The new maid must not be late."

Madeleine von Wildenau made no objection to all this, she was very pale and deeply agitated. Ludwig Gross, who was also just going to the theatre, was obliged to enter the carriage, too; the countess would listen to no refusal. The prince looked coldly at him. Ludwig Gross raised his hat, saying courteously:

"May I request an introduction?"

The lady blushed. "Herr Gross, head-master of the drawing-school!" She paused a moment in embarrassment, Ludwig's bronze countenance still retained its expectant expression.

"The Hereditary Prince of Metten-Barnheim," said the prince, relieving the countess' embarrassment, and raising his hat.

The drawing-master's delicate tact instantly perceived Prince Emil's generous intention.

"Pardon me," he said, with a shade of bashfulness, "I did not know that I was in the presence of a gentleman of such high rank—"

"No, no, you were perfectly right," interrupted Prince Emil, who was pleased with the man's modest confidence, and immediately entered into conversation with him. He asked various questions, and Ludwig described how he was frequently compelled to get suitable figures for his tableau from the forests and the fields, because the better educated people all had parts assigned to them, and how difficult it was to work with this untrained material; especially as he had barely two or three minutes to arrange a tableau containing three hundred persons.

The countess gazed absently at the motley throngs surging toward the Passion Theatre. The fresh morning breeze blew into the carriage. All nature was full of gladness, a

festal joy which even the countess' richly caparisoned horses
seemed to share, for they pranced gaily and dashed swiftly on
as if they would fain vie with the sun-god's steeds above. The
Bavarian flags on the Passion Theatre fluttered merrily against
the blue sky, and now another discharge of cannon announced
the commencement of the performance. The carriage made
its way with much difficulty through the multitude to the entrance, which was surrounded by natives of Ammergau.
Ludwig Gross ordered the driver to stop, and sprang out.
All respectfully made way for him, raising their hats: "Ah,
Herr Gross! The drawing-master! Good-day!"

"Good-day," replied Ludwig Gross, then unceremoni-
ously giving the countess his arm, requested the prince to
follow and led them through several side passages, to which
strangers were not admitted, into the space reserved for boxes,
where two fine-looking young men, also members of the Gross
family, the "ushers" were taking tickets. Ludwig lifted his
hat and left them to go to his work. The prince shook hands
with him and expressed his thanks. "A cultured man!" he
said, after Ludwig had gone. Meanwhile one of the ushers
had conducted the countess to her seat.

There directly before her lay the long-desired goal! A
huge amphitheatre built in the Greek style. Between the
boxes, which overlooked the whole, and the stage, under the
open sky, extended a vast space, whose seats rose to the
height of a house. The orchestra, too, was roofless, as also
were the proscenium and the stage, at whose extreme right
and left stood the houses of Pilate and Caiaphas, between
which stretched the streets of Jerusalem. The chorus was
stationed on the proscenium and here all the great scenes in
which the populace took part were performed. The main
stage, occupying the centre only, as in the Greek theatre, was
a temple-like covered building with a curtain, in a certain
sense a theatre within a theatre, where the scenes that required a smaller frame were set. Beyond, the whole was surrounded by the amphitheatre of the lofty mountains gazing
down in majestic repose, surmounting and crowning all.

The orchestra was playing the last bars of the overture
and the surging and hum of the thousands who were finding
their seats had at last ceased. The chorus came forward, all

the singers clad in the Greek costume, at their head as choragus Johannes Diemer, arrayed in diadem and toga. A majestic figure of true priestly .dignity, he moved across the
stage, fully imbued with the spirit of the sublime drama which
it was his honorable office to open. Deep silence now
reigned throughout the audience. It seemed as if nature herself was listening outside, the whispering morning breeze held
its breath, and not a single bird-note was heard. The repose
of the Sabbath spread its wings protectingly over the whole
scene, that nothing should disturb this consecrated mood.

As the stately figures advanced wearing their costly robes
with as much dignity as if they had never been clad in any
other garments, or would be forced again to exchange them
for the coarse torn blouse of toil; as they began to display
the art acquired with such self-sacrificing devotion after a
wearisome day of labor, and the choragus in the purest,
noblest intonation began the first lines :

> " Sink prostrate, overwhelmed with sacred awe,
> Oh, human race, bowed by the curse of God !"

the countess' heart was suddenly stirred by a new emotion
and tears filled her eyes.

> " Eternal God, Thy stammering children hear,
> For children's language, aye, is stammering."

In these words the devout lips expressed the sacred meaning underlying the childish pastime, and those who heard it
feel themselves once more children—children of the one om-
nipresent Father.

The prologue was over. The curtain of the central stage
rolled up, and the first tableau, the expulsion of Adam and
Eve from Paradise, was revealed. Countess Madeleine gazed
at it with kindly eyes, for Ludwig Gross' refined artistic instinct was visible to her, his firm hand had shaped the rude
material into these graceful lines. A second tableau followed
—the Adoration of the Cross. An empty cross, steeped in
light, stood on a height worshipped by groups of children
and angels. The key-note was thus given and the drama
began.—The first scene was before the temple at Jerusalem—
the Saviour's entry was expected. Madeleine von Wildenau's
heart throbbed heavily. She did not herself know the cause

of her emotion—it almost robbed her of breath—will it be *he* whom she expects, to whom she is bound by some incomprehensible, mysterious spell? Will she find him?

Shouts of "Hosanna!" echoed from the distance—an increasing tumult was audible. A crowd of people, rejoicing and singing praises, poured out of the streets of Jerusalem— the first heralds of the procession appeared, breathlessly announcing His approach.

An indescribable fear overpowered the countess—but it now seemed to her as if she did not dread the man whom she expected to see, but Him he was to personate. The audience, too, became restless, a vibrating movement ran like a faint whisper through the multitude: "He is coming!"

The procession now poured upon the stage, a surging mass —passionately excited people waving palms, and in their midst, mounted on a miserable beast of burden—the Master of the World.

The countess scarcely dared to look, she feared the dismounting, which might shock her æsthetic sense. But lightly as a thought, with scarcely a movement, he had already slipped from the animal, not one of the thousands saw how.

"It is he!" Madeleine's brain whirled, an unspeakable joy overwhelmed her: "When shall I behold thee face to face!" her own words, spoken the evening before, rang in her ears and—the realization was standing before her.

"The Christ!"—a thrill of reverence stirred the throng. Aye, it was He, from head to foot! He had not uttered a word, yet all hearts sank conquered at his feet. Aye, that was the glance, the dignity, the calmness of a God! That was the soul which embraced and cherished a world—that was the heart of love which sacrificed itself for man—died upon the cross.

Now the lips parted and, like an airy, winged genius the words soared upward: A voice like an angel's shouting through the universe: "Peace, peace on earth!"—now clear and resonant as Easter bells, now gentle and tender as a mother's soothing song beside the bed of her sick child. "Source of love—thou art He!"

Mute, motionless, as if transfigured, the countess gazed at the miracle—and with her thousands in the same mood. But from her a secret bond stretched to him—from her alone among the thousands—a prophetic, divine bond, woven by their yearning souls on that night after she had beheld the face from which the God so fervently implored now smiled consent.

The drama pursued its course.

Christ looked around and perceived the traders with their wares, and the tables of the money-changers in the court of the temple. As cloud after cloud gradually rises in the blue sky and conceals the sun, noble indignation darkened the mild countenance, and the eyes flashed with a light which reminded Helios, watching above, of the darts of Zeus.

"My House," saith the Lord, "shall be called a house of prayer, but ye have made it a den of thieves!" And as though His wrath was a power, which emanating from Him acted without any movement of His, a hurricane seemed to sweep over the stands of the traders, while not a single vehement motion destroyed the calmness of the majestic figure. The tables were overthrown, the money rolled on the ground, the cages of the doves burst open, and the frightened birds soared with arrowy speed over the heads of the spectators. The traders raged and shrieked, "My doves, my doves! My money!" and rushed to save the silver coins and scattered wares. But He stood motionless amid the tumult, like the stone of which He said: "Whosoever shall fall upon that stone shall be broken; but on whomsoever it shall fall, it will grind him to powder."

Then, with royal dignity, He swung the scourge over the backs bowed to seize their paltry gains. "Take these things hence, make not my Father's house a house of merchandise!" He did not strike, yet it seemed as though the scourge had fallen, for the dealers fled in wild confusion before the uplifted hand, and terror seized the Pharisees. They perceived that He who stood before them was strong enough to crush them all! His breath had the might of the storm, His glance was consuming flame—His lash felled without striking—He need only will, and "in three days" He would build a new temple as He boasted. Roaring like the sea in a tempest, the exulting populace surrounded Him, yielding to His sway as the waves recede before the breath of the mighty ruler.—Aye, this was the potent spirit of the Jehovah of the Jews, the Zeus of the Greeks, the Jupiter of the Romans. This man was the Son of the God who created Heaven and earth, and it would be an easy matter for the Heir of this power to crush the Pharisees without stirring a finger—if He desired, but that was the point; it was *not* His will, for His mission was a different one! The head once more drooped humbly, the brow, corrugated with anger, smoothed. "I have done my Father's bidding—I have saved the honor of His House!" The storm died away into a whisper, and the mild gaze rested forgivingly upon His foes.

The countess' virile heart almost rebelled against this humility, and would fain have cried out: "Thou *art* the Son of God, help Thyself!" Her sense of justice, formed according to human ideas, was opposed to this toleration, this sacrifice of the most sacred rights! Like Helios in the vault above, she could not understand the grandeur, the divinity of self humiliation, of suffering truth and purity to be judged by falsehood and hyprocrisy—instead of using His own power to destroy them.

As if the personator of Christ suspected her thoughts he suddenly fixed his glance, above the thousands of heads, directly upon her and like a divine message the words fell from his lips : "But in many hearts, day will soon dawn !" Then, turning with indescribable gentleness to His disciples, He added : " Come, let us go into the temple and there worship the Father!" He walked toward it, yet it did not seem as if his feet moved; He vanished from the spectators' eyes noiselessly, gradually, like the fleeting of a happy moment.

The countess covered her eyes with her hand—she felt as if she were dreaming a sadly beautiful dream. The prince watched her silently, but intently. Nods and gestures of greeting came from the boxes on all sides—from the duchess, the diplomatic corps, and numerous acquaintances who happened to be there—but the countess saw nothing.

The drama went on. It was the old story of the warfare of baseness against nobility, falsehood against truth. The Pharisees availed themselves of the injury to the tradesmen's interests to make them their allies. The populace, easily deluded, was incited against the agitator from " Galilee," who wished to rod them of the faith of their fathers and drive the dealers from the temple. So the conspiracy arose and swelled to an avalanche to crush the sacred head! Christ had dealt a rude blow to all that was base in human nature, but baseness was the greater power, to which even God must succumb while He remained a dweller upon earth. But, even in yielding, He conquered—death bestowed the palm of victory!

Between the first and second act was a tableau, "Joseph sold by his Brethren." With thoughtful discrimination every important incident in the Play was suggested by a corresponding event in the Old Testament, represented by a tableau, in order to show the close connection between the Old and the New Testament and verify the words: "that all things which are written may be fulfilled."

At last the curtain rose again and revealed the Sanhedrim assembled for judgment. Here sat the leaders of the people of Israel, and also of Oberammergau. In the midst was Caiaphas, the High-priest, the Chief of the Sanhedrim, the burgomaster of Ammergau and chief manager of the Passion Play. At his right and left sat the oldest members of the community of Ammergau, an old man with a remarkably fine face and long white beard, as Annas, and the sacristan, an impressive figure, as Nathanael. On both sides, in a wide circle, were the principal men in the parish robed as priests and Pharisees. What heads! What figures! The burgomaster, Caiaphas, rose and, with a brief address, opened the discussion. Poor Son of God, how wilt Thou fare in the presence of this mighty one of earth? The burgomaster was the type of the fanatical, ambitious priest, not a blind, dull zealot—nay, he was the representative of the aristocratic hierarchy, the distinguished men of the highest intelligence and culture. A face rigid as though chiselled from stone, yet animated by an intellect of diabolical superiority, which would never confess itself conquered, which no terror could intimidate, no marvel dazzel, no suffering move. Tall and handsome in the very flower of manhood, with eyes whose glances pierced like javelins, a tiara on his haughty head, robed in all the pomp of Oriental priestly dignity, every clanking ornament a symbol of his arrogant, iron nature, every motion of his delicate white hands, every fold of his artistically draped mantle, every hair of his flowing beard a proof of that perfect conscious mastery of outward ceremonial peculiar to those who are accustomed to play a shrewdly planned part before the public. Thus he stood, terrible yet fascinating, repellent yet attractive, nay to the trained eye of an artist who could appreciate this masterly blending of the most contradictory influences, positively enthralling.

This was the effect produced upon Countess Wildenau. The feeling of indignation roused by the incomprehensible humiliation of the divine Martyr almost tempted her to side with the resolute foe who manfully defended his own honor with his god's. A noble-hearted woman cannot withstand the influence of genuine intellectual manfulness, and until the martyrdom of Christ became *heroism*, the firm, unyielding high-priest exerted an irresistible charm over the countess. The conscious mastery, the genius of the performer, the perfection of his acting, roused and riveted the artistic interest of the cultivated woman, and as, with the people of Ammergau, the individual and the actor are not two distinct personages, as among professional artists, she knew that the man before her also possessed a lofty nature, and the nimbus of Ammergau constantly increased, the spirit ruling the whole obtained still greater sway. The sacristan was also an imposing figure as Nathanael, the second high-priest, who, with all the power of Pharisaical superiority and sophistry, appeared as Christ's accuser. The eloquence of these two judges was overpowered, and into the surging waves of passion, Annas, in his venerable dignity, dropped with steady hand the sharp anchor of cold, pitiless resolve. An imposing, sinister assembly was this great Sanhedrim, and every spectator involuntarily felt the dread always inspired by a circle of stern, cruel despots. Poor Lamb, what will be Thy fate?

Destiny pursued its course. In the next act Christ announced His approaching death to the disciples. Now it seemed as though He bore upon His brow an invisible helm of victory, on which the dove of the Holy Spirit rested with outspread wings. Now He was the hero—the hero who *chose* death. Yet meekness was diffused throughout His whole bearing, was the impress of His being; the meekness which spares others but does not tremble for itself. A new perception dawned upon the countess : to be strong yet gentle was the highest nobility of the soul—and as here also the character and its personator were one, she knew that the men before her possessed these attributes : strength and gentleness. Now her defiant spirit at last melted and she longed to take Him to her heart to atone for the injustice of the human race. She thanked Simon for receiving the condemned man under his hospitable roof.

"Aye, love Him—I, too, love Him ?" she longed to cry out to those who were ministering to Him. But when Mary Magdalene touched and anointed Him she averted her eyes, for she grudged her the privilege and thought of her poor, beautiful penitent at home. As He uttered the words: "Rise, Magdalene. Darkness is gathering, and the wintry storms are raging. Yet be comforted! In the early morning, in the Spring garden, thou wilt see me again!" tears streamed form her eyes; "When will the morning dawn that I shall greet Thee —in the Spring garden, redeeming love ?" asked a voice in her heart.

But when Mary appeared and Christ took leave of His mother—when the latter sank upon the breast of her divine son and He consoled her with a voice whose sweetness no ear had ever heard equalled, a feeling which she had never experienced took possession of her: it was neither envy nor jealousy—only a sorrowful longing: If I were only in her place!"

And when Christ said: "My hour is come; now is my soul troubled; and what shall I say ? Father, save me from this hour: but for this cause came I unto this hour!" and Mary, remembering Simeon's words, cried: "Simeon, thy prediction—'a sword shall pierce through thy own soul, also'—is now fulfilled!" the countess, for the first time, understood the meaning of the pictures of Mary with the seven swords in her heart; her own was bleeding from the keenness of her anguish. Now, overpowered with emotion, He again extended His arms: "Mother, mother, receive thy son's fervent gratitude for all the love and faith which thou hast bestowed in the thirty-three years of my life: Farewell, dear mother!"

The countess felt as if she would no longer endure it—that she must sink in a sea of grief and yearning.

"My son, where shall I see Thee again ?" asked Mary.

"Yonder, dear mother, where the words of the Scripture shall be fulfilled: 'He is brought as a lamb to the slaughter, and as a sheep before her shearers is dumb, so he openeth not his mouth.'" Then, while the others were weeping over the impending calamity, Christ said: "Be not overcome in the first struggle. Trust in me." And, as He spoke, the loving soul knew that it might rest on Him and be secure.

He moved away. Serene, noble, yet humble, He went to meet His death.

The curtain fell—but this time there was no exchange of greetings from the boxes, the faces of their occupants were covered to conceal the tears of which they were ashamed, yet could not restrain.

The countess and her companion remained silent. Madeleine's forehead rested on her hand—the prince was secretly wiping his eyes.

"People of God, lo, thy Saviour is near! The Redeemer, long promised, hath come!" sang the chorus, and the curtain rising, showed Christ and his disciples on the way to Jerusalem. It was the moment that Christ wept over Jerusalem. Tears of the keenest anguish which can pierce the heart of a God, tears for the sins of the world! "Jerusalem, Jerusalem, if thou hadst known, even thou, at least in this thy day, the things which belongs unto thy peace! But now they are hid from thine eyes."

The disciples entreated their Master not to enter the hostile city and thus avoid the crime which it was destined to commit. Or to enter and show Himself in His power, to judge and to reward.

"Children, what ye desire will be done in its time, but my ways are ordered by my Father, and thus saith the Lord: 'My thoughts are not your thoughts, neither are your ways my ways.'"

And, loyal and obedient, He followed the path of death. Judas alone lingered behind, resolving to leave the fallen greatness which promised no earthly profit and would bring danger and disgrace upon its adherents. In this mood he was met by Dathan, Andreas Gross, who was seeking a tool for the vengeance of the money changers. Finding it in Judas, he took him before the Sanhedrim.

An impressive and touching tableau now introduced a new period, the gathering of manna in the wilderness, which refreshed the starving children of Israel. A second followed: The colossal bunch of grapes from Canaan. "The Lord miraculously fed the multitude in the desert with the manna and rejoiced their hearts with the grapes of Canaan, but Jesus offers us a richer banquet from Heaven. From the mystery of His body and blood flows mercy and salvation!" sang the chorus. The curtain rose again, Christ was at supper with His disciples. He addressed them in words of calm farewell. But they did not yet fully understand, for they asked who would be *first* in His heavenly kingdom?

His only answer was to lay aside His upper garment, gird, with divine dignity, a cloth about His loins, and kneel to perform for the disciples the humblest service – *the washing of their feet.*

The human race looked on in breathless wonder—viewless bands of angels soared downward and the demons of pride and defiance in human nature fled and hid themselves in the inmost recesses of their troubled hearts.

Aye, the strong soul of the woman, which had at first rebelled against the patience of the suffering God—now understood it and to her also light came, as He had promised and, by the omnipotent feeling which urged her to the feet of Him who knelt rendering the lowliest service to the least of His disciples, she perceived the divinity of *humility!*

It was over. He had risen and put on His upper garment; He stood with His figure drawn up to His full height and gazed around the circle: "Now ye are clean, but not *all!*"—and His glance rested mournfully on Peter, who before the cock crew, would deny Him thrice, and on Judas, who would betray Him for thirty pieces of silver.

Then He again took His seat and, as the presentiment of approaching death transfigures even the most commonplace mortal and illumines the struggling soul at the moment of its separation from the body, so the *God* transfigured the earthly form of the "Son of Man" and appeared more and more plainly on the pallid face, ere he left the frail husk which He had chosen for His transitory habitation. And as the dying man distributes his property among his heirs, *He* bequeathed His. But He had nothing to give, save Himself. As the cloud dissolves into millions of raindrops which the thirsting earth drinks, He divided Himself into millions of atoms which, in the course of the ages, were to refresh millions of human beings with the banquet of love. His body and His blood were his legacy. He divided it into countless portions, to distribute it among countless heirs, yet it remained *one* and the *part* is to every one *the whole.* For as an element remains a great unity, no matter into how many atoms it may dissolve—as water is always water whether in single drops or in the ocean—fire always fire in sparks or a conflagration—so Christ is *always Christ* in the drops of the chalice and the particles of the bread, as well as in His original person, for He, *too,* is an element, *the element of divinity.*

As kindred kneel around the bedside of a loved one who is dying, bedew his hand with tears, and utter the last entreaty: "Forgive us, if we have ever wounded you?" the thousands of spectators longed to kneel, and there was not one who did not yearn to press his lips to the wonderful hand which was distributing the bread, and cry: "Forgive us our sins." But as reverence for the dying restrains loud lamentations, the spectators controlled themselves in order not to sob aloud and thus disturb the divine peace throned upon the Conqueror's brow.

Destiny now relentlessly pursued its course. Judas sold his master for thirty pieces of silver, and they were paid to him before the Sanhedrim. The pieces of silver rang on the stone table upon which they were counted out. It seemed as if the clear sound was sharply piercing the world, like the edge of a scythe destined to mow down the holiest things.

The priests exulted, there was joy in the camp of the foes! All that human arrogance and self-conceit could accomplish, raised its head triumphantly in Caiaphas. The regal priest stood so firmly upon the height of his secular power that nothing could overthrow him, and—Jesus of Nazareth must die!

So the evening came when Christ went with the twelve disciples to the Mount of Olives to await His doom.

"Father, the hour is come; glorify thy Son, that thy Son may also glorify thee! I have finished the work which thou gavest me to do—I have manifested thy name unto men! Father, sanctify them through thy truth; that they all may be one, as thou, Father, art in me and I in thee!"

He climbed the lonely mount in the garden of olive trees to pass through the last agony, the agony of death, which seized upon even the Son of God so long as He was still bound by the laws of the human body.

"Father, if thou be willing, let this cup pass from me!"

Here Freyer's acting reached its height; it was no longer semblance, but reality. The sweat fell in burning drops from his brow, and tears streamed from his eyes. "Yet not *my* will, but *Thine* be done—Thy sacred will!" Clasping his trembling hands, he flung himself prone on the ground, hiding his tear-stained face. "Father—Thy son—hear Him!"

The throng breathed more and more heavily, the tears flowed faster. The heart of all humanity was touched with the anguished cry: "Oh, sins of humanity, ye crush me—oh, the terrible burden—the bitter cup!"

With this anguish the Son of God first drew near to the human race, in this suffering He first bent down to mortals that they might embrace Him lovingly like a mortal brother. And it was so at this moment, also! They would fain have dragged Him from the threatening cross, defended Him with their own bodies, purchased his release at any cost—too late, *this* repentance should have come several centuries earlier.

The hour of temptation was over. The disciples had slept and left him alone—but the angel of the Lord had comforted Him, the angel who God sends to every one who is deserted by men. He was himself again—the Conqueror of the World!

Judas came with the officers and pressed upon the sweet mouth on which the world would fain hang in blissful self-forgetfulness—the traitor's kiss.

"Judas, can you touch those lips and not fall at the feet of Him you have betrayed?" cried a voice in Madeleine von Wildenau's heart. "Can you *kiss* the lips which so patiently endure the death-dealing caress, and not find your hate trans-

5

formed to love? Ah, only the divine can recognize the divine, only sympathetic natures attract one another! Judas is the symbol of the godless world, which would no longer perceive God's presence, even if He came on earth once more. The soldiers, brawny fellows, fell to the ground as He stood before them with the words: "I am Jesus of Nazareth!" and He was forced to say: "Rise!· Fear ye not!" that they might accomplish their work—but Judas remained unmoved and delivered Him up.

Christ was a prisoner and descended step by step into the deepest ignominy. But no matter through what mire of baseness and brutality they dragged Him, haling Him from trial to trial—nothing robbed Him of the majesty of the Redeemer! And if His speech had been full of power, so was His silence! Before the Sanhedrim, before Herŏd, and finally before Pilate, *He* was the king, and the mighty ones of earth were insignificant in *His* presence.

"Who knows whether this man is not the son of some god?" murmured the polytheistic Romans—and shrank from the mystery which surrounded the silent One.

The impression here was produced solely by Freyer's imposing calmness and unearthly eyes. The glance he cast at Herod when the latter ordered him to perform a miracle—darken the judgment chamber or transform a roll of papyrus into a serpent—that one glance, full of dignity and gentleness, fixed upon the poor, short-sighted child of the dust was a greater miracle than all the conjuring tricks of the Egyptian Magicians.

But this very silence, this superiority, filled the priest with furious rage and hastened His doom, which He disdained to stay by a single word.

True, Pilate strove to save Him. The humane Roman, with his aristocratic bearing, as Thomas Rendner personated him with masterly skill, formed a striking contrast to the gloomy, fanatical priests, but he was not the man for violent measures, and the furious leaders understood how to present this alternative. The desire to conciliate, the refuge of all weak souls which shrink in terror from catastrophes, had already wrested from him a shameful concession—he had suffered the Innocent One to be delivered to the scourge.

With clenched teeth the spectators beheld the chaste form, bound to the stake and stained with blood, quiver beneath the lashes of the executioner, without a murmur of complaint from the silent lips. And when He had "had enough," as they phrased it, they placed him on a chair, threw a royal mantle about Him, and placed a sceptre of reeds in the hand of the mock-king. But He remained mute. The tormentors grew more and more enraged—they wanted to have satisfaction, to gloat over the moans of the victim—they dealt Him a blow in the face, then a second one. Christ did not move. They thrust Him from the chair so that He fell on the ground—no one ever forgot the beautiful, pathetic figure—but He was still silent! Then one of the executioners brought a crown made of huge thorns; He was raised again and the martyr's diadem was placed upon His brow. The sharp thorns resisted, they would not fit the noble head, so His tormentors took two sticks, laid cross-ways, and with them forced the spiked coronals so low on His forehead that drops of blood flowed! Christ quivered under the keen agony—but—He was silent! Then He was dragged out of His blood, a spectacle to the populace.

Again Helios above gave the rein to his radiant coursers —he thought of all the horrors in the history of his divine House, of the Danaides, of the chained Prometheus, and of others also, but he could recall nothing comparable to *this*, and *loathed the human race!* Averting his face, he guided his weary steeds slowly downward from the zenith.

The evening breeze blew chill upon the scene of agony.

A furious tumult filled the streets of Jerusalem. The priests were leading the raging mob to the governor's house— fanning their wrath to flame with word and gesture. Caiaphas, Nathanael, the fanatics of Judaism—Annas and Ezekiel, each at the head of a mob, rushed from three streets in an over-whelming concourse. The populace surged like the angry sea, and unchaining yet dominating the elements with word and glance the lofty figure of Caiaphas, the high priest, towered in their midst.

"Shake it off! Cast from you the yoke of the tempter!"

"He has scorned Moses and the prophets—He has blas-phemed God—to the cross with the false Messiah!"

"May a curse rest on every one who does not vote for his

death—let him be cut off from the hereditary rights of our fathers!"

Thus the four leaders cast their watchword like firebrands among the throngs, and the blaze spread tumultuously.

"The Nazarene must die—we demand judgment," roared the people. New bands constantly flocked in. "Oh, fairest day of Israel! Children, be resolute! Threaten a general insurrection. The governor wished to hear the voice of the people—let him hear it!" shrieked Caiaphas, and his passion stirred the mob to fiercer fury. All pressed forward to the house of Pilate. The doors opened and the governor came out. The handsome, classic countenance of the Roman expressed deep contempt, as he surveyed the frantic mob, Behind him appeared the embodiment of sorrow—the picture of all pictures—the Ecce Homo—which all the artists of the world have striven to represent, yet never exhausted the subject. Here it stood personified—before the eyes of men, and even the governor's voice trembled as he pointed to it.

"Behold, *what* a man!"

"Crucify him!" was the answer.

Pilate endeavored to give the fury of the mob another victim: the criminal Barabbas was brought forth and confronted with Christ. The basest of human beings and the noblest! But the spectacle did not move them, for the patience and serenity of the Martyr expressed a grandeur which shamed them all, and *this* was the intolerable offense! The sight of the scourged, bleeding body did not cool their vengeance because they saw that the spirit was unbroken! It *must* be quelled, that it might not rise in judgment against them, for they had gone too far, the ill-treated victim was a reproach to them—he could not be suffered to live longer.

"Release Barabbas! To death with the Nazarene, crucify him!"

Vainly the governor strove to persuade the people. The cool, circumspect man was too weak to defy these powers of hatred—he would fain save Christ, yet was unwilling to drive the fanatics to extremes. So he yielded, but the grief with which he did so, "to avert a greater misfortune," absolved him from the terrible guilt whose curse he cast upon the leaders' head.

The expression with which he pronounced the sentence, uttered the words: "Then take ye Him and crucify Him!" voices the grief of the man of culture for eternal beauty.

The bloodthirsty mob burst into a yell of exultation when their victim was delivered to them—now they could cool their vengeance on Him! "To Golgotha—hence with him to the place of skulls!"

Christ—and Thy sacrifice is for *these*. Alas, the day will come, though perchance not for thousands of years, when Thou wilt perceive that they were not *worthy* of it. But that will be the day of judgment!

A crowd surged through the streets of Jerusalem—in their midst the condemned man, burdened with the instrument of his own martyrdom.

In one corner amid the populace stood Mary, surrounded by a group of friends, and the mother beheld her son urged forward, like a beast which, when it falls, is forced up with lashes and pressed on till it sinks lifeless.

High above in the vaulted heavens, veiled by the gathering dusk of evening, the gods whispered to one another with secret horror as they watched the unprecedented sight. Often as they might behold it, they could never believe it.

The procession stopped before a house—Christ sank to the earth.

A man came out and thrust Him from the threshold.

"Hence, there is no place here for you to rest."

Ahasuerus! The tortured sufferer looked at him with the gaze of a dying deer—a single mute glance of agony, but the man on whom it fell nevermore found peace on earth, but was driven from every resting-place, from land to land, from one spot to another—hunted on ceaselessly through the centuries—wandering forever.

"He will die on the road"—cried the first executioner. Christ had dragged Himself a few steps forward, and fell for the second time.

"Drive him on with blows!" shrieked the Pharisees and the people.

"Oh! where is the sorrow like unto my sorrow?" moaned Mary, covering her face.

"He is too weak, some one must help him," said the executioner. He could not be permitted to die there—the people must see Him on the pillory.

His face was covered with sweat and blood—tears flowed from His eyes, but the mute lips uttered no word of complaint. Then His friends ventured to go and render whatever aid was permitted. Veronica offered Him her handkerchief to wipe His face, and when He returned it, it bore in lines of sweat and blood, the portrait which, throughout the ages, has exerted the silent magic of suffering in legend and in art.

Simon of Cyrene took the cross from the sinking form to bear it for Him to Golgotha, and the women of Jerusalem wept. Christ was standing by the roadside exhausted, but when He saw the women with their children, the last words of sorrow for their lost ones rose from His heart to His lips:

"Daughters of Jerusalem, weep not for me, but weep for yourselves, and your children."

"For, behold, the days are coming, in the which they shall say: Blessed are the barren, and the wombs that never bare, and the paps which never gave suck!"

"Then shall they begin to say to the mountains, Fall on us; and to the hills, Cover us."

"For if they do these things in a green tree, what shall be done in the dry?"

"Drive the women away! Spare him no longer—hence to the place of execution!" the priests commanded.

"To Golgotha—Crucify him!" roared the people. The women were driven away; another message from the governor was unheeded, the procession moved steadily on to death.

But Mary did not leave Him. With the few faithful friends she joined her son's march of suffering, for the steadfastness of maternal love was as great as her anguish.

There was a whispering and a murmuring in the air as if the Valkyries and the gods of Greece were consulting whether they should aid the Son of Man. But they were powerless; the sphere of the Christian's god was closed against them.

The scene changed. The chorus, robed in sable mourning cloaks, appeared and began the dirge for the dying God. The simple chant recalled an ancient Anglo-Saxon song of the cross, composed in the seventh century by the skald

Caedmon, and which for more than a thousand years lay buried in the mysterious spell of the rune.

*Methought I saw a Tree in mid-air hang
Of trees the brightest—mantling o'er with light-streaks;
A beacon stood it, glittering with gold.

All the angels beheld it,
Angel hosts in beauty created.
Yet stood it not a pillory of shame.
Thither turned the gaze
Of spirits blessed,
And of earthly pilgrims
Of noblest nature.
This tree of victory
Saw I, the sin-laden one.

Yet 'mid the golden glitter
Were traces of horror.
Adown the right side
Red drops were trickling.
Startled and shuddering
Noted I the hovering vision
Suddenly change its hue.

Long lay I pondering
Gazing full sadly
At the Saviour's Rood.
When lo, on my ear
Fell the murmur of speech;
These are the words
The forest uttered:

"Many a year ago,
Yet still my mind holds it,
Low was I felled.
The dim forest within
Hacked from my roots,
Haled on by rude woodmen
Bracing sinewy shoulders
Up the steep mountain side,
Till aloft on the summit
Firmly they fastened me.

---

* Part of these lines of Caedmon were put into modern English by Robert Spence Watson.

"I spied the Frey* of man with eager haste
  Approach to mount me ; neither bend nor break
  I durst, for so it was decreed above
  Though earth about me shook.

"Up-girded him then the young hero,
  That was God Almighty,
  Strong and steady of mood,
  Stept he on the high gallows :
  Fearless amongst many beholders
  For he would save mankind.
  Trembled I when that ' beorn ' climbed me,
  But I durst not bow to earth."

There hung the Lord of Hosts
Swart clouds veiled the corpse,
The sun's light vanished   .
'Neath shadows murk.
While in silence drear
All creation wept
The fall of their king.
Christ was on Rood—
Thither from afar
Men came hastening
To aid the noble one.

Everything I saw,
Sorely was I
With sorrows harrowed,
Yet humbly I inclined
To the hands of his servants
Striving much to aid them.

Now from the Rood
The mighty God,
Spear-pierced and blood-besprent,
Gently men lowered ;
They laid him down limb-weary,
They stood at the lifeless head,
Gazing at Heaven's Lord,
And he there rests awhile,
Weary after his mickle death-fight.

---

* Frey is the god of peace. When its Mythological significance was lost, it became an epithet of honor for princes and is found frequently applied to our Lord and God the Father.

Such was the pæan of Caedmon, mighty among the writers of runes, in the seventh century after the Saviour's death. Now, twelve centuries later, it lived again, and the terrible event was once more enacted, just as the skald had sung, just as it happened nearly two thousand years ago.

What is space, what is time to aught that is rooted in love?

The dirge of the chorus had died away. A strange sound behind the curtain accompanied the last verses—the sound of hammering—could it be? No, it would be too horrible. The audience heard, yet *would* not hear. A deathlike stillness pervaded the theatre—the blows of the hammer became more and more distinct—the curtain rolled upward—there He lay with His feet toward the spectators, flat upon the cross. And the executioners, with heavy blows, drove nails through His limbs; they pierced the kind hands which had never done harm to any living creature, but wherever they were gently laid, healed all wounds and stilled all griefs; the feet which had borne the divine form so lightly that it seemed to float over the burning sand of the land and the surging waves of the sea, always on a mission of love. Now He lay in suffering on the ground, stretched upon the accursed timbers—half benumbed, like a stricken stag. At the right and left stood the lower crosses of the two criminals. These men merely had their arms thrown over the cross-beams and tied with ropes, only the feet were fastened with nails. Christ alone was nailed by both hands and feet, because the Pharisees were tortured by a foreboding that He could not be wholly killed. Had they dared, they would have torn Him to pieces, and scattered the fragments to the four winds, in order to be sure that He would not rise on the third day, as He had predicted.

The executioners had completed the binding of the thieves. "Now the King of the Jews must be raised."

"Lift the cross! Take hold!" the captain commanded. The spectators held their breath, every heart stood still! The four executioners grasped it with their brawny arms. "Up! Don't let go!"

The cross is ponderous, the men pant, bracing their shoulders against it—their veins swell—another jerk—it sways—"Hold firm! Once more—put forth your strength!" and in a

wide sweep it moved upward—all cowered back shuddering
at the horrible spectacle.

"It is not, it cannot be!" Yet it *is*, it *can* be! Horror
thrilled the spectators, their limbs trembled. One grasped
another, as if to hold themselves from falling. It was rising,
the cross was rising above the world! Higher—nearer! "Brace
against it—don't let go!"

It stood erect and was firm.

There hung the divine figure of sorrow, pallid and wan.
The nails were driven through the bleeding hands and feet—
and the eye which would fain deny was forced to witness it,
the heart that would have prevented, was compelled to bear
it. But the scene could be endured no longer, the grief re-
strained with so much difficulty found vent in loud sobs, and
the hands trembling with a feverish chill were clasped with the
same feeling of adoring love. Unspeakable compassion was
poured forth in ceaseless floods of tears, and rose gathering in
a cloud of pensive melancholy around the head of the Crucified One to soothe His mortal anguish. By degrees their eyes
became accustomed to the scene and gained strength to gaze at
it. Divine grace pervaded the slender body, and—as eternal
beauty reconciles Heaven and hell and transfigures the most
terrible things—horror gradually merged into devout admiration of the perfect human beauty revealed in chaste repose
and majesty before their delighted gaze. The countess had
clasped her hands over her breast. The world lay beneath
her as if she was floating above with Him on the cross. She
no longer knew whether he was a *man* or Christ Himself—
she only knew that the universe contained *nothing* save that
form.

Her eyes were fixed upon the superhuman vision, tear
after tear trickled down her cheeks. The prince gazed anxiously at her, but she did not notice it—she was entranced.
If she could but die now—die at the foot of the cross, let her
soul exhale like a cloud of incense, upward to Him.

Darkness was gathering. The murmuring and whispering
in the air drew nearer—was it the Valkyries, gathering mournfully around the hero who scorned the aid. Was it the wings
of the angel of death? Or was it a flock of the sacred birds
which, legend relates, strove to draw out the nails that fastened

the Saviour to the cross until their weak bills were crooked and they received the name of "cross-bills."

The sufferer above was calm and silent. Only His lambent eyes spoke, spoke to those invisible powers hovering around Him in the final hour.

Beneath His cross the soldiers were casting lots for His garments—the priests were exulting—the brute cynicism was watching with wolfish greed for the victim to fall into its clutches, while shouting with jeering mocking: If thou be the Son of God, come down from the cross!

He trusted in God; let Him deliver Him now, if He will have Him!—

"Thou that destroyest the temple and buildest it in three days, save thyself. Show thy power, proud King of the Jews!"

The tortured sufferer painfully turned His head.

"Father, forgive them; for they know not what they do.—"

Then one of the malefactors, even in his own death agony, almost mocked Him, but the other rebuked him; "We receive the due reward of our deeds: but this man hath done nothing amiss!" Then he added beseechingly: "Lord, remember me when Thou comest into Thy kingdom."

Christ made the noble answer: "Verily I say unto thee, to-day shalt thou be with me in paradise."

There was a fresh roar of mockery from the Pharisees. "He cannot save himself, yet promises the kingdom of heaven to others."

But the Saviour no longer heard, His senses were failing; He bent His head toward Mary and John. "Woman, behold thy son! Son, behold thy mother!"

The signs of approaching death appeared. He grew restless—struggled for breath, His tongue clung to His palate.

"I thirst."

The sponge dipped in vinegar was handed to him on a long spear.

He sipped but was not refreshed. The agony had reached its climax: "Eloi, Eloi, lama sabachthani?" He cried from the depths of His breaking heart, a wonderful waving motion ran through the noble form in the last throes of death. Then, with a long sigh, He murmured in the tones of an Æolian harp:

"It is finished! Father, into Thy hands I commend my spirit!" gently bowed his head and expired.

A crashing reverberation shook the earth. Helios' chariot rolled thundering into the sea. The gods fled, overwhelmed and scattered by the hurrying hosts of heaven. Dust whirled upward from the ground and smoke from the chasms, darkening the air. The graves opened and sent forth their inmates. In the mighty anguish of love, the Father rends the earth as He snatches from it the victim He has too long left to pitiless torture! The false temple was shattered, the veil rent—and amid the flames of Heaven the Father's heart goes forth to meet the maltreated, patient, obedient Son.

"Come, thou poor martyr!" echoed yearningly through the heavens. "Come, thou poor martyr!" repeated every spectator below.

Yet they were still compelled to see the beloved body pierced with a sharp lance till the hot blood gushed forth—and it seemed as if the thrust entered the heart of the entire world! They were still forced to hear the howling of the wolves disputing over the sacred corpse—but at last the tortured soul was permitted to rest.

The governor's hand had protected the lifeless body and delivered it to His followers.

The multitude dispersed, awe-stricken by the terrible portents—the priests, pale with terror, fled to their shattered temple. Golgotha became empty. The jeers and reviling had died away, the tumult in nature had subsided—and the sacred stillness of evening brooded over those who remained. "He has fulfilled His task—He has entered into the rest of the Father." The drops of blood fell noiselessly from the Redeemer's heart upon the sand. Nothing was heard save the low sobbing of the women at the foot of the cross.

Then pitying love approached, and never has a pæan of loyalty been sung like that which the next hour brought. The first blades were now appearing of that love whose seed has spread throughout the world!

Joseph of Arimathea and Nicodemus came with ladders and tools to take down the body.

Ascending, they wound about the lifeless form long bands of white linen, whose ends they flung down from the cross.

These were grasped by the friends below as a counterpoise to lower it gently down. Joseph and Nicodemus now began to draw out the nails with pincers; the cracking and splintering of the wood was heard, so firm was the iron.

Mary sat on a stone, waiting resignedly, with clasped hands, for her son. "Noble men, bring me my child's body soon!" she pleaded softly.

The women spread a winding sheet at her feet to receive it.

At last the nails were drawn out and—

> "Now from the rood
> The mighty God
> Men gently lowered."

Cautiously one friend laid the loosened, rigid arms of the dead form upon the other's shoulders, that they might not fall suddenly, Joseph of Arimathea clasped the body: "Sweet, sacred burden, rest upon my shoulders."

He descended the ladder with it. Half carried, half lowered in the bands, the lifeless figure slides to the foot of the instrument of martyrdom.

Nicodemus extended his arms to him: "Come, sacred corpse of my only friend, let me receive you."

They bore Him to Mary—

> "They laid Him down limb-weary
> They stood at the lifeless head,"

that the son might rest once more in the mother's lap.

She clasped in her arms the wounded body of the son born in anguish the second time.

Magdalene knelt beside it. "Let me kiss once more the hand which has so often blessed me." And with chaste fervor the Penitent's lips touched the cold, pierced hand of the corpse.

Another woman flung herself upon Him. "Dearest Master, one more tear upon Thy lifeless body!" And the sobbing whisper of love sounded sweet and soothing like vesper-bells after a furious storm.

But the men stood devoutly silent:

> "Gazing at Heaven's Lord,
> And He there rests awhile
> Weary after his mickle death-fight."

CHAPTER VIII.

FREYER.

THE Play was over. "Christ is risen!" He had burst the sepulchre and hurled the guards in the dust by the sight of His radiant apparition. He had appeared to the Penitent as a simple gardener "early in the morning," as He had promised, and at last had been transfigured and had risen above the world, bearing in His hand the standard of victory.

The flood of human beings poured out of the close theatre into the open air. Not loudly and noisily, as they had come— no, reverently and gravely, as a funeral train disperses after the obsequies of some noble man; noiselessly as the ebbing tide recedes after flood raised by a storm. These were the same people, yet they *returned* in a far different mood.

The same vehicles in which yesterday the travelers had arrived in so noisy a fashion, now bore them away, but neither shouts nor cracking of whips was heard—the drivers knew that they must behave as if their carriages were filled with wounded men.

And this was true. There was scarcely one who did not suffer as if the spear which had pierced the Saviour's heart had entered his own, who did not feel the wounds of the Crucified One in his own hands and feet! The grief which the people took with them was grand and godlike, and they treasured it carefully, they did not desire to lose any portion of it, for—we love the grief we feel for one beloved—and to-day they had learned to love Christ.

So they went homeward.

The last carriages which drew up before the entrance were those of the countess and her friends. The gentlemen of the diplomatic corps were already standing below, waiting for Countess Wildenau to assign them their seats in the two landaus. But the lady was still leaning against the pillar which supported one end of the box. Pressing her handkerchief to her eyes, she vainly strove to control her tears. Her heart throbbed violently, her breath was short and quick—she could not master her emotion.

The prince stood before her, pale and silent, his eyes, too, were reddened by weeping.

"Try to calm yourself!" he said firmly. "The ladies are still in their box, the duchess seems to expect you to go to her. A woman of the world, like yourself, should not give way so."

"Give way, do you call it?" repeated Madeleine, who did not see that Prince Emil, too, was moved. "We shall never understand each other."

At this moment the ladies left their box and crossed the intervening space. They were the last persons in the theatre. The duchess, without a word, threw her arms around Countess von Wildenau's neck. Her ladies-in-waiting, too, approached with tearful eyes, and when the duchess at last released her friend from her embrace, the baroness whispered: "Forgive me, I have wronged you as well as many others—even yesterday, forgive me." The same entreaty was expressed in Her Excellency's glance and clasp of the hand as she said: "Whoever sees this must repent every unloving word ever uttered; we will never forget that we have witnessed it together."

"I thank you, but I should have borne you no ill will, even had I known what you have now voluntarily confessed to me!" replied the countess, kissing the ladies with dry, burning lips.

"Shall we go?" asked the duchess. "We shall be locked in."

"I will come directly—I beg you—will your Highness kindly go first? I should like to rest a moment!" stammered the countess in great confusion.

"You are terribly unstrung—that is natural—so are we all. I will wait for you below and take you in my carriage, if you wish. We can weep our fill together."

"Your Highness is—very kind," replied the countess, scarcely knowing what she answered.

When the party had gone down stairs, she passionately seized Prince Emil's arm: "For Heaven's sake, help me to escape going with them. I will not, *cannot* leave. I beseech you by all that is sacred, let me stay here."

"So it is settled! The result is what I feared," said the prince with a heavy sigh. "I can only beg you for your own sake to consider the ladies. You have invited them to dine day after to-morrow—"

"I know it—apologize for me—say whatever you please—you will know—you can manage it—if you have ever loved me—help me! Drive with the ladies—entertain them, that they may not miss me!"

"And the magnificent ovation which the gentlemen have arranged at your home?"

"What do I care for it?"

"A fairy temple awaits you at the Palace Wildenau, and you will stay here? What a pity to lose the beautiful flowers, which must now wither in vain."

"I cannot help it. For Heaven's sake, act quickly—some one is coming!" She was trembling in every limb with fear—but it was no member of the party sent to summon her. A short man with clear cut features stood beside her, shrewd loyal eyes met her glance. "I saw that you were still here, Countess, can I serve you in any way?"

"Thank Heaven, it is Ludwig Gross!" cried the excited woman joyously, taking his arm. "Can you get me to your father's house without being seen?"

"Certainly, I can guide you across the stage, if you wish!"

"Quick, then! Farewell, Prince—be generous and forgive me!"

She vanished.

The prince was too thoroughly a man of the world to betray his feelings even for an instant. The short distance down the staircase afforded him ample time to decide upon his course. The misfortune had happened, and could no longer be averted—but it concerned himself alone. Her name and position must be guarded.

"Have you come without the countess?" called the duchess.

"I must apologize for her, Your Highness. The performance has so completely unstrung her nerves that she is unable to travel to-day. I have just placed her in her landlord's charge promising not only to make her apologies to the ladies, but also endeavor to supply her place."

"Oh, poor Countess Wildenau!" said the duchess, kindly. "Shall we not go to her assistance?"

"Permit me to remind your Highness that we have not a moment to lose, if we wish to catch the train!"

"Is it possible! Then we must hurry."

"Yes—and I think rest will be best for the countess at present," answered Prince Emil, helping the ladies into the carriage.

"Well, we shall see her at dinner on Tuesday? She will be able to travel to-morrow?"

"Oh, I hope so."

"But, Prince Emil! What will become of our flowers?" asked the gentlemen.

"Oh, they will keep until to-morrow!"

"I suppose she has no suspicion?"

"Of course not, and it is far better, for had she been aware of it, no doubt she would have gone to-day, in spite of her illness, and made herself worse."

The gentlemen assented. "Still it's a pity about the flowers. If they will only keep fresh!"

"She will let many a blossom wither, which may well be mourned!" thought the prince bitterly.

"Will you drive with us, Prince?" asked the duchess.

"If Your Highness will permit! Will you go to the Casino to night, as we agreed, gentlemen?" he called as he entered the vehicle.

"Not I," replied Prince Hohenheim. "I honestly confess that I am not in the mood."

"Nor I," said St. Génois. "This has moved me to that—the finest circus in the world might be here and I would not enter! The burgomaster of Ammergau was right in permitting nothing of the kind."

"Yes, I will take back everything I said yesterday; I went to laugh and wept," remarked Wengenrode.

"It has robbed me of all desire for amusement," Cossigny added. "I care for nothing more to-day."

They bowed to the ladies and the prince, and silently entered their carriages. Prince Emil ordered the countess' coachman to drive back with the maid, who sat hidden in one corner, and joined the duchess and her companions.

The equipages rolled away in different directions—one back to the Gross house, the other to Munich, where the florists were toiling busily to adorn the Wildenau Palace for the reception of its fortunate owner, who was not coming.

7

Ludwig Gross led the countess across the now empty stage. It thrilled her with a strange emotion to thread its floor, and in her reverent awe, she scarcely ventured to glance around her at the vast, dusky space. Suddenly she recoiled from an unexpected horror—the *cross* lay before her. Her agitation · did not escape the keen perception of Ludwig Gross, and he doubtless understood it; such things are not new to the people of Ammergau. "I will see whether the house of Pilate is still open, perhaps you may like to step out on the balcony!" he said, and moved away to leave her alone.

The countess understood the consideration displayed by the sympathizing man. Kneeling in the dark wings, she threw herself face downward on the cross, pressed her burning lips on the hard wood which had supported the noble body, on the marks left here also by the nails which had apparently pierced the hands of the crucified one, the red stains made by his painted wounds. Aye, it had become true, the miracle had happened. *The artificial blood also possessed redeeming power.*

Rarely did any pilgrim to the Holy Land ever press a more fervent kiss upon the wood of the true cross, than was now bestowed on the false one.

So, in the days of yore, Helen, the beautiful, haughty mother of the Emperor Constantine, may have flung herself down, after her long sea voyage, when she at last found the long sought cross to press it to her bosom in the unutterable joy of realization.

Ludwig's steps approached, and the countess roused herself from her rapture.

"Unfortunately the house is closed," said Ludwig, who had probably been perfectly aware of it. They went on to the dressing-rooms. "I'll see if Freyer is still here!" and the drawing-master knocked at the first door. The countess was so much startled that she was forced to lean against the wall to save herself from falling. Was it to come now—the fateful moment! Her knees threatened to give way, her heart throbbed almost to bursting—but there was no answer to the knock, thrice repeated. He was no longer there. Ludwig Gross opened the door, the room was empty. "Will you come in?" he asked. "Would it interest you to see the dressing-room?"

She entered. There hung his garments, still damp with perspiration from the severe toil.

Madeleine von Wildenau stooped with clasped hands in the bare little chamber. Something white and glimmering rustled and floated beside her—it was the transfiguration robe. She touched it lightly with her hand in passing, and a thrill of bliss ran through every nerve.

Ah, and there was the crown of thorns.

She took it in her hand and tears streamed down upon it, as though it were some sacred relic. Again the dream-like vision stood before her as she had seen it for the first time on the mountain top with the thorny branches swaying around the brow like an omen. "No, my hands shall defend thee that no thorn shall henceforth tear thee, beloved brow!" she thought, while a strange smile irradiated her face. Then looking up, she met the eyes of Ludwig, fixed upon her with deep emotion as she gazed down at the crown of thorns.

She replaced it and followed him to the door of the next room. Caiaphas! An almost childlike dread and timidity assailed her—the sort of feeling she had had when a young girl at the time of her first presentation at court—she was well-nigh glad that he was no longer there and she had time to calm herself ere she confronted the mighty priest.

"It is too late, they have all gone!" said Ludwig, offering his companion his arm to lead her down the staircase.

Numerous groups of people were standing in front of the theatre and in the street leading to the village.

"What are they doing here?" asked the lady.

"Oh, they are waiting for Freyer! It is always so. He has slipped around again by a side path to avoid seeing anyone, and the poor people must stand and wait in vain. I have often told him that he ought not to be so austere! It would please them so much if he would but give them one friendly word—but he cannot conquer this shyness. He cannot suffer himself to be revered as the Christ, after the Play is over. He ought not to permit the feeling which the people have for the Christ to be transferred to his person—that is his view of the matter."

"It is a lofty and noble thought, but hard for us poor mortals, who so eagerly cling to what is visible. It is impossible not to transfer the impression produced by the character to its representative, especially with a personality like Freyer's!"

Ludwig Gross nodded assent. "Yes, we have had this experience of old. Faith needs an earthly pledge, says our great poet, and Freyer's personation is such a pledge, a guarantee of whose blessed power everyone feels sure."

The countess eagerly pressed Ludwig's hands.

"I have seen people," Ludwig added, "who were happy, if they were only permitted to touch Freyer's garment, as though it could bring them healing like the actual robe of Christ! Would not Christ, also, if He beheld this pious delusion, exclaim: 'Woman, thy faith hath saved thee!'"

A deep flush crimsoned the countess' face, and the tears which she had so long struggled to repress flowed in streams. She leaned heavily on Ludwig's arm, and he felt the violent throbbing of her heart. It touched him and awakened his compassion. He perceived that hers, too, was a suffering soul seeking salvation here, and if she did not find it, would perish. "It shall be yours, poor woman; for rich as you may be, you are still poor—and we will give you what we can!" he thought.

The two companions pursued their way, without exchanging another word. The countess now greeted the old house like a lost home which she had once more regained.

Andreas Gross met her at the door, took off her shawl, and carried it into the room for her.

Josepha had already returned and said that the countess was ill.

"I hope it is nothing serious?" he asked anxiously.

"No, Herr Gross, I am well—but I cannot go; I must make the acquaintance of these people—I cannot tear myself away from this impression!"

She sank into a chair, laid her head on the table and sobbed like a child. "Forgive me, Herr Gross, I cannot help it!" she said with difficulty, amid her tears.

The old man laid his hand upon her shoulder with a gesture of paternal kindness. "Weep your fill, we are accustomed to it, do not heed us!" He drew her gently into the sitting-room.

Ludwig had vanished.

Josepha entered to ask whether she should unpack the luggage which was up in her room.

"Yes," replied the countess, "and let the carriages return to Munich, until I need them again."

"His Highness the Prince has left his valet here for your service," Josepha reported.

"What can he do? Let him go home, too! Let them all go—I want no one except you!" said the countess sternly, hiding her face again in her handkerchief. Josepha went out to give the order. Where could Ludwig Gross be?—He had become a necessity to her now, thus left alone with her overflowing heart! He had been right in everything.—He had told her that she would learn to weep here, he had first made her understand the spirit of Ammergau. Honor and gratitude were his due, he had promised nothing that had not been fulfilled. He was thoroughly genuine and reliable! But where had he gone, did not this man, usually so sympathetic, know that just now he might be of great help to her? Or did he look deeper *still*, and know that he was but a substitute for another, for whom her whole soul yearned? It was so lonely. A death-like stillness reigned in the house and in the street. All were resting after the heavy toil of the day.

Something outside darkened the window. Ludwig Gross was passing on his way toward the door, bringing with him a tall, dark figure, towering far above the low window, a figure that moved shyly, swiftly along, followed by a throng of people, at a respectful distance. The countess felt paralyzed. Was *he* coming? Was he coming in.

She could not rise and look—she sat with clasped hands, trembling in humble expectation, as Danae waited the moment when the shower of gold should fall. Then—steps echoed in the workshop—the footsteps of two—! They were an eternity in passing down its length—but they were really approaching her room—they came nearer—some one knocked! She scarcely had breath to call "come in." She would not believe it—from the fear of disappointment. She still sat motionless at the table—Ludwig Gross opened the door to allow the other to precede him—and *Freyer* entered. He stooped slightly, that he might not strike his head, but that was needless, for—what miracle was this? The door expanded before the countess' eyes, the ceiling rose higher and higher above him. A wide lofty space filled with dazzling light surrounded him. Colors glittered before her vision, figures floated to and fro ; were they shadows or angels ? She knew not, a mist veiled her eyes—for a moment she ceased to think. Then she felt as if she had awaked from a deep slumber, during which she had been walking in her sleep—for she suddenly found herself face to face with Freyer, he was holding her hands in his, while his eyes rested on hers—in speechless silence.

Then she regained her self-control and the first words she uttered were addressed to Ludwig: " You have brought *him*—!" she said, releasing Freyer's hands to thank the man who had so wonderfully guessed her yearning.

Gift and gratitude were equal—and here both were measureless ! She scarcely knew at this moment which she valued more, the man who brought this donation or the gift itself. But from this hour Ludwig Gross was her benefactor.

" You have brought *him* "—she repeated, for she knew not what more to say—that one word contained *all !* Had she possessed the eloquence of the universe, it would not have been so much to Ludwig as that *one* word and the look which accompanied it. Then, like a child at Christmas, which, after having expressed its thanks, goes back happily to its presents, she turned again to Freyer.

Yet, as the child stands timidly before the abundance of its gifts, and, in the first moments of surprise, does not venture to touch them, she now stood, shy and silent before him, her only language her eyes and the tears which streamed down her cheeks.

Freyer saw her deep emotion and, bending kindly toward her, again took her hands in his. Every nerve was still quivering—she could feel it—from the terrible exertion he had undergone—and as the moisture drips from the trees after the rain, his eyes still swam in tears, and his face was damp with perspiration.

" How shall I thank you for coming to me after this day of toil ?" she began in a low tone.

" Oh, Countess," he answered with untroubled truthfulness, "I did it for the sake of my friend Ludwig—he insisted upon it."

"So it·was only on his friend's account," thought the countess, standing with bowed head before him.

He was now the king—and she, the queen of her brilliant sphere, was nothing save a poor, hoping, fearing woman!

At this moment all the vanity of her worldly splendor fell from her—for the first time in her life she stood in the presence of a man where *she* was the supplicant, he the benefactor. What a feeling! At once humiliating and blissful, confusing and enthralling! She had recognized by that one sentence the real state of the case—what to this man was the halo surrounding the Reichscountess von Wildenau with her coronet and her millions? Joseph Freyer knew but one aristocracy—that of the saints in whose sphere he was accustomed to move—and if he left it for the sake of an earthly woman, he would stoop to her, no matter how far, according to worldly ideals, she might stand above him!

Yet poor and insignificant as she felt in his presence—while the lustre of her coronet and the glitter of her gold paled and vanished in the misty distance—*one* thing remained on which she could rely, her womanly charm, and this must wield its influence were she a queen or the child of a wood-cutter! "Then, for the earthly crown you have torn from my head, proud man, you shall give me your crown of thorns, and I will *still* be queen!" she thought, as the spirit of Mother Eve stirred within her and an intoxicating breeze blew from the Garden of Paradise. Not for the sake of a base emotion of vanity and covetousness, nay, she wished to be loved, in order to *bless*. It is the nature of a noble woman to seek to use her power not to receive, but to give, to give without stint or measure. The brain thinks quickly—but the heart is swifter still! Ere the mind has time to grasp the thought, the heart has seized it. The countess had experienced all this in the brief space during which Freyer's eyes rested on her. Suddenly he lowered his lashes and said in a whisper: "I think we have met before, countess."

"On my arrival Friday evening. You were standing on the top of the mountain while I was driving at the foot. Was it not so?"

"Yes," he murmured almost inaudibly, and there was something like an understanding, a sweet familiarity in the soft assent. She felt it, and her hand clasped his more firmly with a gentle pressure.

He again raised his lashes, gazing at her with an earnest, questioning glance, and it seemed as if she felt a pulse throbbing in the part of the hand which bore the mark of the wound—the warning did not fail to produce its effect.

" Christus, my Christus !" she whispered repentantly. It seemed as if she had committed a sin in suffering an earthly wish to touch the envoy of God. He was crucified, dead, and buried. He only walked on earth like a spirit permitted to return from time to time and dwell for a brief space among the living. Who could claim a spirit, clasp a shadow to the heart ? Grief oppressed her, melancholy, akin to the grief we feel when we dream of the return of some beloved one who is dead, and throw ourselves sobbing on his breast, while we are aware that it is only a dream ! But even if but a dream, should she not dream it with her whole soul ? If she knew that he was given to her only a few moments, should she not crowd into them with all the sweeter, more sorrowful strength, the love of a whole life ?

After us the deluge, says love to the moment—and that which does not say it is not love.

But in this *moment*, the countess felt, lay the germ of something imperishable, and when it was past there would begin for her—not annihilation, but *eternity*. To it she must answer for what she did with the moment !

Ludwig Gross was standing by the window, he did not wish to listen what was communicated by the mute language of those eyes. He had perceived, with subtle instinct, the existence of some mysterious connection, in which no third person had any part. They were alone—virtually alone, yet neither spoke, only their tearful eyes expressed the suffering which *he* endured and *she* shared in beholding.

"Come, poor martyr !" cried her heart, and she released one of his hands to clasp the other more closely with both her own. She noticed a slight quiver. " Does your hand still ache—from the terrible nail which seemed to be driven into your flesh ?"

"Oh, no, that would cause no pain; the nail passes between the fingers and the large head extends toward the center of the palm. But to-day, by accident, Joseph of Arimathea in drawing out the nail took a piece of the flesh with it, so that I clenched my teeth with the pain!" he said, smiling, and showing her the wound. "Do you see? Now I am really stigmatized!"

"Good Heavens, there is a large piece of the flesh torn out, and you bore it without wincing?"

"Why, of course!" he said, simply.

Ludwig gazed fixedly out of the window. The countess had gently drawn the wounded hand nearer and nearer; suddenly forgetting everything in an unutterable feeling, she stooped and ere Freyer could prevent it pressed a kiss upon the bloody stigma.

Joseph Freyer shrank as though struck by a thunderbolt, drawing back his hand and closing it as if against some costly gift which he dared not accept. A deep flush crimsoned his brow, his broad chest heaved passionately and he was obliged to cling to a chair, to save himself from falling. Yet unconsciously his eyes flashed with a fire at once consuming and life-bestowing—a Prometheus spark!

"You are weary, pardon me for not having asked you to sit down long ago!" said the countess, making an effort to calm herself, and motioning to Ludwig Gross, in order not to leave him standing alone.

"Only a moment"—whispered Freyer, also struggling to maintain his composure, as he sank into a chair. Madeleine von Wildenau turned away, to give him time to regain his self-command. She saw his intense emotion, and might perhaps have been ashamed of her hasty act had she not known its meaning—for her feeling at that moment was too sacred for him to have misunderstood it. Nor had he failed to comprehend, but it had overpowered him.

Ludwig, who clearly perceived the situation, interposed with his usual tact to relieve their embarrassment: "Freyer is particularly exhausted to-day; he told me, on our way here, that he had again been taken from the cross senseless."

"Good Heavens, does that happen often?" asked the countess.

"Unfortunately, yes," said Ludwig in a troubled tone.

"It is terrible—your father told me that the long suspension on the cross was dangerous. Can nothing be done to relieve it?"

"Something might be accomplished," replied Ludwig, "by substituting a flat cross for the rounded one. Formerly, when we had a smooth, angular one, it did not tax his strength so much! But some authority in archæology told us that the crosses of those days were made of semi-circular logs, and this curve, over which the back is now strained, stretches the limbs too much."

"I should think so!" cried the countess in horror. "Why do you use such an instrument of torture?"

"He himself insists upon it, for the sake of historical accuracy."

"But suppose you should not recover, from one of these fainting fits?" asked the lady, reproachfully.

Then Freyer, conquering his agitation, raised his head. "What more beautiful fate could be mine, Countess, than to die on the cross, like my redeemer? It is all that I desire."

"All?" she repeated, and a keen emotion of jealousy assailed her, jealousy of the cross, to which he would fain devote his life! She met his dark eyes with a look, a sweet, yearning —fatal look—a poisoned arrow whose effect she well knew. She grudged him to the cross, the dead, wooden instrument of martyrdom, which did not feel, did not love, did not long for him as she did! And the true Christ? Ah, He was too noble to demand such a sacrifice—besides, He would receive too souls for one, for surely, in His image, she loved *Him*. He had sent her the hand marked with blood stains to show her the path to Him—He could not desire to withdraw it, ere the road was traversed.

"You are a martyr in the true sense of the word," she said. Her eyes seemed to ask whether the shaft had struck. But Freyer had lowered his lids and sat gazing at the floor.

"Oh, Countess," he said evasively, "to have one's limbs wrenched for half an hour does not make a martyr. That suffering brings honor and the consciousness of serving others. Many, like my friend Ludwig, and other natives of Ammergau, offer to our cause secret sacrifices of happiness which no

audience beholds and applauds, and which win no renown save
in their own eyes and God's. *They* are martyrs, Countess!—
I am merely a vain, spoiled, sinful man, who has enough to do
to keep himself from being dazzled by the applause of the
world and to become worthy of his task."

"To *become !*" the countess repeated. "I think whoever
speaks in that way, *is* worthy already."

Freyer raised his eyes with a look which seemed to Madeleine von Wildenau to lift her into a higher realm. "Who
would venture to say that he was worthy of *this* task ? It requires a saint. All I can hope for is that God will use the
imperfect tool to work His miracles, and that He will accept
my *will* for the deed,—otherwise I should be forced to give
up the part *this very day.*"

The countess was deeply moved.

"Oh, Freyer, wonderful, divinely gifted nature! To us
you are the Redeemer, and yet you are so severe to yourself."

"Do not talk so, Countess ! I must not listen ! I will not
add to all my sins that of robbing my Master, in His garb, of
what belongs to *Him* alone. You cannot suspect how it
troubles me when people show me this reverence; I always
long to cry out, 'Do not confound me with Him—I am
nothing more than the wood—or the marble from which an
image of the Christ is carved, and withal *bad* wood, marble
which is not free from stains.' And when they will not believe
it, and continue to transfer to me the love which they ought to
have for Christ—I feel that I am robbing my Master, and no
one knows how I suffer." He started up. "That is why I
mingle so little with others—and if I ever break this rule I repent it, for my peace of mind is destroyed."

He took his hat. His whole nature seemed changed—
this was the chaste severity with which he had driven the
money changers from the temple, and Madeleine turned pale—
chilled to the inmost heart by his inflexible bearing.

"Are you going ?" she murmured in a trembling voice.

"It is time," he answered, gently, but with an unapproachable dignity which made the words with which she would fain
have entreated him to stay longer, die upon her lips.

"Your Highness will leave to morrow ?"

"The countess intends to remain some time," said Ludwig,

pressing his friend's arm lightly, as a warning not to wound her feelings.

"Ah," replied Freyer, thoughtfully, "then perhaps we shall meet again."

"I have not yet answered what you have said to-day; will you permit me to do so to-morrow?" asked the countess, gently; an expression of quiet suffering hovered around her lips.

"To-morrow I play the Christ again, Countess — but doubtless some opportunity will be found within the next few days."

"As you please—farewell!"

Freyer bowed respectfully, but as distantly as if he did not think it possible that the lady would offer him her hand. Ludwig, on the contrary, as if to make amends for his friend's omission, frankly extended his. She clasped it, saying in a low, hurried tone: "Stay!"

"I will merely go with Freyer to the door, and then return, if you will allow me."

"Yes," she said, dismissing Freyer with a haughty wave of the hand. Then, throwing herself into the chair by the table, she burst into bitter weeping. She had always been sur-rounded by men who sued for her favor as though it were a royal gift. And here—here she was disdained, and by whom? A man of the people—a plebeian! No, a keen pang pierced her heart as she tried to give him that name. If *he* was a plebeian, so, too, was Christ. Christ, too, sprang from the people—the ideal of the human race was born in a *manger.'* She could summon to confront Him only *one* kind of pride, that of the *woman*, not of the high-born lady. Alas—she had not even *this*. How often she had flung her heart away with-out love. For the mess of pottage of gratified vanity or an interesting situation, as the prince had said yesterday, she had bartered the birthright of the holiest feelings. Of what did she dare to be proud? That, for the first time in her life, she really loved? Was she to avenge herself by arrogance upon the man who had awakened this divine emotion because he did not share it? No, that would be petty and ungrateful. Yet what could she do? He was so far above her in his un-assuming simplicity, so utterly inviolable. She was captured by his nobility, her weapons were powerless against him. As she gazed around her for some support by which she might lift herself above him, every prop of her former artificial life snapped in her grasp before the grand, colossal verity of this apparition. She could do nothing save love and suffer, and accept whatever fate he bestowed.

Some one knocked at the door; almost mechanically she gave the permission to enter.

Ludwig Gross came in noiselessly and approached her. Without a word she held out her hand, as a patient extends it to the physician. He stood by her side and his eyes rested on the weeping woman with the sympathy and understanding born of experience in suffering. But his presence was infinitely soothing. This man would allow nothing to harm her! So far as his power extended, she was safe.

She looked at him as if beseeching help—and he understood her.

"Freyer was unusually excited to-day," he said, "I do not know what was passing in his mind. I never saw him in such a mood before! When we entered the garden, he embraced me as if something extraordinary had happened, and then rushed off as though the ground was burning under his feet— of course in the direction opposite to his home, for the whole street was full of people waiting to see him."

The countess held her breath to listen.

"Was he in this mood when you called for him?" she asked.

"No, he was as usual, calm and weary."

"What changed him so suddenly?"

"I believe, Countess, that you have made an impression upon him which he desires to understand. You have thrown him out of the regular routine, and he no longer comprehends his own feelings."

"But I—I said so little—I don't understand," cried the countess, blushing.

"The important point does not always depend on what is said, but on what is *not* said, Countess. To deep souls what is unuttered is often more significant than words."

Madeleine von Wildenau lowered her eyes and silently clasped Ludwig's hand.

" Do you think that he—" she did not finish the sentence, Ludwig spared her.

" From my knowledge of Freyer—either he will *never* return, or—he will come *to-morrow*."

CHAPTER IX.

SIGNS AND WONDERS.

THE great number of strangers who were unable to get tickets the day before had rendered a second performance necessary. The countess did not attend it. To her the play had been no spectacle, but an experience—a repetition would have degraded it to a mere drama. She had spent the day in retirement, like a prisoner, that she might not fall into the hands of any acquaintances. Now the distant rumble of carriages announced the close of the performance. It was a delightful autumn evening. The Gross family came to the window on their return home, and wondered to find the countess still in her room. The sounds of stifled sobs echoed from the work room. The other lodgers in the house had come back from the theatre and, like every one, were paying their tribute of tears. An American had gone to-day for the second time. He sat weeping on the bench near the stove, and said that it had been even more touching than yesterday. Andreas Gross assented: "Yes, Joseph Freyer never played as he did to-day."

The countess, sitting in her room, heard the words and was strangely moved. Why had he never played as he did *to-day ?*

Some one tapped gently on the door.

A burning blush suffused the countess' face—had *he— ?* He might have passed through the garden from the other side to avoid the spectators. "Come in !" she called.

It was Josepha with a telegram in her hand. The messenger was waiting for an answer.

The countess opened it and read the contents. It was from the prince. " Please inform me whether I shall countermand the dinner."

"Very well. I will send the reply."

Josepha withdrew.

"If Ludwig were only here!" thought the countess. "He must be waiting to bring Freyer, as he did yesterday."

The rapid pulsing of her heart almost stifled her. One quarter of an hour passed after another. At last Ludwig came—but alone.

The countess was sitting at the open window and Ludwig paused beside it.

"Well, how was the play to-day?"

"Magnificent," he replied. "I never saw Freyer so superb. He was perfect, fairly superhuman! It is a pity that you were not there."

"Did he inquire for me?"

"Yes. I explained to him that you did not wish to see it a second time—and for what reason. He nodded and said: 'I am glad the lady feels so.'"

"Then—we understand each other!" The countess drew a long breath. "Did you ask him to come here with you?"

"No. I thought I ought not to do that—he must come now of his own free will, or you would be placed in a false position."

"You are right—I thank you!" said the countess, turning pale and biting her lips. "Do you think that — he will come?"

"Unfortunately, no—he went directly home."

"Will you do me a favor?"

"Certainly, Countess."

"Despatch a telegram for me. I have arranged to give a dinner party at home and should like to send a message that I am coming."

"You will not remain here longer?"

"No!" she said in a tone sharp and cutting as a knife which is thrust into one's own heart. "Come in, please."

Ludwig obeyed the command and she wrote with the bearing of a queen signing a death-warrant:

"HEREDITARY PRINCE OF METTEN-BARNHEIM, Munich.

"Will come at five to-morrow. Dinner can be given.

"MADELEINE."

"Here, if you will be so kind," she said, handing the sheet to Ludwig.

The latter gazed earnestly at her, as though he wanted to say: "If only you don't repent it." But he asked the question in the modest wording: "Shall I send it *at once ?*"

"Yes, if you please!" she answered, and her whole manner expressed a coldness which startled Ludwig.

"Can genuine warmth of heart freeze so quickly?" he asked himself. Madeleine von Wildenau felt the mute reproach and disappointment in Ludwig's manner. She felt, too, that he was right, and called him back as he reached the door. "Give it to me," she said, taking the telegram, "I will consider the matter." Then meeting the eyes of the noble man, which now brightened again for her sake, she added earnestly, holding out her hand, "You understand me better than I do myself."

"I thank you for those words—they make me very proud, Countess!" said Ludwig with a radiant glance, placing the telegram on the table. "I will go now that I may not disturb you while you are considering what course to pursue."

He left the room. Twilight was gathering. The countess sat by the table holding the telegram clenched in her little hand.

"The people of Ammergau unconsciously exercise a moral constraint which is irresistible. There is a power of truth in them which prevents even self-deception in their presence!" she murmured half defiantly, half admiringly. What was to be done now? To remain longer here and countermand the dinner meant a positive breach with society. But who was there *here* to thank her for such a sacrifice? Who cared for the Countess Wildenau? She was one of the thousands who came and went, taking with them a lofty memory, without leaving any remembrance in the mind of any one. Why should she hold them accountable if she gave to this impression a significance which was neither intended nor suspected. We must not force upon men sacrifices which they do not desire!

She rested her arm on the table and sat irresolute. Now —now in this mood, to return to the prosaic, superficial

round, after imagining yesterday that she stood face to face
with deity? *Could* she do it? Was not the mute reproach
in Ludwig's glance true? She thoughtfully rested her beautiful face on her hand.

She had not noticed a knock at the door, a carriage was
driving by whose rattle drowned every sound. For the same
reason the person outside, supposing that he had not heard
the "come in!" softly opened the door. At the noise the
countess raised her head—Freyer stood before her.

"You have come, you *did* come!" she exclaimed, starting
up and seizing his hand that the sweet, blissful dream might
not vanish once more.

"Excuse me if I disturb you," he said in a low, timid
tone. "I—I should not have come—but I could not bear to
stay at home, I was so excited to-day. When evening came,
some impulse drove me here—I was—I had—"

"You had a desire to talk to some one who could understand you, and this urged you to me, did it not?"

"Yes, Countess! But I should not have ventured to
come in, had not —"

"Well?"

"Ludwig met me and said that you were going away—"

"Ah—and did you regret it?"

"I wished at least to bid you farewell and thank you for
all your kindness to my unhappy cousin Josepha!" he said
evasively. "I neglected to do so yesterday, I was so embarrassed."

"You are not sincere with me, Herr Freyer!" said the
countess, motioning to him to sit down. "This expression of
thanks does not come from your heart, for you do not care
what I do for Josepha. That is merely the pretext for coming
to me—because you do not wish to confess what really
brought you. Am I not right?"

"Countess!" said Freyer, completely disconcerted, as he
tried to rise.

She gently laid her hand on his, detaining him. "Stay!
Your standard is so rigid in everything—what is your view of
truth?"

Freyer fixed his eyes on the floor.

"Is it *true*, when you say that you came to thank me for

S

Josepha? Were you not drawn hither by the feeling that, of all the thousands of souls who pass you in the course of the summer, perhaps there is not one who could understand you and your task as I do?"

Freyer clasped his hands on his knees and silently bent his head.

"Perhaps you have not thought of me as I have thought of you, all day long, since our eyes met on the mountain, as though some higher power had pointed us out to each other."   .

Freyer remained silent, but as the full cup overflows at the slightest movement, tears again gushed from his eyes.

"Why did you look at me so from head to foot, pouring forth in that gaze your whole soul with a world of grief and joy, as a blossoming tree showers its flowers on the passer-by? Surely not on account of a woman's face, though it may be passably fair, but because you felt that I perceived the Christ in you and that it was *He* for whom I came. Your glance meant to tell me: 'It is I whom you are seeking!' and I believe you. And when at last the promise was fulfilled and the long sought redeemer stood before me, was it by chance that his prophetic eye discovered me among the thousands of faces when he said: 'But in many hearts day will soon dawn!' Did you not seek me, as we look for a stranger to whom we must fulfill a promise given on the journey?"

Freyer now raised his dark eyes and fixed them full upon her, but made no reply.

"And is it true that you came yesterday, only because Ludwig wished it, you who, spite of all entreaties, have kept ladies who had the world at their feet waiting on your stairs for hours? Did you not come because you suspected that I might be the woman with whom, since that meeting, you had had some incomprehensible spiritual bond?"

Freyer covered his eyes with his hand, as if he was afraid more might be read in them.

"Be truthful, Herr Freyer, it is unworthy of you and of me to play a conventional farce. I am compelled to act so many in my life that I would fain for once be frank, as mortal to mortal! Tell me simply, have I judged correctly— yes or no?"

" Yes !" whispered Freyer, without looking up.

She gently drew his hand down. " And to-day—to-day— did you come merely out of gratitude for your cousin ?" she questioned with the archness of her increasing certainty of happiness.

He caught the little hand with which she had clasped his, and raised it ardently to his lips; then, as if startled that he had allowed himself to be carried so far, he flung back his raven locks as if they had deluded his senses, and pushed his chair farther away in order not to be again led into temptation. She did not interfere—she knew that he was in her power— struggle as he might, the dart was fixed. Yet the obstacles she had to conquer were great and powerful. Coquetry would be futile, only the moral force of a *genuine* feeling could cope with them, and of this she was conscious, with a happiness never felt before. Again she searched her own heart, and her rapid glance wandered from the thorn-scarred brow of the wonderful figure before her, to pierce the depths of her own soul. Her love for him was genuine, she was not toying with his heart; she wished, like Mary Magdalene, to sanctify her- self in his love. But she was the Magdalene in the *first* stage. Had Christ been a *man*, and attainable like *this* man, what transformations the Penitent's heart must have undergone, ere its fires wrought true purification.

" Herr Freyer," the countess began in a low, eager tone, "you said yesterday that it troubled you when people showed you idolatrous reverence and you felt that you thereby robbed your Master. Can we give aught to any earthly being without giving it to *God ?*"

Freyer listened intently.

" Is there any soul which does not belong to God, did not emanate from *Him*, is not a part of *His* power ? And does not that which flows from one part to another stream back in a perpetual circle to the *Creator ?* We can *take* nothing which does not come from God, *give* nothing which does not return to Him. Do you know the principle of the preservation of power ?"

" No," said Freyer, confused by his ignorance of something he was asked.

"Well, it can· be explained in a very few words. Science has proved that nothing in the universe can be lost, that even a force which is apparently uselessly squandered is merely transformed into another. Thus in God nothing can be lost, even though it has no direct relation to Him—for he is the *spiritual* universe. True, *every* feeling does not produce a work of God, any more than every effort of nature brings forth some positive result. But as in the latter case the force expended is not lost, because it produces other, though secondary results, so in *God* no sentiment of love and enthusiasm is lost, even though it may relate to Him only in a secondary degree."

"Very true."

"Then if that *is* so,—how can any one rob this God, who surrounds us like the universe, from which we come, into which we pass again, and in which our forces are constantly transformed in a perpetual round of change."

Freyer rested his head on his hand, absorbed in thought.

"And if a feeling is so deeply rooted in religion, so directly associated with God as that which men offer to you, His representative, why should you have these scruples?"

"I have never heard any one talk in this way! Pardon my faint-heartedness, and ignorance—I am a poor, simple-hearted man—you will be indulgent, will you not?"

"Freyer!" cried the countess, deeply moved, and spite of the distance to which he had pushed his chair, held out her hand.

"You see, I had no opportunity to attend a higher school, I was so poor. I lost my parents when a lad of twelve and received only the most necessary instruction. All my knowledge I obtained afterwards by reading, and it is of course defective and insufficient. On our mountains, beside our rushing streams, among the hazel bushes whose nuts were often my only food, I grew up, watching the horses sent to pasture with their colts. Up by St. Gregory's chapel, where the Leine falls over the cliffs, I left the animals grazing in the wide meadows, flung myself down in a field of gentian and, lying on my back, gazed upward into the blue sky and thought it must surely open, the transparent atmosphere *must* at last be pierced—as the bird imagines, when it dashes its head against a pane of glass—so I learned to think of God! And when my brain and heart grew giddy, as if I were destined for something better, when a longing overwhelmed me which my simple meditations could not quell, I caught one of my young horses by the mane, swung myself on its bare back, and swept over the broad plain, feeling myself a king."

He extended his arms, and now his face was suddenly transformed—laughing, bright, joyous as the Swedes imagine their Neck, the kind, friendly water sprite who still retains some of the mythical blood of the Northern god of Spring, Freyer's namesake. "Ah, Countess—that was poetry! Who could restore *those* days; that childish ignorance, that happy hope, that freedom of innocence!"

Again, like the pictures in a kaleidoscope, his expression changed and a gloomy melancholy spread its veil over his brow. "Alas!—that is all over! My light-footed colts have become weary, clumsy animals, dragging loaded wains, and I —I drag no less wearily the burden of life."

"How can you speak so at the moment when, yourself a miracle, you are revealing to men the miracles of God? Is it not ungrateful!"

"Oh, no, Countess, I am grateful! But I do not so separate myself from my part that I could be happy while portraying the sufferings of my Redeemer! Do you imagine that I have merely learned the words by heart? With His form, I have also taken His cross upon me! Since that time all my youth has fled and a touch of pain pervades my whole life."

"Then you are His true follower—then you are doing what Simon of Cyrene did! And do *you* believe that you ought not to accept even the smallest portion of the gratitude which men owe to the Crucified One? Must you share only His sufferings, not His joys, the joys bestowed by the love and faith of moved and converted souls? Surely if you are so narrow-minded, you understand neither yourself nor the love of God, Who has chosen and favored you from among millions to renew to the world the forgotten message of salvation."

"Oh God, oh God!—help me to keep my humility—this is too much."

Freyer started up and pressed his hand upon his brow as if to ward off an invisible crown which was descending upon it.

The countess also rose and approached him. "Freyer, the suffering you endure for Christ's sake, I share with you!

It is the mystery in which our souls found each other. Pain is eternal, Freyer, and that to which it gives birth is imperishable! What do we feel when we stand before a painted or sculptured image of the Crucified One? Pity, the most agonizing pity! I have never been willing to believe it—but since yesterday I have known that it is a solace to the believing soul to bestow a tender embrace upon the lifeless image and to touch the artificial wounds with ardent lips. What must it be when that image loves, feels, and suffers! When it speaks to us in tones that thrill the inmost heart? When we see it quiver and bleed under the lashes of the executioner—when the sweat of agony trickles from the brow and *real* tears flow from the eyes? I ask, *what* must this be to us? Imagine yourself for once the person who *sees this*—and then judge whether it is not overpowering? If faith in the *stone* Christ works miracles— why should not belief in the *living* one do far more? The pious delusion is so much the greater, and *faith* brings blessing."

She clasped her hands upon his breast.

"Come, image of mercy, bend down to me. Let me clasp your beloved head and press upon your tortured brow the kiss of reconciliation for all penitent humanity!" Then, taking his face between her hands, she lightly pressed a fervent kiss upon the brow gently inclined toward her. "Now go and lament that you have robbed your Master of this kiss. He will ask, with a smile: 'Do you know for whom that kiss was meant—*thee* or *me?*' And you will be spared an answer, for when you raise your eyes to Him, you will find it imprinted on *His* brow."

She paused, overpowered by the sacredness of the moment. There are times when our own words influence us like some unknown force, because they express something which has been so deeply concealed in our hearts that we ourselves were ignorant of its existence. This was the case now with the countess. Freyer stood silently with clasped hands, as if in church.

It seemed as though some third person was addressing them—an invisible person whom they must hold their very breath to understand.

It had grown late. The waning moon floated high above the low window and brightened the little room with its cheering rays. The countess nodded. "It is fulfilled!" Then she laid her hands in Freyer's: "For the first time since my childhood I place my soul in the keeping of a human being! For the first time since my childhood, I strip off all the arrogance of reason, for a higher perception is hovering above me, drawing nearer and nearer with blissful certainty! Is it love, is it faith? Whichever it may be—God dwells in *both*. And—if philosophy says: 'I *think*, therefore I *am*,' I say: 'I *love*, therefore I *believe!*' "

She humbly bowed her head. "And therefore I beseech you. Bless me, you who are so divinely endowed, with the blessing which is shed upon and emanates from you!"

Freyer raised his eyes to Heaven as if to call down the benediction she implored, and there was such power in the fervid gaze that Madeleine von Wildenau experienced a thrill almost of fear, as if in the presence of some supernatural being. Then he made the sign of the cross over her: "In the name of the Father, and of the Son, and of the Holy Ghost."

A tremor of foreboding ran through her limbs as if the finger of God had marked her for some mysterious destination and, with this rune, she had been enrolled in the pallid host of those consecrated by sorrow as followers of the deity.

With sweet submission she clasped the hand which had just imprinted the mournful sign on brow and breast: "In the name of God, if only *you* are near me!" Her head drooped on her bosom. Some one knocked at the door, the countess' brain reeled so much that she was forced to cling to Freyer for support.

Josepha timidly asked if she wanted a light.

"Light! Was it *dark?*"

"Very well," she answered absently.

Josepha brought the lamp and enquired when the countess desired to have supper? Freyer took his hat to go.

"I shall eat nothing more to-night!" said the countess in a curt, impatient tone, and Josepha timidly withdrew.

Madeleine von Wildenau covered her face with both hands like a person who had been roused from a beautiful dream to bare reality.

"Alas—that there must be other people in the world, besides ourselves!" She sighed heavily, as if to take breath after the terrible fall.   Freyer, hat in hand, approached her, calm and self-controlled.   Joseph Freyer, addressing Countess Wildenau, had no remembrance of what the penitent soul had just confided to the image of the Redeemer.

"Allow me to take my leave, your Highness," he said in a gentle, but distant tone.

The countess understood the delicate modesty of this conduct.   "Did your blue gentians teach this tact?   It would seem that lonely pastures, whispering hazel copses, and dashing mountain streams are better educators of the heart, for those who understand their mysterious language, than many of our schools."

Freyer was silent a moment, then with eyes bent on the floor, he said: "May I ask when your Highness intends to leave to-morrow?"

"*Must* I go, Freyer?"

"Your Highness—"

"Here is a telegram which announces my arrival at home to-morrow.   Tell me, Freyer, shall I send it?"

"How can *I* decide—" stammered Freyer in confusion.

"I wish to know whether you—*you*, Freyer, would like to keep me here?"

"But Good Heavens, your Highness—is it seemly for me to express such a wish?   Of course it will be a great pleasure to have you remain—but how could I seek to influence you in any way?"

"Mere phrases!" said the countess, disappointed and offended.   Then, if it is a matter of indifference to you whether I go or stay, I will send the telegram." She went to the table to add something.

Suddenly he stood close beside her, with a beseeching, tearful glance—and laid his hand upon the paper.

"No—do not send it."

"Not send it?" asked Madeleine in blissful expectation. "Not send it—then what am I to do?"

His lips moved several times, as if he could not utter the word—but at last it escaped from his closed heart, and with an indescribable smile he murmured: "Stay!"

Ah!   A low cry of exultation escaped the countess, and the telegram lay torn upon the table.   Then with a trembling hand she wrote the second, which she requested him to send at once. It contained only the words: "Am ill—cannot come!"

He was still standing at her side, and she gave it to him to read.

"Is it true?" he asked, after glancing at it, looking at her with timid, sportive reproach. "Are you ill?"

"Yes!" she said caressingly, laying her hand, as if she felt a pang, upon her heart. "I *am*!"

He clasped both in his own and asked softly in a tone which sent a thrill of happiness through every vein: "How shall we *cure* this illness?"

She felt his warm breath on her waving hair—and dared not stir.

Then, with sudden resolution he shook off the thrall: "Good-night, Countess!"

The next moment he was hurrying past the window.

Ludwig, wondering at his friend's hasty departure, entered. "What has happened, Countess?"

"Signs and wonders have happened," she said, extending her arms as if transfigured.

CHAPTER X.

IN THE EARLY MORNING.

"Rise Mary! Night is darkening and the wintry storms are raging—but be comforted, in the early morning, in the Spring garden, you will see me again."

The countess woke from a short slumber as if some one had uttered the words aloud. She glanced around the dusky room, it was still early, scarcely a glimmer of light pierced through the chinks of the shutters. She tried to sleep again, but in vain. The words constantly rang in her ears: "In the early morning you will see me again." Now the chinks in the shutters grew brighter, and one golden arrow after another darted through. The countess threw aside the coverlet and started up. Why should she torment herself with trying to court sleep? Outside a dewy garden offered its temptations.

True, it was an autumn, not a spring garden. Yet for her it was Spring—it had dawned in her heart—the first spring-time of her life.

Up and away! Should she wake Josepha, who slept above her? Nay, no sound, no word must disturb this sacred morning stillness.

She dressed and, half an hour later, glided lightly, unseen, into the garden.

The clock in the church steeple was striking six. A fresh autumn breeze swept like a band of jubilant sprites through the tops of the ancient trees, then rushing downward, tossed her silken hair as though it would fain bear away the filmy strands to some envious wood-nymph to weave nets from it for the poor mortals who might lose themselves in her domain.

On the ground at her feet, too, the grasses and shrubs swayed and rustled as if little gnomes were holding high revel there. A strange mood pervaded all nature.

Madeleine von Wildenau looked upward; there were huge cloud-shapes in the sky, but the sun was shining brightly in a broad expanse of blue. The bells were ringing for early mass. The countess clasped her hands. Everything was silent and lonely, no eye beheld, no ear heard her, save the golden orb above. The birds carolling their matin songs, the flowers whose cups were filled with morning dew, the buzzing, hum-ming bees—all were celebrating the great matins of awakening nature—and she, whose heart was full of the morning dew of the first genuine feeling of her life, was she alone not to join in the chorus of gratitude of refreshed creation?

There is a language whose key we do not possess. It is the Sanscrit of Nature and of the human soul when it com-munes with the deity. The countess sank silently down on the dewy grass. She did not pray in set words—there was an interchange of thought, her heart spoke to God, and reason knew not what it confided to Him.

In the early morning in the spring garden "thou wilt see me again!" There again spoke the voice which had roused her so early! The countess raised her head—but still re-mained kneeling as if spell-bound. Before her stood the Promised One.

She could say nothing save the word uttered by Mary Magdalene : " Master ! "

A loving soul can never be surprised by the object of its love because it expects him always and everywhere, yet it appears a miracle when its expectation becomes fulfilment.

" Have I interrupted your prayer ? I did not see you because you were kneeling "—he said, gently.

" You interrupt my prayer—you who first taught me to pray?" she asked, holding out her hand that he might help her rise. " Tell me, how did you come here ? " .

" I could not sleep—some yearning urged me to your presence—to your garden."

He gently raised her, while she gazed into his eyes as if enraptured. " Master ! " she repeated. " Oh, my friend, I was like Mary Magdalene, my Lord had been taken away and I knew not where they had laid Him. Now I know, He was buried in my own heart and the world had rolled the stone before it, but yesterday—yesterday He rose and the stone was cast aside. So some impulse urged me into the garden early this morning to seek Him and lo—He stands before me as He promised."

" Do not speak so!—I am well aware that the words are not meant for me, but if you associate Christ so closely with my personality, I fear that you will confound Him with me, and that His image will be dimmed, if anything should ever shadow mine! I beseech you, Countess, by all that is sacred —learn to separate Him from me—or you have not grasped the true nature of Christ, and my work will be evil!" He stood before her with hand uplifted in prophecy, the outlines of his powerful form were sharply relieved against the dewy, shining morning air. Purity, chastity, the loftiest, most inspired earnestness were expressed in his whole bearing, all the dignity of the soul and of primeval, divinely created human nature.

Must not she have that feeling of adoration which always seizes upon us whenever, no matter where it may be, the deity is revealed in His creations? No, she did not understand what he meant, she only understood that there was something divine in him, and that the perception of this nearness to God filled her with a happiness never known before. Joseph Freyer was the guarantee of the existence of a God in whom

she had lost faith—why should she imagine Him in any other
form than the one which she had found Him again? "Thou
shalt make thyself no graven image!" Must this Puritani-
cally misunderstood literal statement destroy man's dearest
possession, the *symbol of the reality?* Then the works of
Raphael, Titian, and Rubens must be effaced, and the millions
of miracles of faith, wrought in the souls of the human race
by the representations of the divine nature.

"Oh blessed image-worship, now I understand your meaning!" she joyously exclaimed. "Whoever reviles you has
never felt the ardent desire of the weak human heart, the cap-
tive of the senses, for contact with the unapproachable, the
sight of the face of the ever concealed yet ever felt divinity.
Here, here stands the most perfect image Heaven and
earth ever created, and must I not kneel before it, clasp it with
all the tendrils of my aspiring soul? No! No one ought,
no one can prevent me."

Half defiantly, half imploringly, the words poured from
her inmost soul like molten lava. "Let all misunderstand me
—save *you*, Freyer! You, by whom God wrought the miracle,
ought not to be narrow-minded! *You* ought not to destroy
it for me, you least of all!" Then she pleaded, appealed to
him: "Let saints, let glorified spirits grasp *only* the essence
and dispense with the earthly pledge—I cannot! I am a
type of the millions who live snared by the weaknesses, the
ideas, the pleasures of the world of sense; do you suddenly
require of me the abstract purity and spiritualization of religious thought, to which only the highest innate or required
perfection leads? Be forbearing to me—God has various
ways of drawing the rebellious to Him! To the soul which is
capable of material ideas only, He gives revelations by the
senses until, through pain and sorrow, it has worked its way
upward to intellectual ones. And until I can behold the *real*
God in His shadowy sphere, I shall cling lovingly and devoutly to His *image.*"

She sank on her kness before him in passionate entreaty.
"Do not destroy it for me, rather aid the pious delusion which
is to save me! Bear patiently with the woe of a soul seeking
its salvation, and leave the rest to God!" She leaned her

brow against the hand which hung by his side and was silent from excess of emotion.

The tall, stalwart man stood trembling as Abraham may have stood before the thicket when God stayed his uplifted arm and cried in tender love: " I will not accept thy sacrifice."

He had a presentiment that the victim would be snatched from him also, if he was too stern, and all the floods of his heart burst forth, all the flood gates of love and pity opened. Bending down, he held her head in a close, warm clasp between both hands, and touched her forehead with quivering lips.

A low cry of unutterable bliss, and she sank upon his breast; the next instant she lifted her warm rosy lips to his.

But he drew back a step in agonizing conflict; " No, Countess, for Heavens's sake no, it must not be."

" Why not ? " she asked, her face blanching.

"Let me remain worthy of the miracle God has wrought upon you through me. If I am to represent Christ to you, I must at least feel and think as He did, so far as my human weakness will permit, or everything will be a deception."

The countess covered her face with her hands. "Ah, no one can utter such words who knows aught of love and longing!" she moaned between her set teeth in bitter scorn.

" Do you think so ? " exclaimed Freyer, and the tone in which he spoke pierced her heart like a cry of pain. Drawing her hands from her face, he forced her to meet his glowing eyes: "Look at me and see whether the tears which now course down my cheeks express no love and longing. Look at yourself, your sweet, pouting lips, your sparkling eyes, all your radiant charms, and ask yourself whether a man into whose arms such a woman falls *can* remain unmoved? When you have answered these questions, say to yourself: ' How that man must love his Saviour, if he buys with such sacrifices the right to wear His crown of thorns!' Perhaps you will then better understand what I said just now of the spirit and nature of Christ."

Countess Madeleine made no reply, but wringing her hands, bent her eyes on the ground.

" Have I wounded you, Countess ? "

"Yes, unto death. But it is best so. I understand you.

If I am to love you as Christ, you must *be* Christ. And the more severe you are, the higher you raise me! Alas—the pain is keen!" She pressed her hand upon her heart as though to close a wound, a pathetic expression of resignation rested on her pallid face.

"Oh, Countess, do not make my task too hard for me. I am but mortal! Oh, how can I see you suffer? *I* can renounce everything, but to hurt *you* in doing so—is beyond my power."

"Do not say *you* in this solemn hour! Call me by my name, I would fain hear it once from your lips!"

"And what *is* your name?"

"Maria Magdalena."

"No. You call yourself so under the impression of the Passion Play."

"I was christened Maria Magdalena von Prankenberg."

"Maria Magdalena," he repeated, his eyes resting upon her with deep emotion as she stood before him, she whose bearing was usually so haughty, now humble, silent, submissive, like the Penitent before the Master. Suddenly, overpowered by his feelings, he extended his arms: "*My* Magdalena."

"My Master, my salvation," she sobbed, throwing herself upon his breast. He clasped her with a divine gesture of love in his embrace.

"Oh, God she has flown hither like a frightened dove and nestled in my breast. Poor dove, I will conceal and protect you from every rude breeze, from every base touch of the world! Build your nest in my heart—here you shall rest in the peace of God!" He pressed her head close to his heart.

"How you tremble, dove! May I call you so?"

"Oh, forever!"

"Are you wearied by your long flight? Poor dove! Have you fluttered hither to me across the wild surges of the world, to bring the olive branch, the token of reconciliation, which makes my peace with things temporal and eternal? And must I now thrust you from me, saying as Christ said to Magdàlene! 'Touch me not; for I am not yet ascended to my Father?' Shall I drive you forth again into this chaos, that the faithful wings which bore you on the right way may droop exhausted till you perish in the billows of the world?" He clasped her *still more* closely: "Oh, God! This cannot be Thy will! But *I think* I understand Thee, Omnipotent One—Thou hast *entrusted* this soul to me, and I will guard it for Thee *loyally !*"

It was an hour of sacred happiness. Her head rested on his breast. Not a leaf stirred on the boughs. The dense shadow of the beeches surrounded them, separating them from the world as if the universe contained naught save this one spot of earth, and the dream of this moment.

"Tell me *one* thing," she whispered, "only one, and I will suffer, atone, and purchase this hour of Heaven by any sacrifice: Do you love me?"

He looked at her, his whole soul in his eyes. "Must I *tell* you so?" he asked mournfully. "What can it serve you to put your hand into the wound in my heart, and see how deep it is? You cannot cure it. Have you not felt, from the first moment, that some irresistible spell drew me to you, forcing me, the recluse, to come to you again and yet again? What was it that drove me from my couch early this morning and sent me hither to your closed house and deserted garden? What was it save love?"

"Ever since four o'clock I have wandered restlessly about with my eyes fixed on the shutters of your room, till the impetuous longing of my soul roused you and drew you from your warm bed into the chill morning air. Come, you are shivering, let me warm you, nestle in my arms and feel the glow of my heart."

He sat down on the bench under the arbor, and—he knew not how it happened—she clung to him like a child and he could not repulse her, he *could* not! She stroked his long black locks with her little soft hand and rested her head against his cheek—she was the very embodiment of innocence, simplicity, girlish artlessness. And in low murmurs she poured out her whole heart to him as a child confides in its father. Without reserve, she told him all the bitter sorrow of her whole life— a life which had never known either love or happiness! Having lost her mother when a mere child, she had been educated by a cold-hearted governess and a pessimistic tutor. Her father, wholly absorbed by the whirl of fashionable life, had cared nothing for her, and when scarcely out of the school room had compelled her to marry a rich old man with whom for eight years existence was one long torment. Then, in mortal fear lest her listener would not forgive her, yet faithful to the truth, she confessed also how her eager soul, yearning for love, had striven to find some compensation, rebelling against a law which recognized the utmost immorality as moral, till *sin* itself seemed virtue compared to the wrong of such a bond. But as the forbidden draught did not quench her thirst, a presentiment came to her that she was longing for that spring of which Christ said: "But whosoever drinketh of the water that I shall give him shall never thirst!" This had brought her here, and here had been opened the purifying, redeeming fount of life and love.

"Now you know all! My soul lies open before you! By the self denial with which I risked my highest blessing, *yourself*, and revealed my whole past life to you, you can judge whether I have been ennobled by your love." Slipping from his embrace, she sank on her knees before him: "Now judge the Penitent—I will accept from your hand whatever fate you may impose. But one thing I beseech you to do, whatever you may ask of me: remember *Christ*."

Freyer raised his large dark eyes. "I do remember Him." Bending toward her with infinite gentleness, he lifted her in his strong arms: "Come, Magdalena! I cannot condemn you," he said, and the Penitent again rested in the embrace of compassion.

"There are drops of cold perspiration on your brow," said Madeleine after a long silence. "Are you suffering?"

"I suffer gladly. Do not heed it!" he said with effort.

Then a glance of loving inquiry searched his inmost soul. "Do you regret the kiss which you just denied me?" she asked, scarcely above her breath, but the whispered question made him wince as though a probe had entered some hidden wound. She felt it, and some irresistible impulse urged her to again raise her pouting lips. He saw their rosy curves close to his own, and gently covered them with his hand. "Be true! Let us be loyal to each other. Do not make my lot harder than it is already! You do not know what you are unchaining." Starting up, he clasped his hands upon his breast, eagerly drinking in long draughts of the invigorating morning air. The gloomy fire which had just glowed in his eyes changed again to a pure, calm light. "This is so *beautiful,* do not disturb it," he said gently, kissing her on the forehead. " My child, my dove! Our love shall remain pure and sacred—shall it not?"

" Yes!" she murmured in reverent submission, for now he was once more the image of Christ, and she bent silently to kiss his hand. He did not resist, for he felt that it was a comfort to her. Then he disappeared, calm, lofty, like one who has stripped off the fetters of this world.

Madeleine von Wildenau was left alone. Pressing her forehead against the trunk of the tree, a rude but firm support, she had sunk back upon the bench, closing her eyes. Her heart was almost bursting with its seething tide of emotion. Tears coursed down her cheeks. God had given her so much, that she almost swooned under this wealth of happiness. Only a touch of pain could balance it, or it would be too great for mortal strength to bear. This pain was an unsatisfied yearning, a vague feeling that her destiny could only be fulfilled through this love, and that she was still so far from possessing it. God has ordained that the human heart can bear only a certain measure of happiness and, when this limit is passed, joy becomes pain because we are not to experience here on earth bliss which belongs to a higher stage of development. That is why the greatest joy brings tears, that is why, amid the utmost love, we believe that we have never loved enough, that is why, amid the excess of enjoyment, we are consumed with the desire for a rapture of which this is but a foretaste, that is why every pleasure teaches us to yearn for a new and greater one, so that we may *never* be satisfied, but continually suffer.

There is but one power which, with strong hand, maintains the balance, teaches us to be sparing of joy, helps us endure pain, dams all the streams of desire and sends them back to toil and bear fruit within the soul: asceticism! It cuts with firm touch the luxuriant shoots from the tree of life, that its strength may concentrate within the marrow of the trunk and urge the growth *upward.* Asceticism! The bugbear of all the grown up children of this world. Wherever it appears human hearts are in a tumult as if death were at hand. Like flying ants bearing away their eggs to a place of safety, the disturbed consciences of worldlings anxiously strive to hide their secret desires and pleasures from the dreaded foe! But whoever dares to meet its eyes sees that it is not the bugbear which the apostles of reason and nature would fain represent it, no flesh-less, bloodless shadow which strives to destroy the natural bond between the Creator and creation, but a being with a glowing heart, five wounds, and a brow bedewed with drops of sweat. Its office is stern and gloomy, its labor severe and thankless, for it has to struggle violently with rebellious souls and, save for the aid of the army of priests who have conse-crated themselves to its service, it would succumb in the ceaseless struggle with materialism which is ever developing into higher consciousness! Yet whoever has once given him-self to her service finds her a lofty, earnest, yet gracious god-dess! She is the support of the feeble, the comforter of the unhappy and the solitary, the angel of the self-sacrificing. Whoever feels her hand upon a wounded, quivering heart, knows that she is the *benefactress*, not the taskmistress of humanity.

Nor does she always appear as the gloomy mourner beside the corpse of murdered joys. Sometimes roses wreath the thorn-scarred brow, and she becomes the priestess of love. When the world and its self-created duties rudely sunders two hearts which God created for each other and leaves them to waste away in mortal anguish, *she* is the compassionate one. With sanctifying power she raises the struggling souls above the dividing barrier of temporal things, teaches them to tram-ple the earth under their feet and unites them with an eternal bond in the purer sphere of *intellectual* love. Thus she unites what *morality* severs. *Morality* alone is harsh, not asceticism. Morality pitilessly prescribes her laws, unheeding the weakness of poor human hearts, asceticism helps them to submit to them. Morality *demands* obedience, asceticism *teaches* it. Morality punishes, asceticism corrects. The former judges by appearances, the latter by the reality. Morality has only the reward of the *world*, asceticism of *Heaven!* Morality made Mary Magdalene an outcast, asceticism led her to the Lord and obtained His mercy for her.

And as the beautiful Magdalene of the present day sat with closed eyes, letting her thoughts be swept along upon the wildly foaming waves of her hot blood, she fancied that the bugbear once so dreaded because she had known it only under the guise of the fulfilment of base, loathsome duty was approaching. But this time the form appeared in its pure beauty, bent tenderly over her, a pallid shape of light, and gazed at her with the eyes of a friend! Low, mysterious words, in boding mournful tones, were murmured in her ears. As she listened, her tears flowed more gently, and with childlike humility she clasped the sublime vision and hid her face on its breast. Then she felt upon her brow a chill kiss, like a breath from the icy regions of eternal peace, and the apparition vanished. But as the last words of something heard in a dream often echo in the ears of the person awaking, the countess as she raised her closed lids, remembered nothing save the three words: " On the cross!" . . . .

CHAPTER XI.

MARY AND MAGDALENE.

"On the cross "—was it a consolation or a menace? Who could decipher this rune? It was like all the sayings of oracles. History would explain its meaning, and when this was done, it would be too late, for it would be fulfilled! The countess still sat motionless in the old arbor. Her destiny had commenced on the cross, that was certain. Hitherto she had been a blind blank, driven like thousands by the wheel of chance. She had first entered into communication with the systematic order of divine thought in the hour when she saw Joseph Freyer on the cross. Will her fate *end* as it *began*, upon the cross? An icy chill ran through her veins. She loved the cross, since it bore the man whom she loved, but what farther influence was it to have upon her life! And what had pallid asceticism to do with her? What was the source of all these oppressive, melancholy forebodings, which could only be justified if a conflict with grave duties or constraining circumstances was impending. Why should they not love each other, both were free! But—she not only desired to love him, she wished to be *his*, to claim him *hers*. Every loving woman longs for the fulfilment of her destiny in the man she loves. How was she to

obtain this fulfilment? What is born in morality, cannot exist
in immorality.   He knew this, felt it, and it was the cause of
his sternness. This was the source of her grief, the visit of the
mysterious comforter, and the warning of the cross. But must
the brightest happiness, the beautiful bud of love wither on the
cross, because it grew there? Was there no other sacred soil
where it might thrive and develop to the most perfect flower?
Was there no wedding altar, no sacrament of marriage? She
drew back as if she suddenly stood on the verge of a yawning
abyss. Her brain reeled! A throng of jeering spectres seemed
grinning at her, watching with malicious delight the leap the
Countess Wildenau was about to take, down to a peasant!
She involuntarily glanced around as if some one might have
been listening to the *thought.* But all was still and silent; her
secret, thank Heaven, was still her own.

      " Eternal Providence, what fate hast thou in store for me ?"
her questioning gaze asked the blue sky. What was the meaning of this extraordinary conflict? She loved Freyer as the
God whom he represented, yet he could be hers only as
a *man*; she must either resign him or the divine illusion. She
felt that the instant which made him hers as a man would
break the spell, and she would no longer love him! The God
was too far above her to be drawn down to her level, the man
was too low to be raised to it. Was ever mortal woman thus
placed between two alternatives and told: " Choose!" The
golden shower fell into Danae's lap, the swan flew to Leda,
the bull bore Europa away, and Jupiter did not ask: "In
what form do you wish me to appear?" But to the higher consciousness of the Christian woman the whole responsibility of
free choice is given. And what is the reward of this torturing
dilemma ? If she chooses the God, she must resign the man,
if she chooses the man she must sacrifice the God. Which
can she renounce, which relinquish? She could not decide,
and wrung her hands in agony. Why must this terrible
discord be hers? Had she ventured too boldly into the
sphere of divine life that, as if in mockery, she was given the
choice between the immortal and the mortal in order, in the
struggle between the two, to recognize the full extent of her
weakness ?

      It seemed so ! As if utterly wearied by the sore conflict,

she hid her face in her hands and called to her aid the wan comforter who had just approached so tenderly. But in vain, the revelations were silent, the deity would not aid her!

"You ought to go up the mountain to-day, Countess," called a resonant voice. This time no pale phantom, no grimacing spectre stood before her, but her friend Ludwig, who gazed into her eyes with questioning sympathy. She clasped his hand.

"Whenever you approach me, my friend, I can never help receiving you with a 'Thank Heaven!' You are one of those whose very *presence* is beneficial to the sufferer, as the physician's entrance often suffices to soothe the patient without medicines."

Ludwig sat down on the bench beside the countess. "My sisters and Josepha are greatly troubled because you have not yet ordered breakfast, and no one ventured to ask. So *I* undertook the dangerous commission, and your Highness can see yonder at the door how admiringly my sisters' eyes are following me."

The countess laughed. "Dear me, am I so dreaded a tyrant?"

"No doubt you are a little inclined to be one," replied Ludwig, quizzically; "now and then a sharp point juts from a hidden coronet. I felt one myself yesterday?"

"When—how?"

"May I remind you of it?"

"Certainly."

"When you poured all your wrath upon poor Freyer, and resolved to leave Ammergau at once. Then I was puzzled for a moment."

"Really?" said the countess with charming embarrassment. "Then I was not mistaken—I perceived it, and therefore delayed sending the telegram. People ought not to take such passing ebullitions so seriously."

"Yes, Countess, but that 'passing ebullition,' might have made poor Freyer miserable for a long time. Pray, have more patience and tolerance in future. Natures so powerful and superior as yours fail to exert a destructive influence upon a circle of simple folk like ourselves, only when they show a corresponding degree of generosity, which suffices to excuse all

our awkwardnesses.   Otherwise you will some day thrust us
down from the height to which you have raised us, and that
would be far worse than if we had *never* been withdrawn from
our modest sphere."

"You are right!" said the countess, thoughtfully.

" My fear is that we are capable only of *rousing* your interest, not *fixing* it. We are on too unequal a footing, we feel
and understand your spell, but are too simple and inexperienced not to be dazzled and confused by its ever varying
phantasmagoria.   Therefore, Countess, you are as great a
source of peril as of happiness."

" Hm !   I understand.   But suppose that for the sake of
you people of Ammergau I desired to return to plainness—
and simplicity."

"You cannot, Countess, you are too young."

" What do you mean ?   That would be the very reason I
should be able to do so."

" No, for you have passed the age when people easily accommodate themselves to new circumstances. Too many of
the shoots of luxury have gained a generous growth ; they will
assert their claims and cannot be forced back into the seeds
whence they came.   Not until they have lived out their time
in the world and died can they form the soil for a new and, if
you desire it, more primitive and simple development !—Any
premature attempt of this kind will last only a few moments
and even these would be a delusion.   But what to you would
be passing moments of disappointment, to those who shared
them would be—lifelong destiny. Our clumsy natures cannot
make these graceful oscillations from one feeling to another,
we stake all on one and lose it, if we are deceived."

The countess looked earnestly at him.

"You are a stern monitor, Ludwig Gross!" she said,
thoughtfully.   " Do you fear that I might play a game with
one of you ? "

"An unconscious one, Countess—as the waves toy with a
drifting boat."

" Well, that would at least be no cruel one !" replied the
lady, smiling.

" *Any* sport, Countess, would be cruel, which tore one of
these calm souls from its quiet haven here and set it adrift

rudderless on the high sea of passion." He rose. "Pardon me—I am taking too much liberty."

"Not more than my friendship gave you a right to say. You brought your friend to me; you are right to warn me if you imagine I should heedlessly throw the priceless gift away! But, Ludwig Gross "—she took his hand—"do you know that I prize it so highly that I should not consider *myself* too great a recompense? Do you know that you have just found me in a sore struggle over this problem?"

Ludwig Gross drew back a step as if he could not grasp the full meaning of the words. So momentous did they seem that he turned pale. "Is it possible?" he stammered.

A tremulous gesture of the hand warned him to say no more. "I don't know—whether it is possible! But that I could even *think* of it, will enable you to imagine what value your gift possesses for me. Not a word, I beseech you. Give me time—and trust me. So many marvels have been wrought in me during the past few days, that I give myself up to the impulse of the moment and allow myself to be led by an ever-ruling Providence—I shall be dealt with kindly."

Ludwig, deeply moved, kissed his companion's hand. "Countess, the impulse which moves you at this moment must unconsciously thrill every heart in Ammergau—as the sleeping child feels, even in its dreams, when a good fairy approaches its cradle. And it is indeed so; for, in you conscious culture approaches unconscious nature—it is a sublime moment, when the highest culture, like the fairy beside the cradle, listens to the breathing of humanity, where completion approaches the source of being, and drinks from it fresh vigor."

"Yes," cried the countess, enthusiastically: "That is it. You understand me perfectly. All civilization must gain new strength from the fountain of nature or its sources of life would become dry—for they perpetually derive their nourishment from that inexhaustible maternal bosom. Where this is not accomplished in individual lives, the primeval element, thus disowned, avenges itself in great social revolutions, catastrophes which form epochs in the history of the world. It is only a pity that in such phases of violent renewal the labor of whole epochs of civilization is lost. Therefore souls in harmony with their age must try to reconcile peacfully what, taken collectively, assumes the proportions of contrasts destructive to the universe."

"And where could we find this reconciliation, save in love?" cried Ludwig, enthusiastically.

"You express it exactly: that is the perception toward which minds are more and more impelled, and whose outlines in art and science appear more and more distinctly. That is the secret of the influence of Parsifal, which extends far beyond the domain of art and, in another province, the success of the Passion Play! To one it revealed itself under one guise, to another under another. To me it was here that the very source of love appeared. And as you, who revealed it to me, are pervaded by the great lesson—I will test it first upon you. Brother! Friend! I will aid you in every strait and calamity, and you shall see that I exercise love, not only in words, but that the power working within me will accomplish deeds also." She clasped her hands imploringly: "And if I love one of you *more* than the others, do not blame me. The nearer to the focus of light, the stronger the heat! He, that one, is surely the focus of the great light which, emanating from you, illumines the whole world. I am so near him— could I remain cold?"

"Ah, Countess—now I will cast aside all fears for my friend. In Heaven's name, take him. Even if he consumes under your thrall—pain, too, is godlike, and to suffer for *you* is a grand, a lofty destiny, a thousand-fold fairer and better than the dull repose of an every day happiness."

"Good heavens, when have I ever heard such language!" exclaimed the countess, gazing admiringly at the modest little man, whose cheeks were glowing with the flush of the loftiest feeling. He stood before her in his plain working clothes, his clear-cut profile uplifted, his eyes raised with a searching gaze as if pursuing the vanishing traces of a lofty, unattainable goal.

She rose: "There is not a day, not an hour here, which does not bring me something grand. Woe befall me if I do not show myself worthy of the obligation your friendship imposes, I should be more guilty than those to whom the summons of the ideal has never come; who have never stood face to face with men like you."

Ludwig quietly held out his hand and clasped hers closely in her own. The piercing glance of his artist-eye seemed to read the inmost depths of her soul.

After a long pause Madeleine von Wildenau interrupted the silence: "There stands your sister in great concern over my bodily welfare! Well then, let us remember that we are human—unfortunately! Will you breakfast with me?"

"I thank you, I have already breakfasted," said Ludwig, modestly, motioning to Sephi to be ready.

"Then at least bear me company." Taking his arm, she went with him to the arbor covered with a wild grape-vine where the table was spread. She sat down to the simple meal, while her companion served her with so much tact and grace that she could not help thinking involuntarily: "And these are peasants? What ought we aristocrats to be?" Then, as if in mockery of this reflection, a man in his shirt-sleeves with his jacket flung over his arm and a scythe in his hand passed down the street by the fence. "Freyer!" exclaimed the countess, her face aflame: "The Messiah with a scythe?"

Freyer stopped. "You called me, Countess?"

"Where are you going with that implement, Herr Freyer?" she asked, coldly, in evident embarrassment.

"To mow my field!" he answered quietly. "I have just time, and I want to try to harvest a little hay. Almost everything goes to ruin during the Passion!"

"But why do you cut it yourself"

"Because I have no servant, Countess!" said Freyer, smiling, raised his hat with the dignified gesture characteristic of him, and moved on as firmly and proudly as though the business he was pursuing was worthy of a king. And so it was, when *he* pursued it. A second blush crimsoned Madeleine von Wildenau's fair forehead. But this time it was because she had been ashamed of him for a moment. "Poor Freyer! His little patrimony was a patch of ground, and should it be accounted a degradation that he must receive the scanty gift of nature directly from her hand, or rather win it blade by blade in the sweat of his brow?" So she reasoned.

Then he glanced back at her and she felt that the look, outshining the sun, had illuminated her whole nature. The fiery greeting of a radiant soul! She waved her white hand to him, and he again raised his hat.

"Where is Freyer's field?"

"Not far from us, just outside the village. Would you like to go there?"

"No, it would trouble me. I should not like to see him toiling for his daily bread. Men such as he ought not to find it necessary, and it must end in some way. God sent me here to equalize the injustice of fate."

"You cannot accomplish this with Freyer, Countess, he would have been a rich man long ago, if he had been willing to accept anything. What do you imagine he has had offered by ladies who, from sacred and selfish motives, under the influence of his personation of the Christ, were ready to make any sacrifice? If ever poverty was an honor to a man, it is to Freyer, for he might have been in very different circumstances and instead is content with the little property received from his father, a bit of woodland, a field, and a miserable little hut. To keep the nobility and freedom of his soul, he toils like a servant and cares for house, field, and wood with his own hands."

"Just see him now, Countess," he added, "You have never beheld any man look more aristocratic while at work than he, though he only wields a scythe."

"You are a loyal friend, Ludwig Gross," she answered. "And an eloquent advocate! Come, take me to him."

She hurried into the house, returning with a broad-brimmed hat on her head, which made her face look as blooming and youthful as a girl's. Long undressed kid gloves covered her arms under the half flowing sleeves of her gown, and she carried over her shoulder a scarlet sunshade which surrounded her whole figure with a roseate glow. There was a warmth, a tempting charm in her appearance like the velvety bloom of a ripe peach. Ludwig Gross gazed at her in wonder.

"You are—*fatally* beautiful!" he involuntarily exclaimed, shaking his head mournfully, as we do when we see some inevitable disaster approaching a friend. "No one ought to be so beautiful," he added, disapprovingly.

Madeleine von Wildenau laughed merrily. "Oh! you comical friend, who offers with so sour a visage the most flattering compliments possible. Our young society men might take lessons from you! Pardon me for laughing," she said apologetically, as Ludwig's face darkened. "But it came so unexpectedly, I was not prepared for such a compliment here," and in spite of herself, she laughed again, the compliment was too irresistible.

Her companion was deeply offended. He saw in this outbreak of mirth a levity which outraged his holiest feelings. These were "the graceful oscillations from one mood to another," as he had termed it that day, which he had so dreaded for his friend, and which now perplexed his own judgment!

A moment was sufficient to reveal this to the countess, in the next she had regained her self-control and with it the power of adapting herself to the earnestness of her friend's mood.

He was walking silently at her side with a heavy heart. There had been something in that laugh which he could not fathom, readily as he grasped any touch of humor. To the earnest woman he had seen that morning, he would have confided his friend in the belief that he was fulfilling a lofty destiny; to the laughing, coquettish woman of the world, he grudged him; Joseph Freyer was far too good for such a fate.

They had walked on, each absorbed in thought, leaving the village behind, into the open country. Few people were at work, for during the Passion there is rarely time to till the fields.

"There he is!" Ludwig pointed to a man swinging his scythe with a powerful arm. The countess had dreaded the sight, yet now stood watching full of admiration, for these movements were as graceful as his gestures. The natural symmetry which was one of his characteristic qualities rendered him a picturesque figure even here, while toiling in the fields. His arms described rhythmically returning circles so smoothly, the poise of the elastic body, bending slightly forward, was so noble, and he performed the labor so easily that it seemed like a graceful gymnastic exercise for the training of the marvellous limbs. The countess gazed at him a long time, unseen.

A woman's figure, bearing a jug, approached from the opposite side of the meadow and offered Freyer a drink.

"I have brought some milk. You must be thirsty, it is growing warm," the countess heard her say. She was a gracious looking woman, clad in simple country garb, evidently somewhat older than Freyer, but with a noble, virginal bearing and features of classic regularity. Every movement was dignified, and her expression was calm and full of kindly earnestness.

"I ought to know her," said the countess in a strangely sharp tone.

"Certainly. She is the Mother of God in the Passion Play, Anastasia Gross, the burgomaster's sister."

"Yes, the Mary!" said the countess, and again she remembered how the two, mother and son, had remained clasped in each other's arms far longer than seemed to her necessary. What unknown pang was this which now pierced her heart? "I suppose they are betrothed?" she asked, with quickened breath.

"Who can tell? We think she loves him, but no one knows Freyer's feelings!" said Ludwig.

"I don't understand, since you are such intimate friends, why you should not know!"

"I believe, Countess, if we people of Ammergau have *any* good quality, it is discretion. We do not ask even the most intimate friend anything which he does not confide to us."

Madeleine von Wildenau lowered her eyes in confusion. After a short struggle she said with deadly sternness and bitterness: "You were right this morning—the man must be left *in his sphere*. Come, let us go back!" A glance from Ludwig's eyes pierced her to the heart. She turned back toward the village. But Freyer had already seen her and overtook her with the speed of thought.

"Why, Countess, you here? And"—his eyes, fierce with pain, rested enquiringly on hers as he perceived their cold expression, "and you were going to leave me without a word of greeting? Were you ashamed to speak to the poor peasant who was mowing his grass? Or did my dress shock you?" He was so perfectly artless that he did not even interpret her indignation correctly, but attributed it to an entirely different cause. This did not escape the keen intuition of a woman so thoroughly versed in affairs of the heart. But when a drop of the venom of jealousy has entered the blood, it requires some time ere it is absorbed, even though the cause of the mischief has long been removed. This is an old experience, as well as the fact that, this process once over, repentance is all the sweeter, love the more passionate. But the poor simple-hearted peasant, in his artlessness, could not perceive all this., He was merely ashamed of standing before the countess in his shirt sleeves and hurriedly endeavored, with trembling fingers, to fasten his collar which he had opened while at work, baring his throat and chest. It seemed as if the hot blood could be heard pulsing against the walls of his arched chest, like the low murmur of the sea. The labor, the increasing heat of the sun, and the excitement of the countess' presence had quickened the usually calm flow of his blood till it fairly seethed in his veins, glowing in roseate life through the ascetic pallor of the skin, while the swelling veins stood forth in a thousand beautiful waving lines like springs welling from white stone. Both stood steeped in the fervid warmth, one absorbing, the other reflecting it.

But with the cruelty of love, which seeks to measure the strength of responsive passion by the very pain it has the power to inflict, the beautiful woman curbed the fire kindled in her own pulses and said carelessly : " We have interrupted your tête-à-tête, we will make amends by retiring."

" Countess! " he exclaimed with a look which seemed to say: " Is it possible that you can be so unjust ! My *Mother*, Mary, was with me, she brought her son something to refresh him at his work, why should you interrupt us ? "

The simple words, which to her had so subtle a double meaning, explained everything and Madeleine von Wildenau felt, with deep embarrassment, that he understood her and that she must appear very petty in his eyes.

Ludwig Gross drew out his watch. " Excuse me, it is nine o'clock; I must go to my drawing-school." He bowed and left them, without shaking hands with the countess as usual. She felt it as a rebuke, and a voice in her heart said : " You must become a far better woman ere you are worthy of this man."

" Would not you like to know Mary ? May I introduce her to you ? " asked Freyer, when they were alone.

" Oh, it is not necessary."

" Why, how can you love the son and not care for the mother ? "

" She is *not* your mother," replied the countess.

" And *I* am not the Christ. Why does the illusion affect me, and not Mary ? "

" Because it was perfect in you, but not in her.''

"Then there is still more reason to know her, that her personality may complete what her personation lacked."

The countess cast a gloomy look at the tall maiden, who meanwhile had taken the scythe and was doing Freyer's work.

" She seems to be very devoted to you," she said suspiciously.

" Yes, thank Heaven, we are loyal friends."

" I suppose you call each other thou."

" Yes, all the Ammergau people do that, when they have been schoolmates."

" That is a strange custom. Is it practised by those in both high and low stations ?"

" There are neither high nor low stations among us. We all stand on the same footing, Countess. The fact that one is richer, another poorer, that one can do more for education and external appearances than his neighbor makes no difference with us and, if it did, it would be an honor for me to be permitted to address Anastasia with the familiar thou, for she and the whole Gross family are far above me. Even in your sense of the word, Countess, the burgomaster is an aristocrat, no child of nature like myself, but a man familiar with social usages and thoroughly well educated."

" Well, then," cried the countess, " why don't you marry the lady, if she possesses such superior advantages ? "

" Marry?" Freyer started back as if instead of Madeleine's beautiful face he had suddenly beheld some hideous vision, " I have never thought of it ! "

" Why not ? "

" The Christ wed Mary ? The son the mother? No, though we are not what we represent, *that* would be impossible. I have become so accustomed to regard her as my mother that it would seem to me a profanation."

" But next winter, when the Play is over, it will be different."

"And *you* say this to me, Countess; *you*, after this morning?" cried Freyer, with a trembling voice. "Are you in earnest?"

"Certainly. I cannot expect you, for my sake, to neglect older claims upon your heart!"

"Countess, if I had older claims, would I have spoken to you as I did to-day, would the events have occurred which happened to-day? Can you believe such things of me? You are silent? Well, Countess, that may be the custom in your circle, but not in mine."

"Forgive me, Freyer!" stammered the lady, turning pale.

"Freyer shaded his eyes with his hand as if the sun dazzled him, in order to conceal his rising tears.

"For what are you looking?" asked the countess, who thought he was trying to see more distinctly.

He turned his face, eloquent with pain, full toward her. "I was looking to see where my dove had flown, I can no longer find her. Or was it all a dream?"

"Freyer!" cried the countess, utterly overwhelmed, slipping her hand through his arm and resting her head without regard for possible spectators on his heaving breast. "Joseph, your dove has not flown away, she is here, take her to your heart again and keep her forever, forever, if you wish."

"Take care, Countess," said Freyer, warningly, "there are people moving in all directions."

She raised her head. "Will it cause you any harm?" she asked, abashed.

"Not me, but you. I have no one to question me and could only be proud of your tokens of favor, but consider what would be said in your own circle, if it were rumored that you had rested your head on a peasant's breast."

"You are no peasant, you are an artist."

"In your eyes, but not in those of the world. Even though we do passably well in wood-carving and in the Passion Play, so long as we are so poor that we are compelled to till our fields ourselves, and bring the wood for our carvings from the forest with our own hands, we shall be ranked as peasants, and no one will believe that we are anything else. You will be blamed for having associated with such uncultured people."

"Oh, I will answer for that before the whole world."

"That would avail little, my beloved one, Heaven forbid that I should ever so far forget myself as to boast of your love before others, or permit you to do anything which they would misjudge. God alone understands what we are to each other, and therefore it must remain hidden in His bosom where no profane eye can desecrate it."

The countess clung closer to him in silent admiration. She remembered so many annoyances caused by the indiscretions due to the vanity of men whom she had favored, that this modest delicacy seemed so chivalrous and lofty that she would fain have fallen at his feet.

"Dove, have I found you again?" he said, gazing into her eyes. "My sweet, naughty dove! You will never more wound and wrong me so. I feel that you might break my heart." And pressing her arm lightly to his side, he raised her hand to his burning lips.

A glow of happiness filled Madeleine von Wildenau's whole being as she heard the stifled, passionate murmur of love. And as, with every sunbeam, the centifolia blooms more fully, revealing a new beauty with each opening petal, so too did the soul of the woman thus illumined by the divine ray of true love.

"Come," she said suddenly, "take me to the kind creature who so tenderly ministers to you, perhaps suffers for you. I now feel drawn toward her and will love her for your sake as your mother, Mary."

"Ah, my child, that is worthy of you! I knew that you were generous and noble! Come, my Magdalene, I will lead you to Mary."

They walked rapidly to the field where Anastasia was busily working. The latter, seeing the stranger approach, let down the skirt she had lifted and adjusted her dress a little, but she received the countess without the least embarrassment and cordially extended her hand. *Her* bearing also had a touch of condescension, which the great lady especially noticed. Anastasia gazed so calmly and earnestly at her that she lowered her eyes as if unable to bear the look of this serene soul. The smoothly brushed brown hair, the soft indistinctly marked brows, the purity of the features, and the virginal dignity throned on the noble forehead harmonized with the ideal of the Queen of Heaven which the countess had failed to grasp in the Passion Play. She was beautiful, faultless from head to foot, yet there was nothing in her appearance which could arouse the least feeling of jealousy. There was such spirituality in her whole person—something—the countess could not describe it in any other way—so expressive of the sober sense of age, that the beautiful woman was ashamed of her suspicion. She now understood what Freyer meant when he spoke of the maternal relation existing between Anastasia and himself.

She was the true Madonna, to whom all eyes would be lifted devoutly, reverently, yet whom no man would desire to press to his heart. She was probably not much older than the countess, two or three years at most, but compared with her the great lady, so thoroughly versed in the ways of the world, was but an immature, impetuous child. The countess felt this with the secret satisfaction which it affords every woman to perceive that she is younger than another, and it helped her to endure the superiority which Anastasia's lofty calmness maintained over her. Nay, she even accepted the inferior place with a coquettish artlessness which made her appear all the more youthful. Yet at the very moment she adopted the childish manner, she secretly felt its reality. She was standing in the presence of the Mother of God. Womanly nature had never possessed any charm for her, she had never comprehended it in any form. She had never admired any of Raphael's Madonnas, not even the Sistine. A woman interested her only as the object of a man's love for which she might envy her, the contrary character, the ascetic beauty of an Immaculate was wholly outside of her sphere. Now, for the first time in her life, she was interested in a personality of this type, because she suddenly realized that the Virgin was also the Mother of the Saviour. And as her love for the Christ was first awakened by her love for Joseph Freyer, her reverence for Mary was first felt when she thought of her as his mother! Madeleine von Wildenau, so poor in the treasures of the heart, the woman who had never been a mother, suddenly felt—even while in the act of playing with practised coquetry the part of childlike ignorance—under the influence of the man she loved, the *reality* in the farce and her heart opened to the sacred, mysterious bond between the mother and the child.

10

Thus, hour by hour, she grew out of the captivity of the world and the senses, gently supported and elevated by the might of that love which reconciles earth and heaven.

She held out one hand to Anastasia, the other to Freyer. " I, too, would fain know the dear mother of our Christ! " she said, with that sweet, submissive grace which the moment had taught her. Freyer's eyes rested approvingly upon her. She felt as if wings were growing on her shoulders, she felt that she was beautiful, good, and beloved; earth could give no more.

Anastasia watched the agitated woman with the kindly, searching gaze of a Sister of Charity. Indeed, her whole appearance recalled that of one of these ministering spirits, resigned without sentimentality; gentle, yet energetic; modest, yet impressive.

" I felt a great—" the countess was about to say "admiration," but this was not true, she admired her now for the first time! She stopped abruptly in the midst of her sentence, she could utter no stereotyped compliments at this moment. With quiet dignity, like a princess giving audience, Anastasia came to her assistance, by skilfully filling up the pause : " So this is your first visit to Ammergau ? "

" Yes."

" Then you have doubtless been very much impressed ? "

" Oh, who could remain cold, while witnessing such a spectacle ? "

" Yes, is not our Christ perfect ? " said Anastasia, smiling proudly. " He costs people many tears. But even *I* cannot help weeping, and I have played it with him thirty times." She passed her hand across his brow with a tender, maternal caress, as if she wished to console him for all his sufferings. " Does it not seem as if we saw the Redeemer Himself ? "

The countess watched her with increasing sympathy. "You have a beautiful soul! Your friend was right, people should know you to receive the full impression of Mary."

" Yes, I play it too badly," replied Anastasia, whose native modesty prevented her recognition of the flattery conveyed in the countess' words.

" No—badly is not the word. But the delicate shadings of the feminine nature are lost in the vast space," the other explained.

"It may be so," replied Anastasia, simply. "But that is of no importance; no matter how we others might play—*he* would sustain the whole."

"And your brother, Anastasia, and all the rest—do you forget them?" said Freyer, rebukingly.

"Yes, dear Anastasia." The countess took Freyer's hand. "I have given my soul into the keeping of this Christ—but your brother's performance is also a masterpiece! It seems to me that you are unjust to him. And also to Pilate, whom I admired, the apostles and high-priests."

"Perhaps so. I don't know how the others act—" said Mary with an honesty that was fairly sublime. "I see only him, and when he is not on the stage I care nothing for the rest of the performance. It is because I am his *mother:* to a mother the son is beyond everything else," she added, calmly.

The countess looked at her in astonishment. Was it possible that a woman could love in this way? Yet there was no doubt of it. Had even a shadow of longing to be united to the man she loved rested on the soul of this girl, she could not have had this crystalline transparency and absolute freedom from embarrassment.

These Madonnas are happy beings! she thought, yet she did not envy this calm peace.

Drawing off her long glove with much difficulty, she took a ring from her finger. "Please accept this from me as a token of the secret bond which unites us in love for—your son! We will be good friends."

"With all my heart!" said Anastasia in delight, holding out her sunburnt finger to receive the gift. "What will my brother say when I come home with such a present?" She gratefully kissed the donor's hand. "You are too kind, Countess—I don't know how I deserve it." She stooped and lifted her jug. "I must go home now to help my sister-in-law. You will visit us, won't you? My brother will be so pleased."

"Very gladly—if you will allow me," replied the lady, smiling.

"I beg you to do so!" said Anastasia with ready tact. Then with noble dignity, she moved away across the fields, waving her hand from the distance to the couple she had left behind, as if to say : "Be happy!"

CHAPTER XII.

BRIDAL TORCHES.

"Magdalene—Wife—Angel—what shall I call you?" cried Freyer, extending his arms. "Oh, if only we were not in the open fields, that I might press you to my heart and thank you for being so kind—so *generous* and so kind."

"Does your heart at last yearn for me? Then let us come into the forest, where no one is watching us save holy nature. Take me up one of the mountains. Will you? Can you? Will not your hay spoil?"

"*Let* it spoil, what does that matter? But first you must allow me to go home to put on garments more suitable for your society."

"No, that will be too late! Remain as you are—you are handsome in any clothes," she whispered, blushing faintly, like a girl, while she lowered her eyes from the kingly figure to the ground. A happy smile flitted over her face. Stooping, she picked up the jacket which he had removed while doing his work.

"And you—are you equipped for mountain climbing?"

"Oh, we will not go far. Not farther than we can go and return in time for dinner."

"Come, then. If matters come to the worst, I will take my dove on my shoulder and carry her when she can walk no farther."

"Oh, happy freedom!" cried the countess, joyously! "To wander through the woods, like two children in a fairy tale, enchanted by some wicked fairy and unable to appear again until after a thousand years! Oh, poetry of childhood—for the first time you smile upon me in all your radiance. Come, let us hasten—it is so beautiful that I can hardly believe it. I shall not, until we are there."

She flew rather than walked by his side. "My dove—suppose that we were enchanted and forced to remain in the forest together a thousand years?"

"Let us try it!" she whispered, fixing her eyes on his till he murmured, panting for breath: "I believe—the spell is beginning to work." And his eyes glowed with a gloomy fire as he murmured, watching her: "Who knows whether I am not harboring the Lorelei herself, who is luring me into her kingdom to destroy me!"

"What do you know of the Lorelei?"

Freyer stopped. "Do you suppose I read nothing? What else should I do during the long evenings, when wearied by my work, I am resting at home?"

"Really?" she asked absently, drawing him forward.

"Do you suppose I could understand a woman like you if I had not educated myself a little? Alas, we cannot accomplish much when the proper foundation is lacking. The untrained memory retains nothing firmly except what passes instantly into flesh and blood, the perception of life as it is reflected to us from the mirror of art. But even this reflection is sometimes distorted and confuses our natural thoughts and feelings. Alas, dear one, a person who has learned nothing correctly, and yet knows the yearning for something higher, without being able to satisfy it—is like a lost soul that never attains the goal for which it longs."

"My poor friend, I do know that feeling—to a certain extent it is the same with us women. We, too, have the yearning for education, and finally attain only a defective amount of knowledge! But, by way of compensation, individuality, directness, intuitiveness are developed all the more fully. You did not need to know anything—your influence is exerted through your personality; as such you are great. All knowledge comes from man, and is attainable by him—the divine gift of individuality can neither be gained, nor bestowed, any more than intuition! What is all the logic of reflecting reason compared with the gift of intuition, which enabled you to assume the part of a God? Is not that a greater marvel than the hard-won result of systematic study at the desk?"

"You are a kind comforter!" said Freyer.

"Thinking makes people old!" she continued. "It has aged the human race, too.—Nature, simplicity, love must restore its youth! In them is *direct* contact with the deity; in civilization only an indirect one. Fortunately for me, I have put my lips to their spring. Oh, eternal fountain of human nature, I drink from you with eager draughts."

They had entered the forest—the tree-tops rustled high

above their heads and at their feet rippled a mountain stream. Madeleine von Wildenau was silent—her heart rested on her friend's broad breast, heaving with the rapid throbbing of his heart, her supple figure had sunk wearily down by his side. "Say no more—not a word is needed here." The deep gloom of the woods surrounded them—a sacred stillness and solitude. "On every height there dwells repose!" echoed in soft melody above her head, the marvellous Rubinstein-Goethe song. There was no human voice, it seemed like a mere breath from the distance of a dream—like the wind sweeping over the chords of the cymbal hung by Lenau's gypsy on a tree, scarcely audible, already dying away again. Her ear had caught the notes of that Æolian harp once before: she knew them again; on the cross—with the words: "Into *thy* hands I commend my spirit." And sweet as the voice which spoke at that time was now the tenor that softly, softly hushed the restless spirit of the worldling to slumber. "Wait; soon, soon—" and then the notes gradually rose till the whole buzzing, singing woodland choir seemed to join in the words: "Thou, too, shalt soon rest."

The mysterious sound came from the depths of the great heart on which she rested, as if the soul had quitted the body a few moments and now, returning, was revealing with sweet lamentation what it had beheld in the invisible world.

"Are you weeping?" he asked tenderly, kissing the curls which clustered round her forehead: "*My child.*"

"Oh, when you utter that word, I have a feeling which I never experienced before. Yes, I am, I wish to be a child in your hands. Only those who have ever tasted the delight of casting the burden of their own egoism upon any altar, whether it be religion or love—yielding themselves up, becoming absorbed in another, higher power—*only those* can know my emotions when I lean on your breast and you call me your child! Thus released from ourselves, thus free and untrammelled must we feel when we have stripped off in death the fetters of the body and merged all which is personal to us in God."

"Heaven has destined you for itself, and you already feel how it is loosening your fibres and gradually drawing you up out of the soil in which you are rooted. That is why you

wept when I sang that song to you here in the quiet woodland
solitude. Such tears are like the drops the tree weeps, when
a name is cut upon it. At such moments you feel the hand
of God tearing open the bark which the world has formed
around your heart, and the sap wells from the wounded spot.
Is it not so?" He gently passed his hand over her eyes,
glittering with unshed tears.

"Ah, noble soul! How you penetrate the depths of my
being! What is all the wit and wisdom of the educated
mind, compared with the direct inspiration of your poetic nature. Freyer, Spring of the earth—Christ, Spring of humanity!
My heart is putting forth its first blossom for you, take it."
She threw herself with closed eyes upon his breast, as if blindly.
He clasped her in a close embrace, holding her a long time
silently in his arms. Then he said softly: "I will accept the
beautiful blossom of your heart, my child, but not for myself."
He raised his eyes fervently upward: "Oh, God, Thou hast
opened Thy hand to the beggar, and made him rich that he
may sacrifice to Thee what no king could offer. I thank
Thee."

Something laughed above their heads—it was a pair of
wild-doves, cooing in the green tent over them.

"Do you know why they are laughing?" asked the
countess, in an altered tone. "They are laughing at us!"

"Magdalena!"

"Yes! They are laughing at the self-tormenting doubt of
God's goodness. Look around you, see the torrent foaming,
and the blue gentians drinking its spray, see the fruit-laden
hazel, the sacred tree which sheltered your childhood; see the
bilberries at your feet, all the intoxicating growth and movement of nature, and then ask yourself whether the God who
created all this warm, sunny life is a God who only *takes*—not
gives. Do you believe He would have prepared for us this
Spring of love, that we may let its blossoms wither on the cold
altar of duty or of prejudice? No—take what He bestows—
and do not question."

"Do not lead me into temptation, Magdalena!" he gently
entreated. "I told you this morning that you do not know
what you are unloosening."

He stood before her as if transfigured, his eyes glowed

with the sombre fire which had flashed in them a moment
early that morning, a rustling like eagle's pinions ran through
the forest—Jupiter was approaching in human form.

The beautiful woman sat down on a log with her hands
clasped in her lap.

" A man like me loves but once, but with his whole being.
I *demand* nothing—but what is given to me is given *wholly*,
or not at all ; for if I once have it, I will never give it up save
with my life!

" Not long since a stranger came here, who sang the song
of the Assras, who die when they love. I believe I am of their
race. Woman, do not toy, do not trifle with me ! For know
—I love you with the fatal love of those ' Assras.' "

Madeleine von Wildenau trembled with delight.

" If I once touch your lips, the barrier between us will
have fallen ! Will you forgive me if the flood-tide of feeling
sweeps me away till I forget who you are and what a gulf
divides the Countess Wildenau from the low-born peasant ? "

" Oh, that you can remind me of it—in this hour—! " cried
the countess, with sorrowful reproach.

He looked almost threateningly into her eyes.   The dark
locks around his head seemed to stir like the bristling mane of
a lion : " Woman, you do not know me ! If you deceive me,
you will betray the most sacred emotion ever felt by mortal
man—and it will be terribly avenged. Then the flame you
are kindling will consume either you or me, or both. You see
that I am now a different man. Formerly you have beheld
me only when curbed by the victorious power of my holy task.
You have conjured up the spirits, now they can no longer be
held in thrall—will you not be terrified by the might of a passion which is unknown to you people of the world, with your
calm self-control ? "

" *I*, terrified by you ? " cried the proud woman in a tone
of exultant rapture. " Oh, this is power, this is the very breath
of the gods. Should I fear amid the element for which I
longed—which was revealed to me in my own breast ? Does
the flame fear the fire ? The Titaness dread the Titan ? Ah,
Zeus, hurl thy thunderbolt, and let the forest blaze as the victorious torch of nature at last released from her long bond-
age."

He sat down by her side, his fiery breath fanning her cheek. "Then you will try it, will give me the kiss I dared not take to-day?"

"Yes."

"But it will be a betrothal kiss."

"Yes."

He opened his arms, and as a black moth settles upon a fragrant tea-rose, hovering on its velvet wings above the dewy calyx, he bent his head to hers, shadowing her with his dark locks and pressed his first kiss upon Madeleine von Wildenau's quivering lips.

But such moments tempt the gods themselves, and Jupiter hovered over the pair, full of wrath, for he envied the Christian mortal the beautiful woman. He had heard her laughingly challenge him in the midst of the joy she had stolen from the gods, and the heavens darkened, the hurricane saddled the steeds of the storm, awaiting his beck, and down flashed the fire from the sky—a shrill cry rent the air, the highest tree in the forest was cleft asunder and the bridal torch lighted by Jupiter blazed aloft.

"The gods are averse to it," said Freyer, gloomily. "Defy them!" cried the countess, starting up; "they are powerless—we are in the hands of a Higher Ruler."

"Woman, you do not belong to this world, or you have no nerves which can tremble."

"Tremble?" She laughed happily. "Tremble, by *your* side?" Then, nestling closer still, she murmured: "I am as cowardly as ever woman was, but where I love I have the courage to defy death. Even were I to fall now beneath a thunderbolt, could I have a fairer death than at *this* moment? You would willingly die for your Christ—and I for mine."

"Well then, come, you noble woman, that I may shield you as well as I can! Now we shall see whether God is with us! I defy the elements!" He proudly clasped the object of his love in his arms and bore her firmly on through the chaos into which the whole forest had fallen. The tempest, howling fiercely, burst its way through the woods. The boughs snapped, the birds were hurled about helplessly. The destroying element seemed to come from both heights and depths at the same time, for it shook the earth and tore the

roots of trees from the ground till the lofty trunks fell shattered and, rolling down the mountain, swept everything with
them in the sudden ruin.   With fiendish thirst for battle the
fiery sword flamed from the sky amid the uproar, dealing
thrust after thrust and blow after blow—while here and there
scarlet tongues of flame shot hissing upward through the dry
branches.

A torrent of rain now dashed from the clouds but without
quenching the flames, whose smoke was pressed down into
the tree-tops, closely interlaced by the tempest.   Like a
gigantic black serpent, it rolled its coils from every direction,
stifling, suffocating with the glowing breath of the forest conflagration, and the undulating cloud body bore with it in
glittering, flashing sparks, millions of burning pine needles.

" Well, soul of fire, is the heat fierce enough for you now ? "
asked Freyer, pressing the beautiful woman closer to his side
to shield her with his own body : " Are you content now ? "

" Yes," she said, gasping for breath, and the eyes of both
met, as if they felt only the fire in their own hearts and had
blended this with the external element into a single sea of
flame.

Nearer, closer drew the fire in ever narrowing circles
around the defiant pair, more and more sultry became the
path, brighter grew the hissing blaze through which they were
compelled to force their way.   Now on the left, now on the
right, the red-eyed conflagration confronted them amid the
clouds of smoke and flame, half stifled by the descending
floods of rain, yet pouring from its open jaws hot, scorching
steam—fatal to laboring human chests—and obliged the fugitives to turn back in search of some new opening for escape.

" If the rain ceases, we are lost ! " said the countess with
the utmost calmness.   " Then the fire will be sole ruler."

Freyer made no reply.   Steadily, unflinchingly, he
struggled on, grasping with the strength of a Titan the falling
boughs which threatened the countess' life, shielding with both
arms her uncovered head from the flying sparks, and ever and
anon, sprinkling her hair and garments from some bubbling
spring.   The water in the brooks was already warm.   Throngs
of animals fleeing from the flames surrounded them, and birds
with scorched wings fell at their feet.   It was no longer possi-

ble to go down, the fire was raging below them. They were compelled to climb up the mountain and seek the summit.

"Only have courage—forward!" were Freyer's sole words. And upward they toiled—through the pathless woods, through underbrush and thickets, over roots of trees, rolling stones, and rocks, never pausing, never taking breath, for the flames were close at their heels, threatening them with their fiendish embrace. Where the path was too toilsome, Freyer lifted the woman he loved in his arms and bore her over the rough places.

At last the woods grew thinner, the boundary of the flames was passed, they had reached the top—were saved. The neighing steeds of the wind received them on the barren height and strove to hurl them back into the fiery grave, but Freyer's towering form resisted their assault and, with powerless fury, they tore away the rocks on the right and left and rolled them thundering down into the depths below. The water pouring from the clouds drenched the lovers like a billow from the sea, beating into their eyes, mouths, and ears till, blinded and deafened, they were obliged to grope their way along the cliff. The garments of the beautiful Madeleine von Wildenau hung around her in tatters, heavy as lead, her hair was loosened, dripping and dishevelled, she was trembling from head to foot with cold in the icy wind and rain here on the heights, after the heat and terror below in the smouldering thicket.

"I know where there is a herder's hut, I'll take you to it. Cling closely to me, we must climb still higher."

They silently continued the ascent.

The countess staggered with fatigue. Freyer lifted her again in his arms, and, by almost superhuman exertion, bore her up the last steep ascent to the hut. It was empty. He placed the exhausted woman on the herder's straw pallet, where she sank fainting. When she regained her consciousness she was supported in Freyer's arms, and her face was wet with his tears. She gazed at him as if waking to the reality of some beautiful dream. "Is it really you?" she asked, with such sweet childlike happiness, as she threw her arms around him, that the strong man's brain and heart reeled as if his senses were failing.

" You are alive, you are safe ? "   He could say no more. He kissed her dripping garments, her feet, and tenderly examined her beautiful limbs to assure himself that she had received no injury.   "Thank Heaven!" he cried joyously, amid his tears, " you are safe ! "   Then, half staggering, he rose : " Now, in the presence of the deadly peril we have just escaped, tell me whether you really love me, tell me whether you are mine, *wholly* mine!   Or hurl me down into the blazing forest—it would be more merciful, by Heaven ! than to deceive me."

" Joseph ! " cried the countess, clinging passionately to him. " Can you ask that—now ? "

"Alas ! I cannot understand how a poor ignorant man like me can win the love of such a woman.   What can you love, save the illusion of the Christ, and when that has vanished— what remains ? "

" The divine, the real *love !* " replied the countess with a lofty expression.

" Oh, I believe that you are sincere.   But if you have deceived yourself, if you should ever perceive that you have overestimated me—ah, it would be far better for me to be lying down below amid the flames than to experience *that.* There is still time—consider well, and say—what shall it be ?"

" Consider ? " replied the countess, drawing his head down to hers.   " Tell the torrent to consider ere it plunges over the cliff, to dissolve into spray in the leap.   Tell the flower to consider ere it opens to the sunbeam which will consume it ! Will you be more petty than they ?   What is there to consider, when a mighty impulse powerfully constrains us ?   Is not this moment worth risking the whole life without asking : ' What is to come of it ? '   Ah, then—then, I have been mistaken in you and it will be better for us to part while there is yet time."

" Oh — enchantress !   You are right, I no longer know myself!   Part, now ?   No, it is too late, I am yours, body and soul.   Be it so, then, I will barter my life for this moment, and no longer doubt, for I *can* do nothing else."

Sinking on his knees before her, he buried his face in her lap.   Madeleine von Wildenau embraced him with unspeakable tenderness, yet she felt the burden of a heavy responsibility resting upon her, for she now realized—that she was his destiny. She had what she desired, his soul, his heart, his life —nay, had he possessed immortality, he would have sacrificed that, too, for her sake. But now the "God" had become *human*—the choice was made. And, with a secret tear she gazed upon the husk of the beautiful illusion which had vanished.

"What is the matter?" he asked suddenly, raising his head and gazing into her eyes with anxious foreboding. "You have grown cold."

"No, only sad."

"And why?"

"Alas! I do not know! Nothing in this world can be quite perfect." She drew him tenderly toward her. "This is one of those moments in which the highest happiness becomes pain. The fury of the elements could not harm us, but it is a silent, stealing sorrow, which will appease the envy of the gods for unprecedented earthly bliss: Mourning for my Christus."

Freyer uttered a cry of anguish and starting up, covered his face with both hands. "Oh, that you are forced to remind me of it!" He rushed out of the hut.

What did this mean. The beautiful mistress of his heart felt as if she had deceived herself when she believed him to be exclusively her own, as if there was something in the man over which she had no power! Filled with vague terror, she followed him. He stood leaning against the hut as if in a dream and did not lift his eyes. The sound of alarm-bells and the rattle of fire-arms echoed from the valley. The rain had ceased, and columns of flame were now rising high into the air, forming a crimson canopy above the trees in the forest. It was a wild scene, this glowing sea of fire into which tree after tree gradually vanished, the air quivering with the crash of the falling boughs, from which rose a shower of sparks, and a crowd of shrieking birds eddying amid the flames. Joseph Freyer did not heed it. The countess approached almost timidly. "Joseph—have I offended you?"

"No, my child, on the contrary! When I reminded you to-day of the obligations of your rank, you were angry with me, but I thank you for having remembered what I forgot for your sake."

"Well. But, spite of the warning, I was not ashamed of you and did not disown you before the Countess Wildenau! But you, Joseph, are ashamed of me in the presence of Christ!"

He gazed keenly, sorrowfully at her. "I ashamed of you, I deny you in the presence of my Redeemer, who is also yours? I deny you, because I am forced to confess to Him that I love you beyond everything else—nay, perhaps more than I do *Him*? Oh, my dearest, how little you know me! May the day never come which will prove which of us will first deny the other, and may you never be forced to weep the tears which Peter shed when the cock crowed for the third time."

She sank upon his breast. "No, my beloved, that will never be! In the hour when *that* was possible, you might despise me."

He kissed her forehead tenderly. "I should not do that —any more than Christ despised Peter. You are a child of the world, could treachery to *me* be charged against you if the strong man, the disciple of Christ, was pardoned for treason to the *holiest*."

"Oh, my angel! It would be treason to the 'holiest,'" said the countess with deep emotion, "if I could deny *you!*"

"Why, for Heaven's sake, Herr Freyer," shouted a voice, and the herdsman came bounding down the mountain side: "Can you stand there so quietly—amid this destruction?" The words died away in the distance.

"The man is right," said the countess in a startled tone, "we are forgetting everything around us. Whoever has hands must help. Go—leave me alone here and follow the herdsman."

"There is no hope of extinguishing the fire, the wood is lost!" replied Freyer, indifferently. "It is fortunate that it is an isolated piece of land, so the flames cannot spread."

"But, Good Heavens, at least try to save what can yet be secured—that is only neighborly duty."

"I shall not leave you, happen what may."

"But I am safe, and perhaps some poor man's all, is burning below."

"What does it matter, in this hour?"

"What does it matter?" the countess indignantly ex-

claimed. " Joseph, I do not understand you !   Have you so
little feeling for the distress of your fellow men—and yet play
the Christ ? "

Freyer gazed at the destruction with a strange expression
—his noble figure towered proudly aloft against the gloomy,
cloud-veiled sky. Smiling calmly, he held out his hand to the
woman he loved and drew her tenderly to his breast :   " Do
not upbraid me, my dove—the wood was *mine.*"

CHAPTER XIII.

BANISHED FROM EDEN.

Silence reigned on the height. The winds had died away,
the clouds were scattering swiftly, like an army of ghosts.
The embers of the wood below crackled softly. The trunks
had all been gnawed to the roots by the fiery tooth of the
flames. It was like a churchyard full of clumsy black crosses
and grave-stones on which the souls danced to and fro like
will-o'-the-wisps.

The countess rested silently on Freyer's breast. When he
said : "The wood was mine ! " she had thrown herself, unable to utter a word, into his arms—and had since remained
clasped in his embrace in silent, perfect peace.

Now the misty veil, growing lighter and more transparent,
at last drifted entirely away, and the blue sky once more
arched above the earth in a majestic dome. Here and there
sunbeams darted through the melting cloud-rack and suddenly,
as though the gates of heaven had opened, a double rainbow,
radiant in seven-hued majesty, spanned the vault above them
in matchless beauty.

Freyer bade the countess look up. And when she perceived the exquisite miracle of the air, with her lover in the
midst—encompassed by it, she raised her head and extended
her arms like the bride awaiting the heavenly bridegroom.
Her eyes rested on him as if dazzled: "Be what you will,
man, seraph, God. Shining one, you must be mine ! I will
bring you down from the height of your cross, though you
were nailed above with seven-fold irons. You must be mine.

Freyer, hear my vow, hear it, ye surrounding mountains, hear it, sacred soil below, and thou radiant many-hued bow which, with the grace of Aphrodite, dost girdle the universe, risen from chaos. I swear to be your wife, Joseph Freyer, swear it by the God Who has appeared to me, rising from marvel to marvel, since my eyes first beheld you."

Freyer, with bowed head, stood trembling before her. He felt as if a goddess was rolling in her chariot of clouds above him—as if the glimmering prism above were dissolving and flooding him with a sea of glittering sparks. "You—my wife?" he faltered, sobbing, then flung himself face downward before her. "This is too much—too much—"

"You shall be my husband," she murmured, raising him, "let me call you so now until the priest's hand has united us! When, where, and how this can be done—I do not yet know! Let the task of deciding be left to hours devoted to the consideration of earthly things. This is too sacred, it is our spiritual marriage hour, for in it I have pledged myself to you in spirit and in truth! Our church is nature, our witnesses are heaven and earth, our candles the blazing wood below—your little heritage which you sacrificed for me with a smile! And so I give you my bridal kiss—my husband!"

But Freyer did not return the caress. The old conflict again awoke—the conflict with his duty as the representative of Christ.

"Oh, God—is it not the tempter whom Thou didst send to Thy own son on Mt. Hebron that he might show him all the splendors of the world, saying: 'All shall be thine?' Dare I be faithless to the character of Thy chaste son, if Thou dost appoint me to undergo the same trial? Dare I be happy, dare I enjoy, so long as I wear the sacred mask of His sufferings and sacrifice. Will it not then be a terrible fraud, and dare I enter the presence of God with this lie upon my conscience? Will He not tear the crown of thorns from my head and exclaim: 'Juggler—I wish to rise by the pure and saintly —not by deceivers who *feign* my sufferings and with deceitful art turn the holiest things into a farce. Woe betide me, poor, weak mortal that I am—the trial is too severe. I cannot endure it. Take Thy crown—I place it in Thy hands again— and will personate the Christ no more."

"Joseph!" exclaimed Countess Wildenau, deeply moved. "Must this be? I feel your anguish and am stirred as if we were parting from our dearest possession. She raised her tearful eyes heavenward. "Must the Christ vanish on the very day I plight my troth to him whom I love as Thy image, even as Eve must have loved Adam *for the sake of his likeness to God.* And must I, like Eve, no longer behold Thy face because I have loved the divine in mortal form after the manner of mortals? Unhappy doctrine of the fall of man, which renders the holiest feeling a crime, must we too be driven out of Paradise, must you stand between us and our happy intercourse with the deity? Joseph. Do you believe that the Saviour Who came to bring redemption to the poor human race banished from Eden, will be angry with you if you represent with a happy loving heart the sacrifice by which He saved us? "

"I do not know, my beloved, you may be right. Even the time-honored precepts of our forefathers permit the representative of the Christ to be married. Yet I think differently! The highest demands claim the loftiest service! Whoever is permitted to personate the Saviour should have at that time no other feelings than moved Christ Himself, for *truth* may not be born of *falsehood.*"

He drew the weeping woman to his heart. "You know, sweet wife—to love *you* and call you *mine* is a very different thing from the monotonous commonplace matrimonial happiness which our plain village women can bestow. You demand the *whole* being and every power of the soul is consumed in you."

He clasped her in an embrace so fervent that her breath almost failed, his eyes blazed with the passionate ardor with which the unchained elements seize their prey. "Say what you will, it is on your conscience! I can feel nothing, think of nothing save you! Nay, if they should drive the nails through my own flesh, I should not heed it, in my ardent yearning for you. I have struggled long enough, but you have bewitched me with the sweet promise of becoming my wife—and I am spoiled for personating the Christ. I am yours, take me! Only fly with me to the farthest corner of the world, away from the place where I was permitted to feel myself a part of God, and resigned it for an earthly happiness."

11

"Come then, my beloved, let us go forth like the pair banished from Eden, and like them take upon us, for love's sake, our heavy human destiny! Let us bear it together, and even in exile love and worship, like faithful cast-off children, the Father who was once so near us!"

"Amen!" said Freyer, clasping the beautiful woman who thus devoted her life to him in a long, silent embrace. The rainbow above their heads gradually paled. The radiant splendor faded. The sun was again concealed by clouds, and the warm azure of the sky was transformed into a chill grey by the rising mists. The mountain peak lay bare and cheerless, the earth was rent and ravaged, nothing was visible save rough rubble and colorless heather. An icy fog rose slowly, gathering more and more densely around them. Nothing could be seen save the sterile soil of the naked ridge on which stood the two lonely outcasts from Eden. The gates of their dream paradise had closed behind them, the spell was broken, and in silent submission they moved down the hard, stony path to reality, the cruel uncertainty of human destiny.

CHAPTER XIV.

PIETA.

Twilight was gathering when the pair reached the valley.

The Passion Theatre loomed like a vast shadow by the roadside, and both, as if moved by the *same* impulse, turned toward it.

Freyer, drawing a key from his pocket, opened the door leading to the stage. "Shall we take leave of it?" he said.

"Take leave!"

The countess said no more. She knew that the success of the rest of the performances depended solely upon him—and it burdened her soul like a heavy reproach. Yet she did not tell him so, for hers he must be—at any cost.

The strength of her passion swept her on to her robbery of the cross, as the wind bears away the leaf it has stripped from the tree.

They entered the property room. There stood the stake,

there lay the scourges which lacerated the sacred body. The spear that pierced his heart was leaning in a corner.

Madeleine von Wildenau gazed around her with a feeling of dread. Freyer had lighted a lamp. Something close beside it flashed, sending its rays far through the dim space. It was the cup, the communion cup! Freyer touched it with a trembling hand: "Farewell! I shall never offer you to any one again! May all blessings flow from you! Happy the hand which scatters them over the world and my beloved Ammergau."

He kissed the brim of the goblet, and a tear fell into it, but it glittered with the same unshadowed radiance. Freyer turned away, and his eyes wandered over the other beloved trophies.

There lay the reed sceptre broken on the floor.

The countess shuddered at the sight. A strange melancholy stole over her, and tears filled her eyes.

"My sceptre of reeds—broken—in the dust!" said Freyer, his voice tremulous with an emotion which forced an answering echo in Madeleine von Wildenau's soul. He raised the fragments, gazing at them long and mournfully. "Aye, the sad symbol speaks the truth—my strength is broken, my sovereignty vanished."

A terrible dread overpowered the countess and she fondly clasped the man she loved, as a princess might press to her heart her dethroned husband, grieving amid the ruins of his power. "You will still remain king in my heart!" she said, consolingly, amid her tears.

"You must now be everything to me, my loved one. In you is my Heaven, my justification in the presence of God. Hold me closely, firmly, for you must lift me in your arms out of this constant torture by the redeeming power of love." He rested his head wearily on hers, and she gladly supported the precious burden. She felt at that moment that she had the power to lift him from Hades, that the love in her heart was strong enough to win Heaven for him and herself.

"Womanly nature is drawing us together!" She clung to him, so absorbed in blissful melancholy that his soul thrilled with an emotion never experienced before. Their lips now met in a kiss as pure as if all earthly things were at an end and their rising souls were greeting each other in a loftier sphere.

"That was an angel's kiss!" said Freyer with a sigh, while the air around the stake seemed to quiver with the rustling of angels' wings, the chains which bound him to it for the scourging to clank as though some invisible hand had flung one end around the feet of the fugitives, to bind them forever to the place of the cross.

"Come, I have one more thing to do." He took the lamp from the table and went into the dressing-room.

There hung the raiment in which a God revealed Himself to mortal eyes—the ample garments stirred mysteriously in the draught from the open door. A glimmering white figure seemed to be soaring upward in one corner—it was the Resurrection robe. Inflated by the wind, it floated with a ghost-like movement, while the man divested of his divinity stood with clasped hands and drooping head—to say farewell.

When a mortal strips off his earthly husk he knows that he will exchange it for a brighter one! *Here* a mortal was stripping off his robe of light and returning to the oppressive form of human imperfection. This, too, was a death agony.

The countess clung to him tenderly. "Have you forgotten me?"

He threw his arm around her. "Why, sweet one?"

"I mean," she said, with childlike grace, "that if you thought of *me*, you could not be so sad."

"My child, I forget you at the moment I am resigning Heaven for your sake. You do not ask that seriously. As for the pain, let me endure it—for if I could do this with a *light* heart, would the sacrifice be worthy of you? By the anguish it costs me you must measure the greatness of my love, if you can."

"I can, for even while I rest upon your heart, while my lips eagerly inhale your breath, I pine with longing for your lost divinity."

"And no longer love me as you did when I was the Christ. Be frank—it will come!"

He pressed his hands upon his breast, while his eyes rested mournfully on the shining robe which seemed to beckon to him from the gloom.

"Oh, what are you saying! You sacrifice for me the greatest possession which man ever resigned for woman; the illusion of deity—and I am to punish you for the renunciation by loving you less? Joseph, what *you* give me, no king can bestow. Crowns have been sacrificed for a woman's sake, crowns of gold—but never one like this!"

"My wife!" he murmured in sweet, mournful tones, while his dark eyes searched hers till her very soul swooned under the power of the look.

She clasped her hands upon his breast. "Will you grant me one favor?"

"If I can."

"Ah, then, appear to me once more as the Christ. I will go out upon the stage. Throw the sacred robe over you—let me see Him once more, clasp His knees—let me take farewell, an eternal farewell of the departing One."

"My child, that would be a sin! Are you again forgetting what you yourself perceived this morning with prescient grief—that I am a man? Dare I continue the sacred character outside of the play? That would be working wrong under the mask of my Saviour."

"No, it would be no wrong to satisfy the longing for His face. I will not touch you, only once more, for the last time show my wondering eyes the sublime figure and let the soul pour forth all the anguish of parting to the vanishing God."

"My wife, where is your error carrying you! Did the God-Man I personated vanish because I stripped off His mask? Poor wife, the anguish which now masters you is remorse for having in your sweet womanly weakness destroyed the pious illusion and never rested until you made the imaginary God a man. Oh, Magdalena, how far you still are from the goal gained by your predecessor. Come, I will satisfy your longing; I will lead you where you will perceive that He is everywhere, if we really seek Him, that the form alone is perishable. He is imperishable." Then gently raising her, he tenderly repeated: "Come. Trust me and follow me." Casting one more sorrowful glance around him, he took from the table the crown of thorns, extinguished the lamp, and with a steady arm guided the weeping woman through the darkness. Outside of the building the stars were shining brightly, the road was dis-

tinctly visible.   The countess unresistingly accompanied him.
He turned toward the village and they walked swiftly through
the silent streets.   At last the church rose, dark and solemn,
before them.   He led her in.   A holy-water font stood at the
entrance, and, pausing, he sprinkled her with the water.   Then
they entered.   The church was dark.   No light illumined it
save the trembling rays of the ever-burning lamp and two candles flickering low in their sockets before an image of the Madonna in a remote corner.   They were obliged to grope their
way forward slowly amid the wavering shadows.   At the left
of the entrance stood a " Pieta."   It was a group almost life-
size, carved from wood.   The crucified Saviour in the Ma
donna's lap.   Mary Magdalene was supporting his left hand,
raising it slightly, while John stood at the Saviour's feet.   The
whole had been created by an artist's hand with touching realism.   The expression of anguish in the Saviour's face was very
affecting.   Before the group stood a priedieu on which lay
several withered wreaths.

   The countess' heart quivered ; he was leading her there !
So this was to be the compensation for the living image ?
Mere dead wood ?

   Freyer drew her gently down upon the priedieu.   " Here,
my child, learn to seek him here, and when you have once
found Him, you will never lose Him more.   Lay your hands devoutly on the apparently lifeless breast and you will feel the
heart within throbbing, as in mine—only try."

   " Alas, I cannot, it will be a falsehood if I do."

   "What, *that* a falsehood, and I—was *I* the Christ ? "

   " I could imagine it ! "

   " Because I breathed ?   Ah, the breath of the deity can
swell more than a human breast, sister, and you will hear it !
Collect your thoughts—and pray ! "

   His whisper grew fainter, the silence about her more solemn.   " I cannot pray ; I never have prayed," she lamented,
" and surely not to lifeless wood."

   " Only try—for my sake," he urged gently, as if addressing
a restless child, which ought to go to sleep and will not.

   " Yes ; but stay with me," she pleaded like a child, clinging to his arm.

   " I will stay," he said, kneeling by her side.

"Teach me to pray as you do," she entreated, raising her delicate hands to him. He clasped them in his, and she felt as if the world could do her no further harm, that her soul, her life, lay in his firm hands.

The warmth emanating from him became in her a devout fervor. The pulses of ardent piety throbbing in his finger-tips seemed to communicate a wave-like motion to the surrounding air, which imparted to everything which hitherto had been dead and rigid, an undulating movement that lent it a faint, vibrating life.

Something stirred, breathed, murmured before and above her. There was a rustling among the withered leaves of the garlands at the foot of the Pieta, invisible feet glided through the church and ascended the steps of the high altar; high up the vaulted dome rose a murmur which wandered to the folds of the funeral banner, hanging above, passing from pillar to pillar, from arch to arch, in ghostly echoes which the listening ear heard with secret terror, the language of the silence. And the burning eyes beheld the motionless forms begin to stir. The contours of the figures slowly changed in the uncertain, flickering light, the shadows glided and swung to and fro. The Saviour's lips opened, then slowly closed, the kneeling woman touched the rigid limbs and laid her fevered fingers on the wounded breast. The other hand rested in Freyer's. A chain was thus formed between the three, which thrilled and warmed the wood with the circulating stream of the hot blood. It was no longer a foreign substance—it was the heart, the poor pierced heart of their beloved, divine friend. It throbbed, suffered, bled. More and more distinctly the chest rose and fell with the regular breathing. It was the creative breath of the deity, which works in the conscious and unconscious object, animating even soulless matter. The arm supported by Mary Magdalene swayed to and fro, the fingers of the hand moved gently. The poor pierced hand—it seemed as if it were trying to move toward the countess, as if it were pleading, " Cool my pain."

Urged by an inexplicable impulse, the countess warmed the stiff, slender fingers in her own. She fancied that it was giving relief. Higher and higher swelled the tide of feeling in her heart until it overflowed—and—she knew not how, she had risen and pressed a kiss upon the wounds in the poor little hand, a kiss of the sweetest, most sacred piety. She felt as if she were standing by a beloved corpse whose mute lips we seek, though they no longer feel.

She could not help it, and bending down again the rosy lips of the young widow rested on the pale half-parted ones of the statue. But the lips breathed, a cool, pure breath issued from them, and the rigid form grew more pliant beneath ·the sorrowful caress, as though it felt the reconciling pain of the penitent human soul. But the divine fire which was to purify this soul, blazed far beyond its boundaries in this first ardor. Overpowered by a wild fervor, she flung herself on her knees and adjured the God whose breath she had drunk in that kiss, to hear her. The friend praying at her side was forgotten, the world had vanished, every law of reason was annihilated, all knowledge was out of her mind—every hard-won conquest of human empiricism was effaced. From the heights and from the depths it came with rustling pinions, bearing the soul away on the flood-tide of mercy. The *miracle* was approaching—in unimagined majesty.

Thousands of years vanished, eternity dawned in that *one* moment. All that was and is, *was* not and *is* not—past, present, and future, were blended and melted into a single breath beyond the boundaries of the natural life.

" If it is Thou, if Thou dost live, look at me," she had cried with ardent aspiration, and, lo!—was it shadow or imagination ?—the eyes opened and two large dark pupils were fixed upon her, then the lids closed for an instant to open again. The countess gazed more and more earnestly ; it was distinct, unmistakable. A shudder ran through her veins as, in a burning fever, the limbs tremble with a sudden chill. She tried to meet the look, but spite of the tension in every nerve, the effort was futile. It was too overpowering ; it was the gaze of a God. Dread and rapture were contending for the mastery. Doubtless she said to herself, " It is not *outside* of you, but within you." Once more she ventured to glance at the mysterious apparition, but the eyes were fixed steadily upon her. Terror overpowered her. The chord of the possible snapped and she sank half senseless on the steps of the altar, while the miracle closed its golden wings above her.

CHAPTER XV.

THE CROWING OF THE COCK.

A loud step roused the rapt enthusiast from her visions. The sacristan was passing through the church, extinguishing the candles which, meanwhile, had burned down in their sockets before the Madonna in the distant corner.

"I beg your pardon for disturbing you," he said; "but I wanted to close the church. There is plenty of time, however. Shall I leave a candle? It will be too dark; the lamp alone does not give sufficient light."

"I thank you," replied Freyer, more thoughtful than the countess, who, unable to control herself, remained on her knees with her face buried in her hands.

"I will lock the church when we leave it and bring you the key," Freyer added, and the sacristan was satisfied. The imperious high priest withdrew silently and modestly, that he might not disturb the prayers of the man whom he sentenced to death every week with such fury.

The lovers were again alone, but the door remained open. The shrill crowing of a cock suddenly echoed through the stillness from the yard of the neighboring parsonage. The countess started up. Her eyes were painfully dazzled by the light of the wax candle so close at hand. Before her, the face smeared with shining varnish, lay the wooden Christ, hard and cold in its carven bareness and rigidity. The pale-blue painted eyes gazed with the traditional mournfulness upon the ground.

"What startled you just now?" asked Freyer.

"I don't know whether it was a miracle or a shadow, which created the illusion, but I would have sworn that the statue moved its lids and looked at me."

"Be it what it might, it was still a miracle," said Freyer. "If the finger of God can paint the Saviour's eyes to the excited vision from the wave of blood set in motion by the pulsation of our hearts, or from the shadow cast by a smoking candle, is that any less wonderful than if the stiff lids had really moved?"

The countess breathed a long sigh of relief; " Yes, you are
right.   That is the power which, as you say, can do more
than swell a human breast, it can make, for the yearning soul,
a heart throb even in a Christ carved from wood.   Even if
what I have just experienced could have been done by lifeless
matter, the power which brought us together was divine, and
no one living could have resisted it.   Lay aside your crown of
thorns trustfully and without remorse, you have accomplished
your mission, you have saved the soul for which God destined
you, it was His will, and who among us could resist Him ? "

Freyer raised the crown of thorns, which he still held, to his
lips, kissed it, and laid it at the feet of the Pieta: " Lord, Thy
will be done, in so far as it is Thy will.   And if it is not, forgive the error."

" It is no error, I understand God's purpose better.   He
has sent me His image in you and given it to me in an attainable human form, that I may learn through it to do my duty
to the prototype.   To the feeble power of the novice in faith,
He graciously adds an earthly guide.   Oh, He is good and
merciful ! "

She raised Freyer from his knees :   " Come, thou God-
given one, that I may fulfil the sweetest duty ever imposed on
any mortal, that of loving you and making you happy.   God
and His holy will be praised."

"And will you no longer grieve for the lost Christ ? "

" No, for you were right, He is everywhere ! "

" In God's name then, come and obey the impulse of your
heart, even though I perish."

" Can you speak so to-day, Joseph ? "

" To-day especially.   Would you not just now have sworn to
the truth of an illusion conjured up by a shadow ?   And were you
not disappointed when the light came and the spell vanished ?
The time will come when you will see me, as you now do this
wooden figure, in the light of commonplace reality, and then
the nimbus will vanish and nothing will remain save the dross
as here.   Then your soul will turn away disenchanted and follow the vanished God to loftier heights."

" Or plunge into the depths," murmured the countess.

" I should not fear that, for then my mission would have
been vain !   No, my child, if I did not believe that I was ap-

pointed to save you I should have no excuse in my own eyes for what I am doing.   But come, it is late, we must return home or our absence will occasion comment."

    ✱   ✱   ✱   ✱   ✱   ✱   ✱   ✱   ✱

It was half-past nine o'clock.   An elderly gentleman of distinguished aristocratic bearing was pacing impatiently to and fro.

The two sisters were standing helplessly in the doorway, deeply oppressed by the burden of so haughty a guest.

"If she would only come!" Sephi lamented in the utmost anxiety, for she dreaded the father for the daughter's sake. It was the old Prince von Prankenberg, and his bearing augured nothing good.

It seemed to these loyal souls a democratic impertinence on the part of fate that *such* a gentleman should be kept waiting, and the prince regarded it in precisely the same light. The good creatures would willingly have lent wings to the daughter for whom *such* a father was waiting.   But what did it avail that the noble lord constantly quickened his pace as he walked to and fro, time and his unsuspicious daughter did not do the same.   Prince Prankenberg had reached Ammergau at noon that day and waited in vain for the countess.   On his arrival he had found the whole village in an uproar over the conflagration in the woods, and the countess and Herr Freyer, who had been seen walking together in that direction, were missing.   At last the herder reported that they had been in the mountain pasture with him, and Ludwig Gross, on his return from directing the firemen in the futile effort to extinguish the flames, set off to inform the Countess Wildenau of her father's arrival.   He had evidently failed to find her, for he ought to have returned long before.   So the faithful women had been on coals of fire ever since.   Andreas Gross had gone to the village to look for the absent ones, as if that could be of any service! Josepha was gazing sullenly through the window-panes at the prince, who had treated her as scornfully as if she were a common maid-servant, when she offered to show him the way to the countess' room, and answered: "People can't stay in such a hole!"   Meanwhile night had closed in.

At last, coming from exactly the opposite direction, a

couple approached whose appearance attracted the nobleman's attention. A female figure, bare-headed, with dishevelled hair and tattered, disordered garments, leaning apparently almost fainting on the arm of a tall, bearded man in a peasant's jacket. Could it—no, it was impossible, that *could* not be his daughter.

The unsuspecting pair came nearer. The lady, evidently exhausted, was really almost carried by her companion. It was too dark for the prince to see distinctly, but her head seemed to be resting on the peasant's breast. An interesting pair of lovers! But they drew nearer, the prince could not believe his eyes, it *was* his daughter, leaning on a peasant's arm. There was an involuntary cry of horror from both as Countess Wildenau stood face to face with her haughty father. The blood fairly congealed in Madeleine's veins, her cheeks blanched till their pallor glimmered through the gloom! Yet the habit of maintaining social forms did not desert her: "Oh, what a surprise! Good evening, Papa!"

Her soul had retreated to the inmost depths of her being, and she was but a puppet moving and speaking by rule.

Freyer raised his hat in a farewell salute.

"Are you going?" she said with an expressionless glance. "I suppose I cannot ask you to rest a little while? Farewell, Herr Freyer, and many thanks."

How strange! Did it not seem as if a cock crowed?

Freyer bowed silently and walked on, "Adieu!" said the prince without lifting his hat. For an instant he considered whether he could possibly offer his arm to a lady in *such* attire, but at last resolved to do so—she was his daughter, and this was not exactly the right moment to quarrel with her. So, struggling with his indignation and disgust, he escorted her, holding his arm very far out as though he might be soiled by the contact, through the house into her room. The Gross sisters, with trembling hands, brought in lights and hastily vanished. Madeleine von Wildenau stood in the centre of the room, like an automaton whose machinery had run down. The prince took a candle from the table and threw its light full upon her face. "Pardon me, I must ascertain whether this lady, who looks as if she had just jumped out of a gipsy-cart, is really my daughter? Yes, it is actually she!" he exclaimed in a tone intended to be humorous, but which was merely brutal. "So I find the Countess Wildenau in *this* guise— ragged, worn, with neither hat nor gloves, wandering about with peasants! It is incredible!"

The countess sank into a chair without a word. Her father's large, stern features were flushed with a wrath which he could scarcely control.

"Have you gone out of fashion so completely that you must seek your society in such circles as these, *ma fille?* Could no cavalier be found to escort the Countess Wildenau that she must strike up an intimacy with one of the comedians in the Passion Play?"

"An intimacy? Papa, this is an insult!" exclaimed the countess angrily, for though it was true, she felt that on *his* lips and in *his* meaning it was such! Again a cock crowed at this unwonted hour.

"Well *ma chère*, when a lady is caught half embraced by such a man, the inference is inevitable."

"Dear me, I was so exhausted that I could scarcely stand," replied the countess, softly, as if the cocks might hear: "We were caught by the storm and the man was obliged to support me. I should think, however, that the Countess Wildenau's position was too high for such suspicions."

"Well, well, I heard in Munich certain rumors about your long stay here which accorded admirably with the romantic personage who has just left you. My imaginative daughter always had strange fancies, and as you seem able to endure the peasant odor—I am somewhat more sensitive to it . . ."

"Papa!" cried the countess, frantic with shame. "I beg you not to speak in that way of people whom I esteem."

"Aha!" said the prince with a short laugh, "Your anger speaks plainly enough. I will make no further allusion to these delicate relations."

The countess remained silent a moment, struggling with her emotions. Should she confess all—should she betray the mystery of the "God in man?" Reveal it to this frivolous, prosaic man from whose mockery, even in her childhood, she had carefully concealed every nobler feeling—disclose to him her most sacred possession, the miracle of her life? No, it would be desecration. "I *have* no delicate relations! I scarcely know these people—I am interested in this Freyer as the representative of the Christ—he is nothing more to me."

The cock crowed for the third time.

"What was that? I am continually hearing cocks crow to-night. Did you hear nothing?" asked the countess.

"Not the slightest sound! Have you hallucinations?" asked the prince: "The cocks are all asleep at this hour."

She knew it—the sound was but the echo of her own conscience. She thought of the words Freyer had uttered that day upon the mountain, and his large eyes gazed mournfully, yet forgivingly at her. Now she knew why Peter was pardoned! He would not suffer the God in whom he could not force men to believe to be profaned—so he concealed Him in his heart. He knew that the bond which united him to Christ and the work which he was appointed to do for Him was greater than the cheap martyrdom of an acknowledgment of Him to the dull ears of a handful of men and maid-servants! It was no lie when he said: "I know not the man"—for he really did *not* know the Christ whom *they* meant. He was denying—not *Christ*, but the *criminal*, whom they believed Him to be. It was the same with the countess. She was not ashamed of the man she loved, only of the person her father saw in him and, as she could not explain to the prince what Joseph Freyer was to her, she denied him entirely. But even as Peter mourned as a heavy sin the brief moment in which he faithlessly separated from his beloved Master, she, too, now felt a keen pang, as though a wound was bleeding in her heart, and tears streamed from her eyes.

"You are nervous, *ma fille!* It isn't worth while. Tears for the sake of that worthy villager?" said the prince, with a contemptuous shrug of the shoulders. "Listen, *ma chère*, I believe it would be better for you to marry."

"Papa!" exclaimed the countess indignantly.

The prince laughed: "No offence, when women like you begin to be sentimental—it is time for them to marry! You were widowed too young—it was a misfortune for you."

"A misfortune? May God forgive you the sneer and me the words—it was a misfortune that Wildenau lived so long—nay more: that I ever became his wife, and you, Papa, ought never to remind me of it."

" Why not ? "

" Because I might forget that you *are* my father—as *you* forget it when you sold me to that greybeard ? "

" Sold ? What an expression, *chère enfant!* Is this the result of your study of peasant life here ? I congratulate you on the enlargement of your vocabulary. This is the gratitude of a daughter for whom the most brilliant match in the whole circle of aristocratic families was selected."

" And her soul sold in exchange," the countess interrupted ; "for that my moral nature was not utterly destroyed is no credit of yours."

The prince smiled with an air of calm superiority : "Capital ! Moral nature destroyed ! When a girl is wedded to one of the oldest members of the German nobility and made the possession of a yearly income of half a million ! That is what she calls moral destruction and an outrageous deed, of which the inhuman father must not remind his daughter without forfeiting his *paternal rights.* It is positively delicious !" He laughed and drew out his cigar case : " You see, *ma fille*—I understand a jest. Will you be annoyed if I smoke a Havana in this rural bed-room ? "

" As you please !" replied the countess, who had now regained her former cold composure, holding the candle to him. The prince scanned her features with the searching gaze of a connoisseur as she thus stood before him illumined by the ruddy glow. " You have lost a little of your freshness, my child, but you are still beautiful—still charming. I admit that Wildenau was rather too old for a poetic nature like yours —but there is still time to compensate for it. When were you born ? A father ought not to ask his daughter's age—but the Almanach de Gotha tells the story. You must be now— stop ! You were not quite seventeen when you married Wildenau—you were married nine years—you have been a widow two—that makes you twenty-eight. There is still time, but—not much to lose ! I am saying this to you in a mother's place, my child "—he added, with a repulsive affecta- tion of tenderness. His daughter made no reply.

" It is true, you will lose your income if you give up the name of Wildenau—as the will reads 'exchange it for an- other.' This somewhat restricts your choice, for you can resign this colossal dower only in favor of a match which can partially supply your loss."

The countess turned deadly pale. "That is the curse Wildenau hurled upon me from his grave. It was not enough that I was miserable during his life, no—I must not be happy even after his death."

"Why—who has told you so? You have your choice among any of the handsome and wealthy men who can offer you an equivalent for all that you resign. Prince von Metten-Barn-heim, for instance! He is a visionary, it is true—"

"Prosaic Prince Emil a visionary!" said the countess, laughing bitterly.

"Well, I think that a man who surrounds himself so much with plebeian society, scholars and authors, might properly be termed a visionary! When his father dies, the luckless country will be ruled by loud-voiced professors. What does that matter! He'll suit you all the better, as you are half a scholar yourself. True, it might be said that the Barn-heim family is of inferior rank to ours — the Prankenbergs are an older race and from the days of Charlemagne have not made a single *mesalliance*, while the Barnheim gene-alogical tree shows several gaps—which explains their liberal tendencies. Such things always betray themselves. Yet on the other hand, they are reigning dukes, and we a decaying race—so it is tolerably equal. You are interested in him—so decide at last and marry him, then you will be a happy woman and the curse of the will can have no power."

"Indeed?" cried the countess, trembling with excite-ment. "But suppose that I loved another, a poor man, whom I could not wed unless I possessed some property of my own, however small, and the will made me a *beggar* the moment I gave him my hand—what then? Should I not have a right to hate the jealous despot and the man who sacrificed me to his selfish interests—even though he was my own father?" A glance of the keenest reproach fell upon the prince.

He was startled by this outburst of passion, hitherto un-known in his experience of this apathetic woman. He could make no use of her present mood. Biting off a leaf from his cigar, he blew it into the air with a graceful movement of the lips. Some change had taken place in Madeleine, that was evident! If, after all, she should commit some folly—make a love-match? But with whom? Again the scene he had witnessed that evening rose before his mind! She had let her head rest on the shoulder of a common peasant—that could not be denied, he had *seen* it with his own eyes. Did such a delusion really exist? A woman of her temperament was incomprehensible—she would be quite capable, in a moment of enthusiasm, of throwing her whole splendid fortune away and giving society an unparalleled spectacle. Who could tell what ideas such a " lunatic " might take into her head. And yet—who could prevent it? No one had any power over her—least of all he himself, who could not even threaten her with disinheritance, since it was long since he had possessed anything he could call his own. An old gambler, perpetually struggling with debt, who had come that day, that very day, to—nay, he was reluctant to confess it to himself. And he had already irritated his daughter, his last refuge, the only support which still kept his head above water, more than was wise or prudent—he dared not venture farther.

He had the suppressed brutality of all violent natures which cannot have their own way, are not masters of their passions and their circumstances, and hence are constantly placed in the false position of being compelled to ask the aid of others!

After having busied himself a sufficiently long time with his cigar, he said in a soothing and—for so imperious a man —repulsively submissive tone: " Well, *ma fille*, there is an expedient for that case also. If you loved a man who was too poor to maintain an establishment suitable for you—you might do the one thing without forfeiting the other—Wildenau's will mentions only *a change of name:* you might marry secretly —keep his name and with it his property."

" Papa ! " exclaimed the countess—a burning blush crimsoned her cheeks, but her eyes were fixed with intense anxiety upon the speaker—" I could not expect that from a husband whom I esteemed and loved."

" Why not? If he could offer you no maintenance, he could not ask you to sacrifice yours! Surely it would be enough if you gave him yourself."

12

"If he would accept me under such conditions," she answered, thoughtfully.

"Aha—we are on the right track!" the prince reflected, watching her keenly. "As soon as he perceived that there was no other possibility of making you his—certainly! A woman like you can persuade a man to do anything. I don't wish to be indiscreet, but, *ma fille*—I fear that you have made a choice of which you cannot help being ashamed. Could you think of forming such an alliance except in secret. If, that is, you *must* wed? What would the world say when rumor whispered: 'Countess Wildenau has sunk so low that she'—I dare not utter the word, from the fear of offending you."

The countess sat with downcast eyes.

The world—! It suddenly stood before her with its mocking faces. Should she expose her sacred love to its derision? Should she force the noble simple-mannered man who was the salvation of her soul to play a ridiculous part in the eyes of society, as the husband of the Countess Wildenau? Her father was right—though from very different motives. Could this secret which was too beautiful, too holy, to be confided to her own father—endure the contact of the world?

"But how could a secret marriage be arranged?" she asked, with feigned indifference.

Prince von Prankenberg was startled by the earnestness of the question. Had matters gone so far? Caution was requisite here. Energetic opposition could only produce the opposite result, perhaps a public scandal. He reflected a moment while apparently toiling to puff rings of smoke into the air, as if the world contained no task more important. His daughter's eyes rested on him with suspicious keenness. At last he seemed to have formed his plan.

"A secret marriage? Why, that is an easy matter for a woman of your wealth and independent position! Is the person in question a Catholic?"

Madeleine silently nodded assent.

"Well—then the matter is perfectly simple   Follow the example of Manzoni's *promessi sposi*, with whom we are sufficiently tormented while studying Italian. Go with your chosen husband to the pastor and declare before him, in the presence of two witnesses, who can easily be found among your faithful servants, that you take each other in marriage. According to the rite of the Catholic church, it is sufficient to constitute a valid marriage, if both parties make this declaration, even without the marriage ceremonial, in the presence of an ordained priest—your ordained priest in this case would be our old pastor at Prankenberg. You can play the farce best there. You will thus need no papers, no special license, which might betray you, and if you manage cleverly you will succeed in persuading the decrepit old man not to enter the marriage in the church register. " Then let any one come and say that you are married! There will be absolutely no proof—and when the old pastor dies the matter will go down to the grave with him! You will choose witnesses on whom you can depend. What risk can there be ? "

" Father! But will that be a marriage ? " cried the countess in horror.

" Not according to *our* ideas," said the prince, laconically: " But the point is merely that *he* shall consider himself married, and that *he* shall be bound—not you ? "

" Father—I will not play such a farce ! " She turned away with loathing.

" If you are in earnest—there will be no farce, *ma chère !* It will rest entirely with you whether you regard yourself as married or not. In the former case you will have the pleasant consciousness of a moral act without its troublesome consequences—can go on a journey after the pseudo wedding, roam through foreign lands with a reliable maid, and then return perhaps with one or two ' adopted ' children, whom, as a philanthropist, you will educate and no one can discover anything. The anonymous husband may be installed by the Countess Wildenau under some title on one of her distant estates, and the marriage will be as happy as any—only less prosaic ! But you will thus spare yourself an endless scandal in the eyes of society, keep your pastoral dream, and yet remain the wealthy and powerful Countess Wildenau. Is not that more sensible than in Heaven knows what rhapsody to sacrifice honor, position, wealth, and—your old father ? "

" My father ? " asked the countess, who had struggled with

the most contradictory emotions while listening to the words of the prince.

"Why yes ".—he busied himself again with his cigar, which he was now obliged to exchange for another, "You know, *chère enfant*, the duties of our position impose claims upon families of princely rank, which, unfortunately, my finances no longer allow me to meet. I—h'm—I find myself compelled—unpleasant as it is—to appeal to my daughter's kindness—may I use one of these soap dishes as an ash-receiver? So I have come to ask whether, for the sake of our ancient name—I expect no childish sentimentality—whether you could help me with an additional sum of some fifty thousand marks annually, and ninety thousand to be paid at once—otherwise nothing is left for me—a light, please—*merci*—except to put a bullet through my head!" He paused to light the fresh cigar. The countess clasped her hands in terror.

"Good Heavens, Papa! Are the sums Wildenau gave you already exhausted?"

"What do you mean—can a Prince Prankenberg live on an income of fifty thousand marks? If I had not been so economical, and we did not live in the quiet German style, I could not have managed to make such a trifle hold out so *long!*"

"A trifle! Then I was sold so cheaply?" cried Madeleine Wildenau with passionate emotion. "I have not even, in return for my wasted life, the consciousness of having saved my father? Yes, yes, if this is true—I am no longer free to choose! I shall remain to the end of my days the slave of my dead husband, and must steal the happiness for which I long like forbidden fruit. You have chosen the moment for this communication well—it must be true! You have destroyed the first blossom of my life, and now, when it would fain put forth one last bud, you blight that, too."

The prince rose. "I regret having caused you any embarrassment by my affairs. As I said, you are your own mistress. If I did not put a bullet through my head long ago, it was purely out of consideration for you, that the world might not say: 'Prince von Prankenberg shot himself on account of financial embarrassment because his wealthy daughter would not aid him!' I wished to save you this scandal—that is why

I gave you the choice of helping me if you preferred to
do so."

The countess shuddered. " You know that such threats
are not needed! If I wept, it was not for the sake of the
paltry money, but all the unfortunate circumstances. How
can I ever be happy, even in a secret marriage, if I am constantly compelled to dread discovery for my father's sake ? If
it were for a father impoverished by misfortune, the tears shed
for my sacrifice of happiness would be worthy of execration—
but, Papa, to be compelled to sacrifice the holiest feeling that
ever thrilled a human heart for gambling, race-courses, and
the women of doubtful reputation who consume your property
—that is hard indeed ! "

" Spare your words, *ma fille*, I am not disposed to purchase your help at the cost of a lecture. Either you will relieve me from my embarrassments without reproaches, or you
will be the daughter of a suicide—what is the use of all this
philosophizing ? A lofty unsullied name is a costly article!
Make your choice. *I* for my own part set little value on life.
I am old, a victim to the gout, have grown too stiff to ride or
enjoy sport of any kind, have lost my luck with women—there
is nothing left but gambling. If I must give that up, too, then
rogue la galère! In such a case, there are but two paths—
corriger la fortune—or die. But a Prankenberg would rather
die than to take the former."

" Father! What are you saying! Alas, that matters have
gone so far! Woe betide a society that dismisses an old man
from its round of pleasures so bankrupt in every object, every
dignity, that no alternative remains save suicide or cheating at
the gaming-table—unless he happens, by chance, to have a
wealthy daughter ! "

" My beloved child ! " said the prince, who now found it
advisable to adopt a tone of pathos.

" Pray, say no more, Father. You have never troubled
yourself about your daughter, have never been a father to me
—if you had, you would not now stand before me so miserable, so poor in happiness. This is past change. Alas, that I
cannot love and respect my father as I ought—that I cannot
do what I am about to do more gladly. Yet I am none the
less ready to fulfill my duties towards you. So far as lies in my

power, I will afford you the possibility of continuing your piti-
ful life of shams, and leave it to your discretion how far you
draw upon my income.   It is fortunate that you came in time
—in a few days it might have been too late.   I see now that
I must not give up my large income so long as my father
needs the money.   My dreams of a late, but pure happiness
are shattered!   You will understand that one needs time to
recover from such a blow and pardon my painful excitement."

She rose, with pallid face and trembling limbs: "I will
place the papers necessary to raise the money in your hands
early to-morrow morning, and you will forget this painful scene
sooner than I."

"You have paid me few compliments—but I shall bear no
malice—you are nervous to-day, my fair daughter.   And even
if you do not bestow your aid in the most generous way,
nevertheless you help me.   Let me kiss your liberal hand!
Ah, it is exactly like your mother's.   When I think that those
slender, delicate fingers have been laid in the coarse fist of
Heaven knows what plebeian, I think great credit is due me— "

"Do not go on!" interrupted the countess, imperiously.
"I think I have done my duty, Papa—but the measure is full,
and I earnestly entreat you to let me rest to-day."

"It is the fate of fathers to let their daughters rule them,"
replied the prince in a jesting tone.   "Well, it is better to be
ill-treated by a daughter than by a sweetheart.   You see I,
too, have some moral impulses, since I have been in your
strict society.   May the father whom you judge so harshly be
permitted to kiss your forehead?"

The countess silently submitted—but a shudder ran through
her frame as if the touch had defiled her.   She felt that it was
the Judas kiss of the world, not the caress of a father.

The prince wiped his mouth with a sensation of secret
disgust.   "Who knows what lips have touched that brow to-
day?"   He dared not think of it, or it would make him ill.

"*Ma chère*, however deeply I am indebted to you, I must
assert my paternal rights a few minutes.   You have said so
many bitter things, whose justice I will not deny, that you
will permit me to utter a few truthful words also."   Fixing his
eyes upon her with a stern, cold gaze, he said in a low tone,
placing a marked emphasis on every word: "We have carried

matters very far—you and I—the last of the ancient Prankenberg race! A pretty pair! the father a bankrupt, and the
daughter—on the eve of marrying a peasant."

Madeleine von Wildenau, deadly pale, stood leaning with
compressed lips on the back of her armchair.

The prince laid his hand on her shoulder. "We may
both say that to-day *each* has saved the *other!* This is my
reparation for the humiliating role fate has forced upon me in
your presence. Am I not right? Good-night, my queenly
daughter—and I hope you bear me no ill-will."

CHAPTER XVI.

PRISONED.

The prince had left the room, and she heard him walk
through the work-shop. Silence fell upon the house and the
street. The tortured woman, utterly exhausted, sank upon
her bed—her feet would support her no longer. But she
could get no rest; an indescribable grief filled her heart.
Everything had happened precisely as Freyer had predicted.
Before the cock crowed, she had thrice betrayed him, betrayed him in the very hour when she had sworn fidelity. At
the first step she was to take on the road of life with the man
she loved, at the first glance from the basilisk eyes of conventional prejudice, she shrank back like a coward and could not
make up her mind to acknowledge him. This was her purification, this the effect of a feeling which, as she believed, had
power to conquer the world? Everything was false—she de-
spaired of all things—of her future, of herself, of the power
of Christianity, which she, like all new converts, expected
would have the might to transform sinners into saints in a
single moment. One thing alone remained unchanged, *one*
image only was untouched by any tinge of baseness amid the
turmoil of emotions seething in her heart—Freyer. He alone
could save her—she must go to him. Springing from her bed
she hurried into the work-shop. "Wher is your son?" she
asked Andreas Gross, who was just preparing to retire.

"I suppose he is in his room, Countess."

"Bring him to me at once."

"Certainly, Countess."

"Shall I undress Your Highness?" asked Josepha, who was still waiting for her orders.

Madeleine von Wildenau's eyes rested on the girl with a searching expression, as if she saw her now for the first time. Was she faithful—as faithful as a maid must be to make it possible to carry out the plan her father had suggested? Josepha gazed steadily into the countess' eyes, her frank face expressed nothing but innocent wonder at so long a scrutiny. "Yes—you are faithful," said the countess at last—"are you not?"

"Certainly, Countess," replied the girl, evidently surprised that she needed to give the assurance.

"You know what unhappiness means?"

"I think so!" said Josepha, with bitter emphasis.

"Then you would aid the unhappy so far as you were able?"

"It would depend upon who it was," answered Josepha, brusquely, but the rudeness pleased the countess; it was a proof of character, and character is a guarantee of trustworthiness. "If it were I, Josepha, could I depend upon you in *any* situation?"

"Certainly!" the girl answered simply—"I live only for you—otherwise I would far rather be under the sod. What have I to live for except you?"

"I believe, Josepha, that I now know the reason Providence sent me to you!" murmured her mistress, lost in thought.

Ludwig Gross entered. "Did you wish to see me?"

Madeleine von Wildenau silently took his hand and drew him into her room.

"Oh, Ludwig, what things I have been compelled to hear—what sins I have committed—what suffering I have endured!" She laid her arm on the shoulder of the faithful friend, like a child pleading for aid. "What time is it, Ludwig?"

"I don't know," he replied. "I was asleep when my father called me. I wandered about looking for you and

Freyer until about an hour ago. Then weariness overpowered me." He drew out his watch. " It is half past ten."

"Take me to Freyer, Ludwig. I must see him this very day. Oh, my. friend! let me wash myself clean in your soul, for I feel as if the turbid surges of the world had soiled me with their mire."

Ludwig Gross passed his arm lightly about her shoulders as if to protect her from the unclean element. " Come," he said soothingly, " I will take you to Freyer. Or would you prefer to have me bring him here ? "

"No, he would not come now. I must go to him. for I have done something for which I must atone—there can be no delay."

Ludwig hurriedly wrapped her in a warm shawl. " You will be ill from this continual excitement," he said anxiously, but without trying to dissuade her. "Take my arm, you are tottering."

They left the house before the eyes of the astonished Gross family. " She is a very singular woman," said Sephi, shaking her head. " She gives herself no rest night or day."

It was only five days since the evening that Madeleine von Wildenau had walked, as now, through the sleeping village, and how much she had experienced.

She had found the God whom she was seeking—she had gazed into his eyes, she had recognized divine, eternal love, and had perceived that she was not worthy of it. So she moved proudly, yet humbly on, leaning upon the arm of her friend, to the street where a thrill of reverence had stirred her whole being when Andreas Gross said, " That is the way to the dwelling of the Christ."

The house stood across the end of the street. This time no moonbeams lighted the way. The damp branches of the trees rustled mournfully above them in the darkness. Only a single window on the ground floor of Freyer's house was lighted, and the wavering rays marked the way for the pair. They reached it and looked in. Freyer was sitting on a wooden stool by the table, his head resting on his hand, absorbed in sorrowful thought. A book lay before him, which he had perhaps intended to read, but evidently had not done so, for he was gazing wearily into vacancy.

Madeleine von Wildenau stepped softly in through the unfastened door. Ludwig Gross waited for her outside. As she opened the door of the room Freyer looked up in astonishment. "You?" he said, and his eyes rested full upon her with a questioning gaze—but he rose with dignity, instead of rushing to meet her, as he would formerly have greeted the woman he loved, had she suddenly appeared before him.

"Countess—what does this visit mean—at this hour?" he asked, mournfully, offering her a chair. "Did you come alone?"

"Ludwig brought me and is waiting outside for me—I have only a few words to say."

"But it will not do to leave our friend standing outside. You will allow me to call him in?"

"Do so, you will then have the satisfaction of having a witness of my humiliation," said the countess, quietly.

"Pardon me, I did not think of that interpretation!" murmured Freyer, seating himself.

"May I ask your Highness' commands?"

"Joseph—to whom are you speaking?"

"To the Countess Wildenau!"

She knelt beside him: "Joseph! Am I *still* the Countess Wildenau?"

"Your Highness, pray spare me!" he exclaimed, starting up. "All this can alter nothing. You remain—what you are, and I—what I am! This was deeply graven on my heart to-night, and nothing can efface it." He spoke with neither anger nor reproach—simply like a man who has lost what was dearest to him on earth.

"If that is true, I can certainly do nothing except go again!" she replied, turning toward the door. "But answer for it to God for having thrust me forth unheard."

"Nay, Countess, pray, speak!" said Freyer, kindly. She looked at him so beseechingly that his heart melted with unutterable pain. "Come—and—tell me what weighs upon your heart!" he added in a gentler tone.

"Not until you again call me your dove—or your child."

Tears filled his eyes, "My child—what have you done!"

"That is right—I can speak now! What have I done, Joseph? What you saw; and still worse. I not only treated you coldly and distantly in my father's presence, I afterwards disowned you three times—and I come to tell you so because *you* alone can and—l know—will forgive me."

Freyer had clasped his hands upon his knee and was gazing into vacancy. Madeleine continued: "You see, I have so lofty an opinion of you, and of your love, that I do not try to justify myself. I will only remind you of the words you yourself said to-day: 'May you never be forced to weep the tears which Peter shed when the cock crowed for the third time.' I will recall what must have induced Christ to forgive Peter: 'He knew the disciple's heart!' Joseph—do you not also know the heart of your Magdalena?"

A tremor ran through the strong man's frame and, unable to utter a word, he threw his arm around her and his head drooped on her breast.

"Joseph, you are ignorant of the world, and the bonds with which it fetters even the freest souls. Therefore you must *believe* in me! It will often happen that I shall be forced to do something incomprehensible to you. If you did not then have implicit faith in me, we could never live happily together. This very day I had resolved to break with society, strip off all its chains. But no matter how many false and culpable ideas it has—its principles, nevertheless, rest upon a foundation of morality. That is why it can impose its fetters upon the very persons who have nothing in common with its *immoral* side. Nay, were it merely an *immoral* power it would be easy, in a moment of pious enthusiasm, to shake off its thrall—but when we are just on the eve of doing so, when we believe ourselves actually free, it throws around our feet the snare of a *duty* and we are prisoned anew. Such was my experience to-day with my father! I should have been compelled to sunder every tie, had I told him the truth! I was too weak to provoke the terrible catastrophe—and deferred it, by disowning you."

Freyer quivered with pain.

She stroked his clenched hand caressingly. "I know what this must be. I know how the proud man must rebel when the woman he loved did *that*. But I also expect my angel to know what it cost me!"

She gently tried to loose his clenched fingers, which gradually yielded till the open hand lay soft and unresisting in her own. "Look at me," she continued in her sweet, melting tones: "look at my pallid face, my eyes reddened with weeping—and then answer whether I have suffered during these hours?"

"I do see it!" said Freyer, gently.

"Dear husband! I come to you with my great need, with my great love—and my great guilt. Will you thrust me from you?"

He could hold out no longer, but with loving generosity clasped the pleading woman to his heart.

"I knew it, you are the embodiment of goodness, gentleness—love! You will have patience with your weak, sinful wife—you will ennoble and sanctify her, and not despair if it is a long time ere the work is completed. You promise, do you not?" she murmured fervently amid her kisses, breathing into his inmost life the ardent pleading of her remorse.

And, with a solemn vow, he promised never to be angry with her again, never to desert her until she *herself* sent him away.

She had conquered—he trusted her once more. And now —she must profit by this childlike confidence.

"I thank you!" she said, after a long silence. "Now I shall have courage to ask you a serious question. But let us send home the friend who is waiting outside, you can take me back yourself."

"Certainly, my child," said Freyer, smiling, and went out to seek Ludwig. "He was satisfied," he said returning. "Now speak—and tell me everything that weighs upon your heart—no one can hear us save God." And he drew her into a loving embrace.

"Joseph," the countess began in an embarrassed tone. "The decisive hour has come sooner than I expected and I am compelled to ask, 'Will you be my husband—but only before God, not men.'"

Freyer drew back a step. "What do you mean?"

"Will you listen to me quietly, dearest?" she asked, gently.

"Speak, my child."

"Joseph! I promised to-day to become your wife—and I

will keep the pledge, but our marriage must be a secret one."

"And why ?"

"My husband's will disinherits me, as soon as I give up the name of Wildenau. If I marry you, I shall be dependent upon the generosity of my husband's cousins, who succeed me as his heirs, and they are not even obliged to give me an annuity—so I shall be little better than a beggar."

"Oh, is that all ? What does it matter ? Am I not able to support my wife—that is, if she can be satisfied with the modest livelihood a poor wood-carver like myself can offer ? "

The countess, deeply touched, smiled. "I knew that you would say so. But, my angel, that would only do, if I had no other duties. But, you see, this is one of the snares with which the world draws back those who endeavor to escape its spell. I have a father—an unhappy man whom I can neither respect nor love—a type of the brilliant misery, the hollow shams, to which so many lives in our circle fall victims, a gambler, a spendthrift, but still *my father !* He asks pecuniary aid which I can render only if I remain the Countess Wildenau. Dare I be happy and let my father go to ruin ? "

"No ! " groaned Freyer, whose head sank like a felled tree on the arms which rested folded on the table.

"Then what is left to us—my beloved, save *separation* or a secret marriage ? Surely we would not profane the miracle which God has wrought in us by any other course ? "

"No—never ! "

"Well—then I must say to you : 'choose ! ' "

"Oh, Heaven ! this is terrible. I must not be allowed to assert my sacred rights before men—must live like a dishonored man under ban ? And *where* and *when* could we meet ? "

"Joseph—I can offer you the position of steward of my estates, which will enable us to live together constantly and meet without the least restraint. I can recompense you a hundredfold, for what you resign here, my property shall be yours, as well as all that I am and have—you shall miss nothing save outward appearances, the triumph of appearing before the world as the husband of the Countess Wildenau."

"Oh! God, Thou art my witness that no such thought

ever entered my heart. If you were poor and miserable, starving by the wayside, I would raise you and bear you proudly in my arms into my house. If you were blind and lame, ill and deserted, I would watch and cherish you day and night—nay, it would be my delight to work for you and earn, by my own industry, the bread you eat! When I brought it, I would offer it on my knees and kiss your dear hands for accepting it. But your servant, your hireling, I cannot be! Tell me yourself—could you still love me if I were ? "

" Yes, for my love is eternal ! "

"Do not deceive yourself; you have loved me as a poor, but *free* citizen of Ammergau—as your paid servant you would despise me."

" You shall not be my servant—it is merely necessary to find some pretext before the world which will render it possible for us to be constantly together without exciting suspicion —and the office of a steward is this pretext ! " ·

"Twist and turn it as you will—I shall eat your bread, and be your subordinate. Oh, Heaven, I was so proud and am now so terribly humiliated—so suddenly hurled from the height to which you had raised me ! "

" It will be no humiliation to accept what my love bestows and my superabundance shares with you."

" It *is*, and I could be your husband only on the condition that I might continue to work and earn my own support."

" Oh ! the envious arrogance of the poor, who grudge the rich the noblest privilege—that of doing good. Believe me, true pride would be to say to yourself that your noble nature a thousand times outweighed the petty sacrifice of worldly goods which I could make for you. He who scorns money can accept it from others because he knows that the outward gift is valueless, compared with the treasures of happiness love can offer. Or do you feel so poor In love that you could not pay me the trivial debt for the bit of bread I furnished ? Then indeed—let me with my wealth languish in my dearth of happiness and boast that you sacrificed to your pride the most faithful of women—but do not say that you loved the woman ! "

" My dove ! "

"I am doing what I can!" she continued, mournfully, "I am offering you myself, my soul, my freedom, my future—and you are considering whether it will not degrade you to eat my bread and be apparently my servant, while in reality you are my master and my judge.—I have nothing more to say, you shall have your will, but decide quickly, for what is to be done must be done at once. My father himself (when he perceived that I really intended to marry) advised me to be wedded by our old pastor at Prankenberg. But I know my father, and am aware that he was only luring me into a trap. He will receive from me to-morrow a power of attorney to raise some money he needs—the day after he will invent some new device to keep me in his power. We must take the pastor at Prankenberg by surprise before he can prevent it. Now decide!"

"Omnipotent God!" exclaimed Freyer. "What shall I, what must I do? Oh! my love, I ought not to desert you—and even if I ought—I *could* not, for I could no longer live without you! You know that I must take what you offer, and that my fate will be what you assign! But, dearest, how I shall endure to be your husband and yet regarded as your servant, I know not. If you could let this cup pass from me, it would be far better for us both."

"And did God spare the Saviour the cup? Was Christ too proud to take upon Him His cross and His ignominy, while you—cannot even bear the yoke your wife imposes, is *forced* to impose?"

He bowed his head to the earth. Tears sparkled in his radiant eyes, he was once more the Christ. As his dark eyes rested upon her in the dim light diffused by the lamp, with all the anguish of the Crucified Redeemer, Madeleine von Wildenau again felt a thrill of awe in the presence of something supernatural—a creature belonging to some middle realm, half spirit, half mortal—and the perception that he could never belong wholly to the earth, never wholly to *her*. She could not explain this feeling, he was so kind, so self-sacrificing. Had she had any idea that such a man was destined to absorb *us*, not we *him*, the mystery would have been solved. What she was doing was precisely the reverse. His existence must be sacrificed to hers—and she had a vague suspicion that this was contrary to the laws of his noble, privileged nature.

But he, unconscious of himself, in his modest simplicity, only knew that he must love the countess to the end—and deemed it only just that he should purchase the measureless happiness of calling this woman his by an equally boundless sacrifice. The appeal to Christ had suddenly made him believe that God proposed to give him the opportunity to continue in life the part of a martyr which he was no longer permitted to play on the stage. The terrible humiliation imposed by the woman whom he loved was to be the cross received in exchange for the one he had resigned.

"Very well, then, for the sake of Christ's humility!" he said, sadly, as if utterly crushed. "Give me whatever position you choose, but I fear you will discover too late that you have robbed yourself of the *best* love I have to bestow. Your nature is not one which can love a vassal. You will be like the children who tear off the butterfly's wings and then— throw aside the crawling worm with loathing. My wings were my moral freedom and my self-respect. At this moment I have lost them, for I am only a weak, love-sick man who must do whatever an irresistible woman requires. It is no free moral act, as is usual when a man exchanges an equal existence with his chosen wife.

"If you think *that*, Joseph," said the countess, turning pale, "it will certainly be better—for me to leave you." She turned with dignity toward the door.

"Yes, go!" he cried in wild anguish—"go! Yet you know that you will take me with you, like the crown of thorns you dragged caught in the hem of your dress!" He threw himself on his knees at her feet. "What am I? Your slave. In Heaven's name, be my mistress and take me. I place my soul in your keeping—I trust it to your generosity—but woe betide us both, if you do not give me yours in return. I ask nothing save your soul—but that I want wholly."

The exultant woman clasped him in a passionate embrace: "Yes, give yourself a prisoner to me, and trust your fate to my hands. I will be a gentle mistress to you—you, beloved slave, you shall not be *more* mine than I am yours—that is, *wholly* and *forever*."

CHAPTER XVII.

FLYING FROM THE CROSS.

The burgomaster went to the office every morning at six o'clock, for the work to be accomplished during the day was very great and required an early beginning. Freyer usually arrived about seven to share the task with him. On Fridays, however, he often commenced his labor before the energetic burgomaster. It was on that day that the rush upon the ticket office began, and every one's hands were filled.

But to-day Freyer seemed to be in no hurry. It was after seven—he ought to have arrived long before. He had been absent yesterday, too. The stranger must have taken complete possession of him. The burgomaster shook his head—Freyer's conduct since the countess' arrival, had not pleased him. He had never neglected his duties to the community. And at the very time when the Passion Play had attained unprecedented success. How could any one think of anything else—anything *personal*, especially the man who took the part of the Christ! There were heaps of orders lying piled before him, how could they be disposed of, if Freyer did not help.

This countess was a beautiful woman—and probably a fascinating one. But to the burgomaster there was but *one* beauty—that of the angel of his home. High above the turmoil of the crowd, in quiet, aristocratic seclusion, the lonely man sat at his desk in his bare, plain office. But the angel of Ammergau visited him here; he leaned his weary head upon His breast, *His* kiss rewarded his unselfish labor, *His* radiance illumined the unassuming citizen. No house was so poor and insignificant that at this season the angel of Ammergau did not take up His abode within and shed upon it His own sanctity and dignity. But to him who was the personification of Ammergau, the man who was obliged to care for everything— watch over everything—bear the responsibility of everything, to him the angel brought the reward which men cannot give —the proud consciousness of what he was to his home in these toilsome days. But it was quite time that Freyer should come! The burgomaster rang his bell. The bailiff entered.

"Kleinhofer, see where Herr Freyer is—or the drawing-master. *One* of them can surely be found."

"Yes, Herr Burgomaster." The man left the room.

The burgomaster leaned back in his chair to wait. His eyes rested a few seconds on one of Doré's pictures, Christ condemned by Pontius Pilate. He involuntarily compared the engraving with the grouping on the stage. "Ah, if we could do that! If living beings, with massive bones and clumsy joints, would be as pliable as canvas and brushes!" he thought, sorrowfully. "Wherever human beings are employed there must be defects and imperfections. Perfection, absolute beauty, exist only in the imagination! Yet ought not an inflexible stage manager, by following the lines of the work of art, to succeed in shaping even the rudest material into the artistic idea."

"Much—much remains to be done," said the singular stage manager in pitiless self-criticism, resting his head on his hand. "When one thinks of what the Meininger company accomplishes! But of course they work with *artists*—I with natural talent! Then we are restricted in alloting the parts by dilettante traditional models—and, worst of all, by antiquated statutes and prejudices. The vision of Josepha Freyer rose before him, he keenly felt the blow inflicted on the Passion Play when the beautiful girl, the very type of Mary Magdalene, was excluded. "The whole must suffer under such circumstances! The actors cannot be chosen according to talent and individuality; these things are a secondary consideration. The first is the person's standing in the community! A poor servant would be allowed to play only an inferior part, even if he possessed the greatest talent, and the principal ones are the monopoly of the influential citizens. From a contingent thus arbitrarily limited the manager is compelled to distribute the characters for the great work, which demands the highest powers. It is a gigantic labor, but it will be accomplished, nothing is needed save patience and an iron will! They will grow with their task. The increasing success of the Passion Play will teach them to understand how important it is that artistic interests should supersede all others. Then golden hours will first dawn on Ammergau. May God permit me to witness it!" he added. And he confidently hoped to do so;

for there was no lack of talent, and with a few additions great results might be accomplished. This year the success of the Play was secured by Freyer, who made the audience forget all less skilful performers With him the Passion Play of the present year would stand or fall. The burgomaster's eyes rested with a look of compassion upon the Christ of Doré and the Christ personated by Freyer, as it hovered before his memory – and Freyer bore the test. He had come from the hand of his Creator a living work of art, perfect in every detail. "Thank Heaven that we have him!" murmured the burgomaster, with a nod of satisfaction.

Some one knocked at the door. "At last," said the burgomaster: "Come in!"

It was not the person whom he expected, but Ludwig Gross!

He tottered forward as if his feet refused to obey his will. His grave face was waxen-yellow in its hue and deeply lined –his lips were tightly compressed—drops of perspiration glittered on his brow.

The burgomaster glanced at him in alarm: "What is it? What has happened?"

Ludwig Gross drew a letter from his pocket, "Be prepared for bad news."

"For Heaven's sake, cannot the performance take place? We have sold more than a thousand tickets."

"That would be the least difficulty. Be strong, Herr Burgomaster—I have a great misfortune to announce."

"Has it anything to do with Freyer?" exclaimed the magistrate, with sudden foreboding.

"Freyer has gone—with Countess Wildenau!"

"Run away?" cried the burgomaster, inexorably giving the act the right name.

"Yes, I have just found these lines on his table."

The burgomaster turned pale as if he had received a mortal wound. A peal of thunder seemed to echo in his ears —the thunder which had shattered the temple of Jerusalem, whose priest he was! The walls fell, the veil was rent and revealed the place of execution. Golgotha lay before him. He heard the rustling wings of the departing guardian angel of Ammergau. High above, in terrible solitude, towered the cross, but it was empty—he who should hang upon it—had vanished! Grey clouds gathered around the desolate scene.

But from the empty cross issued a light—not a halo, but like the livid, phosphorescent glimmer of rotten wood! It shone into a chasm where, from a jutting rock, towered a single tree, upon which hung, faithful to his task—Judas!

A peal of jeering laughter rose from the depths. "You have killed yourself in vain. Your victim has escaped. See the conscientious Judas, who hung himself, while the other is having a life of pleasure!"

Shame and disgrace! "The Christ has fled from the cross." Malicious voices echo far and wide, cynicism exults —baseness has conquered, the divine has become a laughing-stock for children—the Passion Play a travesty.

The phosphorescent wood of the cross glimmered before the burgomaster's eyes. Aye, it was rotten and mouldering— this cross—it must crumble—the corruption of the world had infected and undermined it, and this had happened in Ober-ammergau—under *his* management.

The unfortunate man, through whose brain this chain of thoughts was whirling, sat like a stone statue before his friend, who stood waiting modestly, without disturbing his grief by a single word.

What the two men felt—each knew—was too great for utterance.

The burgomaster was mechanically holding Freyer's letter in his clenched hand. Now his cold, stiff fingers reminded him of it. He laid it on the table, his eyes resting dully on the large childish characters of the unformed hand: "Forgive me!" ran the brief contents. "I am no longer worthy to personate the Saviour! Not from lack of principle, but on account of it do I resign my part. Ere you read these lines, I shall be far away from here! God will not make His sacred cause depend upon any individual—He will supply my place to you! For-get me, and forgive the renegade whose heart will be faithful to you unto death!   FREYER!"

Postscript:

" Sell my property—the house, the field, and patch of woods which was not burned and divide the proceeds among the poor of Ammergau. I will send you the legal authority from the nearest city.

" Once more, farewell to all ! "

The burgomaster sat motionless, gazing at the sheet. He could have read it ten times over—yet he still stared at the lines.

Ludwig Gross saw with terror that his eyes were glassy, his features changed. The calmness imposed by the iron will had become the rigidity of death. The drawing-master shook him—now, in the altered position, the inert body lost its balance and fell against the back of the chair. His friend caught the tottering figure and supported the noble head. It was possible for him to reach the bell with his other hand and summon Kleinhofer. "The doctor—quick—tell him to come at once ! " he shouted. The man hurried off in terror.

The news that the burgomaster had been stricken with apoplexy ran through the village like wild fire. Every one rushed to the office. The physician ran bare-headed across the street. The confusion was boundless.

Ludwig could scarcely control the tumult. Supporting the burgomaster with one arm, he pushed the throng back with the other. The doctor could scarcely force his way through the crowded room. He rubbed the temples and arteries of the senseless man. "I don't think it is apoplexy, only a severe congestion of the brain," he said, "but we cannot tell what the result may be. He has long been over-worked and over-excited."

The remedies applied began to act, the burgomaster opened his eyes. But as if he were surrounded by invisible fiends which, like wild beasts were only held in check by the firm gaze of the tamer and, ever ready to spring, were only watching for the moment when they might wrest from him the sacred treasure confided to his care—his dim eyes in a few seconds regained the steady flash of the watchful, imperious master. And the discipline which his unyielding will was wont to exert over his limbs instantly restored his erect bearing. No one save the physician and Ludwig knew what the effort cost him.

" Yes," said the doctor in a low tone to the drawing-master: " This is the consequence of his never granting himself any rest during these terrible exertions."

The burgomaster had gone to the window and obtained a little air. Then he turned to the by-standers. His voice still trembled slightly, but otherwise not the slightest weakness was perceptible, and nothing betrayed the least emotion.

" I am glad, my friends, that we are all assembled—otherwise I should have been compelled to summon you. Is the whole parish here ? We must hold a consultation at once. Kleinhofer, count them."

The man obeyed.

" They are all here," he said.

At that moment the burgomaster's wife rushed in with Anastasia. They had been in the fields and had just learned the startling news of the illness of the husband and brother.

" Pray be calm !" he said, sternly. " There is nothing wrong with me—nothing worth mentioning."

The weeping women were surrounded by their friends but the burgomaster, with an imperious wave of the hand, motioned them to the back of the room. " If you wish to listen—and it is my desire that you should—keep quiet. We have not a moment to lose." He turned to the men of the parish.

" Dear friends and companions ! I have tidings which I should never have expected a native of Ammergau would be compelled to relate of a fellow citizen. A great misfortune has befallen us. We no longer have a Christ ! Freyer has suddenly gone away."

A cry of horror and indignation answered him. A medley of shouts and questions followed, mingled with fierce imprecations.

" Be calm, friends. Do not revile him. We do not know what has occurred. True, I cannot understand how such a thing was possible—but we must not judge where we know no particulars. At any rate we will respect ourselves by speaking no evil of one of our fellow citizens—for that he was, in spite of his act."

Ludwig secretly pressed his hand in token of gratitude.

" This misfortune is sent by God "—the burgomaster continued—" we will not judge the poor mortal who was merely

His tool. Regard him as one dead, as he seems to regard himself. He has bequeathed his property to our poor—we will thank him for that, as is right—in other respects he is dead to us."

The burgomaster took the letter from the table. "Here is his last will for Ammergau, I will read it to you." The burgomaster calmly read the paper, but it seemed as if his voice, usually so firm, trembled.

When he had finished, deep silence reigned. Many were wiping their eyes, others gazed sullenly into vacancy—a solemn hush, like that which prevails at a funeral, had taken possession of the assembly. "We cannot tell," the burgomaster repeated: "Peace to his ashes—for the fire which will be so destructive to us is still blazing in him. We can but say, may God forgive him, and let these be the last words uttered concerning him."

"May God forgive him!" murmured the sorely stricken assemblage.

"Amen!" replied the burgomaster. "And now, my friends, let us consult what is to be done. We cannot deceive ourselves concerning our situation. It is critical, nay hopeless. The first thing we must try to save is our honor. When it becomes known that one of our number, and that one the Christ—has deserted his colors, or rather the cross, we shall be disgraced and our sacred cause must suffer. *Our* honor here is synonymous with the honor of God, and if we do not guard it for ourselves we must for His sake."

A murmur of assent answered him. He continued: "Therefore we must make every effort to keep the matter secret. We can say that Freyer had suddenly succumbed to the exertion imposed by his part, and to save his life had been obliged to seek a warmer climate! Those who *know* us men of Ammergau will not believe that any one would retire on account of his health, nay would prefer death rather than to interrupt the performances—but there are few who do know us."

"God knows that!" said the listeners, mournfully.

"Therefore I propose that we all promise to maintain the most absolute secrecy in regard to the real state of affairs and give the pretext just suggested to the public."

"Yes, yes—we will agree not to say anything else," the men readily assented. "But the women—they will chatter," said Andreas Gross.

"That is just what I fear. I can rely upon you men," replied the burgomaster, casting a stern glance at the girls and women. "The men are fully aware of the meaning and importance of our cause. It is bad enough that so many are not understood and supported by their wives! You—the women of Ammergau—alas that I must say it—you have done the place and the cause more harm by your gossip than you can answer for to the God who honors us with His holy mission. There is chattering and tattling where you think you can do so unpunished, and many things are whispered into the ears of the visitors which afterwards goes as false rumors through the world! You care nothing for the great cause, if you get an opportunity to gratify some bit of petty malice. Now you are weeping, are you not? Because we are ruined—the performances must cease! But are you sure that Joseph Freyer would have been capable of treating us in this way, had it not been for the flood of gossip you poured out on him and his cousin, Josepha? It embittered his mind against us and drove him into the stranger's arms. Has he not said a hundred times that, if it were not for personating the Christ, he would have left Ammergau long ago? Where *one* bond is destroyed another tears all the more easily. Take it as a les-son—and keep silence *this* time at least, if you can govern your feminine weakness so far! I shall make your husbands accountable for every word which escapes concerning this matter." Several of the women murmured and cast spiteful glances at the burgomaster.

"To *whom* does this refer, *who* is said to have tattled?" asked a stout woman with a bold face.

The burgomaster frowned. "It refers to those who feel guilty—and does not concern those who do not!" he cried, sternly. "The good silent women among you know very well that I do not mean them—and the others can take heed."

A painful pause followed. The burgomaster's eyes rested threateningly upon the angry faces of the culprits. Those who felt that they were innocent gazed at him undisturbed.

"I will answer for my wife"—"Nothing shall go from my

house!" protested one after another, and thus at least every effort would be made to save the honor of Ammergau, and conceal their disgrace from the world. But now came the question how to save the Play. A warm debate followed. The people, thus robbed of their hopes, wished to continue the performances at any cost, with any cast of characters. But here they encountered the resolute opposition of the burgomaster: "Either well—or not at all!" was his ultimatum. "We cannot deceive ourselves for a moment. At present, there is not one of us who can personate the Christ—except Thomas Rendner, and where, in that case, could we find a Pilate—who could replace Thomas Rendner?"

There was a violent discussion. "The sacristan, Nathanael, could play Pilate."

"Who then would take Nathanael?"

"Ah, if this one and that one were still in the village! But they had gone away to seek their bread, like so many who could no longer earn a support since the Partenkirch School of Carving had competed with the one in Ammergau. And many more would follow. If things went on in the same fashion, and matters were not improved by the play, in ten years more there might be none to fill the parts, necessity would gradually drive every one away."

"Yes, we are in a sore strait, my friends. The company melts away more and more—the danger to the Passion Play constantly increases. If we can find no help now, penury will deprive us of some of our best performers ere the next time. And yet, my friends, believe me—I say it with a heavy heart: if we now continue with a poor cast of characters—we shall be lost wholly and forever, for then we shall have destroyed the reputation of the Passion Play."

"Thomas Rendner will personate the Christ well—there is no danger on that score."

"And if he does—if Rendner takes the Christ, the sacristan Pilate, and some one else Nathanael—shall we not be obliged to study the whole piece again, and can that be done so rapidly? Can we commence our rehearsals afresh now? I ask you, is it possible?"

The people hung their heads in hopeless discouragement.

"Our sole resource would be to find a Christ among

those who are not in the Play—and all who have talent are already employed. The others cannot be used, if we desire to present an artistic whole."

Despair seized upon the listeners—there was not a single one among them who had not invested his little all in furniture and beds for the strangers, and even incurred debts for the purpose, to say nothing of the universal poverty.

New proposals were made, all of which the hapless burgomaster was compelled to reject.

"The general welfare is at a stake, and the burgomaster thinks only of the *artistic whole.*"

With these words the wrath of the assembly was finally all directed against him, and those who fanned it were mainly the strangers attracted by the Passion Play for purposes of speculation, who cared nothing how much it suffered in future, if only they made their money!

"I know the elements which are stirring up strife here," said the burgomaster, scanning the assembly with his stern eyes. "But they shall not succeed in separating us old citizens of Ammergau, who have held together through every calamity! Friends, let the spirit which our forefathers have preserved for centuries save us from discord—let us not deny the good old Ammergau nature in misfortune."

"And with the good old nature you can starve," muttered the speculators.

"If the burgomaster does not consider your interests of more importance than the fame of his success as stage manager he ought to go to Munich and get the position—there he could give as many model performances as he desired!"

"Yes," cried another, "he is sacrificing our interests to his own vanity."

During this accusation the burgomaster remained standing with his figure drawn up to its full height. Only the dark swollen vein on his weary brow betrayed the indignation seething in his soul.

"I disdain to make any reply to such a charge. I know the hearts of my fellow citizens too well to fear that any one of them believes it."

"No, certainly not!" exclaimed the wiser ones. But the majority were silent in their wrathful despair.

"I know that many of you misjudge me, and I bear you no resentment for it. I admit that in such a period of storm and stress it is difficult to maintain an unprejudiced judgment.

"I know also that I myself have often bewildered your judgment, for it is impossible to create such a work without giving offense here and there. I know that many who feel wounded and slighted secretly resent it, and I do not blame them! Only I beg you to visit the rancor on me *personally*—not extend it to the cause and injure that out of opposition to me. In important moments like these, I beg you to let all private grudges drop and gather around me—in this one decisive hour think only of the whole community, and not of all the wrongs the burgomaster may have done you individually.

"If I had only the interest of Ammergau to guard, all would be well! But I have not only *your* welfare to protect, but the dignity of a cause for which I am responsible to *God* —so long as it remains in my hands. Human nature is weak and subject to external impressions. The religious conceptions of thousands depend upon the greater or less powerful illusion produced by the Passion Play as a moral symbol. This is a heavy responsibility in a time when negation and materialism are constantly undermining faith and dragging everything sacred in the dust. In such a period, the utmost perfection of detail is necessary, that the *form* at least may command respect, where the *essence* is despised. I will try to make this clear to you by an example. The cynic who sneers at our worship of Mary and, with satirical satisfaction, paints the Virgin as the corpulent mother of four or five boys, will laugh at an Altötting Virgin but grow silent and earnest before a Sistine Madonna! For here the divinity in which he does not wish to believe confronts him in the work of art and compels his reverence. It is precisely in a period of materialism like the present that religious representation has its most grateful task—for the deeper man sinks into sensualism, the more accessible he is to sensual impressions, and the more easily religion can influence him through visible forms, repelling or attracting according to the defective or artistic treatment of the material. The religious-sensuous impetus is the only one which can influence times like these, that is why the Passion Play is more important now than ever!

" God has bestowed upon me the modest talent of organization and a little artistic culture, that I may watch over it, and see that those who come to us trustfully to seek their God, do not go away with a secret disappointment—and that those who come to *laugh* may be quiet—and ashamed.

"This is the great task allotted to me, which I have hitherto executed without regard for personal irritability, and the injury of petty individual interests, and hope to accomplish even under stress of the most dire necessity.

"If you wish to oppose it, you should have given the office I occupy to some one who thinks the task less lofty, and who is complaisant enough to sacrifice the noble to the petty. But see where you will end with the complaisant man, who listens to every one. See how soon anarchy will enter among you, for where individual guidance is lacking, and every one can assert his will, the seed of discord shoots up, overgrowing everything. Now you are all against *me*, but then you will be against *one another*, and while you are quarreling and disputing, time will pass unused, and at last the first antiquated model will be seized because it can be most easily and quickly executed. But the modern world will turn away with a derisive laugh, saying: ' We can't look at these peasant farces any more '

" Then answer for robbing thousands of a beautiful illusion and letting them return home poorer in faith and reverence than they came—answer for it to God, whose sublime task you have degraded by an inferior performance, and lastly to yourselves for forgetting the future in the present gain, and to profit by the Passion Play a few more times now, ruin it for future decades. You do not believe it because, in this secluded village, you cannot know what the taste of our times demands. But I do, for I have lived in the outside world, and I tell you that whoever sees these incomplete performances will certainly not return, and will make us a reputation stamping us as bunglers forever !"

The burgomaster pressed his hand to his head ; a keen pang was piercing his brain—and his heart also.

" I have nothing more to add," he concluded, faintly. " But if you know any one whom you believe could care for

Ammergau better than I—I am ready at any moment to place my office in his hands."

Then, with one accord, every heart swelled with the old lofty feeling for the sacred cause of their ancestors and grateful appreciation of the man who had again roused it in them. No, he did not deserve that they should doubt him—he had again taught them to think like true natives of Ammergau, aye, they felt proudly that he was of the true stock—it was Ammergau blood that flowed in his veins and streamed from the wounds which had been inflicted on his heart that day! They saw that they had wronged him and they gathered with their old love and loyalty around the sorely-beset man, ready to atone with their lives, for these hot-blooded, easily influenced artist-natures were nevertheless true to the core.

The malcontents were forced to keep silence, no one listened to them. All flocked around the burgomaster. "We will stand by you, Burgomaster—only tell us what we are to do—and how we can help ourselves. We rely wholly upon you."

" Alas! my friends, I must reward your restored confidence with unpalatable counsel. Let us bear the misfortune like men! It is better to fell trees in the forest, go out as day laborers—nay, *starve*—rather than be faithless to the spirit of our ancestors! Am I not right?" A storm of enthusiasm answered him.

It was resolved to announce the close of the Passion Play for this decade. The document was signed by all the members of the community.

" So it is ended for this year! For many of us perhaps for this life!" said the burgomaster. " I thank all who have taken part in the Play up to this time. I will report the receipts and expenditures within a few days. In consideration of the painful cause, we will dispense with any formal close."

A very different mood from the former one now took possession of the assembly. All anxiety concerning material things vanished in the presence of a deeper sorrow. It was the great, mysterious grief of parting, which seized all who had to do anything connected with the " Passion." It seemed as if the roots of their hearts had become completely interwoven with it and must draw blood in being torn away, as if a part of their lives went with it. The old men felt the pang most keenly. "For the last time for this life!" are words before whose dark portal we stand hesitating, be it where it may—but if this "for the last time" concerns the highest and dearest thing we possess on earth, they contain a fathomless gulf of sadness! Old Barabbas, the man of ninety, was the first, to express it—the others joined in and the greybeards who had been young together and devoted their whole lives to the cause which to them was the highest in the world, sank into one another's arms, like a body of men condemned to death.

Then one chanted the closing line of the choragus: "Till in the world beyond we meet"—and all joined as with a *single* voice, the unutterable anguish of resigning that close communion with Deity, in which every one of them lived during this period, created its own ceremonial of farewell and found apt expression in those last words of the Passion Play.

Then they shook hands with one another, exchanging a life-long farewell. They knew that they should meet again the next day—in the same garments—but no longer what they now were, Roman governor and high-priests, apostles and saints. They were excluded from the companionship of the Lord, for their Christ had not risen as usual—he had fled and faithlessly deserted his flock, ere their task could be fulfilled. It was doubly hard!

Old Judas, the venerable Lechner, was so much moved that they were obliged to support him down the stairs: Judas weeping over Christ! The loyal man had suffered unutterably from the necessity of playing the traitor's part—the treachery now practised toward the sacred cause by the personator of Christ himself—fairly broke his heart! "That I must live to witness this!" he murmured, wringing his hands as he descended the steps. But Thomas Rendner shook his handsome head and mournfully repeated the momentous words of Pilate: "What is truth?" With tears in his eyes, he held out his sinewy right hand consolingly to Caiaphas.

"Don't take it so much to heart, Burgomaster; God is still with us!" Then he cast a sorrowful glance toward the corner of the room. "Poor Mary! I always thought so!" he muttered compassionately, under his breath, and followed the others.

The burgomaster and Ludwig were left behind alone and followed the direction of Rendner's glance. There—it almost broke their hearts—there sat the burgomaster's sister—the " Mary " in the corner, with her hands clasped in her lap, the very attitude in which she waited for the body of her Crucified Son.

" Poor sister," said the burgomaster, deeply moved. " For what are you waiting? They will never bring him to you again."

" He will come back, the poor martyr!" she replied, her large eyes gazing with prophetic earnestness into vacancy. "·He will come, weary and wounded—perhaps betrayed by all."

" Then I will have nothing to do with him," said the burgomaster in a low, firm tone.

" You can do as you please, you are a man. But I, who have so long personated his mother—I will wait and receive and comfort him, as a mother cheers her erring child."

" Oh, Anastasia !" A cry of pain escaped Ludwig's lips, and, overwhelmed by emotion, he turned away.

The burgomaster, with tender sympathy, laid his hand upon his shoulder.

" Ah, sister, Freyer is not worthy that you should love him so !"

" How do I love him?" replied the girl. " I love him as Eternal Compassion loves the poor and suffering. He *is* poor and suffering. Oh ! do not think evil of him—he does not deserve it. He is good and noble! Believe me, a mother must know her child better," she added, with the smile that reveals a breaking heart.

She looked the drawing-master kindly in the face : " Ludwig, we both understand him, do we not? *We* believe in him, though all condemn."

Ludwig could not speak—he merely nodded silently and pressed Anastasia's hand, as if in recognition of the pledge. He was undergoing a superhuman conflict, but, with the strength peculiar to him, succeeded in repressing any display of emotion.

The burgomaster stood mutely watching the scene, and neither of the three could decide which suffered most.

He gazed in speechless grief at the clasped hands of his sister and his friend. How often he had wished for this moment, and now—? What *parted* alone united them, and what united, divided.

"Aye, Freyer has brought much misery upon us!" he said, with sullen resentment. "I only hope that he will never set foot again upon the soil of his forefathers!"

"Oh, Brother, how can you speak so—you do not mean it. I know that his heart will draw him back here; he will seek his home again, and he shall find it. You will not thrust him from you when he returns from foreign lands sorrowing and repentant. God knows how earnestly I wish him happiness, but I do not believe that he will possess it. And as he will be loyal to us in his inmost soul, we will be true to him and prepare a resting place when the world has nailed his heart upon the cross. Shall we not, Ludwig?"

"Yes, by Heaven, we will!" faltered Ludwig, and his tears fell on the beautiful head of the girl, who still sat motionless, as if she must wait here for the lost one.

"Woman, behold thy son—son, behold thy mother!" stirred the air like a breath.

CHAPTER XVIII.

THE MARRIAGE.

On a wooded height, hidden in the heart of the forests of the Bavarian highlands, stood an ancient hunting castle, the property of the Wildenau family. A steep mountain path led up to it, and at its feet, like a stone sea, stretched the wide, dry bed of a river, a Griess, as it was called in that locality. Only a few persons knew the way; to the careless glance the path seemed wholly impassable.

Bare, rugged cliffs towered like a wall around the hunting castle on its mossy height, harmonizing in melancholy fashion with the white sea of stone below, which formed a harsh foreground to the dreary scene. Ever and anon a stag emerged from the woods, crossing the Griess with elastic tread, the brown silhouette of its antlers sharply relieved against the colorless monotony of the landscape. The hind came forward from the opposite side, slowly, reluctantly, with nostrils vibrating. The report of a rifle echoed from beyond the river bed, the antlers drooped, the royal creature fell upon its knees, then rolled over on its back; its huge antlers, flung backward in the death agony, were thrust deep down among the loose pebbles. The hind had fled, the poacher seized his prey—a slender rill of blood trickled noiselessly through the stones, then everything was once more silent and lifeless.

This was the hiding-place where, for seven years, Countess Wildenau had hidden the treasure filched from the cross—the rock sepulchre in which she intended to keep the God whom the world believed dead. Built close against the cliff, half concealed by an overhanging precipice, the castle seemed to be set in a niche. Shut out from the sunshine by the projecting crag which cast its shadow over it even at noonday, it was so cold and damp that the moisture trickled down the walls of the building, and, moreover, was surrounded by that strange atmosphere of wet moss and rotting mushrooms which awakens so strange a feeling when, after a hot walk, we pause to rest in the cool courtyard of some ruined castle, where our feet sink into wet masses of mouldering brown leaves which for decades no busy hand has swept away. It seems as if the sun desired to associate with human beings. Where no mortal eyes behold its rays, it ceases to shine. It does not deem it worth while to penetrate the heaps of withered leaves, or the tangle of wild vines and bushes, or the veil of cobwebs and lime-dust which, in the course of time, accumulates in heaps in the masonry of a deserted dwelling.

As we see by a child's appearance whether or not it has a loving mother, so the aspect of a house reveals whether or not it is dear to its owner, and as a neglected child drags out a joyless existence, so a neglected house gradually becomes cold and inhospitable.

This was the case with the deserted little hunting seat. No foot had crossed its threshold within the memory of man. What could the Countess Wildenau do with it? It was so remote, so far from all the paths of travel, so hidden in the woods that it would not even afford a fine view. It stood as an outpost on the chart containing the location of

14

the Wildenau estates. It had never entered the owner's mind to seek it out in this—far less in reality.

Every year an architect was sent there to superintend the most necessary repairs, because it was not fitting for a Wildenau to let one of these family castles go to ruin. This was all that was done to preserve the building. The garden gradually ran to waste, and became so blended with the forest that the boughs of the trees beat against the windows of the edifice and barred out like a green hedge the last straggling sunbeams. A castle for a Sleeping Beauty, but without the sleeping princess. Then Fate willed that a blissful secret in its owner's breast demanded just such a hiding-place in which to dream the strangest fantasy ever imagined by woman since Danæ rested in the embrace of Jove.

Madeleine von Wildenau sought and found this forgotten spot in her chart, and, with the energy bestowed by the habit of being able to accomplish whatever we desire, she discovered a secret ford through the Griess, known only to a trustworthy old driver, and no one was aware of Countess Wildenau's residence when she vanished from society for days. There were rumors of a romantic adventure or a religious ecstacy into which the Ammergau Passion Play had transported her years before. She had set off upon her journey to the Promised Land directly after, and as no sea is so wide, no mountain so lofty, that gossip cannot find its way over them, it even made its way from the Holy Sepulchre to the drawing rooms of the capital.

A gentleman, an acquaintance of so-and-so, had gone to the Orient, and in Jerusalem, at the Holy Sepulchre, met a veiled lady, who was no other than Countess Wildenau. There would have been nothing specially remarkable in that. But at the lady's side knelt a gentleman who bore so remarkable a resemblance to the pictures of Christ that one might have believed it was the Risen Lord Himself who, dissatisfied with heaven, had returned repentant to His deserted resting-place.

How interesting! The imagination of society, thirsting for romance, naturally seized upon this bit of news with much eagerness.

Who could the gentleman with the head of Christ be, save the Ammergau Christ? This agreed with the sudden interruption of the Passion Play that summer, on account of the illness of the Christ—as the people of Ammergau said, who perfectly understood how to keep their secrets from the outside world.

But as they committed the imprudence of occasionally sending their daughters to the city, one and another of these secrets of the community, more or less distorted, escaped through the dressing-rooms of the mistresses of these Ammergau maids.

Thus here and there a flickering ray fell upon the Ammergau catastrophe: The Christ was not ill—he had vanished—run away—with a lady of high rank. What a scandal! Then lo! one day Countess Wildenau appeared—after a journey of three years in the east—somewhat absentminded, a little disposed to assume religious airs, but without any genuine piety. Religion is not to be obtained by an indulgence of religious-crotic rapture with its sweet delusions —it can be obtained only by the hard labor of daily self-sacrifice, of which a nature like Madeleine von Wildenau's has no knowledge.

So she returned, somewhat changed—yet only so far as that her own ego, which the world did not know, was even more potential than before.

But she came alone! Where had she left her pallid Christ? All inquiries were futile. What could be said? There was no proof of anything—and besides; proven or not—what charge would have overthrown Countess Wildenau? That would have been an achievement for which even her foes lacked perseverance?

It is very amusing when a person's moral ruin can be effected by a word carelessly uttered! But when the labor of producing proof is associated with it, people grow good-natured from sheer indolence—let the victim go, and seek an easier prey.

This was the case with the Countess Wildenau! Her position remained as unshaken as ever, nay the charm of her person exerted an influence even more potent than before. Was it her long absence, or had she grown younger? No matter—she had gained a touch of womanly sweetness which rendered her irresistible.

In what secret mine of the human heart and feeling had she garnered the rays which glittered in her eyes like hidden treasures on which the light of day falls for the first time?

When a woman conceals in her heart a secret joy men flock around her, with instinctive jealousy, all the more closely, they would fain dispute the sweet right of possession with the invisible rival. This is a trait of human nature. But one of the number did so consciously, not from a jealous instinct but with the full, intense resolve of unswerving fidelity—the prince! With quiet caution, and the wise self-control peculiar to him, he steadily pursued his aim. Not with professions of love; he was only too well aware that love is no weapon against love! On the contrary, he chose a different way, that of cold reason.

"So long as she is aglow with love, she will be proof against any other feeling—she must first be cooled to the freezing-point, then the chilled bird can be clasped carefully to the breast and given new warmth."

It would be long ere that point was reached—but he knew how to wait!

Meanwhile he drew the Countess into a whirl of the most fascinating amusements.

No word, no look betrayed the still hopeful lover! With the manner of one who had relinquished all claims, but was too thoroughly a man of the world to avoid an interesting woman because he had failed to win her heart, he again sought her society after her return. Had he betrayed the slightest sign of emotion, he would have been repulsive in her present mood. But the perfect frankness and unconcern with which he played the "old friend" and nothing more, made his presence a comfort, nay even a necessity of life! So he became her inseparable companion—her shadow, and by the influence of his high position stifled every breath of slander, which floated from Ammergau to injure his beautiful friend.

During the first months after her return she had the whim —as she called it—of retiring from society and spending more time upon her estates. But the wise caution of the prince prevented it.

" For Heaven's sake, don't do that. Will you give free
play to the rumors about your Ammergau episode and the
pilgrimage to Jerusalem connected with it, by withdrawing
into solitude and thus leaving the field to your slanderers,
that they may disport at will in the deserted scenes of your
former splendor ?"

" This," he argued, " is the very time when you must take
your old position in society, or you will be—pardon my frankness—a fallen star."

The Countess evidently shrank from the thought.

" Or—have you some castle in the air whose delights outweigh the world in your eyes ?" he asked with relentless in-
sistence :

This time the Countess flushed to the fair curls which
clustered around her forehead.

Since that time the drawing-rooms of the Wildenau palace
had again been filled with the fragrance of roses—lighted, and
adorned with glowing Oriental magnificence, and the motley
tide of society, amid vivacious chatter, flooded the spacious
apartments. Glittering with diamonds, intoxicated by the
charm of her own beauty whose power she had not tested for
years, the Countess was the centre of all this splendor—while
in the lonely hunting-seat beyond the pathless Griess, the
solitary man whom she had banished thither vainly awaited
—his wife.

The leaves in the forest were turning brown for the sixth
time since their return from Jerusalem, the autumn gale was
sweeping fresh heaps of withered leaves to add to the piles
towering like walls around the deserted building, the height
was constantly growing colder and more dreary, the drawing-rooms below were continually growing warmer, the Palace
Wildenau, with its Persian hangings and rugs and cosy nooks
behind gay screens daily became more thronged with guests.
People drew their chairs nearer and nearer the blazing fire on
the hearth, which cast a rosy light upon pallid faces and made
weary eyes sparkle with a simulated glow of passion. The
intimate friends of the Countess Wildenau, reclining in comfortable armchairs, were gathered in a group, the gentlemen
resting after the fatigues of hunting—or the autumn manœu-
vres, the ladies after the first receptions and balls of the

season, which are the more exhausting before habit again asserts its sway, to say nothing of the question of toilettes, always so trying to the nerves at these early balls.

What is to be done at such times? It is certainly depressing to commence the season with last year's clothes, and one cannot get new ones because nobody knows what styles the winter will bring? Parisian novelties have not come. So one must wear an unassuming toilette of no special style in which one feels uncomfortable and casts aside afterwards, because one receives from Paris something entirely different from what was expected!

So the ladies chatted and Countess Wildenau entered eagerly into the discussion. She understood and sympathized with these woes, though now, as the ladies said, she really could not "chime in" since she had a store of valuable Oriental stuffs and embroideries, which would supply a store of "exclusive" toilettes for years. Only people of inferior position were compelled to follow the fashions—great ladies set them and the costliness of the material prevented the garments from appearing too fantastic. A Countess Wildenau could allow herself such bizarre costumes. She had a right to set the fashions and people would gladly follow her if they could, but two requirements were lacking, on one side the taste—on the other the purse. The Countess charmingly waived her friends' envious compliments; but her thoughts were not on the theme they were discussing; her eyes wandered to a crayon picture hanging beside the mantel-piece, the picture of a boy who had the marvellous beauty of one of Raphael's cherubs.

"What child is that?" asked one of the ladies who had followed her glance.

"Don't you recognize it?" replied the Countess with a dreamy smile. "It is the Christ in the picture of the Sistine Madonna."

"Why, how very strange—if you had a son one might have thought it was his portrait, it resembles you so much."

"Do you notice it?" the Countess answered. "Yes, that was the opinion of the artist who copied the picture; he gave it to me as a surprise." She rose and took another little picture from the wall. "Look, this is a portait of me when I was three years old—there really is some resemblance."

The ladies all assented, and the gentlemen, delighted to have an opportunity to interrupt the discussion of the fashions, came forward and noticed with astonishment the striking likeness between the girl and the boy.

"It is really the Christ child in the Sistine Madonna—very exquisitely painted!" said the prince.

"By the way, Cousin," cried a sharp, high voice, over Prince Emil's shoulder, a voice issuing from a pair of very thin lips shaded by a reddish moustache, "do you know that you have the very model of this picture on your own estates?"

The Countess, with a strangely abrupt, nervous movement, pushed the copy aside and hastily turned to replace her own portrait on the wall. The gentlemen tried to aid her, but she rejected all help, though she was not very skillful in her task, and consequently was compelled to keep her back turned to the group a long time.

"It is possible—I cannot remember," she replied, while still in this position. "I cannot know the children of all my tenants."

"Yes," the jarring voice persisted, "it is a boy who is roaming about near your little hunting-castle."

Madeleine von Wildenau grew ghastly pale.

"Apropos of that hunting box," the gentleman added— he was one of the disinherited Wildenaus—"you might let me have it, Cousin. I'll confess that I've recently been looking up the old rat's nest. Schlierheim will lease his preserves beyond the government forests, but only as far as your boundaries, and there is no house. My brother and I would hire them if we could have the old Wildenau hunting-box. We are ready to pay you the largest sum the thing is worth. You know it formerly belonged to our branch of the family, and your husband obtained it only forty years ago. At that time it was valueless to us, but now we should like to buy it again."

The Countess shivered and ordered more wood to be piled on the fire. She had unconsciously drawn nearer to Prince Emil, as if seeking his protection. Her shoulder touched his. She was startlingly pale.

"The recollection of her husband always affects her in this way," the prince remarked.

"Well, we will discuss the matter some other time, *belle cousine!*" said Herr Wildenau, sipping a glass of Chartreuse which the servant offered.

Prince Emil's watchful gaze followed the little scene with the closest attention.

"Did you not intend to have the little castle put in order for your father's residence, as the city air does not agree with him in his present condition?" he said, with marked emphasis.

"Yes, certainly—I—we were speaking of it a short time ago," stammered the Countess. Besides, I am fond of the little castle. I should not wish to sell it."

"Ah, you are *fond* of it. Pardon me—that is difficult to understand! I thought you set no value upon it—the whole place is so neglected."

"That is exactly what pleases me—I like to have it so," replied the Countess in an irritated tone. "It does not need to have everything in perfect order. It is a genuine forest idyl!"

"A forest idyl?" repeated the cousin. "H'm. Ah, yes! That's a different matter. Pardon me. Had I known it, I would not have alluded to the subject!" His keen gray eyes glittered with a peculiar light as he kissed her hand and took his leave.

The others thought they must now withdraw also, and the Countess detained no one—she was evidently very weary.

The prince also took leave—for the sake of etiquette—but he whispered, with an expression of friendly anxiety, "I will come back soon." And he kept his promise.

An hour had passed. Madeleine von Wildenau, her face still colorless, was reclining on a divan in a simple home costume.

Prince Emil's first glance sought the little table on which stood the crayon picture of the infant Christ—it had vanished.

The Countess followed his look and saw that he missed it—their eyes met. The prince took a chair and sat down by her side, as if she were an invalid who had just sustained a severe operation and required the utmost care. He himself was very pale. Gently arranging the pillows behind her, he gazed sympathizingly into her face.

"Why did you not tell me this before?" he murmured, almost inaudibly, after a pause. "All this should have been very differently managed!"

"Prince, how could I suppose that you were so generous —so noble"—she could not finish the sentence, her eyes fell, the beautiful woman's face crimsoned with shame.

He gazed earnestly at her, feeling at this moment the first great sorrow of his life, but also perceiving that he could not judge the exquisite creature who lay before him like a statue of the Magdalene carved by the most finished artist—because he could not help loving her in her sweet embarrassment more tenderly than ever.

"Madeleine," he said, softly, and his breath fanned her brow like a cooling breeze, "will you trust me? It will be easier for you."

She clasped his hand in her slender, transparent fingers, raising her eyes beseechingly to his with a look of the sweetest feminine weakness, like a young girl or an innocent child who is atoning for some trivial sin. "Let me keep my secret," she pleaded, with such touching embarrassment that it almost robbed the prince of his calmness.

"Very well," he said, controlling himself with difficulty. "I will ask no farther questions and will not strive to penetrate your secret. But if you ever need a friend—and I fear that may happen—pray commit no farther imprudences, and remember that, in me, you possess one who adds to a warm heart a sufficiently cool head to be able to act for you as this difficult situation requires! Farewell, *chère amie!* Secure a complete rest."

Without waiting for an answer, like the experienced physician, who merely prescribes for his patients without conversing with them about the matter, he disappeared.

The countess was ashamed—fairly oppressed by the generosity of his character. Would it have been better had she told him the truth?

Should she tell him that she was married? Married! Was she wedded? Could she be called a wife? She had played a farce with herself and Freyer, a farce in which, from her standpoint, she could not believe herself.

On their flight from Ammergau they had hastened to

Prankenberg, surprised the old pastor in his room, and with Josepha and a coachman who had grown gray in the service of the Wildenau family for witnesses, declared in the presence of the priest that they took each other for husband and wife.

The old gentleman, in his surprise and perplexity, knew not what course to pursue. The countess appealed to the rite of the Tridentine Council, according to which she and Freyer, after this declaration, were man and wife, even without a wedding ceremony or permission to marry in another diocese. Then the loyal pastor, who had grown gray in the service of the Prankenbergs, as well as of his church, could do nothing except acknowledge the fact, declare the marriage valid, and give them the marriage certificate.

So at the breakfast-table, over the priest's smoking coffee, the bond had been formed which the good pastor was afterwards to enter in the church register as a marriage. But even this outward proof of the marriage between the widowed Countess Wildenau and the Ammergau wood-carver Freyer was removed, for the countess had been right in distrusting her father and believing that his advice concerning the secret marriage was but a stratagem of war to deter her from taking any public step.

On returning from the priest's, her carriage dashed by Prince von Prankenberg's.

Ten minutes after the prince rushed like a tempest into the room of the peaceful old pastor, and succeeded in preventing the entry of the "scandal," as he called it, in the church register. So the proofs of the fact were limited to the marriage certificate in the husband's hands and the two witnesses, Josepha and Martin, the coachman—a chain, it is true, which bound Madeleine von Wildenau, yet which was always in her power.

What was this marriage? How would a man like the prince regard it? Would it not wear a totally different aspect in the eyes of the sceptic and experienced man of the world than in those of the simple-hearted peasant who believed that everything which glittered was gold? Was such a marriage, which permitted the exercise of none of the rights and duties which elevate it into a moral institution, better than an illegal relation? Nay, rather worse, for it perpetrated a robbery of God—it was an illegal relation which had stolen a sacred name!

But—what did this mean? To-day, for the first time, she felt as if fate might give the matter the moral importance which she did not willingly accord it—as if the Deity whose name she had abused might take her at her word and compel her to turn jest into earnest.

Her better nature frankly confessed that this would be only moral justice! To this great truth she bowed her head as the full ears bend before the approaching hail storm.

Spite of the chill autumn evening, there was an incomprehensible sultriness in the air of the room.

Something in the brief conversation with Herr Wildenau and especially in the manner in which the prince, with his keen penetration, understood the episode, startled the Countess and aroused her fears.

Why had Herr Wildenau gone to the little hunting-box? How had he seen the child?

Yet how could she herself have been so imprudent as to display the picture? And still—it was the infant Christ of Raphael. Could she not even have one of Raphael's heads in her drawing-room without danger that some one would discover a suspicious resemblance!

She sprang from the cushions indignantly, drawing herself up to her full height. Who was she? What did she dread?

"Anything but cowardice, Madeleine," she cried out to herself. "Woe betide you, if your resolution fails, you are lost! If you do not look the brute gossip steadily in the eye, if so much as an eye-lash quivers, it will rend you. Do not be cowardly, Madeleine, have no scruples, they will betray you, will make your glance timid, your bearing uncertain, send a flush to your brow at every chance word. But "—she sank back among her cushions—" but unfortunately this very day the misfortune has happened, all these people may go away and say that they saw the Countess Wildenau blush and grow confused—and why?—Because a child was mentioned—"

She shuddered and cowered—a moan of pain escaped her lips!

"Yet you exist, my child—I cannot put you out of the

world—and no mother ever had such a son. And I, instead of being permitted to be proud of you, must feel ashamed.

"Oh, God, thou gavest me every blessing: the man I loved, a beautiful child—all earthly power and splendor—yet no contentment, no happiness! What do I lack?" She sat a long time absorbed in gloomy thought, then suddenly the cause became clear. She lacked the moral balance of service and counter-service.

That was the reason all her happiness was but theft, and she was forced, like a thief, to enjoy it in fear and secrecy. Her maternal happiness was theft—for Josepha, the stranger, filled a mother's place to the boy, and when she herself pressed him to her heart she was stealing a love she had not earned. Her conjugal happiness was a theft, for so long as she retained her fortune, she was not permitted to marry! That was the curse! Wherever she looked, wherever she saw herself, she was always the recipient, the petitioner—and what did she bestow in return? Where did she make any sacrifice? Nothing—and nowhere! Egotism was apparent in everything. To enjoy all—possess all, even what was forbidden and sacrifice nothing, must finally render her a thief—in her own eyes, in those of God, and who knows, perhaps also in those of men, should her secret ever be discovered!

"Woe betide you, unhappy woman—have you not the strength to resign one for the other? Would you rather live in fear of the betrayer than voluntarily relinquish your stolen goods? Then do not think yourself noble or lofty—do not deem yourself worthy of the grace for which you long!"

She hid her face in the cushions of the divan, fairly quivering under the burden of her self-accusation.

"I beg your pardon, your Highness, I only wanted to ask what evening toilette you desired."

Madeleine von Wildenau started up. "If you would only cease this stealing about on tip-toe!" she angrily exclaimed. "I beg pardon, I knocked twice and thought I did not hear your 'come in.'"

"Walk so that you can be heard—I don't like to have my servants glide about like spies, remember that!"

"At Princess Hohenstein's we were all obliged to wear felt slippers. Her Highness could not endure any noise."

"Well I have better nerves than Princess Hohenstein."—

"And apparently a worse conscience," muttered the maid, who had not failed to notice her mistress' confusion.

"May I ask once more about the evening toilette?"

"Street costume—I shall not go to the theatre, I will drive out to the estates. Order Martin to have the carriage ready."

The maid withdrew.

The countess felt as if she were in a fever—must that inquisitive maid see her in such a condition? It seemed as though she was surrounded like a hunted animal, as though eyes were everywhere watching her.

There was something in the woman's look which had irritated her. Oh, God, had matters gone so far—must she fear the glance of her own maid?

Up and away to nature and her child, to her poor neglected husband on the cliff.

Her heart grew heavy at the thought that the time since she had last visited the deserted man could soon be counted by months.

Her *interest* in the simple-hearted son of nature was beginning to wane, she could not deny it. Woe betide her if *love* should also grow cold; if that should happen, then—she realized it with horror—she would have no excuse for the whole sensuous—supersensuous episode, which had perilled both her honor and her existence!

CHAPTER XIX.

AT THE CHILD'S BEDSIDE.

The stars were already twinkling above the Griess, here and there one looked as if impaled on a giant flagstaff, as they sparkled just above the tops of the lofty firs or the sharp pinnacles of the crags. Countless shooting stars glided hither and thither like loving glances seeking one another.

The night was breathing in long regular inhalations. Every five minutes her sleeping breath rustled the tree-tops.

Four horses drawing a small calash whose wheels were

covered with rubber glided across the Griess as noiselessly as a spectral equipage. The animals knew the way, and their fiery spirit urged them forward without the aid of shout or lash, though the mountain grew steeper and steeper till the black walls of the hunting seat at last became visible in the glimmering star-light.

Josepha was standing at the window of the little sitting-room upstairs :

"I think the countess is coming." At a table, by the lamp, bending over a book, sat "the *steward*."

He evidently had not heard the words, for he did not look up from the volume and it seemed as if the gloomy shadow above his eyes grew darker still.

"Joseph, the countess is coming!" cried Josepha in a louder tone.

"You are deceiving yourself again, as usual," he replied in the wonderful voice which gave special importance to the simplest words, as when a large, musical bell is rung for some trivial cause.

"No, this time it really is she," Josepha insisted.

"I don't believe it."

Josepha shook her head. "You must receive her."

"She is not coming on my account, it is only to see the child."

"Then *I* will go. Oh, Heaven, what a life!" sighed Josepha, going out upon the green moss-covered steps of the half ruined stone stairs where the carriage had just stopped.

"Is that you, Josepha?" asked the countess, in a disappointed tone, "where—where is Freyer?"

"He is within, your Highness, he would not believe that your Highness was really coming!"

The countess understood the bitter meaning of the words.

"I did not come to endure ill-temper!" she murmured. "Is the boy asleep?"

"Yes, we have taken him into the sitting-room, he is coughing again and his head is burning, so I wanted to have him in a warmer room."

"Isn't it warm here?"

"Since the funnel fell out, we cannot heat these rooms; Freyer tried to fit it in, but it smokes constantly. I wrote to your Highness last month asking what should be done. Freyer, too, reported a fortnight ago that the stove ought to be repaired, and the child moved to other apartments before the cold weather set in if Your Highness approved, but—we have had no answer. Now the little boy is ill—it is beginning to be very cold."

Madeleine von Waldenau bit her lips. Yes, it was true, the letters had been written—and in the whirl of society and visits she had forgotten them.

Now the child was ill—through her fault. She entered the sitting-room. Freyer stood waiting for her in a half defiant, half submissive attitude—half master, half servant.

The bearing was unlovely, like everything that comes from a false position. It displeased the countess and injured Freyer, though she had herself placed him in this situaion. It made him appear awkward and clownish.

When, with careless hand, we have damaged a work of art and perceive that instead of improving we have marred it, we do not blame ourselves, but the botched object, and the innocent object must suffer because we have spoiled our own pleasure in it. It is the same with the work of art of creation—a human being.

There are some natures which can never leave things undisturbed, but seek to gain a creative share in everything by attempts at shaping and when convinced that it would have been better had they left the work untouched, they see in the imperfect essay, not their own want of skill, but the inflexibility of the material, pronounce it not worth the labor bestowed—and cast it aside.

The countess had one of these natures, so unconsciously cruel in their artistic experiments, and her marred object was—Freyer.

Therefore his bearing did not, could not please her, and she allowed a glance of annoyance to rest upon him, which did not escape his notice. Passing him, she went to their son's bed.

There lay the "infant Christ," a boy six or seven years old with silken curls and massive brows, beneath whose shadow the closed eyes were concealed by dark-lashed lids. A single ray from the hanging lamp fell upon the forehead of the little

Raphael, and showed the soft brows knit as if with unconscious pain.

The child was not happy—or not well—or both. He
breathed heavily in his sleep, and there was a slight nervous
twitching about the delicately moulded nostrils.

" He has evidently lost flesh since I was last here!" said
the countess anxiously.

Freyer remained silent.

" What do you think ? " asked the mother.

" What can I think ? You have not seen the boy for so
long that you can judge whether he has altered far better than
I."

" Joseph ! " The beautiful woman drew herself up, and a
look of genuine sorrow rested upon the pale, irritated countenance of her husband. " Whenever I come, I find nothing
save bitterness and cutting words—open and secret reproaches.
This is too much. Not even to-day, when I find my child ill,
do you spare the mother's anxious heart. This is more than
I can endure, it is ignoble, unchivalrous."

" Pardon me," replied her husband in a low tone, " I could
not suppose that a mother who deserts her child for months
could possibly possess so tender a nature that she would instantly grow anxious over a slight illness or a change in his
appearance. I am a plain man, and cannot understand such
contradictions ! "

" Yes, from your standpoint you are right—in your eyes I
must seem a monster of heartlessness. I almost do in my
own. Yet, precisely because the reproach appears merited it
cuts me so deeply, that is why it would be generous and noble
to spare me! Oh! Freyer, what has become of the great
divine love which once forgave my every fault ? "

" It is where you have banished it, buried in the depths of
my heart, as I am buried among these lonely mountains,
silent and forgotten."

The countess, shaking her head, gazed earnestly at him.
" Joseph, you see that I am suffering. You must see that it
would be a solace to rest in your love, and you are ungenerous
enough to humble my bowed head still more."

" I have no wish to humble you. But we can be generous
only to those who need it. I see in the haughty Countess

Wildenau a person who can exercise generosity, but not require it."

"Because you do not look into the depths of my heart, tortured with agonies of unrest and self-accusation?" As she spoke tears sprang to her eyes, and she involuntarily thought of the faithful, shrewd friend at home whose delicate power of perception had that very day spared her the utterance of a single word, and at one glance perceived all the helplessness of her situation.

True, the *latter* was a man of the world whom the tinsel and glitter which surrounded her no longer had power to dazzle, and who was therefore aware how poor and wretched one can be in the midst of external magnificence.

The *former*—a man of humble birth, with the childish idea of the value of material things current among the common people, could not imagine that a person might be surrounded by splendor and luxury, play a brilliant part in society, and yet be unhappy and need consideration.

But, however, she might apologize for him, the very excuses lowered him still more in her eyes! Each of these conflicts seemed to widen the gulf between them instead of bridging it.

Such scenes, which always reminded her afresh of his lowly origin, did him more injury in her eyes than either of them suspected at the moment. They were not mere ebullitions of anger, which yielded to equally sudden reactions—they were not phases of passion, but the result of cool deliberation from the standpoint of the educated woman, which ended in hopeless disappointment.

The continual refrain: "You do not understand me!" with which the countess closed such discussions expressed the utter hopelessness of their mutual relations.

"You wonder that I come so rarely!" she said bitterly. "And yet it is you alone who are to blame—nay, you have even kept me from the bedside of my child."

"Indeed?" Freyer with difficulty suppressed his rising wrath. "This, too!"

"Yes, how can you expect me to come gladly, when I always encounter scenes like these? How often, when I could at last escape from the thousand demands of society,

15

and hurried hither with a soul thirsting for love, have you repulsed me with your perpetual reproaches which you make only because you have no idea of my relations and the claims of the fashionable world.   So, at last, when I longed to come here to my husband and my child, dread of the unpleasant scenes which shadow your image, held me back, and I preferred to conjure before me at home the Freyer whom I once loved and always should love, if you did not yourself destroy the noble image.   With *that* Freyer I have sweet intercourse by my lonely fireside—with *him* I obtain comfort and peace, if I avoid *this* Freyer with his petty sensitiveness, his constant readiness to take umbrage."   A mournful smile illumined her face as she approached him; "You see that when I think of the Freyer of whom I have just spoken—the Freyer of my imagination—my heart overflows and my eyes grow dim!   Do you no longer know that Freyer?   Can you not tell me where I shall find him again if I seek him very, *very* earnestly?"

Freyer opened his arms and pointed to his heart: "Here, here, you can find him, if you desire—come, my beloved, loved beyond all things earthly, come to the heart which is only sick and sensitive from longing for you."

In blissful forgetfulness she threw herself upon his breast, completely overwhelmed by another wave of the old illusion, losing herself entirely in his ardent embrace.

"Oh, my dear wife!" he murmured in her ear, "I know that I am irritable and unjust!   But you do not suspect the torment to which you condemn me.   Banished from your presence, far from my home, torn from my native soil, and not yet rooted in yours.   What life is this?   My untrained reason is not capable of creating a philosophy which could solve this mystery.   Why must these things be?   I am married, yet not married.   I am your husband, yet you are not my wife.   I have committed no crime, yet am a prisoner, am not a dishonored man—yet am a despised one who must conceal himself in order not to bring shame upon his wife!

"So the years passed and life flits by!   You come often, but—I might almost say only to make me taste once more the joys of the heaven from which I am banished.

"Ah, it is more cruel than all the tortures of hell, for the condemned souls are not occasionally transferred to Heaven only to be again thrust forth and suffer a thousandfold. Even the avenging God is not so pitiless."

The countess, overwhelmed by this heavy charge, let her head sink upon her husband's breast.

"See, my wife," he continued in a gentle, subdued tone, whose magic filled her heart with that mournful pleasure with which we listen to a beautiful dirge even beside the corpse of the object of our dearest love. "In your circles people probably have sufficient self-control to suppress a great sorrow. I know that I only weary and annoy you by my constant complaints, and that you will at last prefer to avoid me entirely rather than expose yourself to them!

"I know this—yet I cannot do otherwise. I was not trained to dissimulation—self-control, as you call it—I cannot laugh when my heart is bleeding or utter sweet words when my soul is full of bitterness. I do not understand what compulsion could prevent you, a free, rich woman, from coming to the husband whom you love, and I cannot believe that you could not come if you longed to do so—that is why I so often doubt your love.

"What should you love in me? I warned you that I cannot always move about with the crown of thorns and sceptre of reeds as Ecce Homo, and you now perceive that you were deceived in me, that I am only a poor, ordinary man, your inferior in education and intellect! And so long as I am not a real Ecce Homo—though that perhaps might happen—so long I am not what you need. But however poor and insignificant I may be—I am not without honor— and when I think that you only come occasionally, out of compassion, to bring the beggar the crumbs which your fine gentlemen have left me—then, I will speak frankly—then my pride rebels and I would rather starve than accept alms."

"And therefore you thrust back the loving wife when, with an overflowing heart, she stole away from the glittering circles of society to hasten to your side, therefore you were cold and stern, disdaining what the others *sought in vain!*— For, however distant you may be, there has not been an hour of my life which you might not have witnessed—however free and independent of you I may stand, there is not a fibre in my

heart which does not cling to you! Ah, if you could only
understand this deep, sacred tie which binds the freest spirit
to the husband, the father of my child. If I had wings to
soar over every land and sea—I should ever be drawn back
to you and would return as surely as 'the bird bound by
the silken cord.' No one can part me from you except *you
yourself.* That you are not my equal in education, as you
assert, does not sever us, but inferiority of *character* would
do so, for nothing but *greatness* attracts me—to find you base
would be the death-knell of our love! Even the child would
no longer be a bond between us, for to intellectual natures
like mine the ties of blood are mere animal instincts, unless
pervaded and transfigured by a loftier idea. The greatest
peril which threatens our love is that your narrow views prevent your attaining the standpoint from which a woman like
myself must be judged. I have great faults which need
great indulgence and a superiority which is not alarmed by
them. Unfortunately, my friend, you lack both. I have a
great love for you—but you measure it by the contracted
scales of your humdrum morality, and before this it vanishes
because its dimensions far transcend it.—Where, where, my
friend, is the grandeur, the freedom of the soul which I need ? "

" Alas, your words are but too true," said Freyer, releasing
her from his embrace. " Every word is a death sentence.
You ask a grandeur which I do not possess and shall never
obtain. I grew up in commonplace ideas, I have never seen
any other life than that in which the husband and wife belonged together, the father and mother reared, tended, and
watched their children together, and love in this close, tender
companionship reached its highest goal. This idea of quiet
domestic happiness embodied to me all the earthly bliss
allotted by God to Christian husbands and wives. Of a love
which is merely incidental, something in common with all the
other interests of life, and which when it comes in conflict
with them, must move aside and wait till it is permitted to
assert itself again, of such a love I had no conception—at
least, not in marriage ! True, we know that in the dawn of
love it is kept secret as something which must be hidden.
But this is a state of restless torture, which we strive to end as
soon as possible by a marriage. That such a condition of

affairs would be possible in marriage would never have entered my mind, and say what you will, a—marriage like ours is little better than an illegal relation."

The countess started—she had had the same thought that very day.

" And I "—Freyer inexorably continued—" am little more than your lover! If you choose to be faithful to me, I shall be grateful, but do not ask the ' grandeur ' as you call it, of my believing it. Whoever regards conjugal duties so lightly— whoever, like you, feels bound by no law ' which was only made for poor, ordinary people ' will keep faith only—so long as it is agreeable to do so."

The countess, gazing into vacancy, vainly strove to find a reply.

" This seems very narrow, very ridiculous from your lofty standpoint. You see I shall always be rustic. It is a misfortune for you that you came to me. Why did you not remain in your own aristocratic circle—gentlemen of noble birth would have understood you far better than a poor, plain man like me. I tell myself so daily—it is the worm which gnaws at my life. Now you have the ' greatness ' you desire, the only ' greatness ' I can offer—that of the perception of our misery."

Madeleine nodded hopelessly. " Yes, we are in an evil strait. I despair more and more of restoring peace between us—for it would be possible only in case I could succeed in making you comprehend the necessity of the present certainly unnatural form of our marriage. Yet you cannot and will not see that a woman like me cannot live in poverty, that wealth, though it does not render me happy, is nevertheless indispensable, not on account of the money, but because with it honor, power, and distinction would be lost. You know that this would follow an acknowledgement of our marriage, and I would die rather than resign them. I was born to a station too lofty to be content in an humble sphere. Do you expect the eagle to descend to a linnet's nest and dwell there? It would die, for it can breathe only in the regions for which it was created."

" But the eagle should never have stooped to the linnet," said Freyer, gloomily.

" I believed that I should find in you a consort, aspiring enough to follow me to my heights, for the wings of your genius rustled with mighty strokes above me when you hung upon the cross. Oh, can one who, like you, has reached the height of the cross, sink to the Philistine narrowness of the ideas of the lower classes and thrust aside the foaming elixir of love, because it is not proffered in the usual wooden bowl of the daily performance of commonplace duties? It is incredible, but true. And lastly you threaten that I shall make you an Ecce Homo! If you were, it would be no fault of mine but because, even in daily life, you could not cease to play the Christ."

The countess had spoken with cutting sharpness and bitterness; it seemed as if the knife she turned against the man she loved must be piercing her own heart.

Freyer's breath came heavily, but no sound betrayed the anguish of the wound he had received. But the child, as if feeling, even in its sleep, that its mother was about to sunder, with a fatal blow, the chord of life uniting her to the father and itself, quivered in pain and flung its little hands into the air, as though to protect the mysterious bond whose filaments ran through its heart also.

" See, the child feels our strife and suffers from it!" said Freyer, and the unutterable pain in the words swept away all hardness, all defiance. The mother, with tearful eyes, sank down beside the bed of the suffering child—languishing under the discord between her and its father like a tender blossom beneath the warfare of the elements. " My child!" she said in a choking voice, "how thin your little hands have grown! What does this mean?"

She pressed the boy's transparent little hands to her lips and when she looked up again two wonderful dark eyes were gazing at her from the child's pale face. Yes, those were the eyes of the infant Redeemer of the World in the picture of the Sistine Madonna, the eyes which mirror the foreboding of the misery of a world. It was the expression of Freyer's, but spiritualized, and as single sunbeams dance upon a dark flood, it seemed as if golden rays from his mother's sparkling orbs had leaped into his.

What a marvellous child! The mother's delicate beauty,

blended with the deep earnestness of the father, steeped in the loveliness and transfiguration of Raphael. And she could wound the father of this boy with cruel words? She could scorn the wonderful soul of Freyer, which gazed at her in mute reproach from the eyes of the child, because the woe of the Redeemer had impressed upon it indelible traces; disdain it beside the bed of this boy, this pledge of a love whose supernatural power transformed the man into a god, to rest for a moment in a divine embrace? "Mother!" murmured the boy softly, as if in a waking dream; but Madeleine von Wildenau felt with rapture that he meant *her*, not Josepha. Then he closed his eyes again and slept on.

Kneeling at the son's bedside, she held out her hand to the father; it seemed as if a trembling ray of light entered her soul, reflected from the moment when he had formerly approached her in all the radiance of his power and beauty.

"And *we* should not love each other?" she said, while burning tears flowed down her cheeks. Freyer drew her from the child's couch, clasping her in a close embrace. "My dove!" He could say no more, grief and love stifled his voice.

She threw her arms around his neck, as she had done when she made her penitent confession with such irresistible grace that he would have pardoned every mortal sin. "Forgive me, Joseph," she said softly, in order not to wake the boy who, even in sleep, turned his little head toward his parents, as a flower sways toward the sun. "I am a poor, weak woman; I myself suffer unutterably under the separation from you and the child; if you knew how I often feel—a rock would pity me! It is a miserable condition—nothing is mine, neither you, my son, nor my wealth, unless I sacrifice one for the other, and that I cannot resolve to do. Ah, have compassion on my weakness. It is woman's way to bear the most unendurable condition rather than form an energetic resolve which might change it. I know that the right course would be for me to find courage to renounce the world and say: ' I am married, I will resign, as my husband's will requires, the Wildenau fortune; I will retire from the stage as a beggar—I will starve and work for my daily bread.' I often think how beautiful and noble this would be, and that perhaps we might be happy so—

happier than we are now—if it were only *done !*   But when I
seriously face the thought, I feel that I cannot do it."

" Yet you told me in Ammergau,"cried Freyer, "that it was
only on your father's account that you could not acknowledge
the marriage.   Your father is now a paralytic, half-foolish old
man, who cannot live long, then this reason will be removed."

"Yes, when we married it *was* he who prevented me from
announcing it ; I wished to do so, and it would have been easy.
But if I state the fact now, after having been secretly married
eight years, during which I have illegally retained the property,
I shall stamp myself a cheat.   Take me to the summit of the
Kofel and bid me leap down its thousand feet of cliff—I cannot, were it to purchase my eternal salvation.   Hurl me down
—I care not—but do not expect me voluntarily to take the
plunge, it is impossible.   Unless God sends an angel to bear
me over the chasm on its wings, all pleading will be futile."

She pressed her cheek, burning with the fever of fear, tenderly against his : " Have pity on my weakness, forgive me !
Ah, I know I am always talking about greatness—yet with me
it exists only in the imagination.   I am too base to be capable of what is really noble."

" You see me now, as God Himself beholds me.   He will
judge me—but it is the privilege of marital love to forgive.
Will you not use this sweet right ?   Perhaps God will show me
some expedient.   Perhaps I shall succeed in making an agreement with the relatives or gaining the aid of the king, but for
all this I must live in the world—in order to secure influence
and scope for my plans.   Will you have patience and forbear-
ance with me till there is a change ? "

" That will never be, any more than during the past eight
years.   But I will bear with you, poor wife ; in spite of *everything* I will trust your love, I will try to repress my discontent
when you come and gratefully accept what you bestow, without remonstrance or fault-finding.   I will bear it as long as I
can.   Perhaps—it will wear me out, then we shall both be released.   I would have removed myself from the world long
ago—but that would be a sin, and would not have benefited
you.   Your heart is too kind not to be wounded and the
suicide's bloody shade would not have permitted you to enjoy
your liberty."

"Oh, Heaven, what are you saying! My poor husband, is that your condition?" cried the countess, deeply stirred by the tragedy of these calmly uttered words. She shuddered at this glimpse of the dark depths of his fathomless soul and what, in her opinion, he might lack in broadness of view was now supplied by the extent of his suffering; at this moment he again interested her. Throwing herself on his breast, she overwhelmed him with caresses. She sought to console him, make him forget the bitterness of his grief by the magic potion of her love. She herself did not know that even now—carried away by a genuine emotion of compassion—she was yielding to the demoniac charm of trying upon his pain the power of her coquetry, which she had long since tested sufficiently upon *human beings.* But where she would undoubtedly have succeeded with men of cultivation, she failed with this child of nature, who instinctively felt that this sweet display of tenderness was not meant for him but was called forth by the struggle against a hostile element which she desired to bribe or conquer. His grief remained unchanged; it was too deeply rooted to be dispelled by the love-raptures of a moment. Yet the poor husband, languishing for the wife so ardently beloved, took the poisoned draught she offered, as the thirsting traveller in the desert puts his burning lips to the tainted pool whence he knows he is drinking death.

CHAPTER XX.

CONFLICTS.

It was morning! The lamp had almost burned out! Josepha and the countess were busied with the boy, whose sleep was disturbed by a short, dry cough. The mother had remained at the little castle all night and rested only a few hours. When with the little one there were times when her maternal affection was roused. Then she was seized with dread lest God should recall a precious gift because she had not known its value. It would be only just, she was aware of that—and because of its justice it seemed probable, and her heart strove to make amends in a few hours for the neglect of

years. Perhaps thereby she might escape the punishment. But
when she had gone, the little pale star in her horizon receded
into the background before the motley phenomena of the
world in which she lived, and only in isolated moments did
she realize, by a dull pain, that feelings were slumbering within
her soul which could not be developed—like a treasure which
lies concealed in a spot whence it cannot be raised.   It was
akin to the parable of the servant who did not put out his talent at interest.   This talent which God entrusted to men is
love.   A lofty noble sentiment which we suppress is the buried
treasure which God will require of us, when the period for
which He loaned it has expired.   There were hours when the
unhappy woman realized this.   Then she accused everything—
the world and herself!   And the poor little child felt in his
precocious soul the grief of the "beautiful lady," in whom he
presciently loved his mother without knowing that it was she.
Ordinary children, like animals, love best those who provide
for their physical wants and therefore frequently cling more
fondly to the nurse than to the mother.   Not so this boy.   He
was almost ungrateful to Josepha, who nursed him the more
faithfully, the more he was neglected by the countess.

Josepha was passionately attached to the boy.   All the
sorrowful love which she had kept in her desolate heart for
her own dead son was transferred from the first hour to this
delicate, motherless creature.   It reminded her so much of her
own poor child : the marked family likeness between him and
Freyer —the mystery with which he must be surrounded.   A
mother who was ashamed of him, like Josepha at the time—it
seemed as though her own dead child had returned to life.
And besides she passed for his mother.

The boy was born while the countess was travelling in the
East, and it was an easy matter to arrange with the author-
ities.   The countess, while in Jerusalem, took the name of
Josepha Freyer—Josepha that of Countess Wildenau, and the
child was baptized under the name of Freyer.   It was entered
in the register as an illegitimate child, and Josepha bore the
disgrace, and returned to Germany as the boy's mother.

What was lacking to complete Josepha's illusion that the
child was hers, and that she might love it as a mother ?
Nothing, save the return of her affection.   And this was a

source of bitter pain. She might give and do what she would, devote her days and nights to him, sacrifice her already failing health—nothing availed. When after weeks and months of absence the "beautiful lady," as he called her, came, his melancholy eyes brightened and he seemed to glow with new life as he stretched out his little arms to her with a look that appeared to say: "Had you not come soon, I should have died!" Josepha no longer existed for him, and even his father, whom he usually loved tenderly as his god-father— " Goth," as the people in that locality call it—was forgotten. This vexed Josepha beyond endurance. She performed a mother's duties in all their weariness, her heart cherished a mother's love with all its griefs and cares and, when that other woman came, who deserved nothing, did nothing, had neither a mother's heart nor a mother's rights—she took the child away and Josepha had naught save the trouble and the shame! The former enjoyed hurriedly, lightly, carelessly, the joys which alone could have repaid Josepha's sacrifices, the child's sweet smiles, tender caresses, and coaxing ways, for which she would have given her life. She ground her sharp white teeth and a secret jealousy, bordering on hatred, took root in her embittered mind. What could she esteem in this woman? For what should she be grateful to her? She was kind to her —because she needed her services—but what did she care for Josepha herself! "She might give me less, but do her duty to her husband and child—that would suit me better," she secretly murmured. "To have such a child and not be a mother to him, not give him the sunshine, the warmth of maternal love which he needs—and then come and take away from another what she would not earn for herself."

To have such a husband, the highest blessing Josepha knew on earth—a man to whom the whole world paid homage as if to God, a man so devout, so good, so modest, so faithful —and desert him, conceal him in a ruinous old castle that no one might note the disgrace of the noble lady who had married a poor wood-carver! And then to come and snatch the kisses from his lips as birds steal berries, when no one was looking, he was good enough for that! And he permitted it —the proud, stern man, whom the whole community feared and honored. It was enough to drive one mad.

And she, Josepha, must swallow her wrath year after year
—and dared not say anything—for woe betide her if she com-
plained of the countess! He would allow no attack upon her
—though this state of affairs was killing him. She was forced
to witness how he grieved for this woman, see him gradually
lose flesh and strength, for the wicked creature bewitched
every one, and charmed her husband and child till they were
fairly dying of love for her, while she was carrying on her
shameless flirtations with others.

Such were the terrible accusations raging in Josepha's
passionate soul against the countess, charges which effaced the
memory of all she owed her former benefactress.

"I should like to know what she would do without me"
was the constant argument of her ungrateful hatred. "She
may well be kind to me—if I chose, her wicked pranks
would soon be over. She would deserve it—and what do I
care for the pay? I can look after myself, I don't need the
ill-gotten gains. But—then I should be obliged to leave the
boy—he would have no one. No, no, Josepha, hold out as
long as possible—and be silent for the child's sake."

Such were the conflicts seething in the breast of the silent
dweller in the hunting-castle, such the gulfs yawning at the
unsuspicious woman's feet.

It was the vengeance of insulted popular morality, to
which she imagined herself so far superior. This insignificant
impulse in the progress of the development of mankind, insignificant because it was the special attribute of the humble
plain people, will always conquer in the strife against the
emancipation of so-called "more highly organized" natures,
for it is the destiny of individual giants always to succumb in
the war against ordinary mortals. Here there is a great,
eternal law of the universe, which from the beginning gathered
its contingent from the humble, insignificant elements, and in
so-called "plebian morality" is rooted—Christianity. Therefore, the former will conquer and always assert its right, even
where the little Philistine army, which gathers around its standard, defeats a far nobler foe than itself, a foe for whom the
gods themselves would mourn! Woe betide the highly gifted
individuality which unites with Philistine elements—gives them
rights over it, and believes it can still pursue its own way—in

any given case it will find pity before *God*, sooner than before the judgment seat of this literal service, and the spears and shafts of its yeomanry.

Something like one of these lance-thrusts pierced the countess from Josepha's eyes, as she bent over the waking child.

Josepha tried to take the boy, but he struggled violently and would not go to her. With sparkling, longing eyes he nestled in the arms of the " beautiful lady." The countess drew the frail little figure close to her heart. As she did so, she noticed the stern, resentful expression of Josepha's dry cracked lips and the hectic flush on the somewhat prominent cheek bones. There was something in the girl's manner which displeased her mistress. Had it been in her power, she would have dismissed this person, who " was constantly altering for the worse." But she was bound to her by indissoluble fetters, nay, was dependent upon her—and must fear her. She felt this whenever she came. Under such impressions, every visit to the castle had gradually become a penance, instead of a pleasure   Her husband, out of humor and full of reproaches, the child ill, the nurse sullen and gloomy. A spoiled child of the world, who had always had everything disagreeable removed from her path, could not fail at last to avoid a place where she could not breathe freely a single hour.

" Will you not get the child's breakfast, Josepha ?" she said wearily, the dark circles around her eyes bearing traces of her night vigil.

" He must be bathed first !" said Josepha, in the tone which often wounded the countess—the tone by which nurses, to whose charge children are left too much, instruct young mothers that, " if they take no care of their little ones elsewhere, they have nothing to say in the nursery."

The countess, with aristocratic self-control, struggled to maintain her composure. Then she said quietly, though her voice sounded faint and hoarse : " The child seems weak, I think it will be better to give him something to eat before washing him."

" Yes," pleaded the little fellow, " I am thirsty." The words reminded the countess of his father, as he said on the cross : " I thirst." When these memories came, all the an-

guish of her once beautiful love—now perishing so miserably
—overwhelmed her. She lifted the boy—he was light as a
vapor, a visoin of mist—from the bed into her lap, and
wrapped his little bare feet in the folds of her morning dress.
He pressed his little head, crowned with dark, curling locks,
against her cheek. Such moments were sweet, but out·
weighed by too much bitterness.

"Bring him some milk—fresh milk!" Madeleine von
Wildenau repeated in the slightly imperious tone which seems
to consider opposition impossible.

"That will be entirely different from his usual custom,"
remarked Josepha, as if the countess' order had seriously in-
terfered with the regular mode of life necessary to the child.

The mother perceived this, and a faint flush of shame and
indignation suffused her face, but instantly vanished, as if
grief had consumed the wave of blood which wrath had stirred.

"Is your mother—Josepha—kind to you?" she asked,
when Josepha had left the room.

The boy nodded carelessly.

"She does not strike you, she is gentle?"

"No, she doesn't strike me," the little fellow answered.
"She loves me."

"Do you love her, too?" the countess went on.

"Wh—y—Yes!" said the child, shrugging his shoulders.
Then he looked tenderly into her face. "I love you better."

"That is not right, Josepha is your mother—you must love
her best."

The boy shook his head thoughtfully. "But I would
rather have you for my mamma."

"That cannot be—unfortunately—I must not."

The child gazed at her with an expression of sorrowful
disappointment. At last he found an expedient. "But in
Heaven—when I go to Heaven—*you* will be my mother
there, won't you?"

The countess shuddered—an indescribable pain pierced
her heart, yet she was happy, a blissful anguish! Tears
streamed from her eyes and, clasping the child tenderly, she
gently kissed him.

"Yes, my child! In Heaven—perhaps I may be your
mother!"

Josepha now brought in the milk and wanted to give it to him, but the boy would not take it from her, he insisted that the countess must hold the bowl. She did so, but her hand trembled and Josepha was obliged to help her, or the whole contents would have been spilled. She averted her face.

"She cannot even give her child anything to drink," thought Josepha, as she moved about the room, putting it in order.

"Josepha, please leave me alone a little while," said the countess, almost beseechingly.

"Indeed ? " Josepha's cheeks flushed scarlet, it seemed as if the bones grew still more prominent. "If I am in your Highness' way—I can go at once."

"Josepha!" said the countess, now suddenly turning toward her a face wet with tears. "Surely I might be allowed to spend fifteen minutes alone with my child without offending any one! I will forgive your words—on account of your natural jealousy—and I think you already regret them, do you not? "

"Yes," replied Josepha, somewhat reluctantly, but so conquered by the unhappy mother's words that she pressed a hard half reluctant kiss upon the countess' hand with her rough, parched lips. Then, with a passionate glance at the child, she gave place to the mother whose claim she would fain have disputed before God Himself, if she could.

But when the door had closed behind her, the countess could bear no more. Placing the child in his little bed, she flung herself sobbing beside it. "My child—my child, forgive me," she cried, forgetting all prudence "—pray for me to God."

Just at that moment the door opened and Freyer entered. All that was stirring the mother's heart instantly became clear to him, as he saw her thus broken down beside the boy's bed.

"Calm yourself—what will the child think ! " he said, bending down and raising her.

"Don't cry, Mamma ! " said the boy, stroking the soft hair on the grief-bowed head. He did not know why he now suddenly called her " mamma "—perhaps it was a prospect of the heaven where she would be his mother, and he said it in advance.

"Oh, Freyer, kill me—I am worthy of nothing better—cut

short the battle of a wasted life! An animal which cannot
recover is killed out of pity, why not a human being, who feels
suffering doubly?"

"Magdalena—Countess—I do not know you in this
mood."

"Nor do I know myself! What am I? What is a
mother who is no mother—a wife who cannot declare herself
a wife? A fish that cannot swim, a bird that cannot fly!
We kill such poor crippled creatures out of sheer compassion.
What kind of existence is mine? An egotist who nevertheless
feels the pain of those whom she renders unhappy; an aristocrat who cannot exist outside of her own sphere and yet
pines for the eternal verity of human nature; a coquette who
trifles with hearts and yet would *die* for a genuine feeling—
these are my traits of character! Can there be anything more
contradictory, more full of wretchedness?"

"Let us go out of doors, Countess, such conversation is
not fit for the child to hear."

"Oh, he does not understand it."

"He understands more than you believe, you do not know
what questions he often asks—ah, you deprive yourself of the
noblest joys by being unable to watch the remarkable development of this child."

She nodded silently, absorbed in gazing at the boy.

"Come, Countess, the sun has risen—the cool morning
air will do you good, I will ring for Josepha to take the boy,"
he said quietly, touching the bell.

The little fellow sat up in bed, his breathing was hurried
and anxious, his large eyes were fixed imploringly on the
countess: "Oh, mamma—dear mamma in Heaven—stay—
don't go away."

"Ah, if only I could—my child—how gladly I would stay
here always. But I will come back again presently, I will
only walk in the sunshine for half-an-hour."

"Oh, I would like to go in the sunshine, too. Can't I go
with you, and run about a little while?"

"Not to-day, not until your cough is cured, my poor little
boy! But I'll promise to talk and think of nothing but you
until I return! Meanwhile Josepha shall wash and dress you,
I don't understand that—Josepha can do it better."

"Oh! yes, I'm good enough for that!" thought the girl, who heard the last words just as she entered.

"My beautiful mamma has been crying, because she is a bird and can't fly—" said the child to Josepha with sorrowful sympathy. "But you can't fly either—nor I till we are angels —then we can!" He spread out his little arms like wings as if he longed to soar upward and away, but an attack of coughing made him sink back upon his pillows.

The husband and wife looked at each other with the same sorrowful anxiety.

The countess bent over the little bed as if she would fain stifle with kisses the cough that racked the little chest.

"Mamma, it doesn't hurt—you must not cry," said the boy, consolingly. "There is a spider inside of my breast which tickles me—so I have to cough. But it will spin a big, big net of silver threads like those on the Christmas tree which will reach to Heaven, then I'll climb up on it!"

The countess could scarcely control her emotion. Freyer drew her hand through his arm and led her out into the dewy morning.

"You are so anxious about our secret and yet, if *I* were not conscientious enough to help you guard it, you would betray yourself every moment, you are imprudent with the child, it is not for my own interest, but yours that I warn you. Do not allow your newly awakened maternal love to destroy your self-control in the boy's presence. Do not let him call you 'Mamma.' Poor mother—indeed I understand how this wounds you—but—it must be one thing or the other. If you cannot—or *will* not be a mother to the child—you *must* renounce this name."

She bowed her head. "You are as cruel as ever, though you are right! How can I maintain my self-control, when I hear such words from the child? What a child he is! Whenever I come, I marvel at his intellectual progress! If only it is natural, if only it is not the omen of an early death!"

Freyer pitied her anxiety.

"It is merely because the child is reared in solitude, associating solely with two sorrowing people, Josepha and myself; it is natural that his young soul should develop into a graver

16

and more thoughtful character than other children," he said, consolingly.

They had gone out upon a dilapidated balcony, overgrown with vines and bushes. It was a beautiful morning, but the surrounding woods and the mouldering autumn leaves were white with hoar frost. Freyer wrapped the shivering woman in a cloak which he had taken with him. Under the cold breath of the bright fall morning, and her husband's cheering words, she gradually grew calm and regained her composure.

"But something must be done with the child," she said earnestly. "Matters cannot go on so, he looks too ethereal. — I will send him to Italy with Josepha."

"Good Heavens, then I shall be entirely alone!" said Freyer, with difficulty suppressing his dismay.

"Yet it must be," replied the countess firmly.

"How shall I endure it? The child was my all, my good angel—my light in darkness! Often his little hands have cooled my brow when the flames of madness were circling around it. Often his eyes, his features have again revealed your image clearly when, during a long separation, it had become blurred and distorted. While gazing at the child, the dear, beautiful child, I felt that nothing could sever this sacred bond. The mother of this boy could not desert her husband —for the sake of this child she must love me! I said to myself, and learned to trust, to hope, once more. And now I am to part from him. Oh, God!—Thy judgment is severe. Thou didst send an angel to comfort Thy divine son on the Mount of Olives—Thou dost take him from me! Yet not my will, but Thine, be done!"

He bent his head sadly: "If it must be, take him."

"The child is ill, I have kept him shut up in these damp rooms too long, he needs sunshine and milder air. If he were obliged to spend another winter in this cold climate, it would be his death. But if it is so hard for you to be separated from the boy—go with him. I will hire a villa for you and Josepha somewhere on the Riviera. It will do you good, too, to leave this nook hidden among the woods—and I cannot shelter you here in Bavaria where every one knows you, without betraying our relation."

Freyer gazed at her with a mournful smile: "And you

think—that I would go?" He shook his head. " No, I cannot make it so easy for you. We are still husband and wife,
I am still yours, as you are mine. And though you so rarely
come to me—if during the whole winter there was but a single
hour when you needed a heart, you must find your husband's,
I must be here!" He drew her gently to his breast. " No,
my wife, it would have been a comfort, if I could have kept
the child—but if you must take him from me, I will bear this,
too, like everything which comes from your hand, be it life or
death—nothing shall part me from you, not even love for my
boy."

There was something indescribable in the expression with
which he gazed at her as he uttered the simple words, and she
clung to him overwhelmed by such unexampled fidelity, which
thus sacrificed the only, the last blessing he possessed for a
single hour with her.

" My husband—my kind, noble husband! The most
generous heart in all the world!" she cried, caressing him
again and again as she gazed rapturously at the beautiful face,
so full of dignity: " You shall not make the sacrifice for a
single hour, your wife will come and reward your loyalty with
a thousand-fold greater love. Often—often. Perhaps oftener
than ever! For I feel that the present condition of affairs
cannot last. I must be permitted to be wife and mother—I
realized to-day at the bedside of my child that my *guilt*, too,
was growing year by year. It is time for me to atone. When
I return home I will seriously consider what can be done to
make an arrangement with my relatives! I need not confess
that I am already married—I could say that I might marry if
they would pay me a sufficient sum, but I would *not* do so, if
they refused me the means to live in a style which befitted my
rank. Then they will probably prefer to make a sacrifice
which would enable me to marry, thereby giving them the
whole property, rather than to compel me, by their avarice, to
remain a widow and keep the entire fortune." That would be
a capital idea! Do you see how inventive love is?" she said
with charming coquetry, expecting his joyful assent.

But he turned away with clouded brow—it seemed as
though an icy wind had suddenly swept over the whole sunny
landscape, transforming everything into a wintry aspect.

" Falsehood and deception everywhere—even in the most sacred things. When I hear you speak so, my heart shrinks! So noble a woman as you to stoop to falsehood and deceit, like one of the basest !"

The countess stood motionless, with downcast lids, shame and pride were both visible on her brow. Her heart, too, shrank, and an icy chill encompassed it.

" And what better proposal would you make ?"

" None!" said Freyer in a low tone, " for the only one I could suggest you would not accept. It would be to atone for the wrong you have committed, frankly confess how everything happened, and then retire with your husband and child into solitude and live plainly, but honestly. The world would laugh at you, it is true, but the noble-hearted would honor you. I cannot imagine that any moral happiness is to be purchased by falsehood and deceit—there is but one way which leads to God—the way of truth—every other is delusive !"

The beautiful woman gazed at him in involuntary admiration. This was the inward majesty by which the lowly man had formerly so awed her; and deeply as he shamed and wounded her, she bowed to this grandeur. Yet she could no longer bear his gaze, she felt humbled before him, her pleasure in his companionship was destroyed. She stood before the man whom she believed so far beneath her, like a common criminal, convicted of the most petty falsehood, the basest treachery. She fairly loathed herself. Where was there anything to efface this brand ? Where was the pride which could raise her above this disgrace ? In her consciousness of rank ? Woe betide her, what would her peers say if they knew her position ? Would she not be cast out from every circle ? What was there which would again restore her honor ? She knew no dignity, no honor save those which the world bestows, and to save them, at any cost and by any means—she sank still lower in her own eyes and those of the poor, but honorable man who had more cause to be ashamed of her than she of him.

She must return home, she must again see her palace, her servants, her world, in order to believe that she was still herself, that the ground was still firm under her feet, for everything in and around her was wavering.

" Please order the horses to be harnessed !" she said, turning toward the half ruined door through which they had come out of the house.

It had indeed grown dull and cold. A pallid autumnal fog was shrouding the forest. It looked doubtful whether it was going to rain or snow.

" I have the open carriage—I should like to get home before it rains," she said, apologetically, without looking at him.

Freyer courteously opened the heavy ancient iron door. They walked silently along a dark, cold, narrow passage to the door of the boy's room.

" I will go and have the horses harnessed," said Freyer, and the countess entered the chamber.

She took an absent leave of the child. She did not notice how he trembled at the news that she was going home, she did not hear him plead : " Take me with you !" She comforted him as usual with the promise that she would soon come again, and beckoned Josepha out of the room. The boy gazed after her with the expression of a dying roe, and a few large tears rolled down his pale cheeks. The mother saw it, but she could not remain, her stay here was over for that day. Outside she informed Josepha of the plan of sending her and the child to Italy, but the latter shook her head.

"The child needs nothing but its mother," she said, pitilessly, " it longs only for *you*, and if you send it still farther away, it will die."

The countess stood as if sentenced.

" When you are with him, he revives, and when you have gone, he droops like a flower without the sun !"

"Oh Heaven !" moaned the countess, pressing her clasped hands to her brow : " What is to be done !"

" If you could take the boy, it would be the best cure. The child need's a mother's love ; that would be more beneficial to him than all the travelling in the world. You have no idea how he clings to his mother. It really seems as if you had bewitched him. All day long he wears himself out listening and watching for the roll of the carriage, and when evening comes and the hour that you usually drive up arrives, his little hands are burning with fever from expectation. And then he sees how his father longs for you. A child like him notices everything and, when his father is sad, he is sorrowful, too. 'She is not coming to-day!' he said a short time ago, stroking his father's cheek; he knew perfectly well what troubled him. A delicate little body like his is soon worn out by constant yearning. Every kid, every fawn, cries for its mother. Here in the woods I often hear the young deer, whose mother has been shot, wail and cry all night long, and must not a child who has sense and affection long for its mother? You sit in your beautiful rooms at home and don't hear how up here in this dreary house with us two melancholy people, the poor child asks for the mother who is his all."

"Josepha, you will kill me!"

The countess clung to the door-post for support, her brain fairly whirled.

"No, I shall not kill you, Countess, I only want to prevent your killing the child," said Josepha with flaming eyes. "Do you suppose that, if I could supply a mother's place to the boy, I would beg you for what is every child's right, and which every mother who has a mother's heart in her breast would give of her own accord? Certainly not. I would *steal* the child's heart, which you are starving—ere I would give you one kind word, and you might beg in vain for your son's love, as I now beseech his mother's for him. But the poor little fellow knows very well who his mother is, and no matter what I do—he will not accept me! That is why I tell you just how matters are. Do what you choose with me —I no longer fear anything—if the child cannot be saved I am done with the world! You know me—and know that I set no value on life. You have made it no dearer to me than it was when we first met."

Just at that moment the door opened and a small white figure appeared. The boy had heard Josepha's passionate tone and came to his mother's assistance: " Mamma, my dear mamma in Heaven, what is she doing to you? She shan't hurt you. Wicked mamma Josepha, that's why I don't like you, you are always scolding the beautiful, kind lady."

He threw his little arm around his mother's neck, as if to protect her.

"Oh, you angel!" cried the countess, lifting him in her arms to press him to her heart.

The rattle of wheels was heard outside—the countess' four horses were coming. To keep the fiery animals waiting was impossible. Freyer hastily announced the carriage, the horses were very unruly that day. The countess gave the boy to Josepha's care. Freyer silently helped her into the equipage, everything passed like a flash of lightning for the horses were already starting—one gloomy glance was exchanged between the husband and wife—the farewell of strangers—and away dashed the light vehicle through the autumn mists. The mother fancied she heard her boy weeping as she drove off, and felt as if Josepha had convicted her of the murder of the child. But she would atone for it—some day—soon! It seemed as if a voice within was crying aloud: "My child, my child!" An icy moisture stood in drops upon her brow; was it the sweat of anxiety, or dew? She did not know, she could no longer think, she was sinking under all the anxieties which had pressed upon her that day. She closed her eyes and leaned back in the carriage as if fainting, while the horses rushed swiftly on with their light burden toward their goal.

The hours flew past. The equipage drove up to the Wildenau palace, but she was scarcely conscious of it. All sorts of plans and resolutions were whirling through her brain. She was assisted from the carriage and ascended the carpeted marble stairs. Two letters were lying on the table in her boudoir. The prince had been there and left one, a note, which contained only the words: "You will perceive that at the present time you *dare* not refuse this position.

"*The friend who means most kindly.*"

The other letter, in a large envelope, was an official document. Countess Wildenau had been appointed mistress of ceremonies!

CHAPTER XXI.

UNACCOUNTABLE.

A MOMENT—and a turning point in a life!

The countess was "herself" again, as she called it. "Thank God!"

The Ammergau episode—with all its tragic consequences

—belonged to the past.   To-day, under the emotional impressions and external circumstances at that luckless castle, where everything conspired against her, she had thought seriously of breaking with her traditions and the necessities of life, faced the thought of poverty and shame so boldly that this appointment to the highest position at court saved her from the gulf of ruin.   Stopped at the last moment, tottering, giddy, the startled woman sought to find a firm footing once more.   She felt like a suicide, who is not really in earnest, and rejoices when some one prevents his design.

She stood holding the document in her hand.   This was truth, reality, the necessity for self-destruction was imagination. The disgrace whose brand she already felt upon her brow could no longer approach her !

She set her foot upon the shaggy skin of a lion—the earth did not yet reel beneath her.   She pressed her burning brow against a slender marble column—this, too, was still firm! She passed her slender fingers over the silk plush of the divan on which she reclined and rejoiced that it was still hers.   Her eye, intoxicated with beauty, wandered over the hundreds of art-treasures, pictures and statues from every land with which she had adorned her rooms—nothing was lacking.   Upon a pedestal   stood the Apollo Belvedere, whose pure marble glowed warmly in a sunbeam shining through red curtains, as if real blood were circulating in the stone.   The wondrous face smiled in divine repose upon the motley array, which the art and industry of centuries had garnered here.

The past and the present here closed their bewitching chain.   Yonder stood a Venus de Milo, revealing to the charming owner the majesty of her own beauty.   In a corner filled with flowers, a bathing nymph, by a modern master, timidly concealed herself.   In a Gothic niche a dying Christ closed his eyes to the splendor of the world and the senses. It was a Christ after the manner of Gabriel Max, which opened and shut its eyes.   Not far away the portrait of the countess, painted with the genius of Lenbach stood forth from the dark frame—the type of a drawing-room blossom.   Clad in a soft white robe of Oriental stuff embroidered with gold, heavy enough to cling closely to the figure—light enough to float away so far as to reveal all that fashion and propriety permit-

ted to be seen of the beauty of a wonderful neck and arm.
And, as Lenbach paints not only the outward form but the
inward nature, a tinge of melancholy, of yearning and thought-
fulness rested upon the fair face, which made the beholder almost forget the beauty of the form in that of the soul, while
gazing into the spiritual eyes which seemed to seek some other
home than this prosaic earth. Just in the direction of her
glance, Hermes, the messenger of death, bent his divine face
from a group of palms and dried grasses. It seemed as if she
beheld all these things for the first time—as if they had been
newly given back to her that day after she had believed them
lost. Her breath almost failed at the thought that she had
been on the point of resigning it all—and for what? All these
treasures of immortal beauty and art—for a weeping child and
a surly man, who loved in her only the housewife, which any
maid-servant can be, but understood what she really was,
what really constituted her dignity and charm no more than
he would comprehend Lenbach's picture, which reflected to
her her own person transfigured and ennobled. She gazed at
herself with proud satisfaction. Should such a woman sacrifice
herself to a man who scarcely knew the meaning of beauty !
Destroy herself for an illusion of the imagination ? She rang
the bell—she felt the necessity of ordering something, to be
sure that she was still mistress of the house.

The lackey entered. "Your Highness ? "

Thank Heaven ! Her servants still obeyed her.

"Send over to the Barnheim Palace, and invite the Prince
to dine with me at six. Then serve lunch."

"Very well. Has Your Highness any other orders ? "

"The maid."

"Yes, Your Highesss."

The man left the room with the noiseless, solemn step of
a well-trained lackey.

"How can any one live without servants ? " the countess
asked herself, looking after him. "What should I have done,
if I had dismissed mine ? " She shuddered. Now that regal
luxury again surrounded her she was a different person from this
morning. No doubt she still felt what she had suffered that
day, but only as we dimly, after waking from a fevered dream,
realize the tortures we have endured.

Some one knocked, and the maid entered.

" I will take a bath before lunch. I feel very ill. Pour a bottle of *vinaigre de Bouilli* into the water. I will come directly."

The maid disappeared.

Everything still went on like clock-work. Nothing had changed—no one noticed what she had *almost* done that day. The struggle was over. The royal order, which it would have been madness to oppose, had determined her course.

But her nerves were still quivering from the experiences of the day.

The child, if only she were not hampered by the child ! That was the only thing which would not allow her to breathe freely—it was her own flesh and blood. That was the wound in her heart which could never be healed. She would always long for the boy—as he would for her. Yet, what did this avail, nothing could be changed, she must do what reason and necessity required. At least for the present; nay, there was even something beautiful in a sorrow borne with aristocratic dignity ! By the depth of the wound, we proudly measure the depth of our own hearts.

She pleased herself with the idea of doing the honors as mistress of ceremonies to kings and emperors, while yearning in the depths of her soul for a poor orphaned child, the son of the proud Countess Wildenau—whose husband was a peasant. Only a nature of the elasticity of Madeleine von Wildenau's could sink so low and yet soar so high, without losing its equilibrium.

These were the oscillations which Ludwig Gross once said were necessary to such natures—though their radii passed through the lowest gulfs of human misery to the opposite heights. Coquetry is not only cruel to others, but to itself—in the physical tortures which it endures for the sake of an uncomfortable fashion, and the spiritual ones with which it pays for its triumphs.

This was the case with the countess. During her first unhappy marriage she had learned to control the most despairing moods and be " amusing " with an aching heart. What marvel that she deemed it a matter of course that she must subdue the gnawing grief of her maternal love. So she coquetted even with suffering and found pleasure in bearing it gracefully.

She sat down at her writing-desk, crowned with Canova's group of Cupid and Psyche, and wrote:

"MY DEAR HUSBAND! In my haste I can only inform you that I shall be unable to come out immediately to arrange Josepha's journey. I have been appointed mistress of ceremonies to the queen and must obey the summons. Meanwhile, let Josepha prepare for the trip, I will send the directions for the journey and the money to-day. Give the boy my love, kiss him for me, and comfort him with the promise that I will visit him in the Riviera when I can. Amid the new scenes he will soon forget me and cease waiting and expecting. The Southern climate will benefit his health, and we shall have all the more pleasure in him afterward. He must remain there at least a year to regain his strength.

"I write hastily, for many business matters and ceremonies must be settled within the next few days. It is hard for me to accept this position, which binds me still more closely in the fetters I was on the eve of stripping off! But to make the king and queen my enemies at the very moment when I need powerful friends more than ever, would be defying fate! It will scarcely be possible for me now to come out as often as I promised you to-day. But, if you become too lonely, you can occasionally come in as my "steward," ostensibly to bring me reports—in this way we shall see each other and I will give orders that the steward shall be admitted to me at any time, and have a suitable office and apartments assigned to him 'as I shall now be unable to look after the estates so much myself.'

"If I cannot receive you at once, you will wait in your room until your wife, freed from the restraint and duties of the day, will fly to your arms.

"Is not this admirably arranged? Are you at last satisfied, you discontented man?

"You see that I am doing all that is possible! Only do not be angry with me because I also do what reason demands. I must secure to my child the solid foundations of a safe and well-ordered existence, since we must not, for the sake of sentiment, aimlessly shatter our own destiny. How would it

benefit the sick child if I denounced myself and was compelled to give up the whole of my private fortune to compensate my first husband's relatives for what I have spent
illegally since my second marriage? I could not even do
anything more for my son's health, and should be forced to
see him pine away in some mountain hamlet—perhaps Ammergau itself, whither I should wander with my household
goods and you, like some vagrant's family. The boys there
would stone him and call him in mockery, the 'little Count.'
The snow-storms would lash him and completely destroy his
delicate lungs.

"No, if I did not fear poverty for *myself*, I must do so for
you. How would you endure to have the Ammergau people—
and where else could you find employment—point their fingers
at you and say: 'Look, that is Freyer, who ran away with a
countess! He did a fine thing'—and then laugh jeeringly.

"My Joseph! Keep your love for me, and let me have
judgment for you, then all will be well. In love,

YOUR M."

She did not suspect, when she ended her letter, very well
satisfied with her dialectics, that Freyer after reading it would
throw the torn fragments on the floor.

This cold, frivolous letter—this change from the mood of
yesterday—this act after all her promises! He had again
been deceived and disappointed, again hoped and believed in
vain. All, all on which he had relied was destroyed, the
moral elevation of his beloved wife, which would at last restore
to her husband and child their sacred rights—was a lie, and
instead, by way of compensation, came the offer—of the position of a lover.

He was to seek his wife under the cover of the darkness,
as a man seeks his inamorata—he, her husband, the father of
her child! "No, Countess, the steward will not steal into
your castle, in order when you have enjoyed all the pleasures
of the day, to afford you the excitement of a stolen intrigue.

"Though the scorn and derision of the people of my native
village would wound me sorely, as you believe—I would rather
work with them as a day-laborer, than to play before your
lackeys the part which you assign me." This was his only
answer. He was well aware that it would elicit only a shrug

of the shoulders, and a pitying smile, but he could not help it.

It was evening when the countess' letter reached him, and while, by the dim light of the hanging lamp, in mortal anguish he composed at the bedside of the feverish child this clumsy and unfortunately mis-spelled reply, the folding-doors of the brilliantly lighted dining-room in the Wildenau palace, were thrown open and the prince offered his arm to the countess.

She was her brilliant self again. She had taken a perfumed bath, answered the royal letter, made several sketches for new court costumes and sent them to Paris.

She painted with unusual skill, and the little water-color figures, which she sent to her modistes, were real works of art, far superior to those in the fashion journals.

"Your Highness might earn your bread in this way"—said the maid flatteringly, and a strange thrill stirred the countess at these words. She had made herself a costume book, in which she had painted all the toilettes she had worn since her entrance into society, and often found amusement in turning the leaves; what memories the sight of the old clothes evoked! From the heavy silver wrought brocade train of old Count Wildenau's young bride, down to the airy little summer gown which she had worn nine years ago in Ammergau. From the stiff, regulation court costume down to the simple woolen morning gown in which she had that morning spent hours of torture on account of that Ammergau "delusion." But at the maid's words she shut the book as if startled and rose: "I will give you the dress I wore this morning, but on condition that I never see it."

"Your Highness is too kind, I thank you most humbly," said the delighted woman, kissing the sleeve of the countess' combing-mantle—she would not have ventured to kiss her hand.

The dinner toilette was quickly completed, and when the countess looked in the glass she seemed to herself more beautiful than ever. The melancholy expression around her eyes, and a slight trace of tears which she had shed, lent the pale tea-rose a tinge of color which was marvellously becoming.

The day was over, and when the prince came to dinner at six o'clock she received him with all her former charm.

" To whom do I owe this—Prince ?" she said smiling, holding out the official letter.

" Why do you ask me ?"

" Because *you* only can tell !"

" I ?"

" Yes, you. Who else would have proposed me to their Majesties ? Don't try to deceive me by that air of innocence. I don't trust it. You, and no one else would do me this friendly service, for everything good comes through you. You are not only a great and powerful man—you are also a good and noble one—my support, my Providence! I thank you."

She took both his hands in hers and offered him her forehead to kiss, with a glance of such sincere admiration and gratitude, that in his surprise and joy he almost missed the permitted goal and touched her lips instead. But fortunately, he recollected himself and almost timidly pressed the soft curls which quivered lightly like the delicate tendrils of flowers.

" I cannot resist this gratitude! Yes, my august cousin, the queen, did have the grace to consider my proposal as ' specially agreeable ' to her. But, my dear Countess, you must have been passing through terrible experiences to lavish such undue gratitude upon the innocent instigator of such a trifle as this appointment as mistress of ceremonies, for whose acceptance we must be grateful to you. There is a touch of almost timidity in your manner, my poor Madeleine, as if you had lost the self-control which, with all your feminine grace, gave your bearing so firm a poise. You do yourself injustice. You must shake off this oppression. That is why I ventured to push the hands of the clock of life a little and secured this position, which will leave you no time for torturing yourself with fancies. That is what you need most. Unfortunately I cannot lift from those beautiful shoulders the burden you yourself have probably laid upon them; but I will aid you gradually, to strip it off.

" The world in which you are placed needs you—you must live for it and ought not to withdraw your powers, your intellect, your charm. You are created for a lofty position! I do not mean a subordinate one—that of a mistress of ceremonies. This is merely a temporary palliative—I mean that of a reigning princess, who has to provide for the physical and intellectual welfare of a whole nation. When in your present office you have become reconciled to the world and its conditions—perhaps the day will come when I shall be permitted to offer you that higher place !"

The countess stood with her hands resting on the table and her eyes bent on the floor. Her heart was throbbing violently—her breath was short and hurried. *One* thought whirled through her brain. " You might have had all this and forfeited it forever ! " The consciousness of her marred destiny overwhelmed her with all its power. What a contrast between the prince, the perfect product of culture, who took into account all the demands of her rank and character, and the narrow, limited child of nature, her husband, who found cause for reproach in everything which the trained man of the world regarded as a matter of course. Freyer tortured her and humbled her in her own eyes, while the prince tenderly cherished her. Freyer—like the embodiment of Christian asceticism—required from her everything she disliked while Prince Emil desired nothing save to see her beautiful, happy, and admired, and made it her duty to enjoy life as suited her education and tastes ! She would fain have thrown herself exultingly into the arms of her preserver and said: " Take me and bear me up again on the waves of life ere I fall into the power of that gloomy God whose power is nurtured on the blood of the murdered joys of His followers."

Suddenly it seemed as if some one else was in the room gazing intently at her. She looked up—the eyes of the Christ in the Gothic niche were bent fixedly on her. " Are you looking at me again ?" asked a voice in her terror-stricken soul. " Can you never die ?"

It was even so; He could not die on the cross, He cannot die in her heart. Even though it was but a moment that He appeared to mortal eyes in the Passion Play, He will live for ever to all who experienced that moment.

Her uplifted arms fell as if paralyzed, and she faltered in broken sentences : " Not another word, Prince—in Heaven's name—do not lead me into temptation. Banish every thought of me—you do not know—oh ! I was never worthy of you, have never recognized all your worth—and now when I do—

now it is too late." She could say no more, tears were trembling on her lashes. She again glanced timidly at the painted Christ—He had now closed His eyes, His expression was more peaceful.

The prince gazed at her earnestly, but quietly. "Ah, there is a false standpoint which must be removed. It will cost something, I see. Calm yourself—you have nothing more to fear from me—I was awkward—it was not the proper moment, I ought to have known it. Do you remember our conversation nine years ago, on the way to the Passion Play? At that time a phantom stood between us. It has since assumed a tangible form, has it not? I saw this coming, but unfortunately could not avert it. But consider—it is and will always remain—a phantom! Such spectres can be fatal only to eccentric imaginative women like you who, in addition to imagination, also possess a strongly idealistic tendency which impresses an ethical meaning upon everything they feel. With a nature like yours things which, in and of themselves, are nothing except romantic episodes, assume the character of moral conflicts in which you always feel that you are the guilty ones because you were the superior and have taken a more serious view of certain relations than they deserved."

"Yes, yes! That is it. Oh, Prince—you understand me better than any one else!" exclaimed the countess, admiringly.

"Yes, and because I understand you better than any one else, I love you better than any one else—that is the inevitable consequence. Therefore it would be a pity, if I were obliged to yield to that phantom—for never were two human beings so formed for each other as we." He was silent, Madeleine had not heard the last words. In her swift variations of mood reacting with every changing impression, a different feeling had been evoked by the word "phantom" and the memories it awakened. Even the cleverest man cannot depend upon a woman. The phantom again stood between them—conjured up by himself.

As if by magic, the Kofel with its glittering cross rose before her, and opposite at her right hand the glimmering sunbeams stole up the cliff till, like shining fingers, they rested on a face whose like she had never seen—the eyes, dark yet sparkling, like the night when the star led the kings to the child in the manger! There he stood again, the One so long imagined, so long desired.

And her enraptured eyes said: "Throughout the whole world I have sought you alone." And his replied: "And I you!" And was this to be a lie—this to vanish? It seemed as if Heaven had opened its gates and suffered her to look in, and was all this to be delusion? The panorama of memory moved farther on, leading her past the dwellings of the high priest and apostles in Ammergau to the moonlit street where her ear, listening reverently, caught the words: This is where Christus lives! And she stood still with gasping breath, trembling with expectation of the approach of God.

Then the following day—the great day which brought the fulfilment of the mighty yearning when she beheld this face "from which the God so long sought smiled upon her!" The God whom she had come to seek, to confess! What! Could she deny, resign this God, in whose wounds she had laid her fingers.

Again she stood in timid reverence, with a glowing heart, while before her hovered the pierced, bleeding hand—Heaven and earth turned upon the question whether she dared venture to press her lips upon the stigma; she did venture, almost swooning from the flood of her feelings—and lo, in the kiss the quivering lips felt the throbbing of the warm awakening life in the hand of the stern "God," and a feeling of exultation stirred within her. "You belong to me! I will steal you from the whole human race." And now, scarcely nine years later—must the joy vanish, the God disappear, the faith die? What a miserable, variable creature is man!

"Dinner is served, and Baron St. Génois has called—shall I prepare another place?"

The countess started from her reverie—had she been asleep where she stood? Where was she?

The lackey was obliged to repeat the announcement and the question. A visitor now? She would rather die—yet Baron St. Génois was an intimate friend, he could come to dinner whenever he pleased—he was not to be sent away.

She nodded assent to the servant. Her emotions were repressed and scattered, her throbbing heart sank feebly back

17

to its usual pulsation—pallid despair whispered: " Give up
the struggle—you cannot be saved ! "

A few minutes after the little party were celebrating in the
brilliantly lighted dining-room in sparkling sack the " event
of the day," the appointment of the new mistress of ceremonies.

CHAPTER XXII.

FALLING STARS.

" THE new mistress of ceremonies isn't popular."

" Countess Wildenau is said to have fallen into disgrace
already; she did not ride in the queen's carriage at the recent
great parade."

" That is perfectly natural. It was to be expected, when a
lady so unaccustomed to put any constraint upon herself as
Countess Wildenau was appointed to such a position."

" She is said to make constant blunders. If she chooses,
she keeps the queen and the whole court waiting. She is
reported to have arrived at court fifteen minutes too late a
short time ago."

" And to have forgotten to present a number of ladies."

" People are indignant with her."

" Poor woman, she takes infinite trouble, but the place is
not a suitable one for her—she is absent-minded and makes
mistakes, which are unpardonable in a mistress of ceremonies."

" Yes, if the queen's cousin, the Hereditary Prince of
Metten-Barnheim did not uphold her, the queen would have
dropped her long ago. She is seen at court only when she is
acting as representative. She has not succeeded in establish-
ing personal relations with Her Majesty."

Such, at the end of a few months, were the opinions of
society, and they were just.

It seemed as though the curse of those whom she had
deserted, rested upon her—do what she would, she had no
success in this position.

As on the mountain peak towering into the upper air,
every warm current condenses into a cloud, so in the cool,
transparent atmosphere of very lofty and conspicuous positions

the faintest breath of secret struggles and passions seems to condense into masses of clouds which often gather darkly around the most brilliant personalities, veiling their traits. The passionate, romantic impulse, which was constantly at war with the aristocratic birth and education of the countess, was one of those currents which unconsciously and involuntarily must enter as an alien element in the crystalline clearness of these peaks of society.

This was the explanation of the mystery that the countess, greatly admired in private life and always a welcome guest at court, could not fill an official position successfully. The slight cloud which, in her private life, only served to surround her with a halo of romance which rendered the free independent woman of rank doubly interesting, was absolutely unendurable in a lady of the court representing her sovereign! There everything must be clear, calm, official. The impersonal element of royalty, as it exists in our day, especially in the women of reigning houses, will not permit any individuality to make itself prominent near the throne. All passionate emotions and peculiarities are abhorrent, because, even in individuals, they are emanations of the seething popular elements which sovereigns must at once rule and fear.

Countess Wildenau's constant excitement, restless glances, absence of mind, and feverish alternations of mood unconsciously expressed the vengeance of the spirit of the common people insulted in her husband—and the queen, in her subtle sensibility, therefore had a secret timidity and aversion to the new mistress of ceremonies which she could not conquer. Thus the first mists in the atmosphere near the throne arose, the vapors gathered into clouds—but the clouds were seen by the keen-eyed public—as the sun of royal favor vanished behind them.

It is far better never to have been prominent than to be forced to retire. The countess was a great lady, whose power seemed immovable and unassailable, so long as she lived independently—now it was seen that she was on the verge of a downfall! And now there was no occasion for further consideration of the woman hitherto so much envied. Vengeance could fearlessly be taken upon her for always having handsomer toilettes, giving better dinners, attracting more admirers—and being allowed to do unpunished what would be unpardonable in others.

"A woman who is continually occupied with herself cannot be mistress of ceremonies, I see that clearly," she said one day to the prince. "If any position requires self-denial, it is this. And self-denial has never been my forte. I ought to have known that before accepting the place. People imagine that the court would be the very field where the seeds of egotism would flourish most abundantly! It is not true; whoever wishes to reap for himself should remain aloof, only the utmost unselfishness, the most rigid fulfilment of duty can exist there. But I, Prince, am a spoiled, ill-trained creature, who learned nothing during the few years of my unhappy marriage save to hate constraint and shun pain! What is to be done with such a useless mortal?"

"Love her," replied Prince Emil, as quietly as if he were speaking of a game of chess, "and see that she is placed in a position where she need not obey, but merely command. Natures created to rule should not serve! The pebble is destined to pave the path of daily life—the diamond to sparkle. Who would upbraid the latter because it serves no other purpose? Its value lies in itself, but only connoisseurs know how to prize it!" Thus her friend always consoled her and strengthened her natural tendencies. But where men are too indulgent to us, destiny is all the more severe—this is the amends for the moral sins of society, the equalization of the undeserved privileges of individuals compared with the sad fate of thousands.

Prince Emil's efforts could not succeed in soothing the pangs of Madeleine von Wildenau's conscience—for he did not know the full extent of her guilt. If he knew all, she would lose him, too.

Josepha took care to torture the mother's heart by the reports sent from Italy.

Freyer was silent. Since that bitter letter, which he wrote, she had heard nothing more from him. He had hidden himself in his solitary retreat as a sick lion seeks the depths of its cave, and she dared not go to him there, though a secret yearning often made her start from her sleep with her husband's name on her lips, and tears in her eyes.

In addition to this she was troubled by Herr Wildenau, who was becoming still more urgent in his offers to purchase the hunting-castle, and often made strangely significant remarks, as though he was on the track of some discovery. The child with the treacherous resemblance was far away— but if this man was watching—*that* fact itself might attract his notice because it dated from the day when he made the first allusions. She lay awake many nights pondering over this mystery, but could not discover what had given him the clew to her secret. She did not suspect that it was the child himself who, in an unwatched moment, had met the curious stranger and made fatal answers to his cunning questions, telling him of " the beautiful lady who came to see ' Goth ' who had been God—in Ammergau! And that he loved the beautiful lady dearly—much better than Mother Josepha!"

Question and answer were easy, but the inference was equally so. It was evident to the inquisitor that a relation existed here quite compromising enough to serve as a handle against the countess, if the exact connection could be discovered. Cousin Wildenau and his brother resolved from that day forth to watch the countess' mysterious actions sharply— this was the latest and most interesting sport of the disinherited branch of the Wildenau family.

But the game they were pursuing had a powerful protector in the prince, they must work slowly and cautiously.

At court also it was his influence which sustained her. The queen, out of consideration for him, showed the utmost patience in dealing with the countess spite of her total absence of sympathy with her. Thus the unfortunate woman lived in constant uncertainty. Her soul was filled with bitterness by the experiences she now endured. She felt like dagger thrusts the malevolence, the contempt with which she had been treated since the sun of royal favor had grown dim. She lost her self-command, and no longer knew what she was doing. Her pride rebelled. A Wildenau, a Princess von Prankenberg, need not tolerate such treatment! Her usual graciousness deserted her and, in its place, she assumed a cold, haughty scorn, which she even displayed while performing the duties of her office, and thereby still more incensed every one against her. Persons, whom she ought to have

honored she ignored. Gradations of rank and lists of noble
families, the alpha and omega of a mistress of ceremonies, were
never in her mind. People entitled to the first position were
relegated to the third, and similar blunders were numerous.
Complaints and annoyances of all kinds poured in, and at a
state dinner in honor of the visit of a royal prince, she was
compelled to endure, in the presence of the whole court, a rebuke from the queen who specially distinguished a person
whom she had slighted.

This dinner became fateful to her. Wherever she turned,
she beheld triumphant or sarcastic smiles—wherever she approached a group, conversation ceased with the marked sud-
denness which does not seek to conceal that the new-comer
has been the subject of the talk. Nay, she often encountered
a glance which seemed to say: "Why do you still linger
among us?"

It happened also that the prince had been summoned to
Cannes by his father's illness and was not at hand to protect
her. She had hoped that he would return in time for the
dinner, but he did not come. She was entirely deserted. A
few compassionate souls, like the kind-hearted duchess whom
she met at the Passion Play, her ladies-in-waiting, and some
maids of honor, joined her, but she felt in their graciousness a
pity which humbled her more than all the insults. And her
friends! The gentlemen who belonged to the circle of her
intimate acquaintances had for some time adopted a more
familiar tone, as if to imply that she must accept whatever
they choose to offer. She was no longer even beautiful—a
pallid, grief-worn face, with hollow eyes gazing hopelessly into
vacancy, found no admirers in this circle. And as every look,
every countenance wore a hostile expression, her own image
gazed reproachfully at her from the mirror, the dazzling fair
neck with its marvellous contours, supported a head whose
countenance was weary and prematurely aged. "It is all over
with you!" cried the mirror! "It is all over with you!"
smiled the lips of society. "It is all over with you, you may
be glad if we still come to your dinners!" the wine-scented
breath of her former intimate friends insultingly near her
seemed to whisper.

Was this the world, to which she had sacrificed her heart

and conscience? Was this the honor for which she hourly suffered tortures. And on the wintry mountain height the husband who had naught on earth save the paltry scrap of love she bestowed, was perishing—she had avoided him for months because to her he represented that uncomfortable christianity whose asceticism has survived the civilization of thousands of years. Yes! This christianity of the Nazarene who walked the earth so humbly in a laborer's garb is the friend of the despised and humbled. It asks no questions about crowns and the favor of courts, human power and distinction. And she who had trembled and sinned for the wretched illusions, the glitter of the honors of this brief life—was she to despise a morality which, in its beggar's garb, stands high above all for which the greatest and most powerful tremble? Again the symbol of the renewed bond between God and the world— the cross—rose before her, and on it hung the body of the Redeemer, radiant in its chaste, divine beauty—that body which for *her* descended from the cross where it hung for the whole world and, after clasping it in her arms, she repined because it was only the *image* of what no earthly desire will ever attain, no matter how many human hearts glow with the flames of love so long as the world endures.

"My Christus—my sacrificed husband!" cried a voice in her heart so loudly that she did not hear a question from the queen. "It is incredible!" some one exclaimed angrily near her. She started from her reverie. "Your Majesty?" The queen had already passed on, without waiting for a reply— whispers and nods ran through the circle, every eye was fixed upon her. What had the queen wanted? She tried to hurry after her. Her Majesty had disappeared, she was already going through the next hall—but the distance was so great— she could not reach her, the space seemed to increase as she moved on. She felt that she was on the verge of fainting and dragged herself into a secluded room.

The members of the court were retiring. Confusion arose —the mistress of ceremonies was absent just at the moment of the *Congé!* No one had time to seek her. All were assembling to take leave, and then hurrying after servants and wraps. Carriage after carriage rolled away, the rooms were empty, the lackeys came to extinguish the lights. The countess lay on a sofa, alone and deserted in the last hall of the suite.

"In Heaven's name, is your Highness ill?" cried an old major-domo, offering his assistance to the lady, who slowly rose. "Is it all over?" she asked, gazing vacantly around. "Where is my servant?"

"He is still waiting outside for Your Highness," replied the old gentleman, trying to assist her. "Shall I call a doctor or a maid?"

"No, thank you, I am well again. It was only an attack of giddiness," said the countess, walking slowly out of the palace.

"Who is driving to-night?" she asked the footman, as he put her fur cloak over her bare shoulders.

"Martin, Your Highness."

"Very well, then go home and say that I shall not come, but visit the estates."

"It is bitterly cold, Your Highness!" observed the major domo, who had attended her to the equipage.

"That does not matter—is the beaver robe in the carriage?"

"Certainly, Your Highness!"

"What time is it? Late?"

"Oh no; just nine, Your Highness."

"Forward, then!"

Martin knew where.

The major-domo closed the door and away dashed the horses into the glittering winter night along the familiar, but long neglected road. It was indeed a cold drive. The ground was frozen hard and the carriage windows were covered with frost flowers. The countess' temples were throbbing violently, her heart beat eagerly with longing for the husband whom she had deserted for this base world! The mood of that Ammergau epoch again asserted its rights, and she penitently hastened to seek the beautiful gift she had so thoughtlessly cast aside. With a heart full of rancor over the injustice and lovelessness experienced in society, her soul plunged deeply into the sweet chalice of the love and poesy of those days—a love which was religion—a religion which was *love*. "Though I speak with the tongues of men and of angels, and have not charity, I am become as sounding brass or a tinkling cymbal!"

Aye, for sounding brass and a tinkling cymbal she had squandered warm heart's blood, and the sorrowing soul of the people from whose sacred simplicity her wearied soul was to have drawn fresh youth, gazed tearfully at her from the eyes of her distant son.

The horses went so slowly to-night, she thought—no pace is swift enough for a repentant heart which longs to atone!

He would be angry, she would have a bitter struggle with him—but she would soften his wrath—she would put forth all her charms, she would be loving and beautiful, fairer than he had ever seen her, for she had never appeared before him in full dress, with diamonds sparkling on her snowy neck, and heavy gold bracelets clasping her wonderful arms.

She would tell him that she repented, that everything should be as of yore when she plighted her troth to him by the glare of the bridal torches of the forest conflagration and, feeling Valkyrie might in her veins, dreamed Valkyrie dreams.

She drew a long breath and compared the pallid court lady of the present, who fainted at a proof of disfavor and a few spiteful glances, with the Valkyrie of those days! Was it a mere delusion which made her so strong? No—even if the God whom she saw in him was a delusion, the love which swelled in her veins with that might which defied the elements was divine and, by every standard of philosophy, asthetics, and birth, as well as morality, had a right to its existence.

Then why had she been ashamed of it? On account of trivial prejudices, petty vanities: in other words, weakness!

Not Freyer, but *she* was too petty for this great love! "Yet wait—wait, my forsaken husband. Your wife is coming to-day with a love that is worthy of you, ardent enough to atone in a single hour for the neglect of years."

She breathed upon the frost-coated pane, melting an opening in the crust of ice. The castle already stood before her, the height was almost reached. Then—a sudden jolt—a cry from the coachman, and the carriage toppled toward the precipice. With ready nerve the countess sprang out on the opposite side.

"What is it?"

"Why, the horses shied at sight of Herr Freyer!" said the coachman, as Freyer, with an iron hand, curbed the rearing animals. The countess hastened toward him. Aided by the coachman, he quieted the trembling creatures.

" I beg your pardon, Your Highness," said Freyer, still panting from the exertion he had made. " I came out of the wood unexpectedly, and the dark figure frightened them. Fortunately I could seize their reins."

" Drive on, Martin," the countess ordered, " I will walk with Herr Freyer." The coachman obeyed. She put her hand through Freyer's arm. " No wonder that the horses shied, my husband, you look so strange. What were you doing in the woods in the middle of the night ?"

" What I always do—wandering about."

" That is not right, you ought to sleep."

" Sleep ?" Freyer repeated with a bitter laugh.

" Is this my reception, Joseph ?"

" Pardon me—it makes me laugh when you talk of sleeping ! Look "—he raised his hat : " Even in the starlight you can see the white hairs which have come since you were last here, sent my child away, and made me wholly a hermit. No sleep has come to my eyes and my hair has grown grey."

The countess perceived with horror the change which had taken place in him. Threads of silver mingled with his black locks, his eyes were sunken, his whole figure was emaciated, his chest narrowed—he was a sick man. She could not endure the sight—it was the most terrible reproach to her ; she fixed her eyes on the ground : " I had made such a lovely plan—Martin has the key of the outside door—I was going to steal gently to the side of your couch and kiss your sleeping lips."

" I thank you for the kind intention. But do you imagine that I could have slept after receiving that letter which brought me the news that I was betrayed—betrayed once more and, after all the sacred promises made during your last visit, you had done exactly the opposite and accepted a position which separated you still farther from your husband and child, bound you still more firmly to the world ? Do you imagine that the *days* are enough to ponder over such thoughts ? No, one must call in the nights to aid. You know that well, and I should be far better satisfied if you would say honestly : ' I know that I am killing you, that your strength is being consumed with sorrow, but I have no wish to change this state of affairs!' instead of feigning that you cannot understand why I should not sleep quietly and wondering that I wander all night in the forest? But fear nothing, I am perfectly calm—I shall reproach you no farther," he added in a milder tone, "for I have closed accounts with myself—with you—with life. Do not weep, I promised that when you sought your husband you should find him—I will not be false to my pledge. Come, lay your little head upon my breast—you are trembling, are you cold? Lean on me, and let us walk faster that I may shelter you in the warm room. Wandering dove—how did you happen suddenly to return to your husband's lonely nest in the cold night, in this bitter winter season? Why did not you stay in the warm cote with the others, where you had everything that you desire? Do you miss anything? Tell me, what do you seek with me, for what does your little heart long?" His voice again sank to the enthralling whisper which had formerly made all her pulses throb with a sensation of indescribable bliss. His great heart took all its pains and suffering and ceased to judge her. The faithless dove found the nest open, and his gentle hand scattered for her the crumbs of his lost happiness, as the starving man divides his last crust with those who are poorer still.

She could not speak—overpowered by emotion she leaned against him, allowing herself to be carried rather than led up the steep ascent. But she could not wait, even as they moved her lips sought his, her little hands clasped his, and a murmur tremulous with emotion: "*This* is what I missed!"—answered the sweet question. The stars above sparkled with a thousand rays—the whole silent, glittering, icy winter night rejoiced.

At last the castle was reached and the "warm" room received them. It did not exactly deserve the name, for the fire in the stove had gone out, but neither felt it—the glow in their hearts sufficed.

"You must take what I can offer—I am all alone, you know."

"*All alone!*" she repeated with a happy smile which he

could see by the starlight shining through the open window. Another kiss—a long silent embrace was exchanged.

" Now let me light a lamp, that I may take off your cloak and make you comfortable! Or, do you mean to spend the night so?" He was bewitching in his mournful jesting, his sad happiness.

" Ah, it is so long since I have seen you thus," Madeleine murmured. " World, I can laugh at you now!" cried an exultant voice in her heart, for the old love, the old spell was hers once more. And as he again appeared before her in his mild greatness and beauty, she desired to show herself his peer—display herself to him in all the dazzling radiance of her beauty. As he turned to light the lamp she let the heavy cloak fall and stood in all her loveliness, her snowy neck framed by the dark velvet bodice, on which all the stars in the firmament outside seemed to have fallen and clung to rest there for a moment.

Freyer turned with the lamp in his hand—his eyes flashed —a faint cry escaped his lips! She waited smiling for an expression of delight—but he remained motionless, gazing at her as if he beheld a ghost, while the glance fixed upon the figure whose diamonds sparkled with a myriad rays constantly grew more gloomy, his bearing more rigid—a deep flush suffused his pallid face. " And this is my wife?" at last fell in a muffled, expressionless tone from his lips. " No—it is not she."

The countess did not understand his meaning—she imagined that the superb costume so impressed him that he dared not approach her, and she must show him by redoubled tenderness that he was not too lowly for this superb woman. " It *is* your wife, indeed it is, and all this splendor veils a heart which is yours, and yours alone!" she cried, throwing herself on his breast and clasping her white arms around him.

But with a violent gesture he released himself, drawing back a step. " No—no—I cannot, I will not touch you in such a guise as this."

" Freyer!" the countess angrily exclaimed, gazing at him as if to detect some trace of insanity in his features. " What does this mean?"

"Have you—been in society—in *that* dress?" he asked in a low tone, as if ashamed for her.

"Yes.   And in my impatience to hasten to you I did not stop to change it.   I thought you would be pleased."

Freyer again burst into the bitter laugh from which she always shrank.   "Pleased, when I see that you show yourself to others so—"

"How?" she asked, still failing to understand him.

"So naked!" he burst forth, unable to control himself longer.   "You have uncovered your beauty thus before the eyes of the gentlemen of your world?   And this is my wife— a creature so destitute of all shame?"

"Freyer!" shrieked the countess, tottering backward with her hand pressed upon her brow as if she had just received a blow on the head: "This to *me—to-day!*"

"To-day or to-morrow.   On any day when you display the beauty at which I scarcely dare to glance, to the profane eyes of a motley throng of strangers, who gaze with the same satisfaction at the booths of a fair—on any day when you expose to greedy looks the bosom which conceals the heart that should be mine—on any such day you are unworthy the love of any honest man."

A low cry of indignation answered him, then all was still. At last Madeleine von Wildenau's lips murmured with a violent effort: "This is the last!"

Freyer was striving to calm himself.   He pressed his burning brow against the frosty window-panes with their glittering tangle of crystal flowers and stars.   The sparkling firmament above gazed down in its eternal clearness upon the poor earthling, who in his childlike way was offering a sacrifice to the chaste God, whose cold home it was.

"Whenever I come—there is always some new torture for me—but you have never so insulted and outraged me as today," said the countess slowly, in a low tone, as if weighing every word.   Her manner was terribly calm and cold.

"I understand that it may be strange to you to see a lady in full dress—you have never moved in a circle where this is a matter of course and no one thinks of it.   To the pure all things are pure, and he who is not stands with us under the law of the etiquette of our society.   Our village lasses must muffle themselves to the throat, for what could protect them from the coarse jests and rudeness of the village lads?"

Freyer winced, he felt the lash.

"To add to the splendor of festal garments," she went on, "a little of the natural beauty of the divinely created human body is a tribute which even the purest woman can afford the eye, and whatever is kept within the limits of the artistic sense can never be shameless or unseemly. Woe betide any one who passes these bounds and sees evil in it—he erases himself from the ranks of cultured people. So much, and no more, you are still worthy that I should say in my own justification!"

She turned and took up the cloak to wrap herself in it: "Will you be kind enough to have the horses harnessed?"

"Are you going?" asked Freyer, who meanwhile had regained his self-control.

"Yes."

"Alas, what have I done!" he said, wringing his hands. "I have not even asked you to sit down, have not let you rest, have offended and wounded you. Oh, I am a savage, a wretched man."

"You are what you can be!" she replied with the cutting coldness into which a proud woman's slighted love is quickly transformed.

"What such an uncultivated person can be! That is what you wish to say!" replied Freyer. "But there lies my excuse. Aye, I am a native of the country, accustomed to break my fruit, wet with the morning-dew, from the tree ere any hand has touched it, or pluck from the thorny boughs in the dewy thicket the hidden berries which no human eye has beheld;—I cannot understand how people can enjoy fruits that have been uncovered for hours in the dust of the market-place. The aroma is gone—the freshness and bloom have vanished, and if given me—no matter how costly it might be, I should not care for it—the wild berries in the wood which smiled at me from the leafy dusk with their glittering dew-drops, would please me a thousand times better! This is not meant for a comparison, only an instance of how people feel when they live in the country!"

"And to carry your simile further—if you believe that the

fruit so greatly desired has been kept for you alone—will it not please you to possess what others long for in vain ?"

"No," he said simply, " I am not envious enough to wish to deprive others of anything they covet—but I will not share, so I would rather resign!"

" Well, then—I have nothing more to say on that point— let us close the conversation."

Both were silent a long time, as if exhausted by some great exertion.

" How is our—the child ?   Have you any news from Josepha?" the countess asked at last.

" Yes, but unfortunately nothing good."

" As usual!" she answered, hastily; " it is her principle to make us anxious. Such people take advantage of every opportunity to let us feel their power. I know that."

" I do not think so. I must defend my cousin. She was always honest, though blunt and impulsive," answered Freyer. " I fear she is writing the truth, and the boy is really worse."

" Go there then, if you are anxious, and send me word how you find him."

" I will not travel at your expense—except in your service, and my own means are not enough," replied Freyer in a cold, stern tone.

" Very well, this *is* in my service. So—obey and go at my expense !"

Freyer gazed at her long and earnestly. " As your steward ?" he asked in a peculiar tone.

" I should· like to have a truthful report—not a biassed one, as is Josepha's custom," she replied evasively. " There is nothing to be done on the estates now—I beg the ' steward ' to represent my interests in this matter. If you find the child really worse, I will get a leave of absence and go to him."

" Very well, I will do as you order."

" But have the horses harnessed now, or it will be morning before I return."

" Will it not be too fatiguing for you to return to-night ? Shall I not wake the house-maid to prepare your room and wait on you !"

" No, I thank you."

" As you choose," he said, quietly going to order the

horses, which had hardly been taken from the carriage, to be harnessed again. The coachman remonstrated, saying that the animals had not had time to rest, but Freyer replied that there must be no opposition to the countess' will.

The half-hour which the coachman required was spent by the husband and wife in separate rooms. Freyer was arranging on his desk a file of papers relating to his business as steward; bills and documents for the countess to look over. He worked as quietly as if all emotion was dead within him. The countess sat alone in the dimly-lighted, comfortless sitting room, gazing at the spot where her son's bed used to stand. Her blood was seething with shame and wrath; yet the sight of the empty wall where the boy no longer held out his arms to her from the little couch, was strangely sad—as if he were dead, and his corpse had already been borne out. Her heart was filled with grief, too bitter to find relief in tears, they are frozen at such a moment. She would fain have called his name amid loud sobs, but something seemed to stand beside her, closing her lips and clutching her heart with an iron hand, the *vengeance* of the sorely insulted woman. Then she fancied she saw the child fluttering toward her in his little white shirt. At the same moment a door burst open, a draught of air swept through the room, making her start violently—and at the same moment a star shot from the sky, so close at hand, that it appeared as if it must dart through the panes and join its glittering fellows on the countess' breast.

What was that? A gust of wind so sudden, that it swept through the closed rooms, burst doors open, and appeared to hurl the stars from the sky? Yet outside all was still; only the wainscoting and beams of the room creaked slightly— popular superstition would have said: "Some death has been announced!" The excited woman thought of it with secret terror. Was it the whir of the spindle from which one of the Fates had just cut the thread of life? If it were the life-thread of her child—if at that very hour—her blood congealed to ice! She longed to shriek in her fright, but again the gloomy genius of vengeance sealed her lips and heart. *If* it were— God's will be done. Then the last bond between her and Freyer would be sundered. What could she do with *this* man's child? Nothing that fettered her to him had a right to exist

—if the child was dead, then she would be free, there would
be nothing more in common between them! He had slain
her heart that day, and she was slaying the last feeling which
lived within it, love for her child! Everything between them
must be over, effaced from the earth, even the child. Let
God take it!

Every passionate woman who is scorned feels a touch of
kinship with Medea, whose avenging steel strikes the husband
whom it cannot reach through the children, whether her own
heart is also pierced or not. Greater far than the self-denial
of *love* is that of *hate*, for it extends to self-destruction! It
fears no pain, spares neither itself nor its own flesh and blood,
slays the object of its dearest love to give pain to others—even
if only in *thought*, as in the modern realm of culture, where
everything formerly expressed in deeds of violence now acts
in the sphere of mental life.

It was a terrible hour! From every corner of the room,
wherever she gazed, the boy's large eyes shone upon her
through the dusk, pleading: "Forgive my father, and do not
thrust me from your heart!" But in vain, her wrath was too
great, her heart was incapable at that moment of feeling anything else. Everything had happened as it must; she had
entered an alien, inferior sphere, and abandoned and scorned
her own, therefore the society to which she belonged now exiled her, while she reaped in the sphere she had chosen in-
gratitude and misunderstanding.

Now, too late, she was forced to realize what it meant to
be chained for life to an uneducated man! "Oh, God, my
punishment is just," murmured an angry voice in her soul, "in
my childish defiance I despised all the benefits of culture by
which I was surrounded, to make for myself an idol of clay
which, animated by my glowing breath, dealt me a blow in
the face and returned to its original element! I have thrown
myself away on a man, to whom any peasant lass would be
dearer! Why—why, oh God, hast Thou lured me with Thy
deceitful mask into the mire? Dost Thou feel at ease amid
base surroundings? I cannot follow Thee there! A religion
which stands on so bad a footing with man's highest blessings,
culture and learning, can never be *mine*. Is it divine to steal
a heart under the mask of Christ and then, as if in mockery,

18

leave the deceived one in the lurch, after she has been caught in the snare and bound to a narrow-minded, brutal husband? Is this God-like? Nay, it is fiendish! Do not look at me so beseechingly, beautiful eyes of my child, I no longer believe even in you! Everything which has hitherto bound me to your father has been a lie; you, too, are an embodied falsehood. It is not true that Countess Wildenau has mingled her noble blood with that of a low-born man; that she has given birth to a bastard, wretched creature, which could be at home in no sphere save by treachery! No—no, I cannot have forgotten myself so far—it is but a dream, a phantasy of the imagination and when I awake it will be on the morning of that August day in Ammergau after the Passion Play. Then I shall be free, can wed a noble man who is my peer, and give him legitimate heirs, whose mother I can be without a blush!"

What was that? Did her ears deceive her? The hoof-beats of a horse, rushing up the mountain with the speed of the wind. She hurried to the window. The clock was just striking two. Yes! A figure like the wild huntsman was flitting like a shadow through the night toward the castle. Now he turned the last curve and reached the height and the countess saw distinctly that he was her courier. What news was he bringing—what had happened—at so late an hour?

Was the evil dream not yet over?

What new blow was about to strike her?

"What you desired—nothing else!" said the demon of her life.

The courier checked his foaming horse before the terrace. The countess tried to hurry toward him, but could not leave the spot. She clung shuddering to the cross-bars of the window, which cast its long black shadow far outside.

Freyer opened the door; Madeleine heard the horseman ask: "Is the Countess here?"

"Yes!" replied Freyer.

"I have a telegram which must be signed, the answer is prepaid."

Freyer tore off the envelope. "Take the horse round to the stable, I will attend to everything."

He entered and approached the door, through which the child had come to his mother's aid the last time she was there, to protect her from Josepha. The countess fancied that the little head must be again thrust in ! But it was only Freyer with the despatch. The countess mechanically signed her name to the receipt as if she feared she could not do so after having read the message. Then, with a trembling hand, she opened the telegram, which contained only the words :

" Our angel has just died, with his mother's name on his lips. Please send directions for the funeral.

JOSEPHA."

A cry rang through the room like the breaking of a chord —a death-like silence followed. The countess was on her knees, with her face bowed on the table, her hand clasping the telegram, crushed before the God whose might she felt for the first time in her life, whom only a few moments before she had blasphemed and defied. He had taken her at her word, and her words had condemned her. The child, the loyal child who had died with her name on his lips, she had wished but a few minutes before that God would take out of the world—she could betray him for the sake of an aristocratic legitimate brother, who never had existed. She could think of his death as something necessary, as her means of deliverance ? Now the child *had* released her. Sensitive and modest, he had removed the burden of his poor little life, which was too much for her to bear and vanished from the earth where he found no place—but his last word was the name of all love, the name " mother !" He had not asked " have you fulfilled a mother's duties to me ?"—have you loved me ?" He had loved his mother with that sweet child-love, which demands nothing—only gives.

And she, the avaricious mother, had been niggardly with her love—till the child died of longing. She had let it die and did not bestow the last joy, press the last kiss upon the little mouth, permit the last look of the seeking eyes to rest upon the mother's face !

Outraged nature, so long denied, now shrieked aloud, like an animal for its dead young ! But the brute has at least done its duty, suckled its offspring, warmed and protected it with its own body, as long as it could. But she, the more highly organized creature—for only human beings are capable of such unnatural conduct—had sacrificed her child to so-

called higher interests, had neither heeded Josepha's warning,
nor the voice of her own heart. Now came pity for the dead
child, now she would fain have taken it in her arms, called it
by every loving name, cradled the weary little head upon her
breast. Too late! He had passed away like a smiling good
genius, whom she had repulsed—now she was alone and free,
but free like the man who falls into a chasm because the rope
which bound him to the guide broke. She had not known
that she possessed a child, while he lived, now that he was
dead she knew it. *Maternal joy* could not teach her, for she had
never experienced it—*maternal grief* did—and she was forced
to taste it to the dregs. Though she writhed in her torture,
burying her nails in the carpet as if she would fain dig the
child from the ground, she could find no consolation, and letting her head sink despairingly, she murmured : " My child—
you have gone and left me with a guilt that can never be
atoned !"

 "You can be my mother in Heaven," he had once said.
This, too, was forfeited ; neither in Heaven nor on earth
had she a mother's rights, for she had denied her child, not
only before the world but, during this last hour, to herself
also.

Freyer bore the dispensation differently. To him it was
no punishment, but a trial, the inevitable consequence
of unhappy, unnatural relations. He could not reproach
himself and uttered no reproaches to others. He was no
novice in suffering and had one powerful consolation, which
she lacked : the perception of the divinity of grief—this made
him strong and calm ! Freyer leaned against the window
and gazed upward to the stars, which were so peacefully pursuing their course. "You were far away from me when you
lived in a foreign land, my child—now you are near, my poor
little boy ! This cold earth had no home for you ! But to
your father you will still live, and your glorified spirit will
brighten my path—the dark one I must still follow ! " Tears
flowed silently down his cheeks. No loud lamentations
must profane his great, sacred anguish. With clasped hands
he mutely battled it down and as of old on the cross his eyes
appealed to those powers ever near the patient sufferer in the
hour of conflict. However insignificant and inexperienced

he might be in this world, he was proportionally lofty and superior in the knowledge of the things of another.

"Come, rise!" he said gently to the bewildered woman, bending to help her. She obeyed, but it was in the same way that two strangers, in a moment of common disaster, lend each other assistance. The tie had been severed that day, and the child's death placed a grave between them.

"I fear your sobbing will be heard downstairs. Will you not pray with me?" said Freyer. "Do what we may, we are in God's hands and must accept what He sends! I wish that you could feel how the saints aid a soul which suffers in silence. Loud outcries and unbridled lamentations drive them away! God does not punish us to render us impatient, but patient." He clasped his hands: "Come, let us pray for our child!" He repeated in a low tone the usual, familiar prayers for the dying—we cannot always command words to express our feelings. An old formula often stands us in good stead, when the agitation of our souls will not suffer us to find language, and our thoughts, swept to and fro by the tempest of feeling, gladly cling to a familiar form to which they give new life."

The countess did not understand this. She was annoyed by the commonplace phraseology, which was not hallowed to her by custom and piety—she was contemptuous of a point of view which could find consolation for *such* a grief by babbling "trivialties." Freyer ended his prayer, and remained a moment with his hands clasped on his breast. Then he dipped his fingers in the holy water basin beside the place where the child's couch had formerly stood and made the sign of the cross over himself and the unresponsive woman. She submitted, but winced as if he had cut her face with a knife and destroyed its beauty. It reminded her of the hour in Ammergau when he made the sign of the cross over her for the first time! Then she had felt enrolled by this symbol in a mysterious army of sufferers and there her misery began.

"We must now arrange where we will have the child buried," said Freyer; "I think we should bring him here, that we may still have our angel's grave!"

"As you choose!" she said in an exhausted tone, wiping away her tears. "It will be best for you to go and attend to everything yourself. Then you can bring the—body!" The word again destroyed her composure. She saw the child in his coffin with Josepha, the faithful servant who had nursed him, beside it, and an unspeakable jealousy seized her concerning the woman to whom she had so indifferently resigned all her rights. The child, always so ready to lavish its love, was lying cold and rigid, and she would give her life if it could rise once more, throw its little arms around her neck, and say "my dear mother." "Pearl of Heaven—I have cast you away for wretched tinsel and now, when the angels have taken you again, I recognize your value." She tore the jewels from her breast. "There, take these glittering stars of my frivolous life and put them in his coffin—I never want to see them again—let their rays be quenched in my child's grave."

"The sacrifice comes too late!" said Freyer, pushing the stones away. He did not wish to be harsh, but he could not be untruthful. What was a handful of diamonds flung away in a moment of impulse to the Countess Wildenau? Did she seek to buy with them pardon for her guilt toward her dead child? The father's aching heart could not accept *that* payment on account! Or was it meant for the symbol of a greater sacrifice—a sacrifice of her former life? Then it came too late, too late for the dead and for the living; it could not avail the former, and the latter no longer believed in it!

She had understood him and the terrible accusation which he unwittingly brought against her! Standing before him as if before a judge, she felt that God was with him at that moment—but she was deserted, her angel had left her, there was no pity for her in Heaven or on earth—save from one person! The thought illumined the darkness of her misery. There was but one who would pour balm upon her wounds, one who had indulgence and love enough to raise the drooping head, pardon the criminal—her noble, generous-hearted friend, the Prince! She would fly to him, seek shelter from the gloomy spirit which had pursued her ever since she conjured up in Ammergau the cruel God who asked such impossible things and punished so terribly.

"Pray, order the carriage—I must leave here or I shall die."

Freyer glanced at the clock. " The half-hour Martin re-quired is over, he will be here directly."

"Is it only half an hour? Oh! God—is it possible—so much misery in half an hour! It seems an eternity since the news came! "

" We can feel more grief in one moment than pleasure in a thousand years!" answered Freyer. " It is probably be-cause a just Providence allots to each an equal measure of joy and pain—but the pain must be experienced in this brief existence, while we have an eternity for joy. Woe betide him, who does the reverse—keeps the pain for eternity and squand-ers the joy in this world. He is like the foolish virgins who burned their oil before the coming of the 'bridegroom.'"

The countess nodded. She understood the deep signifi-cance of Freyer's words.

" But we of the people say that 'whom God loveth, He chasteneth,'" he continued, "and I interpret that to mean that He *compels* those whom He wishes to save to bear their por-tion here below, that the joy may be reserved for them in Heaven! To such favored souls He sends an angel with the cup of wormwood and wherever it flees and hides—he finds it. Nearer and nearer the angel circles around it on his dark pinions, till it sinks with fatigue, and fainting with thirst like the Saviour on the Cross—drinks the bitter draught as if it were the most delicious refreshment."

The countess gazed into his face with timid admiration. He seemed to her the gloomy messenger of whom he spoke, she fancied she could hear the rustle of his wings as he drew nearer and nearer in ever narrowing circles, till escape was no longer possible. Like a hunted animal she took to flight—seeking deliverance at any cost. Thank Heaven, the car-riage! Martin was driving up. A cold: " Farewell, I hope you may gain consolation and strength for the sad journey! " was murmured to the father who was going to bring home the body of his dead child—then she entered the carriage.

Freyer wrapped the fur robe carefully around the delicate form of his wife, but not another word escaped his lips. What he said afterward to his God, when he returned to the deserted house, Countess Wildenau must answer for at some future day.

CHAPTER XXIII.

NOLI ME TANGERE.

"I have attracted you by a Play—for you were a child, and children are taught by games. But when one method of instruction is exhausted it is cast aside and exchanged for a higher one, that the child may ripen to maturity." Thus spoke the voice of the Heavenly Teacher to the countess as, absorbed in her grief, she drove through the dusk of a wintry morning. She almost wondered, as she gazed out into the grey dawn, that the day-star was not weary of pursuing its course. Aye, the mysterious voice spoke the truth: the play was over, that method of instruction was exhausted, but she did not yet feel ready for a sterner one and trembled at the thought of it.

Instead of the divine Kindergarten instructor, came the gloomy teacher death, forcing the attention of the refractory pupil by the first pitiless blow upon her own flesh and blood! Day was dawning—in nature as well as in her own soul, but the sun shone upon a winding sheet, outside as well as in, a world dead in the clasp of winter. Where was the day when the redeeming love for which she hoped would appear to her in the spring garden? Woe to all who believed in spring. Their best gift was a cold winter sunlight on snow-covered graves.

The corpse of her spring dream was lying on the laughing shores of the Riviera.

The God whom she sought was very different from the one she intended to banish from her heart. The new teacher seized her hand with bony fingers and forced her to look closely at the God whom she herself had created, and whom she now upbraided with having deceived her. "What kind of God would this creature of your imagination be?" rang in her ears with pitiless mockery. Aye, she had believed Him to be the Jupiter who loved mortal women, only in the course of the ages he had changed his name and now appeared as Christ. But she was now forced to learn that He was no off-spring of the sensual fancy of the nations, but a contrast to

every natural tendency and desire—a *true* God, not a creation
of mankind. Were it not so, men would have invented a
more complaisant one. Must not that be a divine power
which, in opposition to all human, all earthly passions, with
neither splendor, nor power, with the most insignificant means
has established an empire throughout the world? Aye, she recognized with reverent awe that this was a God, though unlike the one whom she sought, Christ was not Jupiter—and
Freyer was not Christ. The *latter* cannot be clasped in the
arms, does not yield to earthly yearning, no matter how fervently devout. Spirit as He is, He vanishes, even where He
reveals Himself in material form, and whoever thinks to grasp
Him, holds but the poor doll, whom He gave for a momentary
support to the childish mind, which seeks solely what is
tangible!

Mary Magdalene was permitted to serve and anoint Him
when He walked on earth in human form, but when she tried
to clasp the risen Lord the " *noli me tangere* " thundered in
her ears, and God withdrew from mortal touch. In Mary
Magdalene, however, the love kindled by the visible Master
was strong enough to burn on for the invisible One—she no
longer sought Him among the living, but went into solitude
and lived for the vanished Christ. But the countess had not
advanced so far. What " God of Love " was this, who imposed conditions which made the warm blood freeze, killed
the warm life-pulses? What possession was this, which could
only be obtained by renunciation, what joy that could be attained solely by mortification? Her passionate nature could
not comprehend this contradiction. She longed to clasp His
knees and wipe His feet with her hair, at least that, nothing
more, only that—she would be modest! But not even that
was allowed her.

This was the great impulse of religious materialism, in
which divinity and humanity met, the Magdalene element in
the history of the conversion of mankind, which attracted souls
like that of Madeleine von Wildenau, made them feel for an
instant the bliss of the immediate presence of God, and then
left them disappointed and alone until they perceived that in
that one instant wings have grown—strong enough to bear
them up to Heaven, if they once learned to use them.

Thus quivering and forsaken, the heart of the modern Magdalene lay on the earth when the first *noli me tangere* echoed in her ears. She had never known that there were things which could not be had, and now that she wanted a God and could not obtain Him, she murmured like a child which longs in vain for the stars until it attains a higher consciousness of ownership than lies in mere personal possession, the feeling which in quiet contemplation of the starry firmament fills us with the proud consciousness: " This is yours !"

Everything is ours—and nothing, according to our view of it. To expand our breasts with its mighty thoughts—to merge ourselves in it and revel in the whirling dance of the atoms, *in that sense* the universe is ours. But absorb and contain it we cannot; in that way it does not belong to us. It is the same with God. Greatness cannot enter littleness—the small must be absorbed by the great; but its power of possession lies in the very fact that it can do this and still retain its own nature. How long will it last, and what will it cost, ere the impatient child attains the peace of this realization ?

In the faint glimmer of the dawn the countess drove past a little church in the suburbs of Munich. It was the hour for early mass. A few sleepy, shivering old women, closely muffled, were shuffling over the snow in big felt shoes toward the open door. A dim ray of light streamed out, no organ notes, no festal display lured worshippers, for it was a "low mass." It was cold and gloomy outside, songless within. Yet the countess suddenly stopped the carriage.

" I am going into the church a moment," she said, tottering forward with uncertain steps, for she was exhausted both physically and mentally. The old women eyed her malignantly, as if asking: " What do you want among poor ugly crones who drag their crooked limbs out of bed so early to go to their Saviour, because later they must do the work of their little homes and cannot get away ? What brings you to share with us the bitter bread of poverty, the bread of the poor in spirit, with which our Saviour fed the five thousand and will feed thousands and tens of thousands more from eternity to eternity ? Of what use to you are the crumbs scattered here for a few beggars ?"

She felt ashamed as she moved in her long velvet train and

costly fur cloak past the cowering figures redolent of the
musty straw beds and close sleeping rooms whence they had
come, and read these questions on the wrinkled faces peering
from under woollen hoods and caps, as if she, the rich woman,
had come to take something from the poor. She had gone
forward to the empty front benches near the altar, where the
timid common people do not venture to sit, but—she knew
not why—as she was about to kneel there, she suddenly felt
that she could not cut off a view of any part of the altar from
the people behind, deprive them of anything to which she had
no right, and turning she went back to the last seat. There,
behind a trembling old man in a shabby woollen blouse, who
could scarcely bend his stiff knees and sat coughing and gasping, and a consumptive woman, who was passing the beads of
her rosary between thin, crooked fingers, she knelt down.
She was more at ease now—she felt that she had no rights
here, that she was the least among the lowliest.

The church was still dark, it had not yet been lighted, the
sacristan was obliged to be saving—every one knew that.
The faint ray which streamed through the door came from the
candle ends brought by the congregation, who set them in
front of the praying-desks to read their prayer-books. The
first person was compelled to use a match, the others lighted
their candles from his and were glad to be able to save the
matches. It was a silent agreement, which every one knew.
Here and there a tiny light glowed brightly—ever and anon
in some dark corner the slight snap of a mateh was heard and
directly after a column or the image of some saint emerged
from the wavering shadows, now fainter, now more distinct,
according as the light flashed up and down, till it burned
clearly. Then the nave grew bright and the breath of the
congregation rose through the cold church over the little
flames like clouds of incense. The high-altar alone still lay
veiled in darkness. The light of a wax-candle on the bench
in front shone brightly into the countess' eyes. The woman
in the three-cornered kerchief with the sunken temples and
bony hands glanced back and gazed mournfully, almost reproachfully, into her face and at her rich fur cloak. Madeleine
von Wildenau was ashamed of her beauty, ashamed that she
wore furs while the woman in front of her scarcely had her

shoulders covered. She felt burdened, she almost wanted to excuse herself. If she were poor also—she would have no cause to be ashamed. She gently drew out her purse and slipped the contents into the woman's hand. The latter drew back startled, she could not believe, could not understand that she was really to take it, that the lady was in earnest.

"May God reward you! I'll pray for you a thousand times!" she whispered, and a great, unutterable emotion filled the countess' soul as she met the poor woman's grateful glance. Then the kneeling crone nudged her neighbor, the coughing, stammering old man, and pressed a gold coin into his hand.

"There's something for you! You're poor and needy too."

The latter looked at the woman, who was a stranger, as though she were an apparition from another world. "Why, what is this?" he murmured with difficulty.

"The lady behind gave it to me," said the woman, pointing backward with her thumb.

The old man nodded to the lady, as well as his stiff neck would permit, and the woman did not notice that he ought to have thanked her, as the money was given to her and she had voluntarily shared it with him.

Countess Wildenau experienced a strange emotion of satisfaction as if now, for the first time, she had a right here, and with the gift she had purchased her share of the " bread of poverty."

At last there was a movement near the high altar. A sleepy alcolyte shuffled in, made his reverence before it and lighted a candle, which would not burn because he did not wait till the wax, which was stiffened by the cold, had melted. While he was lighting the second, the first went out and he was obliged to begin his task anew. The wand wavered to and fro a long time in the boy's numb hands, but at last the altar was lighted, the boy bowed again, and went down the stone steps into the vestry-room. This was ordinary prose, but the devout worshippers did not perceive it. They all knew the wondrous spell of fire, with which the Catholic church consecrates candles and gives their light the power to scatter the princes of darkness, and rejoiced in the victorious rays from which the evil spirits fled, they saw their gliding shadows dart in wild haste through the church and the sleepy boy who had wrought the miracle by means of his lighter disappear. *The light shines, no matter who kindles it.* The poor dark souls, illumined by no ray of earthly hope, eagerly absorbed its cheering rays and so long as the consecrated candles burned, the ghosts of care, discord, envy, and all the other demons of poverty were spell-bound! Now the priest entered, clad in his white robes, accompanied by two attendants.

A deathlike stillness reigned throughout the church. In a low, almost inaudible whisper he read the Latin text, which no one understood, but whose meaning every one knew, even the countess.

Everything which gives an impulse to the independent activity of the soul produces more effect than what is received in a complete form. During the incomprehensible muttering, the countess had time to recall the whole mighty drama to which it referred better and more vividly than any distinct prosaic theological essay could have described it. Again she experienced all the horrors of the Passion, as she had done in the Passion Play—only this time invisibly, instead of visibly—spiritually instead of materially—"Noli me tangere!"

The priest stooped and kissed the altar, it meant the Judas kiss. Can you kiss those lips and not fall down to worship?" cried a voice in the countess' heart, as it had done nine years before, and a nameless longing seized upon her for the divine contact which had fallen to the traitor's lot—but "Noli me tangere" rang in the ears of the penitent Magdalene. Before her stood an altar and a priest, not Christ nor Judas, and the kiss she envied was imprinted upon white linen, not the Saviour's lips. She pressed her hands upon her heart and a few bitter tears oozed from beneath her drooping lashes. She was like the blind princess in Henrik Hertz' wonderful poem, who, when she suddenly obtained her sight, no longer knew herself among the objects which she had formerly recognized only by touch, and fancied that she had lost everything which was dear and familiar—because she had gained a new sense which she knew not how to use—a *higher* one than that of her groping finger tips.

Then in her fear she turned to the *invisible* world and recognized *it* only, it alone had not changed with outward phenomena because alike to the blind and those who had sight it revealed itself only to the *mind*. It was the same with the countess. The world which she could touch with her fingers had vanished and before her newly awakened sense lay a boundless space filled with strange forms, which all seemed so unattainably distant; one only remained the same: the God whom she had *never* seen. And now when everything once familiar and near was transformed and removed to a vast distance, when everything appeared under a wholly different guise, it was He to whom her heart, accustomed to blindness, sought and found the way.

The priest was completely absorbed in his prayer-book. What he beheld the others felt with mysterious awe. It was like looking through a telescope into a strange world, while those who were not permitted to do so stood by and imagined what the former beheld.

The Sursum corda fell slowly from the lips of the priest. The bell sounded. "Christ is present!" The congregation, as if dazzled, bowed their faces and crossed themselves in the presence of the marvel that Heaven itself vouchsafed to descend to their unworthy selves. Again the bell sounded for the transformation, and perfect silence followed—while the miracle was being wrought by which God entered the mouths of mortals to be the bread of life to mankind.

This was the bread of the poor and simple-hearted, whose crumbs the Countess Wildenau had that day stolen and was eating with secret shame.

The mass was over, the priest pronounced the benediction and withdrew to the vestry-room. The people put out their bits of wax candles—clouds of light smoke filled the church. It was like Christmas Eve, after the children have gone to bed and the candles on the tree are extinguished—but their hearts are still full of Christmas joy. The countess knew not why the thought entered her mind, but she suddenly recollected that Christmas was close at hand and she no longer had any child on whom she could bestow gifts. True, she had never done this herself, but always left Josepha to attend to the matter. This year, however, she had thought she would do it, now it was too late. Suddenly she saw a child's eyes gazing happily at a lighted tree and below it a manger, with the same eyes sparkling back. The whole world, heaven and earth were glittering with children's beaming eyes, but the most beautiful of all—those of her own boy, were closed— no grateful glance smiled upon her amid the universal joy, for her there was no Christmas, for it was the mother's day, and she was *not* a mother. "Child in the manger, bend down to the sinner who mourns neglected love at Thy feet." Sinking on the kneeling bench, she sobbed bitterly. It was dark and silent. The congregation had gone, the candles on the altar had been extinguished as fast as possible—the ever-burning lamp cast dull red rays upon the altar, dawn was glimmering through the frost-covered window panes. All was still—only in the distance the cocks were crowing. Again she remembered that evening when her father came and she had knelt with Freyer in the church before the Pieta, until the crowing of the cock reminded her how easy it was to betray love and fidelity. Rising wearily from her knees, she dragged herself to a Pieta above a side altar, and pressed her lips upon the wounds of the divine body. She gazed to see if the eyes would not once more open, but it remained rigid and lifeless, this time no echo answered the mute pleading of the warm lips. No second miracle was wrought for her, the hand which guided her had been withdrawn, and like the poorest and most humble mortal she was forced to grope her way wearily along the arid path of tradition;—it was just, she had deserved nothing better, and the great discovery which came to her that day was that this path also led to God.

While thus absorbed in contemplation, a voice suddenly startled her so that she almost fainted: "What does this mean, Countess? You here at early mass, in a court-train! Are you going to write romances—or live them? I have often asked you the question, but never with so much justification as now!" Prince Emil was standing before her. She could almost have shrieked aloud in her delight. "Prince—my dear Prince!"

"Unfortunately, Prince no longer, but Duke of Metten-Barnheim, in which character I again lay myself at your feet and beg for a continuation of your favor!" said the prince with a touch of humor. Raising her from her knees, he led her into the little corridor of the church. " My father," he went on, " feels so well at Cannes that he wants to spend his old age there in peace, and summoned me by telegram to sign the abdication documents and take the burden of government upon my young shoulders. I was just coming from the station and, as I drove by, saw your carriage waiting before this poor temple. I stopped and obtained with difficulty from the half frozen coachman information concerning the place where his mistress was seeking compensation from the ennui of a court entertainment! A romantic episode, indeed! A beautiful woman in court dress, weeping and doing penance at six o'clock in the morning, among beggars and cripples in a little church in the suburbs. A swearing coachman and two horses stiff from the cold waiting outside, and lastly a faithful knight, who comes just at the right time to prevent a moral suicide and save a pair of valuable horses—what more can be desired in our time, in the way of romance ? "

" Prince—pardon me, Duke, your mockery hurts me."

" Yes, I suppose so, you are far too wearied, to understand humor. Come, I will take you to the carriage. There, lean on me, you are ill, *machère Madeleine*, you cannot go on in this way. What—you will take holy water, into which Heaven knows who has dipped his fingers. Well, to the pure all things are pure. Fortunately the doubtful fluid is frozen!"

Talking on in this way he led her out into the open air. A keen morning wind from the mountains was sweeping through the streets and cut the countess' tear-stained face. She involuntarily hid it on the duke's breast. The latter put his arm gently around her and lifted her into the carriage. His own coachman was waiting near, but the duke looked at her beseechingly. " May I go with you ? I cannot possibly leave you in this state."

The countess nodded. He motioned to his servant to drive home and entered the Wildenau equipage. " First of all, Madeleine," he said, warming her cold hands in his, " tell me : *Are* you already a saint—or do you wish to *become* one ? Whence dates this last caprice of my adored friend ? "

" No saint, Duke—neither now, nor ever, only a deeply humbled, contrite heart, which would fain fly from this world ! "

"But is this world so unlovely that one would fain try Heaven, while there are people who can be relied on under any circumstances!"

"Yes," replied the countess bitterly, but the sweetness of the true warmth of feeling revealed through her friend's humor was reviving and strengthening to her brain and heart. In his society it seemed as if there was neither pain nor woe on earth, as if all gloomy spirits must flee from his unruffled calmness. His apparent coldness produced the effect of champagne frappé, which, ice-cold when drunk, warms the whole frame.

"Oh, thank Heaven, that you are here—I have missed you sorely," she said from the depths of her soul. "Oh, my friend, what is to be done—I am helpless without you!"

"So much the better for me, if I am indispensable to you —you know that is the goal of my desires! But dearest friend —you are suffering and I cannot aid you because I do not know the difficulty! What avail is a physician, who cures only the symptoms, not the disease. You are simply bungling about on your own responsibility and every one knows that is the worst thing a sick person can do. Consumptives use the hunger-cure, anæmics resort to blood letting. You, my dear Madeleine, I think, do the same thing. Mortification, when your vital strength is waning, moral blood-letting, while the heart needs food and warmth. What kind of cure is it to be up all night long and wander about in cold churches, with the thermometer marking below freezing, early in the morning. I should advise you to edit a book on the physiology of the nerves. You are like the man in the fairy-tale who wanted to learn to shiver." An involuntary smile hovered about the countess' lips.

"Duke—your humor is beginning to conquer. No doubt you are right in many things, but you do not know the state of my mind. My life is destroyed, the axe is laid at the root, happiness, honor—all are lost."

"For Heaven's sake, what has happened to thus overwhelm you?" asked the duke, still in the most cheerful mood.

She could not tell him the truth and pleaded some incident at court as an excuse. Then in a few words she told him of

19

the queen's displeasure, the malice of her enemies, her imperilled position.

"And do you take this so tragically?" The prince laughed aloud: "Pardon me, *chère amie*—but one can't help laughing! A woman like you to despair because a few stiff old court sycophants look askance at you, and the queen does not understand you which, with the dispositions you both have, was precisely what might have been expected. It is too comical! It is entirely my own fault—I ought to have considered it—but I expected you to show more feminine craft and diplomacy. That you disdained to employ the petty arts which render one a *Persona grata* at court is only an honor to you, and if a few fops presumed to adopt an insolent manner to you, they shall receive a lesson which will teach them that *your* honor is *mine!* Nay, it ought to amuse you, to feign death awhile and see how the mice will all come out and dance around you to scatter again when the lioness awakes. Do you talk of destroyed happiness and roots to which the axe is laid? Oh, women—women! You can despair over a plaything! For this position at court could never be aught save a toy to you!"

"But to retire thus in shame and disgrace—would *you* endure it—if it should happen to you? Ought not a woman to be as sensitive concerning her honor as a man?"

"I don't think your honor will suffer, because the restraint of court life does not suit you! Or is it because you do not understand the queen? Why, surely persons are not always sympathetic and avoid one another without any regret; does the fact become so fateful because one of you wears a crown? In that case I beg you to remember that a crown is hovering over your head also—a crown that is ready to descend whenever that head will receive it, and that you will then be in a position to address Her Majesty as 'chère cousine!' You, a Princess von Prankenberg, a Countess Wildenau, fly like a rebuked child at an ungracious glance from the queen and her court into a corner of a church?" He shook his head. "There must be something else. What is it? I shall never learn, but you cannot deceive me!"

The countess was greatly disconcerted. She tried to find another plausible pretext for her mood and, like all natures to whom deception is not natural, said precisely what betrayed her: "I am anxious about the Wildenaus—they are only watching for the moment when they can compromise me unpunished, and if the queen withdraws her favor, they need show me no farther consideration."

The duke frowned. "Ah! ah!"—he said slowly, under his breath: "What do you fear from the Wildenaus, how can they compromise you?"

The countess, startled, kept silence. She saw that she had betrayed herself.

"Madeleine"—he spoke calmly and firmly—"everything must now be clearly understood between us. What connection was there between Wildenau and that mysterious boy? I must know, for I see that that is the quarter whence the danger which you fear is threatening you, and I must know how to avert it—you have just heard that *your* honor is *mine*." There was a shade of sternness in his tone, the sternness of an resolve to take this weak, wavering woman under his protection.

"The child"—she faltered, trembling from head to foot— "ah, no—there is nothing more to be feared from him—he is dead!"

"Dead?" asked the duke gently. "Since when?"

"Since yesterday!" And the proud countess, sobbing uncontrollably, sank upon his breast.

A long silence followed.

The duke passed his arm around her and let her weep her fill. "My poor Madeleine—I understand everything." An indescribable emotion filled the hearts of both. Not another word was exchanged.

The carriage rolled up to the entrance of the Wildenau palace. Her little cold hands clasped his beseechingly.

"Do not desert me!" she whispered hurriedly.

"Less than ever!" he replied gravely and firmly.

"Her Highness is ill!" he said to the servants who came hurrying out and helped the tottering woman up the steps. She entered the boudoir, where the duke himself removed her cloak. It was a singular sight—the haughty figure in full evening dress, adorned with jewels, in the light of the dawning day—like some beautiful spirit of the night, left behind by her companions who had fled from the first sunbeams, and now stood terrified, vainly striving to conceal herself in darkness. " Poor wandering sprite, where is the home your tearful eyes are seeking ?" said the prince, overwhelmed by pity as he saw the grief-worn face. " Yes, Madeleine, you are too beautiful for the broad glare of day. Such visions suit the veil of evening—the magical lustre of drawing-rooms! By day one feels as if the night had been robbed of an elf, who having lost her wings by the morning light was compelled to stay among common mortals." Carried away by an outburst of feeling, he approached her with open arms. A strange conflict of emotion was seething in her breast. She had longed for him, as for the culture she had despised—she felt that she could not live without him, that without him she could not exorcise the spirits she had conjured up to destroy her, her ear listened with rapture to the expression of love in cultured language, but when he strove to approach her—it seemed as if that unapproachable something which had cried " Noli me tangere !" had established its throne in her own heart since she had knelt among the beggars early that morning, and now, in spite of herself, cried in its solemn dignity from her lips the " Noli me tangere " to another.

And, without words, the duke understood it, respected her mute denial, and reverently drew back a step.

" Do you not wish to change your dress, you are utterly exhausted. If it will be a comfort to you to have me stay, I will wait till you have regained your strength. Then I will beg permission to breakfast with you !" he said with his wonted calmness.

" Yes, I thank you !" she answered—with a two-fold meaning, and left the room with a bearing more dignified than the duke had ever seen, as though she had an invisible companion of whom she was proud.

CHAPTER XXIV.

ATTEMPTS TO RESCUE.

THE countess remained absent a long time, while the duke
sat at the window of the boudoir gazing out into the frosty
winter morning, but without seeing what was passing outside.
Before him lay a shattered happiness, a marred destiny. The
happiness was his, the destiny hers. "There is surely nothing weaker than a woman—even the strongest!" he thought,
shaking his head mournfully. Ought we not to punish this
personator of Christ, who used his mask to break into the cit-
adel of our circle and steal what did not belong to him?
Pshaw, how could the poor fellow help it if an eccentric
woman out of ennui—ah, no, we should not think of it! But
—what is to be done now? Shall I sacrifice this superb
creature to an insipid prejudice, because she sacrificed herself
and everything else to a childish delusion? Where is the
man pure enough to condemn you because when you give,
you give wholly, royally, and in your proud self-forgetfulness
fling what others would outweigh with kingly crowns into the
lap of a beggar who can offer you nothing in exchange, not
even appreciation of your value—which he is too uncultured
to perceive.

"Alas! such a woman—to be thrown away on such a
man! And should I not save her? Should I weakly desert
her—I, the only person who can forgive because I am the
only one who *understands* her?—No! It would be against
all the logic of destiny and reason, were I to suffer such a life
to be wrecked by this religious humbug. What is the use of
my cool brain, if I lose my composure *now? Allons donc!*
I will bid defiance to fate and to every prejudice, clasp her in
my arms, and destroy the divine farce!"

Such was the train of the duke's thoughts. But his pale
face and joyless expression betrayed what he would not acknowledge to himself: that his happiness was shattered. He
gathered up the fragments and tried to join them together—
but with the secret grief with which we bear home some loved
one who could not be witheld from a dangerous path, know-

ing that, though the broken limbs may be healed, he can never regain his former strength.

"So grave, Duke?" asked a voice which sent the blood to his heart. The countess had entered—her step unheard on the soft carpet.

He started up: "Madeleine—my poor Madeleine! I was thinking of you and your fate!"

"I have saddened you!" she said, clasping her hands penitently.

"Oh, no!" he drew the little hands down to his lips, and with a sorrowful smile kissed them.

"My cheerfulness can bear some strain—but the malapert must be permitted to be silent sometimes when there are serious matters to be considered."

"You are too noble to let me feel that you are suffering. Yet I see it—you would not be the man you are if you did not suffer to-day."

The duke bit his lips, it seemed as if he were struggling to repress a tear: "Pshaw—we won't be sentimental! You have wept enough to-day! The world must not see tear-stains on your face. Give me a cup of coffee—I do not belong to the chosen few whom a mental emotion raises far above all the needs of their mortal husk."

The countess rang for breakfast.

The servant brought the dishes ordered into the boudoir, as the dining-room was not yet thoroughly heated. In the chimney-corner beside the blazing fire the coffee was already steaming in a silver urn over an alcohol lamp, filling the cosy room with its aroma and musical humming.

"How pleasant this is!" said the duke, throwing himself into an armchair beside the grave mistress of the house.

"I will pour it myself," she said to the servant who instantly withdrew. The countess was now simply dressed in black, without an ornament of any kind, and with her hair confined in a plain knot.

"What a contrast!" the duke remarked, smiling—"you alone are capable of such metamorphoses. Half an hour ago in a court costume, glittering with diamonds, an aching heart, and hands half frozen from being clasped in prayer in the chilled church, now a demure little housewife, peacefully watching the coffee steam in a cosy little room, waiting intently for the moment when the water will boil, as if there were no task in the whole world more important than that of making a good decoction."

A faint smile glided over the countess' face—she had nearly allowed the important moment to pass. Now she poured out the coffee, extinguished the spirit lamp, and handed her companion a cup of the steaming beverage.

" A thousand thanks! Ah, that's enough to brighten the most downcast mood! What comfort! Now let us enjoy an hour of innocent, genuine plebeian happiness. Ah—how fortunate the people are who live so every day. I should be the very man to enjoy such bliss!" His glance wandered swiftly to the countess' empty cup. " Aha! I thought so! A great sorrow must of course be observed by mortifying the body, in order to be sure to succumb to it. Well, then the guest must do the honors of the hostess! There, now *ma chère Madeleine* will drink this, and dip this buscuit into it! One can accomplish that, even without an appetite. Who would wish to make heart and stomach identical!"

The countess, spite of her protestations, was forced to obey. She saw that the duke had asked for breakfast only to compel her to eat.

" There. You see that it can be done. I enjoy with a touch of emotion this coffee which your dear hands have prepared. If you would do the same with the cup I poured out what a sentimental breakfast it would be!" A ray of the old cheerfulness sparkled in the duke's eyes.

" Ah, I knew that with you alone I should find peace and cheer!" said the countess, brightening.

"So much the better." The duke lighted a cigarette and leaned comfortably back in his chair.

The countess ordered the coffee equipage to be removed and then sat down opposite to him with her hands clasped in her lap.

"The main point now, my dear Madeleine, if I may be allowed to speak of these things to you, is to release you from the cause of all the trouble—I need not name him. Of course I do not know how easy or how difficult this may be, because I am ignorant how far you are involved in this relation and unfortunately lack the long locks of the Christ, which would enable me successfully to play the part of the 'Good Shepherd,' who freed the imprisoned lamb from the thicket."

"As if it depended on that!" said the countess.

"Not at all? Oh, women, women! What will not a few raven locks do? The destiny of your lives turns upon just such trifles. Imagine that Ammergau Christus with close-cropped hair and a bristling red beard! Would that mask have suited the illusion to which you sacrificed yourself? Hardly!"

The countess made no reply, silenced by the pitiless truth, but at last she thought she must defend herself. "And the religious impression, the elevation, the enthusiasm—the revelations of the Passion Play, do you count these nothing?"

"Certainly not! I felt them myself, but, believe me, you would not have transferred them to the person, if the representative of Christ had worn a wig, and the next day had appeared before you with stiff, closely-cropped red hair."

The countess made a gesture of aversion.

"There, now you see the realist again. Yet, say what you will, a few locks of raven hair formed the net in which the haughty, clever Countess Wildenau was prisoned!"

"You may be right, the greatest picture consists of details, and may be spoiled by a single one. I will confess it—Yes! The harmony of the whole person, down to the most trifling detail, with the Christ tradition, enthralled me, and had the locks been wanting, the impression would not have been complete. But, however I may have been deceived in the image, I cannot let myself and him sink so low in your opinion as to permit you to believe that it was nothing save an ensnaring outward semblance which sealed my fate! Had not his spiritual nature completed the illusion—matters would never have gone so far."

"Yes, yes, I can imagine how it happened. You prompted the part, and he had skill enough to play to the prompter, as it is called in the parlance of the stage."

"'Skill' is not the right word, he was influenced precisely as I was."

"Ah! He probably would not have been so foolish as to refuse such a chance. A wealthy, beautiful woman—like you—"

" No, no, do not speak of him in that way. I cannot let that accusation rest upon him. He is not base! He is uncultured, has the narrow-minded views of a peasant, is sensative and capricious, an unfortunate temperament, with which it is impossible to live happily—but I know no one in the world, to whom any ignoble thought is more alien."

The prince gazed at her admiringly. Tears were sparkling in her eyes. " I don't deny that I am bitterly dissappointed in him—but though I love him no longer, I must not allow him to be insulted. He loved me and sacrificed his poor life for mine—that the compensation did not outweigh the price was no fault of his, and I ought not to make him responsible for it."

The duke became very thoughtful. The countess was silent, she had clasped her hands on her knee, and was gazing, deeply moved, into vacancy.

" You are a noble woman, Madeleine!" he said in a low tone. " I always ranked you high, but never higher than at this moment! I will never again wound your feelings. But however worthy of esteem Freyer may be, deeply as I pity the unfortunate man—you are my first consideration— and you cannot, must not continue in this relation. Throughout the whole system of the universe the lower existence must yield to the higher. You are the higher—therefore Freyer must be sacrificed! You are a philosopher—accept the results of your view of the world, be strong and resolve to do what is inevitable quickly. You yourself say that you no longer love him—whether you have ever done so, I will not venture to decide! If he is really what you describe him to be, he must feel this and—I believe, that he, too, is not to be envied. What kind of respite is this which you are granting the hapless man under the sword of the executioner. Pardon me, but I should term it torture. You feign, from motives of compassion, feelings you no longer have, and he feels the deception. So he is continually vibrating between the two extremes of fear and hope—a prey to the most torturing doubts. So you permit the victim whom you wish to kill to live, in order to destroy him slowly. You pity him—and for pity are cruel."

The countess cast a startled glance at him. " You are terribly truthful."

"I must say that I am sorry for that man," the duke went on in his usual manner. "I think it is your duty to end this state of things. If he has a good, mentally sound character, he will conquer the blow and shape his life anew. But such a condition of uncertainty would unnerve the strongest nature. This cat and mouse sport is unworthy of you! You tried it with me ten years ago in a less painful way—I, knowing women, was equal to the game, so no harm was done, and I could well allow you the graceful little pastime. It is different with Freyer. A man of his stamp, who stakes his whole life upon a single feeling, takes the matter more tragically, and the catastrophe was inevitable. But must romance be carried to tragedy? See, my dear friend, that it is confined within its proper limits. Besides, you have already paid for it dearly enough—it has left an indelible impress upon your soul— borne a fruit which matured in suffering and you have buried with anguish because destiny itself, though with a stern hand, tried to efface the consequences of your error. Heed this portent, for your sake and his own! I speak in his behalf also. My aim is not only to win you, but to see the woman whom I have won worthy of herself and the high opinion I cherish of her."

The countess' features betrayed the most intense emotion. What should she do? Should she tell this noble man all— confess that she was *married*. The hour that he discovered it, he would desert her. Must she lose him, her last support and consolation? No, she dared not. The drowning woman clung to him; she knew not what was to come of it—she only knew that she would be lost without him—and kept silence.

"Where is he? In the old hunting-box of which your cousin Wildenau spoke?" asked the duke after a long pause.

"Yes."

"As what?"

"As steward."

"Steward? H'm!"

The duke shook his head. "What a relation; you made the man you loved your servant, and believed that you could love him still? How little you knew yourself! Had you seen him on the mountains battling with wind and storm as a wood-cutter, a shepherd, but free, you might have continued to love him. But as 'the steward' at whom the servants look with one eye as their equal, with the other as their mistress' favorite—never! You placed him in a situation where he could not help despising himself—how could *you* respect him? But a woman like you no longer loves where she can no longer esteem!" He was silent a moment, then with sudden determination exclaimed: "Do you understand what I say now? Not free yourself from him—but free *him* from *himself!* You have done the same thing as the giantess who carried the farmer and his plough home in her apron. Do you understand what a deep meaning underlies Chamisso's comical tale? The words with which the old giant ordered her to take her prize back to the spot where she found it, say everything: 'The peasant is no plaything.' Only in the sphere where a man naturally belongs is he of value, but this renders him too good for a toy. You have transplanted Freyer to a sphere in which he ceased to have any value to you and are now making him play a part there which I would not impose on my worst enemy."

"Yes, you are right."

"Finally we owe it to those who were once dear to us, not to make them ridiculous! Or do you believe that Freyer, if he had the choice, would not have pride enough to prefer the most cruel truth to a compassionate lie?"

"Certainly."

"And still more. We owe it to the law of truthfulness, under which we stand as moral beings, not to continue deliberately a deception which was perhaps unconsciously begun. When self-respect is lost—all is lost."

The duke rose: "It is time for me to go. Consider my advice, I can say nothing more in your interest and his."

"But what shall I do—how am I to find a gentle way—oh! Heaven, I don't know how to help myself."

"Do nothing at present, everything is still too fresh to venture upon any positive act—the wounds would bleed, and what ought to be severed would only grow together the more firmly. Go away for a time. You are out of favor with the queen. What is more natural than to go on a journey and sulk. To the so-called steward also, this must at present serve for a pretext to avoid a tragical parting scene."

"Go now! Now!—leave—you?" she whispered, blushing as she spoke.

"Madeleine," he said gently, drawing her hand to his
breast. "How am I to interpret this blush? Is it the sign
of a sweeter feeling, or embarrassment because circumstances
have led you to say something which I might interpret differently from your intention?"

She bent her head, blushing still more deeply.

"Perhaps you do not know yourself—I will not torture
you with questions, which your agitated heart cannot answer·
now. But if anything really does bind you to me, then—I
would suggest your joining my father at Cannes. If even the
faintest feeling of affection for me is stirring within you, you
will understand that we could never be nearer to each other
than while you were learning to be my old father's daughter!
Will you?"

"Yes!" she whispered with rising tears, for ever more beautiful, ever purer rose before her a happiness which she had forfeited, of which she would no longer be worthy, even could
she grasp it.

The duke, usually so sharp-sighted, could not guess the
source of these tears; for the first time he was deceived and
interpreted favorably an emotion aroused by the despairing
perception that all was vain.

He gazed down at her with a ray of love shining in his
clear blue eyes, and pressed a kiss on her drooping brow.
Then raising his hand, he pointed upward. "Only have
courage, and hold your head high. All will yet be well.
Adieu!"

He moved away as proudly, calmly and firmly as if success was assured; he did not suspect that he was leaving a
lost cause.

CHAPTER XXV.

DAY IS DAWNING.

In the quiet chamber in the ancient hunting-castle, on the spot formerly occupied by the little bed, a casket now stood on two chairs near a wooden crucifix.

Freyer had returned, bringing the body of his child. He had telegraphed to the countess, but received in reply only a few lines: "She was compelled to set off on a journey at once, her mind was so much affected that her physician had advised immediate change of scene to avert worse consequences."

A check was enclosed to defray the funeral expenses and bestow a sum on Josepha "as a recognition of her faithful service," sufficient to enable her to live comfortably in case she wished to rest. Josepha understood that this was a gracious form of dismissal. But the royal gift which expressed the countess' gratitude did not avail to subdue the terrible rancor in her soul, or the harshness of this dismissal.

Morning was dawning. Josepha was changed by illness almost beyond recognition, yet she had watched through the night with Freyer beside the coffin. Now she again glanced over the letter which had come the evening before. "She doesn't venture to send me away openly, and wants to satisfy me with money, that I may go willingly. Money, always money! I was forced to give up the child, and now I must lose you, too, the last thing I have in the world?" she said to Freyer, who was sitting silently beside the coffin of his son. Tearing the cheque, she threw it on the floor. "There are the fragments. When the child is buried, I know where I shall go."

"You will not leave here, Josepha, as long as I remain. Especially now that you are ill. I have been her servant long enough. But this is the limit where I cease to yield to her caprices. She cannot ask me to give you up also, my relative, the only soul in my boundless solitude. If she did, I would not do it, for—no matter how lowly my birth, I am still her husband; have I no rights whatever? You will stay with me, I desire it, and can do so the more positively as my salary is sufficient to support you. So you need accept no wages from her."

"Yes, tell her so, say that I want nothing—nothing except to stay with you, near my angel's grave." Sobs stifled her words. After a time, she continued faintly: "I shall not trouble her long, you can see that."

"Oh, Josepha, don't fancy such things. You are young and will recover!" said Freyer consolingly, but his eyes rested anxiously upon her.

She shook her head. "The child was younger still, yet he died of longing for his mother, and I shall die of the yearning for him."

"Then let me send for a doctor—you cannot go on in this way."

"Oh, pray don't make any useless ado—it would only be one person more to question me about the child, and I shall be on thorns while I am deceiving him. You know I never could lie in my life. Leave me in peace, no doctor can help me."

Some one rang. Josepha opened the door. The cabinet-maker was bringing in a little coffin, which was to take the place of the box containing the leaden casket. Her black dress and haggard face gave her the semblance of a mother mourning her own child. Nothing was said during the performance of the work. Josepha and Freyer lifted the metal casket from the chest and placed it in the plain oak coffin. The man was paid and left the room. Freyer hastened out and shook the snow from some pine branches to adorn the bier. A few icicles which still clung to them thawed in the warm room, and the drops fell on the coffin—the tears of the forest! The last scion of the princely House of Prankenberg lay under frost-covered pine boughs; and a peasant mourned him as his son, a maid servant prepared him for his eternal rest. This is the bloodless revolution sometimes accomplished amid the ossified traditions of rank, which affords the insulted idea of universal human rights moments of loving satisfaction.

The two mourners were calm and quiet. They seemed to have a premonition that this moment possessed a significance which raised it far above personal grief.

An hour later the pastor came—a few men and maid-servants formed the funeral procession. Not far from the castle, in the wood, stood a ruinous old chapel. The countess had permitted the child to be buried there because the churchyard was several leagues away. " It is a great deal of honor· for Josepha's child to be placed in the chapel of a noble family!" thought the people. "If haughty old Count Wildenau knew it, he would turn in his grave!" The coffin was raised and borne out of the castle. Josepha, leaning on Freyer, followed silently with fixed, tearless eyes and burning cheeks. Yet she succeeded in wading through the snow and standing on the cold stone floor in the chilly chapel beside the grave. But when she returned home, the measure of her strength was exhausted. Her laboring lungs panted for breath; her icy feet could not be warmed; her heart, throbbing painfully, sent all the blood to her brain, which burned with fever, while her thoughts grew confused. The terrible chill completed the work of destruction commenced by grief. Freyer saw it with unutterable sorrow.

" I must get a doctor!" he said gently. " Come, Josepha, don't stare steadily at the empty space where the body lay. Come, I will take you to my room and put you on the bed. Everything there will not remind you of the boy."

" No, I will stay here," she said, with that cruelty to herself, peculiar to sick persons who do not fear death. "Just here!" She clung to the uncomfortable sofa on which she sat as if afraid of being dragged away by force.

Freyer hastily removed the chairs which had supported the coffin, the crucifix, and the candles.

" Yes, put them out, you will soon need them for me. Oh, you kind-hearted man. If only you could have the happiness you deserve. You merited a better fate. Ah, I will not speak of what she has done to me, but her sins against you and the child nothing can efface—nothing!" A fit of coughing almost stifled her. But it seemed as if her eyes continued to utter the words she had not breath to speak, a feverish vengeance glittered in their depths which made Freyer fairly shudder.

" Josepha," he said mildly, but firmly. " Sacrifice your hate to God, and be merciful. If you love me, you must forgive her whom I love and forgive."

" Never !" gasped Josepha with a violent effort. " Joseph
—oh ! this pain in my chest—I believe it is inflammation of the
lungs !"

" Alas !—and there is no one to send for the doctor. The
men are all in the woods. Go to bed, I beg you, there is not
a moment to be lost, I must get the doctor myself. I will
send the house-maid to you. Keep up your courage, I will
be as quick as I can !"

And he hurried off, forgetting his grief for his child in his
anxiety about the last companion of his impoverished life.

The house-maid came in and asked if she could do anything, but Josepha wanted no assistance. The anxious girl
tried to persuade her to go to bed, but Josepha said that she
could not breathe lying down. At last she consented to eat
something. The nourishment did her good, her weakness
diminished and her breathing grew easier. The girl put
some wood in the stove and returned to her work in the
kitchen. Josepha remained lost in thought. To her, death
was deliverance—but Freyer, what would become of him if he
lost her also? This alone rendered it hard to die. The
damp wood in the stove sputtered and hissed like the voices
of wrangling women. It was the " fire witch," which always
proclaims the approach of any evil. Josepha shook her head.
What could be worse than the evil which had already befallen
her poor cousin and herself? The fire witch continued to
shriek and lament, but Josepha did not understand her. A
pair of crows perched in an old pine tree outside the window
croaked so suddenly that she started in terror.

Ah, it was very lonely up here ! What would it be when
Freyer lived all alone in the house and waited months in vain
for the heartless woman who remembered neither her husband
nor her child ? She had not troubled herself about the living,
why should she seek the little grave where lay the *dead ?*

A loud knock on the door of the house echoed through
the silence.

Josepha listened. Surely it could not be the doctor already ?

The maid opened it. Heavy footsteps and the voices of
men were heard in the entry, then a dog howled. The stupid
servant opened the door of the room and called : " Jungfer

Josepha, here are two hunters, who are so tired tramping over the snow that they would like to rest awhile. Can they come in? There is no fire anywhere else!"

Josepha, though so ill, of course could not refuse admittance to the freezing men, who were already on the threshold. Rising with an effort from the sofa, she pushed some chairs for the strangers near the stove. "I am ill," she said in great embarrassment—"but if you wish to rest and warm yourselves here, I beg—"

"We are very grateful," said one of the hunters, a gentleman with a red moustache and piercing eyes. "If we do not disturb you, we will gladly accept your hospitality. We are not familiar with the neighborhood and have lost our way. We came from beyond the frontier and have been wading through the snow five hours."

Meanwhile, at a sign from Josepha, the maid-servant had taken the gentlemen's cloaks and hunting gear.

"See, this is our booty," said the other hunter. "If we might invite you to dine with us, I should almost venture to ask if this worthy lass could not roast the hare for us? Our cousin, Countess Wildenau, will surely forgive us this little trespass upon her preserves."

"Are you relatives of Countess Wildenau?"

"Certainly, her nearest and most faithful ones!"

Josepha, in her mortal weakness felt as if crushed by the presence of these strangers—with their heavy hunting-boots and loud voices. She tried to take refuge in the kitchen on the pretense of roasting the hare herself. But both gentlemen earnestly protested against it.

"No, indeed, that would be fine business to drive you out of your room when you are ill! In that case, we must leave the house at once."

The red-bearded gentleman—Cousin Wildenau himself—sprang from his chair and almost forced Josepha to go back to her sofa.

"There, my dear—madam—or miss? Now do me the honor to take your seat again and allow us to remain a short time until the roast is ready, then you must dine with us."

A faint smile hovered around Josepha's parched lips. "I thank you, but I am too ill to eat."

" You are really very ill "—said the stranger with kindly
solicitude. " You are feverish. I fear we are disturbing you
very much. Pray send us away if we annoy you." Yet he
knew perfectly well that she could not help asking the unbid-
den guests to stay.

" But my dear—madam—or miss ?"—Josepha never answered the question—" are you doing nothing to relieve your
illness, have you had no physician ?"

" No we are in such a secluded place, a physicain cannot
always be had. But I am expecting one to-day."

" Why, it is strange to live in this wilderness. And how
uncomfortable you are, you haven't even a stool," said the red-
haired cousin putting his huge hunting-muff, after warming it
at the stove, under her feet.

Josepha tried to refuse it, but he would not listen.

" You need not mind us, we are sick nurses ourselves, we
commanded a sanitary battalion in the war. So we understand a little what to do. You are suffering from asthma, it is
difficult for you to breathe, so you must sit comfortably.
There! Now put my cousin's muff at your back. That's
better, isn't it ?"

" But pray—"

" Come, come, come—no contradiction. You must be
comfortable."

Josepha was ashamed. The gentlemen were so kind, so
solicitous about her—there were good people in the world!
The neglected, desolate heart gratefully appreciated the unusual kindness.

" But I am really astonished to find everything so primitive. Our honored cousin really ought to have done something more for your comfort. Not even a sofa-cushion, no
carpet! I should have thought she would have paid more attention to so faithful a—" he courteously suppressed the word
" servant "—and correcting himself, said : " assistant !"

Josepha made no answer, but her lips curled bitterly,
significantly.

Wildenau noted it. " Dissatisfied!" escaped his lips, so
low that only his companion heard it.

" You have been here a long time, I suppose—how many
years ?

" Have I been with her ?" said Josepha frankly. " Since the last Passion Play. That will be ten years next summer."

" Ah—true—you are a native of Ammergau!" said the baron, with the manner of one familiar with the facts, whose memory has failed for an instant. " I suppose you came to the countess at the same time as the Christus ?"

" Yes."

" Is he a relative of yours ?"

" Yes, my cousin."

" He is here still, isn't he ?"

" Why, of course."

" He is—her—what is his title ?"

" Steward."

" Is he at home ?"

" No, he has gone to the city for a doctor."

" Oh, I am very sorry. We should have been glad to make his acquaintance. We have heard so many pleasant things about him. A man in whom our cousin was so much interested—"

" Then she speaks of him ?"

" Oh—to her intimate friends—certainly !" said Wildenau equivocally gazing intently at Josepha, whose face beamed with joy at the thought that the countess spoke kindly of Freyer.

" Why is he never seen in the city ? He must live like a hermit up here."

" Yes, Heaven knows that."

" He ought to visit my cousin sometimes in the city, everybody would be glad to know the Ammergau Christus."

" But if she doesn't wish it—!" said Josepha thoughtlessly.

" Why, that would be another matter certainly, but she has never told me so. Why shouldn't she wish it ?" murmured Wildenau with well-feigned surprise.

" Because she is ashamed of him !"

" Ah !" Wildenau almost caught his breath at the significance of the word. " But, tell me, why does Herr Freyer—isn't that his name—submit to it ?"

Josepha shrugged her shoulders. " Yes, what can he do about it ?"

A pause ensued. Josepha stopped, as if fearing to say too much. The two gentlemen had become very thoughtful.

At last Wildenau resumed the conversation. " I don't understand how a man who surely might find a pleasant position anywhere, can be so dependent on a fine lady's whims. You won't take it amiss, I see that your kinsman's position troubles you—were I in his place I would give up the largest salary rather than—"

" Salary?" interrupted Josepha, with flashing eyes. " Do you suppose that my cousin would do anything for the sake of a salary? Oh, you don't know him. If the countess described him to you in that way, the shame is hers !"

Wildenau listened intently. " But, my dear woman, that isn't what I meant, you would not let me finish ! I was just going to add that such a motive would not affect your kinsman, that it could be nothing but sincere devotion, which bound him to our cousin—a loyalty which apparently wins little gratitude."

" Yes, I always tell him so—but he won't admit it—even though his heart should break."

Two dark interlaced veins in Josepha's sunken, transparent temples throbbed feverishly.

" But—how do you feel ? We are certainly disturbing you!" said the baron.

" Oh, no ! It does not matter !" replied Josepha, courteously.

" Could you not take us into some other room—the countess doubtless comes here constantly—there must be other apartments which can be heated."

" Yes, but no fire has been made in them for weeks; the stoves will smoke."

" Has not the countess been here for so long ?"

" No, she scarcely ever comes now."

" But the time must be very long to you and your cousin —you were doubtless accustomed to the countess' visits."

" Certainly," replied Josepha, lost in thought—" when I think how it used to be—and how things are now !"

Wildenau glanced around the room, then said softly: " And the little son—he is dead."

Josepha stared at him in terror. " Do you know that ?"

"I know all. My cousin has his picture in her boudoir, a splendid child."

Josepha's poor feverish brain was growing more and more confused. The tears she had scarcely conquered flowed again. "Yes, wasn't he—and to let such a child die without troubling herself about him!"

"It is inexcusable" said Wildenau.

"If the countess ever speaks of it again, tell her that Josepha loved it far more than she, for she followed it to the grave while the mother enjoyed her life—she must be ashamed then."

"I will tell her. It is a pity about the beautiful child— was it not like an Infant Christ?"

"Indeed it was—and now I know what picture you mean. In Jerusalem, where the child was christened, a copy as they called it of the Infant Christ hung in the chapel over the baptismal font. The countess afterwards bought the picture on account of its resemblance to the boy."

"I suppose it resembles Herr Freyer, too?" the baron remarked carelessly.

"Somewhat, but the mother more!"

Baron Wildenau began to find the room too warm—and went to the window a moment to get the air, while his companion, horrified by these disclosures, shook his head. He would gladly have told the deluded woman that they had only learned the child's death from a wood-cutter whom they met in the forest—but he dared not "contradict" his cousin. After a pause, Wildenau again turned to Josepha. He saw that there was danger in delay, for at any moment the fever might increase to such a degree that she would begin to rave and no longer be capable of making a deposition: The truth must be discovered, now or never! He felt, however, that Josepha's was no base nature which could be led to betray her employer by ordinary means. Caution and reflection were necessary.

"I am really touched by your fidelity to my cousin. Any one who can claim such a nature is fortunate. I thank you in her name."

He held out his hand. But she replied with her usual blunt honesty: "I don't deserve your thanks, sir. I have not remained here for the sake of the countess, but on account of the child and my unfortunate cousin. She has been kind to me—but—if I should see her to-day, I would tell her openly that I would never forgive her treatment of the child and Joseph—no matter what she did. The child is dead and my cousin will die too. Thank Heaven, I shall not live to witness it."

"I understand you perfectly—oh, I know my cousin. And—my poor dear Fräulein Josepha—I may call you Fräulein now, may I not, since you are no longer obliged to pass for the child's mother?—it was an unprecedented sacrifice for you—! Alas! My dear Fräulein, you and your cousin must be prepared to fare still worse, to be entirely forgotten, for I can positively assure you that the countess is about to wed the Hereditary Prince of Metten-Barnheim."

"What?" Josepha shrieked loudly.

Wildenau watched her intently.

"She has just gone to Cannes, where the old duke is staying, and the announcement of the engagement is daily expected."

"It is impossible—it cannot be!" murmured Josepha, trembling in every limb.

"But why not? She is free—has a right to dispose of her hand—" Wildenau persisted.

"No—she is not—she cannot marry," cried Josepha, starting from her sofa in despair and standing before them with glowing cheeks and red hair like a flame which blazes up once more before expiring. "For Heaven's sake—it would be a crime!"

"But who is to prevent it?" asked Wildenau breathlessly.

"I!" groaned Josepha, summoning her last strength.

"You?—My dear woman, what can you do?"

"More than you suppose!"

"Then tell me, that we may unite to prevent the crime ere it is too late."

"Yes, by Heaven! Before I will allow her to do Joseph this wrong—I will turn traitor to her."

"But Herr Freyer has no right to ask the countess not to marry again—"

"No right?" she repeated with terrible earnestness, "are you so sure of that?"

"He is only the countess' lover—"

" Her lover ?" sobbed Josepha in mingled wrath and anguish : " Joseph, you noble upright man—must *this* be said of you—!"

" I don't understand. If he is not her lover—what is he ?"

Josepha could bear no more. " He is her husband—her legally wedded husband."

The baron almost staggered under this unexpected, unprecedented revelation. Controlling himself with difficulty, he seized the sick woman's hand, as if to sustain her lest she should break down, ere he had extorted the last disclosure from her—the last thing he must know. " Only tell me where and by whom the marriage ceremony was performed."

As if under the gaze of a serpent the victim yielded to the stronger will : " At Prankenburg—Martin and I—were witnesses." She slipped from his hand, her senses grew confused, her eyes became glassy, her chest heaved convulsively in the struggle for breath, but the one word which she still had consciousness to utter—was enough for the Wildenaus.

When, a few hours later, Freyer returned with the physician and the priest, whom he had thoughtfully brought with him, he found Josepha alone on the sofa, speechless, and in the last agonies of death.

The physician, after examining her, said that an acute inflammation of the lungs had followed the tuberculosis from which she had long suffered and hastened her end. The priest gave her the last sacrament and remained with Freyer, sitting beside the bed in which she had been laid. The death-struggle was terrible. She seemed to be constantly trying to tell Freyer something which she was unable to utter. Three times life appeared to have departed, and three times she rallied again, as if she could not die without having relieved her heart of its burden. Vain ! It was useless for Freyer to put his ear to her lips, he could not understand her faltering words. It was a terrible night! At last, toward morning, she grew calm, and now she could die. Leaning on his breast, she ceased her struggles to speak, and slowly breathed her last. *She* had conquered and she now knew that *he* would conquer also. She bowed her head with a smile, and her last glance was fixed on him, a look of reconciliation rested on her features—her soul soared upward—day was dawning !

CHAPTER XXVI.

THE LAST SUPPORT.

THERE was alarm in the Wildenau Palace. The countess
had suddenly returned, without notifying the servants—in
plain words, without asking the servants' permission. She had
intended to remain absent several months—they were not prepared, had nothing ready, nothing cleaned, not even a single
room in her suite of apartments heated.

She seemed absent-minded, went to her rooms at once,
and locked herself in. Then her bell rang violently—the servants who were consulting together below scattered, the maids
darted up the main staircase, the men up a side flight.

"I want the coachman, Martin!" was the unexpected
order.

"Martin isn't here," the footman ventured to answer—"as
we did not know . . . ."

"Then send for him!" replied the countess imperiously.
She did not appear even to notice the implied reproof. Then
she permitted the attendant to make a fire on the hearth, for
it was a raw, damp day in early spring, and after her stay in
Cannes, the weather seemed like Siberia.

Half an hour elapsed. Meanwhile the maids were unpacking, and the countess was arranging a quantity of letters
she had brought with her. They were all numbered, and of
ancient date. Among them was one from Freyer, written
four weeks previously, containing only the words:

"Even in death, Josepha has filled a mother's place to our
child—she has rested in the chapel with him since this morning. I think you will not object to her being buried there.

JOSEPH."

The countess again glanced at the letter, her eyes rested
on the errors in orthography. Such tragical information, with
so terrible a reproach between the lines—and the effect—a
ludicrous one! She would gladly have effaced the mistakes in
order not to be ashamed of having given this man so important a part in the drama of her life—but they stood there with
the distinctness of a boy's unpractised hand. A man who
could not even write correctly! She had not noticed it before,

he wrote rarely and always very briefly—or had she possessed no eyes for his faults at that time? Yes, she must have been blind, utterly blind. She had not answered the letter. Now she tore it up and threw it into the fire. Josepha's death would have been a deliverance to her, had she not a few weeks later received another letter which she now read once more, panting for breath. But, however frequently she perused its contents, she found only that old Martin entreated her to return—Josepha had "blabbed."

That one word in the stiff hand of the faithful old servant, which looked as if it might have been scrawled with a match upon paper redolent of the odors of the stable, had so startled the countess that she left Cannes by the first train, and traveled day and night to reach home. A nervous restlessness made the sheet tremble in her hand as she thrust it into the flames. Then she paced restlessly to and fro. Martin was keeping her waiting so long.

A little supper had been hurriedly prepared and was now served. But the countess scarcely touched the food and, complaining that the dining-room was cold, crept back to her boudoir. At last, about half past nine, Martin was announced. He had gone to bed and they had been obliged to rouse him.

"Is Your Highness going out?" asked the footman, who could not understand the summons to Martin.

"If I am, you will receive orders for the carriage," replied his mistress, and a flash from her eyes silenced the servant. "Let Martin come in!" she added in a harsh, imperious tone.

The man opened the door.

"You are dismissed for to-night. The lights can be put out," she added.

Martin stood, hat in hand, awaiting his mistress' commands. A few minutes passed, then the countess noiselessly went to the door to see that the adjoining rooms were empty and that no one was listening. When she returned she drew the heavy curtains over the door to deaden every sound. Then her self-control gave way and rushing to the old coachman she grasped his hand. "Martin, for Heaven's sake, what has happened?"

Tears glittered in Martin's eyes, as he saw his mistress' alarm, and he took her trembling hands as gently as if they were the reins of a fiery blooded horse, on which a curb has been placed for the first time. "Ho—ho—dear Countess, only keep quiet, quiet," he said in the soothing tones used to his frightened steeds: "All is not lost! I didn't let myself be caught, and there's no proof of what Josepha blabbed."

"So they tried to catch you? Tell me"—she was trembling—"how did they come to you?"

"Well," said Martin clumsily, "this is how it was. They seem to have driven Josepha into a corner. At her funeral the cook told me that just before she died, two strangers came to the house and had a long conversation with the sick woman. When the hare she was ordered to cook was done, she carried it up. But the people in the room were talking so loud that she didn't dare go in and stood at the door listening. Something was said about the countess' favor and a crime, and Josepha was terribly excited. Suddenly she heard nothing more, Josepha stammered a few unintelligible words, and the gentlemen came out with faces as red as fire. They left the hare in the lurch—and off they went. Josepha died the same night. Then I thought they might be the Barons von Wildenau, because their coachman had often tried to pump me about our countess, and I said to myself, 'now I'll do the same to him.' And sure enough I found out that the gentlemen had gone away, and where? To Prankenberg!"

The countess turned pale and sank into an arm-chair. "There, there—Your Highness, don't be troubled," Martin went on calmly—"that will do them no good, the church books don't lie open on the tavern tables like bills of fare, and the old pastor will not let everybody meddle with them."

"The old pastor?" cried the countess despairingly—"he is dead, and since my father, the prince, has grown weak-minded, the patronage has lapsed to the government. The new pastor has no motive for showing us any consideration."

"So the old pastor is dead? H'm, H'm!" Martin for the first time shook his head anxiously. "If one conld only get a word from His Highness the Prince—just to find out whether the marriage was really entered in the record."

"Yes, if we knew that!"

Martin smiled with a somewhat embarrassed look. "I ventured to take a little liberty—and went—I thought I would

try whether I could find out anything from him? Because
His Highness—you remember—followed us to Prankenberg."

"Very true!" The countess nodded in the utmost excitement. "Well?"

"Alas!—it was useless! His Highness doesn't know anybody, can remember nothing. When you go over to-morrow,
you will see that he can't live long. His Highness is perfectly childish. Then he got so excited that we thought he
would lose his breath, and at last had to be put to bed. I
could not help weeping when I saw it—such a stately gentleman—and now so helpless!"

The countess listened to this report with little interest.
Her father had been nothing to her while he retained his
mental faculties—now, in a condition of slow decay, he was
merely a poor invalid, to whom she performed the usual filial
duties.

"Go on, go on," she cried impatiently, "you are not telling the story in regular order. When did you see my father?"

"A week ago, after my talk with the gentlemen."

"That is the main thing—tell me about that."

"Why, it was this way: I was sitting quietly at the tavern
one night, when Herr von Wildenau's coachman came to me
again and said that his master wanted to talk with me about
our bay mare with the staggers which he would like to harness
with his bay. I was glad that we could get the mare off on
him."

"Fie, Martin!"

"Why—if nobody tried to cheat, there wouldn't be any
more horse-trading! So I told him I thought the countess
would sell the mare—we had no mate for her and I would inform Your Highness. No, the gentleman would write directly
to Her Highness—only I must go to them, they wanted to
talk with me. Well—I went, and they shut all the doors and
pulled the curtains over them, just as your Highness did, and
then they began on the bay and promised me a big fee, if I
would get her cheap for them. Every coachman takes a fee,"
the old man added in an embarrassed tone, "it's the custom—
you won't be vexed, Countess—so I made myself a bit important and pretended that it depended entirely on me, and I
would make Her Highness so dissatisfied with the mare that

she would be glad to get rid of her cheap, and—all the rest of the things we coachmen say ! So the gentlemen thought because I bargained with them about one thing, I would about another. But *that* was quite different from a horse-trade, and my employers are no animals to be sold, so they found that they had come to the wrong person. If I would make a little extra money by getting rid of a poor animal, which we had long wanted to sell, I'm not the rascal to take thousands from anybody to deprive my employers of house and home. And the poor old Prince, who can no longer help himself, would perhaps be left to starve in his old age. No, the gentlemen were mistaken in old Martin, they don't know what it is"—tears were streaming down the old man's wrinkled cheeks—" to put such a little princess on a horse for the first time and place the reins in her tiny hands."

" Please go on Martin," said the countess gently, scarcely able to exert any better control over herself. " What did they offer you ?"

" A great deal of money, if I would bear witness in court that you were married."

" Ah !"—the terrified woman covered her face with her hands.

" There—there, Countess," said Martin, soothingly. " I haven't finished ! Hold your head up, Your Highness, I beg you, this is no time to be faint-hearted, we must be on the watch and keep the reins well in hand, that they may not get the start of us."

" Yes, yes ! Go on !"

" Well, they tried to catch me napping. They knew everything, and I had been a witness of the wedding at Prankenberg !"

" Good Heavens !" The countess seemed paralyzed.

Martin laughed. " But I didn't let myself be caught—I looked as stupid as if I couldn't bridle a horse, and had never heard of any wedding in all my days except our Princess' marriage to the late Count. Of course I was at the church then, with all the other servants. Then the gentlemen muttered something in French—and asked what wages I had, and when I told them, they said they were too low for such rich employers, and began to make me offers till they reached fifty thousand marks, if I would state what they wanted. Yes, and then they told me you were capable of marrying two men and meant to take the duke as well as the steward, and they didn't want to have such a crime in the family—so I must help them prevent it. But this didn't move me at all, and I said: 'That's no concern of mine; my mistress knows what to do!' So off I went, and left the gentlemen staring like balky horses when they don't want to pass anything. Then I went to the Prince, and as I could learn nothing there, I knew of no other way than to write to Your Highness. I hope you'll pardon the liberty."

"Oh, Martin, you trusty old servant! Your simple loyalty shames me; but I fear that your sacrifice is useless—they know all, Martin, nothing can save me."

Martin smiled craftily into the bottom of his hat, as if it was the source of his wisdom, "I think just this: If the gentlemen *do* know everything, they have got to *prove* it, for Josepha is dead, and if they had found the information they wanted at Prankenberg, they needn't offer so much money for my testimony!"

The countess pressed her hand upon her head: "I don't know, I can't think any more. Oh, Martin, how shall I thank you? If the stroke of the pen which will give you the fifty thousand marks you scorned to receive from the Wildenaus can repay you—take it, but I shall still be your debtor." She hurriedly wrote a few words. "There is a check for fifty thousand marks, cash it early to-morrow morning. Don't delay an hour, any day may be the last that I shall have anything to give. Take it quickly."

But Martin shook his head. "Why, what is Your Highness thinking of? I don't want to be paid, like a bribed witness, for doing only my duty. There would have been no credit in refusing the money, if I took it afterward from Your Highness. No, I thank you most humbly—but I can't do it."

The countess was deeply ashamed. "But if I lose my property, Martin, if they begin a law-suit—I can no longer reward your fidelity. Have you considered that everything can be taken from me if they succeed in proving that I am married?"

Martin nodded: "Yes, yes, I know our late master's will.

I believe he was jealous and wanted to prevent the countess from marrying again. But you needn't be troubled about me, I've saved enough to buy a little home which, in case of need, might shelter the countess and Herr Freyer, too. I have had it all from you!" Martin's broad face beamed with joy at the thought.

"Martin!"—she could say no more. Martin did not know what had happened—surely the skies would fall—the countess had sunk upon his breast, the broad old breast in which throbbed such a stupid, honest heart! He stood as motionless as a post or the pile of a bridge, to which a drowning person clings. But, during all the sixty-five years his honest heart had beat under the Prankenberg livery, it had never throbbed so violently as at this moment. His little princess! She was in his arms again as in the days when he placed her in the saddle for the first time. Then she wept and clung to him whenever the horse made a spring, but he held her firmly and she felt safe in his care—now she again wept and clung to him in helpless terror—but now she was a stately woman who had outgrown his protection!

"There—there, Countess," he said, soothingly. "God will help you. Go to rest. You are wearied by the long journey. To-morrow you will see everything with very different eyes. And, as I said before, if all the ropes break—then you will find lodging with old Martin. You always liked peasants' fare. Don't you remember how you used to slip in to the coachman's little room and shared my bread and cheese till the governess found it out and spoiled our fun? Yes, yes, bread and cheese were forbidden dainties, and yet they were God's gift which even the poorest might enjoy. You must remember the coachman's little room and how they tasted! Well, we haven't gone so far yet, and Your Highness' friends will not suffer it. Yet, if matters ever *did* come to that, I believe Your Highness would rather accept a home from me than from any of these noblemen."

"You may be right there!" said the countess, with a thoughtful nod.

"May God guard Your Highness from either.—Has Your Highness any farther orders?"

"Yes, my good Martin. Go early to-morrow morning to

the Prince—or rather the Duke of Metten-Barnheim—and ask him to call on me at ten o'clock."

"Alas—the duke went to shoot black cock this morning—I suppose he didn't know that Your Highness was coming?"

"Certainly not. How long will he be away?"

"Till the end of the week, his coachman told me."

"This too!" She stood in helpless despair.

"The coachman said that His Highness was going to Castle Sternbach—perhaps Your Highness might telegraph there!"

"Yes, my good old friend—you are right!" And with eager haste she wrote a telegram. "There it is, Martin, it will reach him somewhere!"

And she remembered the message despatched nine years before, after the Passion Play, to the man whom she was now recalling as her last support. At that time she informed him that she should stay in Ammergau and let the roses awaiting her at home wither—now she remained at home and let the roses that bloomed for her in Ammergau languish.

The coachman, as if reading the mute language of her features and the bitter expression of her compressed lips, asked timidly: "I suppose Your Highness will not drive to the Griess."

"No!" she said, so curtly and hastily that it cut short any farther words.

For the first time a shadow flitted over honest Martin's face. Sadly, almost reproachfully, he wished his beloved mistress "a good night's rest," and stumbled wearily out. It had hurt him,—but "the last thing he had discovered" he did not venture, out of respect to his employer, to express even to himself.

CHAPTER XXVII.

BETWEEN POVERTY AND DISGRACE.

THREE weary days had passed. The countess was ill. At least she permitted her household to believe that she was unable to leave her room. No one was allowed to know that she had returned, and the windows of the Wildenau Palace remained closed, as when the owner was absent. Thus condemned to total inactivity in the twilight of her apartments, she became the helpless prey of her gnawing anxiety. The third day brought a glimmer of hope, a telegram from the duke: " I will come at six this evening."

The countess trembled and turned pale as she read the lines. What was to be done now? She did not know, she only felt that the turning-point of her life had come.

" The Duke of Metten-Barnheim will call this evening and must be admitted, but no one else !" were the orders given to the servant.

Then, to pass away the time, she changed her dress. If she was to be poor and miserable, to possess nothing she formerly owned; she would at least be beautiful, beautiful as the setting sun which irradiates everything with rosy light.

And with the true feminine vanity which coquets with death and finds a consolation in being beautiful even in the coffin, she chose for the momentous consultation impending one of the most bewitching negligeé costumes in her rich wardrobe. Ample folds of rose-colored *crêpe de chine* were draped over an under-dress of pink plush, which reflected a thousand shades from the deepest rose to the palest flesh color, the whole drapery loosely caught with single grey pearls. How long would she probably possess such garments? She perhaps wore it to-day for the last time. Her trembling hand was icy cold, as she wound a pink ribbon through her curls and fastened it with a pearl clasp.

There she stood, like Aphrodite, risen from the foam of the sea, and—she smiled bitterly—she could not even raise herself from the mire into which a single error had lured her. Then she was again overwhelmed by an unspeakable consciousness of misery, her disgrace, which made all her splendor seem a mockery. She was on the point of stripping off the glittering robe when the duke was announced. It was too late to change.

She hurried into the boudoir to meet him—floating in like a roseate cloud.

" How beautiful !" exclaimed the duke, admiringly; " you look like a bride ! It must be some joyful cause which brought you back here so soon and made you send for me."

"On the contrary, Duke—a bride of misfortune—a penitent who would fain varnish the ugliness of her guilt in her friend's eyes by outward beauty."

"H'm! That would be at any rate a useless deed, Madeleine; for beautiful as you are, I do not love you for your beauty's sake. Nor is it for your virtues—you never aspired to be a saint, not even in Ammergau, where you least succeeded! What I love is the whole grand woman with all her faults, who seems to have been created for me, in spite of the obstacles reared between us by temperament and circumstances. The latter are accidents which may prevent our union, but which cannot deprive me of my share in you, the part which *I* alone understand, and which I shall love when I see you before me as a white-haired matron, weary of life— perhaps then for the first time."

Emotion stifled the countess' words. She drew him down upon a chair by her side and sank feebly upon the cushions of her divan.

"Oh, how cold your hands are!" said the duke, gazing with loving anxiety into her eyes. "You alarm me. Spite of your rosy glimmer, you are pale as your own pearls. And now pearls in your eyes too? Madeleine—my poor tortured Madeleine—what has happened?"

"Oh, Duke—help, advise me—or all is lost. The Wildenaus have discovered my secret. Josepha, that half-crazy girl from Ammergau, has betrayed me!"

"So that is her gratitude for the life you saved." The duke nodded as if by no means surprised. "It was to be expected from that sort of person. Why did you preserve the fool?"

"I could not let her leap into the water."

"Perhaps it would have been better! This sham-saint had not even sufficient healthful nature in her to be grateful?"

"Ah, she had reason to hate me, she loved my child more than any earthly thing and reproached me for having neglected it. These people can imagine love only in the fulfillment of lowly duties and physical attendance. That a woman can have no time or understanding of these things, and yet love, is beyond their comprehension."

"A fine state of affairs, where the servant makes herself

21

the judge of her mistress—nay even discovers in her conduct an excuse for the basest treachery. A plain maid-servant, properly reared by her parents, would have fulfilled her duty to her employers without philosophizing."

The countess nodded, she was thinking of old Martin.

"But," the duke continued, "extra allowance must of course be made for these Ammergau people."

"We will let her rest; she is dead. Who knows how it happened, or the struggles through which she passed?"

"Is she dead?"

"Yes, she died just after the child."

"Indeed?" said the duke, thoughtfully, in a gentler tone: "Well, then at least she has atoned. But, my dear Madeleine, this does not undo the disaster. The Wildenaus will at any rate try to make capital out of their knowledge of your secret, and, as the dear cousins are constantly incurring gaming and other debts—especially your red-haired kinsman Fritz—they will not let slip the opportunity of making their honored cousin pay for their discretion the full amount of their notes!"

"Ah, if that were all!"

"That all! What more could there be? I admit that it is unspeakably painful for you to know that your honor and your deepest secrets are in such hands—but how long will it be ere, if it please God, you will be in a position which will remove you from it all, and I—!"

"Duke—Good Heavens!—It is far worse," cried the countess, wringing her hands: "Oh, merciful God—at last, at last, it must be told. You do not know all, the worst—I had not courage to tell you—are you aware of the purport of my late husband's will?"

"Certainly—it runs that you must restore the property, of which he makes you sole heiress, to the cousins, if you marry again. What of that—do you suppose I ever thought of your millions?" He laughed gayly: "I flatter myself that my finances will not permit you to feel the withdrawal of your present income when you are my wife."

"Omnipotent Father!—You do not understand me! This is the moment I have always dreaded—oh, had I only been truthful. Duke, forgive me, pity me, I am the most miserable creature under the sun. I shall not be your wife, but a beggar

—for I am married, and the Wildenaus know it through Josepha!"

There are moments when it seems as if the whole world was silent—as if the stars paused in their courses to listen, and we hear nothing save the pulsing of the blood in our ears. It is long ere we perceive any other sound. This was the case with the duke. For a long time he seemed to himself both deaf and blind. Then he heard the low hissing of the gas jets, then heavy breathing, and at last the earth began to turn on its axis again and things resumed their natural relations.

Yet his energetic nature did not need much time to recover its poise. One glance at the hopeless, drooping woman showed him that this was not the hour to think of himself—that he never had more serious duties to perform than to-day. Now he perceived for the first time that he had unconsciously retreated from her half the length of the room.

She held out her hand imploringly, and with the swiftness of thought he was once more at her side, clasping it in his own. "I have concealed this, deceived your great, noble love —for years—because I perceived that you were as necessary to my life as reason and science and all the other gifts I once undervalued. I did not venture to reveal the secret, lest I should lose you. The moment has come—you will leave me, for you must now make another choice—but do not be angry, grant me the *one* consolation of parting without rancor."

"We have not yet gone so far. I told you ten minutes ago that the accidents of temperament and circumstance may divide us, but cannot rob you of what was created for me, we do not part so quickly.—You have not deceived me, for you have never told me that you loved me or would become my wife, and your bearing was blameless. Your husband might have witnessed every moment of our intercourse. Believe me, the slightest coquetry, the smallest concession in my favor at your husband's expense would find in me the sternest possible judge. But though an unhappy wife, you were a loyal one— to that I can bear witness. If I yielded to illusions, it is no fault of yours—who can expect a nature so delicately strung as yours to make an executioner of the heart of her best friend? Those are violent measures which would not accord with the sweet weakness, which renders you at once so guilty and so excusable."

The countess hid her face as if overwhelmed by remorse and shame.

" Do not let us lose our composure and trust to me to care for you still, for your present position requires the utmost caution and prudence. But now, Madeleine—you have no farther pretext for not telling me the whole truth ! Now I must know *all* to be able to act. Will you answer my questions ?"

" Yes."

" Then tell me—are you really married to Freyer ?"

" Yes !"

" So the farce must end tragically !" murmured the duke. " I cannot, will not believe it—it is too shocking that a woman like you should be ruined by the Ammergau farce."

" Not by that; by the presumption with which I sought to draw the deity down to me. Oh, it is a hard punishment. I prayed so fervently to God and, instead of His face, He showed me a mask and then left me to atone for the deception by the repentance of a whole life."

" Ah, can you really believe that the Highest Wisdom would have played so cruel a masquerade with you ? Why should you be so terribly punished ? No, *ma chère amie*, God has neither deceived nor wished to punish you. He showed Himself in response to your longing, or rather your longing made you imagine that you saw Him—and had you been content with that, you would have returned home happy with the vision of your God in your heart, like thousands who were elevated by the Passion Play. But you wanted *more ;* you possess a sensuous religious nature, which cannot separate the essence from the *appearance* and, after having *seen*, you desired to *possess* Him in the precise form in which He appeared to you ! Had it depended upon you, you would have robbed the world of its God ! Fortunately, it was only Herr Freyer whom you stole, and now that you perceive your error you accuse God of having deceived you. You talk constantly of your faith in God, and yet have so poor an opinion of Him ? What had God to do with your imagining that the poor actor in the Passion Play, who wore His mask, must be Himself, and therefore wedded him !"

The countess made no reply. This was the tone which she could never endure. He was everything to her—her sole confidant and counselor—but he could not comprehend what she had experienced during the Passion Play.

"I am once more the dry sceptic who so often angered you, am I not?" said the Prince, whose keen observation let nothing escape. "But I flatter myself that you will be more ready to view matters from a sober standpoint after having convinced yourself of the dangers of intercourse with 'phantoms' and demi-gods, who lure their victims into devious paths where they are liable morally to break their necks."

The countess could not help smiling sorrowfully. "You are incorrigible!"

"Well, we must take things as they are. As you will not confess that you—pardon the frankness—have committed a folly and ruined your life for the sake of a fanciful whim, the caprice must be elevated to the rank of a 'dispensation of Providence,' and the inactive endurance of its consequences a meritorious martyrdom. But I do not believe that God is guilty either of your marriage or of your self-constituted martyrdom, and therefore I tell you that I do not regard your marriage, to use the common parlance, one of those 'made in Heaven'—in other words, an *indissoluble* one."

The countess shrank as though her inmost thoughts were suddenly pointing treacherous fingers at her. "Do you take it so lightly, Duke?"

"That I do not take it lightly is proved by the immense digression which I made to remove any moral and religious scruples. The practical side of the question scarcely requires discussion. But to settle the religious moral one first, tell me, was your marriage a civil or religious one?"

"Religious."

"When and where?"

"At Prankenberg, after the Passion Play. It will be ten years next August."

"How did it all happen?"

"Very simply: My father, who suddenly sought me, as usual when he was in debt, saw that I wanted to marry Freyer and, fearing a public scandal, advised me, in order to save the property—which he needed almost more than I—to marry *secretly.* Wherever the Tridentine Council ruled, the sole requisite of a valid marriage was that the two persons should state, in the presence of an ordained priest and two witnesses, that they intended to marry. As my father was never very reliable, and might change his opinion any day, I hastened to follow his advice before it occurred to him to put any obstacles in my way, as the pastor at Prankenberg was wholly in his power. So I set off with Freyer and Josepha that very night. An old coachman, Martin, whose fidelity I had known from childhood, lived at Prankenberg. I took him and Josepha for witnesses, and we surprised the old pastor while he was drinking his coffee."

The prince made a gesture of surprise. " What—over his coffee ?"

" Yes—before he could push back his cup, we had made our statement—and the deed was done."

The prince started up; his eyes sparkled, his whole manner betrayed the utmost agitation. " And you call that being married ? And give me this fright ?" He drew a long breath, as if relieved of a burden. " Madeleine, if you had only told me this at once !"

" But why ? Does it change the matter ?"

" Surely you will not persuade yourself that this farce with the old pastor in his dressing-gown and slippers, his morning-pipe and the fragrance of Mocha—was a wedding ? You will not expect me as a Protestant, or any enlightened Catholic, to regard it in that light ?"

" But what does the form matter ? Protestantism cares nothing for the form—it heeds only the meaning."

" But the meaning was lacking—at least to you—to you it was a mere form which you owed to the sanctity of your lover's mask of Christus." He seized her hand with unwonted passion. " Madeleine, for once be truthful to yourself and to me —am I not right ?"

" Yes !" she murmured almost inaudibly.

" Well, then—if the *meaning* was lacking and the chosen form an *illegal* one—what binds you ?"

Madeleine was silent. This question was connected with her secret, which he would never understand. His nature was too positive to reckon with anything except facts. The duke

felt tnat she was withholding an answer, not because she had
none, but because she did not wish to give the true one.   But
he did not allow himself to be disconcerted.   " Did the old
pastor give you any written proof of this 'sacred rite'—we will
give it the proud name of a marriage certificate."

" Yes." .

" Who has the document ?"

" Freyer !"

" That is unfortunate; for it gives him an apparent right to
consider himself married and make difficulties, which compli-
cate the case.   But we can settle with Freyer—I have less fear
of him.   Your situation is more imperilled by this tale of a secret marriage, which Josepha, in good faith, brought to the
ears of the Wildenaus.   This is a disaster which requires
speedy remedy.   In other respects everything is precisely as
it was when you went to Cannes.   This complication changes
nothing in my opinion.   I hold the same view.   If you no
longer *love* Freyer, break with him; the way of doing so is a
minor matter.   I leave it to you.   But break with him and
give me your hand—then the whole spectre will melt.   We
will gladly restore the Wildenau property to the cousins, and
they will then have no farther motive for pursuing the affair."

" Is that true ?   Could you still think seriously of it—and
I, good Heavens, must I become doubly a criminal ?"

" But, *chère amie*, look at things objectively a little."

" Even if I do look at them objectively, I don't understand
how I could marry again without being divorced, and to apply
for a divorce now would be acknowledging the marriage."

" Who is to divorce you, if no one married you ?   According to civil law, you are still single, for you are not registered
in accordance with your rank—according to religious law you
are not married, at least not in the opinion of the great majority of Christian countries and sects, to whom the Tridentine
Council is not authoritative !   Will you insist upon sacrificing
your existence and honor to a sentimental scruple ?   Will you
confess to the Wildenaus that you are married ?   In that case
you must not only restore the property, but also the interest
you have illegally appropriated for nine years, which will swallow your little private property and rob you of your sole
means of support.   What will follow then ?   Do you mean to

retire with the 'steward' from the scene amid the jeering laughter of society, make soup for him at his home in Ammergau, live by the labor of his hands, and at Christmas receive the gift of a calico gown?"

The countess shuddered, as though shaken by a feverish chill.

"Or will you continue to live on with Freyer as before and suffer the cousins to begin an inquiry against you, and afford the world the spectacle of seeing you wrangle with them over the property? Then you must produce the dogmatic and legal proof that you are not married. This certainly would not be difficult—but I must beg you to note certain possibilities. If it is decided that your marriage was *illegal*, then the question will be brought forward—how did *you yourself* regard it? And it might occur to the Wildenaus' lawyers that, no matter whether correctly or not, you considered yourself married and intentionally defrauded them of the property!"

"Merciful Heaven!"

"Or will you then escape a criminal procedure by declaring that you regarded your connection with Freyer as an illegal marriage?"

"Oh!" the countess crimsoned with shame.

"There the vindication would be more dishonoring than the accusation—so you must renounce *that*. You see that you have been betrayed into a *circulus vitiosus* from which you can no longer escape. Wherever you turn—you have but the choice between poverty or disgrace,—unless you decide to become Duchess of Metten-Barnheim and thus, at one bound, spring from the muddy waves which now threaten you, into the pure, unapproachable sphere of power and dignity to which you belong. My arms are always open to save you— my heart is ready to love and to protect you—can you still hesitate?"

The tortured woman threw herself at his feet. "Duke— Emil—save me—I am *yours!*"

CHAPTER XXVIII.

PARTING.

SEVERAL minutes have passed—to the duke a world of happiness—to the countess of misery. The duke bent over the beautiful trembling form to clasp her in his arms for the first time.

"Have I won you at last—my long-sought love ?" he exclaimed, rapturously. "Do you now perceive what your dispensations of Providence mean ? The shrewdness and persistence of a single man who knows what he wants, has baffled them, and driven all the heroes of signs and wonders from the field ! Do you now believe what I said just now : that we are our own Providence ?"

"That will appear in due time, do not exalt yourself and do not blaspheme, God might punish your arrogance !" she said faintly, slipping gently from his embrace.

"Madeleine—no betrothal kiss—after these weary years of waiting and hoping."

"I am *still* Freyer's wife," she said, evasively—"not until I am parted from him."

"You are right ! I will not steal my bride's first kiss from another. I thank you for honoring my future right in his." His lips touched her brow with a calm, friendly caress. Then he rose : "·It is time to go, I have not a moment to lose." He glanced at the clock : "Seven ! I will make my preparations at once and set out for Prankenberg to-morrow."

"What do you wish to do ?"

"First of all to see what is recorded in the church register, and to ascertain what kind of a man the Catholic pastor is, that I may form some idea of what the Wildenaus have discovered and how much proof they have obtained. Then we can judge how far we must dissimulate with these gentlemen until your relation with Freyer can be dissolved without any violent outbreak or without being compelled to use any undue haste. I will also go to Barnheim and quietly prepare everything there for our marriage. The more quickly all these business matters are settled, the sooner our betrothal can be announced. And that I am ardently longing to be at last permitted to call you mine, you will—I hope, understand ?"

" But my relation with Freyer must first be arranged," said the countess, evasively. " We cannot dispose of him like an ordinary business matter. He is a man of heart and mind—we must remember that I could not be happy for an hour, if I knew that he was miserable."

" Yet you have left him alone for weeks and months without any pangs of conscience," said the duke with a shade of sternness.

" It was not *I*, but the force of circumstances. What happens now *I* shall do—and must bear the responsibiltty. Help me to provide that it is not too heavy." Her face wore a lofty, beautiful expression as she spoke, and deeply moved, he raised her hand to his lips.

" Certainly, Madeleine ! We will show him every consideration and do everything as forbearingly as possible. But remember that, as I just respected *his* rights, you must now guard *mine*, and that every hour in which you retain this relation to him longer than necessary—is treason to *both*. It cannot suit your taste to play such a part—so do not lose a moment in renouncing it."

" Certainly—you are right."

" Will you be strong—will you have the power to do what is unavoidable—and do it soon ?"

" I have always been able to do what I desired—I can do this also."

The duke took her hand and gazed long and earnestly into her eyes. " Madeleine—I do not ask : do you love me ? I ask only : do you believe that you *will* love me ?"

The profound modesty of this question touched her heart with indescribable melancholy, and in overflowing gratitude for such great love, which gave all and asked nothing, she bowed her head : " Yes—I do believe it."

The duke's usual readiness of speech deserted him—he had no words to express the happiness of this moment.

What was that ? Voices in the ante-room. The noise sounded like a dispute. Then some one knocked violently at the door.

" Come in !" cried the countess, with a strange thrill of

fear. The footman entered hurriedly with an excited face.
" A gentleman, he calls himself 'Steward Freyer,' is there, is
following close at my heels—he would not be refused admittance." He pointed backward to where Freyer already appeared.

The countess seemed turned to stone. " Request the
steward to wait a moment !" she said at last, with the imperi-
ousness of the mistress.

The man stepped back, and they saw him close the door
almost by force.

" Do not carry matters too far," said the duke ; " he seems
to be very much excited—such people should not be irritated.
Admit him before he forces the door and makes a scandal in
the presence of the servant. He comes just at the right time
—in this mood it will be easy for you to dismiss him. So end
the matter ! But be *calm*, have no scene—shall I remain at
hand ?"

" No—I am not afraid—it would be ignoble to permit you
to listen to him. Trust me, and leave me to my fate."

At this time the voices again grew louder, then the door
was violently thrown open. Freyer stood within the room.

" What does this mean — am I assaulted in my own
house ?" cried the countess, rebelling against this act of violence.

Freyer stood trembling from head to foot ; they could hear
his teeth chatter : " I merely wished to ask whether it was the
Countess Wildenau's desire that I should be insulted by her
servant."

" Certainly not !" replied the countess with dignity. " If
my servant insulted you, you shall have satisfaction—only I
wish you had asked it in a less unseemly way."

The duke quietly took his hat and kissed the countess'
hand : " *Restez calme !*" Then he passed out, saluting Freyer
with that aristocratic courtesy which at once irritates and
disarms.

Freyer stepped close to the countess, his eyes wandered
restlessly, his whole appearance was startling : " Everything
in the world has its limit, even patience—mine is exhausted.
Tell me, are you my wife—you who stand here in this gay
masquerade of laces and pearls—are you the mourning mother

. of a dead child ? Is this my wife who decks herself for another, shuts herself up with another, or at least gives orders
not to be disturbed—who has her lackeys keep her wedded
husband at bay outside with blows—and deems it unseemly
if the last remnant of manly dignity in his soul rebels and he
demands satisfaction from his wife.   Where is the man, I
ask, who would not be frenzied ? Where is the woman, I ask,
who once loved me ? Is it you, who desert, betray, make me
contemptible to myself and others ? Where—where—in the
wide world is there a man so deceived, so trampled under foot,
as I am by you ? Have you any answer to this, woman ?"

The countess turned deadly pale, terror almost stifled her.
For the first time, she beheld the Gorgon, popular fury, in
his face and while turning to stone the thought came to her:
" Would you live *with that ?*" Horror stole over her—she did
not know whether her feeling was fear or loathing, she only
knew that she must fly from the " turbid waves" ever rolling
nearer.

There is no armor more impenetrable than the coldness of
a dead feeling.   Madeleine von Wildenau armed herself with
it. " Tell me, if you please, how you came here, what you
desire, and what put you into such excitement."

" What—merciful Heaven, do you still ask ? I came here
to learn where you were now, to what address I could write,
as you made no reply to my announcement of Josepha's death
—and I wished to say that I could no longer endure this life!
While talking with the servant at the door, old Martin passed
and told me that you were here. I wanted to say one last
word to you—I went upstairs, found the footman, and asked,
entreated him to announce me, or at least to inquire when I
could speak to you! You had a visitor and could not be disturbed, was his scornful answer. Then the consciousness of
my just rights awoke within me, and I *commanded* him
to announce me. You refused to receive me: ' I must
wait'—I—must wait in the ante-room while you, as I saw
through the half-opened door, were whispering familiarly
with you former suitor ! Then I forgot everything and approached the door—the servant tried to prevent me, I flung
him aside, and then—he dealt me a blow in the face—that
face which you had once likened to the countenance of your

God — he, your servant. If I had not had sufficient self-control at the moment to say to myself that the lackey was only your tool—I should have torn him to pieces with my own hands, as I should now tear you, if you were not a woman and sacred to me, even in your sin."

" I sincerely regret what has happened and do not blame you for making me—at least indirectly responsible. I will dismiss the servant, of course—although he has the excuse that you provoked him, and that he did not know you."

" Yes, he certainly cannot know me, when I am never permitted to appear."

" No matter, he should not venture to treat even a stranger so, and therefore must be punished with dismissal."

" Because he should not venture to treat even a *stranger* so ?" Freyer laughed sadly, bitterly: " I thank you, keep your servant—I will renounce this satisfaction."

" I do not know what else you desire."

" You do not know ? Oh, Heaven, had this happened earlier, what would your feelings have been ! Do you remember your emotion in the Passion Play, when I received only the *semblance* of a blow upon the cheek ? Did it not, as you said, strike your own heart ? How should you feel when you saw it in reality ? Oh, tears should have streamed down your cheeks with grief for the poor deserted husband, who the only time he crossed your threshold, was insulted by your lackey. If you still retained one spark of love for me, you would feel that a single kiss pressed compassionately on my cheek to efface the brand would be a greater satisfaction than the dismissal of a servant whom you would have sacrificed to any stranger. But that is over, we no longer understand each other !"

The countess struggled a moment between pity and repugnance. But at the thought of pressing her lips to the face her servant's hand had struck, loathing overwhelmed her and she turned away.

" Yes, turn your back upon me—for should you look me in the eyes now, you would be forced to lower your own and blush with shame."

" I beg you to consider that I am not accustomed to such outbreaks, and shall be compelled to close the conversation, if your manner does not assume a form more in accord with the standard of my circle."

" Yes, I understand! You dread the element you have unchained ? A peasant was very well, by way of variety, was he not ? He loved differently, more ardently, more fiercely than your smooth city gentlemen. The strength and the impetuosity of the untutored man were not too rude when I bore you through the flaming forest, and caught the falling branches which threatened to crush you—then you did not fear me, you did not thrust me back within the limits of your social forms; on the contrary, you rejoiced that the world still contained power and might, and felt yourself a Titaness. Why have you suddenly become so weak-nerved. and cannot endure this might—because it has turned against you ?"

" No," said the countess, with a flash of deadly hatred in her fathomless grey eyes: " Not on that account—but because at that time I believed you to be different from what you really are. Then I believed I beheld a God, now I perceive that it was a—" She paused.

" Go on—put no constraint on yourself—now you perceive that it was a *peasant.*"

" You just called yourself by that name."

Freyer stood as though a thunder-bolt had struck him. He seemed to be struggling for breath. " Yes," he said at last in a low tone, " I did call myself by that name, but—*you* should not have done so – *not you !*" He grasped the back of a chair to steady himself.

" It is your own fault," said the countess, coldly. " But— will you not sit down? We have only a few words to say to each other. You have in this moment stripped off the mask of Christus and torn the last illusion from my heart. I can no longer see in the person who stood before me so disfigured by fury the image of the Redeemer."

" Was not the Christ also angry, when He saw the money-changers in the temple ? And you, you bartered the most sacred treasures of your heart and mine for paltry·pelf and useless baubles—but I must not be angry ! Scarcely a year ago, by the bedside of our sick child, you reproached me with being unable to cease playing the Christ—now—I have not kept up the part ! But it does not matter, whatever I might be, I should no longer please you, for the *love* which rendered the peasant a God is lacking. Yet one thing I must add; if now, after nine years marriage with you, I am still rough and a peasant, the reproach does not fall on me alone. You might have raised, ennobled me, my soul was in your keeping"—tears suddenly filled his eyes: " Woman, what have you done with my soul ?"

He sank into a chair, his strength was exhausted. Madeleine von Wildenau made no reply, the reproach struck home. She had never taken the trouble to develop his powers, to expand his intellectual faculties. After his poetical charm was exhausted—she flung him aside like a book whose contents she had read.

" You knew my history. I had told you that I grew up in the meadow with the horses and had gained the little I knew by my own longing. I would have been deeply grateful, if you had released me from the ban of ignorance and quenched the yearning which those who are half educated always feel for the treasures of culture, of which they know a little, just enough to show them what they lack. But whenever I sought to discuss such subjects with you, you impatiently made me feel my shortcomings, and this shamed and intimidated me. So I constantly deteriorated in my lonely life —grew more savage, instead of more cultivated. Do you know what is the hardest punishment which can be inflicted upon criminals ? Solitary confinement. It can be imposed for a short time only, because they go *mad*. Since the child and Josepha died, I have been one of those unfortunates, and you—did not even write me a line, had no word for me ! I felt that my mind was gradually becoming darkened ! Woman, even if you had power over life and death—you must not murder my soul, you have no right to that—even the law slays the *body* only, not the soul. And where it imposes the death penalty, it provides that the torture shall be shortened as much as possible. You are more cruel than the law—for you destroy your victim slowly--intellectually and physically."

" Terrible !" murmured the countess.

" Ay, it is terrible! You worldlings come and entice and sigh and kiss the hem of our robes, as long as the delusion of your excited imagination lasts, and your delusion infects us till we at last believe ourselves that we are gods—and then you thrust us headlong into the depths. Here you strew the miasma of the mania for greatness and vanity, yonder money and the seeds of avarice—there again you wished to sow your culture, tear us from our ignorance, and but half complete your work. Then you wonder because we become misshapen, sham, artificial creatures, comedians, speculators, misunderstood geniuses—everything in the world except true children of Ammergau!" He wiped his forehead, as if it were bleeding from the scratches of thorns. " I was a type of my people when, still a simple shepherd boy, I was brought from my herd to act the Christ, when in timid amazement, I suddenly felt stirring within me powers of which I had never dreamed—and I am so once more in my wretchedness, my mental conflicts, my marred life. I shall be so at last in my defeat or victory— as God is gracious to me. And since everything has deserted me—since I saw Josepha, the last thing left me of Ammergau, lying in her coffin—since then it has seemed as if from her grave, and that of all my happiness, my home, my betrayed, abandoned home, once more rose before me, and I felt a strange yearning for the soil to which I have a right, the earth where I belong. Ah, only when the outside world abandons us do we know what home is! Unfortunately I forgot it long enough, while I believed that you loved and needed me. Now that I know that you no longer care for me—the matter is very different! Like a true peasant, I believed that I had only duties, no rights, but in my loneliness I have pondered over many things, and so at last perceived that you, too, had duties and expected more from me than I can honorably endure! That I bore it *so long* gave you a right to despise me, for the husband who sits angrily in a corner and sees his wife daily betray, deny, and mock him—deserves no better fate. So I have come to ask what you intend and to tell you my resolve."

"What do you desire ?"

" That you will go with me to Ammergau, that you will cast aside the wealth, distinction, and splendor which I was not permitted to share with you, and in exchange accept with me my scanty earnings, my simplicity, my honest, plebeian name.

For, poor and humble as I am, I am not so contemptible in the eyes of Him, who bestowed upon me the dignity and honor of personating His divine Son, that you need feel ashamed to be my wife in the true Christian meaning."

The countess uttered a sigh of relief. "You anticipate me," she answered, blushing. "I see that you feel the untenableness of our relation. Your ultimatum is a proof that you will have strength to do what is inevitable, and I have delayed so long only from consideration for you. For—you know as well as I that I could never assent to your demand. It will be a sacred duty, so long as you live, to see that you want for nothing, but we must *part.*"

Freyer turned pale. "Part? We must part—for ever?"

"Yes."

"Merciful Heaven—is nothing sacred to you, not even the bond of marriage?"

"You know that I am a Rationalist, and do not believe in dogmas; as such I hold that every marriage can be dissolved whenever the moral conditions under which it was formed prove false. Unfortunately this is the case with us. You did not learn to accommodate yourself to the circumstances, and you never will—the conflict has increased till it is unendurable, we cannot understand each other, so our marriage-bond is spiritually sundered. Why should we maintain its outward semblance? I have lost through you nine years of my life, sacrificed to you the duties imposed by my rank, by renouncing marriage with a man of equal station. Matters have now progressed so far that I shall be ruined if you do not release me! Will you nevertheless cross my path and thrust yourself into my sphere?"

"Oh God—this too!" cried Freyer in the deepest anguish. "When have I thrust myself into your sphere? How, where, have I crossed your path? During the whole period of my marriage I have lived alone on the solitary mountain peak as your servant Have I boasted of my position as your husband? I waited patiently until every few weeks, and later, every few months, you came to me. I disdained all the gifts of your lavish generosity, it was my pride to work for you in return for the morsel of food I ate. I asked nothing from your wealth, your position, took no heed, like others, of the

22

splendor of your establishment. I wanted nothing from you save the immortal part. I was the poorest, the most insignificant of all your servants! My sole possession was your love, and that I was forced to conceal from every inquisitive eye, like a theft, in order to avoid the scorn of my fellow-citizens and all who could not understand the relation in which I stood to you. But this disgrace also I bore in silence, when a word would have vindicated me—bore it, that I might not drag you down from your brilliant position to mine—and you call that thrusting myself into your sphere? I will grant that I gradually became morose and embittered and by my ill-temper and reproaches deterred you more and more from coming, but I am only human and was forced to bear things beyond human endurance. The intention was good, though the execution might have been faulty. I lost your love—I lost my child—I lost my faithful companion, Josepha, yet I bore all in silence! I saw you revelling in the whirl of fashionable society, saw you admired by others and forget me, but I bore it—because I loved you a thousand times better than myself and did not wish to cause you pain. I often thought of secretly vanishing from your life, like a shadow which did not belong there. But the inviolability of the marriage-bond held me, and I wished to try once more, by the power of the vow you swore at the altar, to lead you back to your duty, for I cannot dissolve the sacrament which unites us, and which you voluntarily accepted with me. If it does not bind *you*—it still binds *me!* I am your husband, and shall remain so; if *you* break the bond you must answer for it to God; as for me, I shall keep it—unto death!"

"That would be a needless sacrifice, which neither church nor state would require. I will not release myself and leave you bound. You argue from a mistaken belief that we were legally married—it is time to explain the error, both on your account and mine. You speak of a vow which I made you before the altar, pray remember that we have never stood before one."

"Never?" muttered Freyer, and the vein on his forehead swelled with anger.

"Was the breakfast-table of the Prankenberg pastor an altar?"

" No, but wherever two human beings stand before a priest in the name of God, there is a viewless altar."

" Those are subjective Catholic opinions which I do not understand—I do not consider myself married, and you need not do so either."

" Not married ? Do you know what you are saying ?"

" What I *must* say, to loose *your* bonds as well as *mine*."

" Good Heavens, what will it avail if you loose my bonds and at the same time cut an artery so that I bleed to death ? No, no, you cannot be so cruel. You cannot be in earnest. Omnipotent Father—you did not say it, take back the words. Lord, forgive her, she does not know what she is doing ! Oh, take back those words—I will not believe that my wife, my dear wife, can be so wicked !"

" Moderate your expressions ! I guarantee my standpoint ; ask whom you choose, you will hear that we are not married !"

Freyer rushed up to her and seized her by the shoulders, shaking her as a tempest shakes a young birch-tree. " Not married—do you know then what you are !" He waited vainly for an answer, he seemed fairly crazed. " Shall I tell you, shall I ? Then for nine years you were a ——"

" Do not finish !" shrieked the countess, wrenching herself with a desperate effort from the terrible embrace and hurling him from her.

" Yes, I will finish, and you deserve that the whole world should hear and point the finger of scorn at you. I ought to shout to all the winds of Heaven that the Countess Wildenau, who is too proud to be called a poor man's wife, was not too proud to be his ——"

" Traitor, ungrateful, dishonorable traitor ! Is this your return for my love ? Take a knife and thrust it into my heart, it would be more seemly than to threaten me with degrada-tion !" She drew herself up to her full height and raised her hand as if to take an oath : " Accursed be the hour I raised you from the dust to my side. Curses on the false humanity which strove to efface the distinctions of rank, curses on the murmur of ' the eternal rights of man ' which removes the fetters from brutishness, that it may set its foot upon the neck of culture ! It is like the child which opens the door to the whin-

ing wolf to be torn to pieces by the brute. Yes, take yourself
out of my life, gloomy shadow which I conjured from those
seething depths in which ruin is wrought for us—take yourself away, you have no longer any part in me !—Your right is
doubly, trebly forfeited, your spell is broken, your strength re-
coils from the shield of a noble spirit, under whose protection
I stand.   Dare to lay hands on me again and—you will insult
the betrothed bride of the Duke of Barnheim and must account to him."

A cry—a heavy fall—Freyer lay senseless on the ground.

The countess timidly stroked the pallid face—a strange
memory stole over her—thus he lay prostrate on the ground
when he was nailed to the cross.   She could not help looking
at him again and again: Oh, that all this should be a lie!
Those features—that noble brow, on which the majesty of suffering was throned—the very image of the Saviour ! Yet only
an image, a mask ! She looked away, she would gaze no
longer, she would not again fall a victim to the old delusion—
she would not let herself be softened by the wonderful, delusive face ! But what was she to do ? If she called her servants, she would be the talk of the whole city on the morrow.
She must aid him, try to restore him to consciousness alone.
Yet if she now roused him from the merciful stupor, if the
grief and rage which had overwhelmed him should break forth
again—would he not murder her ? Was it strange that she re
mained so calm in the presence of this thought ? A contemptuous indifference to death had taken possession of her:
" If he kills me, he has a right to do so."

She was too lofty to shun punishment which she had deserved, though it were her death.   So she awaited her fate.

She brought a little bottle filled with a pungent essence
from her sleeping-room, and poured a few drops into his
mouth.   It was long ere he gave any sign of life—it seemed
as though the soul was reluctant to awake, as if it would not
return to consciousness.   At last he opened his eyes ;—they
rested as coldly on the little trembling hand which was busied
about him as if he had never clasped it, never kissed it, never
pressed it to his throbbing heart.   The storm had spent its
fury—he was calm !

The countess had again been mistaken in him, as usual—

his conduct was always unlike her anticipations. He rose as quickly as his strength permitted, passed his hand over his disordered hair, and looked for his hat: " I beg your pardon for having startled you—forget this scene, which I might have spared you and myself, had I known what I do now. I deeply lament that the error which clouded your life has lasted so long !"

" Yes," she said, and the words fell from her lips with the sharp sound of a diamond cutting glass: " Yes, it was not *worth* it !"

Freyer turned and gave her one last look—she felt it through her lowered lids. She had sunk on the sofa and fixed her eyes on the ground. A death-like chill ran through her limbs—she waited in her position as if paralysed. All was still for a moment, then she heard a light step cross the soft carpet of the room—and when she looked up, the door had closed behind Joseph Freyer.

CHAPTER XXIX.

IN THE DESERTED HOUSE.

THE night had passed, day was shining through the closed curtains—but Countess Wildenau still sat in the same spot where Freyer had left her. Yes, he had gone " silently, noiselessly as a shadow "—perhaps vanished from her life, as he had said ! She did not know what she felt, she would fain have relieved her stupor by tears, but she dared not weep—why should she ? Everything was proceeding exactly as she wished. True, she had been harsh, too severe and harsh, and words had been uttered by both which neither could forgive the other ! Yet it was to be expected that the bond between them would not be sundered without a storm—why was her heart so heavy, as if some misfortune had happened—greater than aught which could befall her. Tears ! What would the duke think ? It would be an injustice to him. And it was not true that she felt anything; she had no emotion whatever, neither for the vanished man nor for the duke ! Honor—honor was the only thing which could still be saved ! But—his sudden

silence when she mentioned her betrothal to the duke—his
going thus, without a farewell—without a word! He despised
her—she was no longer worthy of him. That was the cause
of his sudden calmness. There w s a crushing grandeur and
dignity in this calmness after the outbursts of fierce despair.
The latter expressed a conflict, the former a victory—and *she*
was vanquished, hers was the shame, the pangs of conscience,
and a strange, inexplicable grief.

So she sat pondering all night long, always imagining that
she had seen what she had not witnessed, the last look he had
fixed upon her, and then—his noiseless walk through the
room. It seemed as though time had stopped at that moment,
and she was compelled, all through the night, to experience
that *one* instant!

Some one tapped lightly on the door, and the maid entered with a haggard face. "I only wanted to ask," she said,
in a weary, faint tone, "whether I might go to bed a little
while. I have waited all night long for Your Highness to
ring—"

"Why, have you been waiting for me?" said the countess,
rising slowly from the sofa. "I did not know it was so late.
What time is it?"

"Nearly six o'clock. But Your Highness looks so pale!
Will you not permit me to put you to bed?"

"Yes, my good Nannie, take me to my bedroom. I cannot walk, my feet are numb."

"You should lie down at once and try to get warm. You
are as cold as ice!" And the maid, really alarmed by the
helplessness of her usually haughty mistress, helped the drooping figure to her room.

The countess allowed herself to be undressed without re-
sistance, sitting on the edge of the bed as if paralysed and
waiting for the maid to lift her in. "I thank you," she said
in a more gentle tone than the woman had ever heard from
her lips, as the maid voluntarily rubbed the soles of her feet.
Her head instantly sank upon the pillows, which bore a large
embroidered monogram, surmounted by a coronet. When her
feet at last grew warm, she seemed to fall asleep, and the maid
left the room. But Madeleine von Wildenau was not asleep,

she was merely exhausted, and, while her body rested, she constantly beheld *one* image, felt *one* grief.

The maid had determined not to rouse her mistress, and left her undisturbed.

At last, late in the morning, the weary woman sank into an uneasy slumber, whence she did not wake until the sun was high in the heavens.

When she opened her eyes, she felt as if she was paralysed in every limb, but attributed this to the terrible impressions of the previous day, which would have shaken even the strongest nature.

She rang the bell for the maid and rose. She walked slowly, it is true, and with great effort—but she *did* walk. After she had been dressed and her breakfast was served she wrote:

"The footman Franz is dismissed for rude treatment of the steward Freyer, and is not to appear in my presence again. The intendant is to settle the matter of wages.

COUNTESS WILDENAU."

Another servant now brought in a letter on a silver tray.

The countess' hand trembled as she took it—the envelope was one of those commonly used by Freyer, but the writing was not his.

"Is any one waiting for an answer?" she asked in a hollow tone.

"No, Your Highness, it was brought by a Griess wood-cutter."

The countess opened the letter—it was from the maid-servant at the hunting castle, and contained only the news that the steward had left suddenly and the servants did not know what to do.

The countess sat motionless for a moment unable to utter a word. Everything seemed whirling around her in a dizzy circle, she saw nothing save dimly, as if through a veil, the servant clearing away the breakfast.

"Let old Martin put the horses in the carriage," she said, hoarsely, at last.

How the minutes passed before she entered it—how it was possible for her to assume, in the presence of the maid, the quiet bearing of the mistress of the estate, who "must see that things were going on right," she did not know. Now she sat with compressed lips, holding her breath that she might seem calm in her own eyes. What will she find on the height? Two graves of the past, and the empty abode of a former happiness. She fancied that a dark wing brushed by the carriage window, as if the death angel were flying by with the cup of wormwood of which Freyer had once spoken!

She had a horror of the deserted house, the spectres of solitude and grief, which the vanished man might have left behind. When a house is dead, it must be closed by the last survivor, and this is always a sorrowful task. But if he himself has driven love forth, he will cross the deserted threshold with a lagging step, for the ghost of his own act will stare at him everywhere from the silent rooms.

Evening had closed in, and the shadows of the mountain were already gathering around the house, from whose windows no loving eye greeted her. The carriage stopped. No one came to meet her—everything was lifeless and deserted. Her heart sank as she alighted.

"Martin—drive to the stable and see if you can find the maid servant," said the countess in a low tone, as if afraid of rousing some shape of horror. Martin did not utter a word, his good natured face was unusually grave as he drove off around the house in the direction of the stables.

The countess stood alone before the locked door. The evening wind swept through the trees and shook the boughs of the pines. A few broken branches swayed and nodded like crippled arms; they were the ones from which Freyer had taken the evergreen for the child's coffin. At that time they were stiff with ice, now the sap, softened by the Spring rain, was dripping from them. Did she understand what the boughs were trying to tell her? Were her cheeks wet by the rain or by tears? She did not know. She only felt unutterably deserted. She stood on the moss grown steps, shut out from her own house, and no voice answered her call.

A cross towered above the tree-tops, it was on the steeple of the old chapel where they both lay—Josepha and the child. A bird of prey soared aloft from it and then vanished in the neighboring grove to shield its plumage from the rain. It had its nest there.

Now all was still again—as if dead, only the cloud rising above the wood poured its contents on the Spring earth. At last footsteps approached. It was the girl bringing the keys.

"I beg the countess' pardon—I did not expect Your Highness so late, I was in the stable unlocking the door," she said. Then she handed her the bunch of keys. "This one with the label is the key of the steward's room, he made me promise not to give it to anybody except the countess, if she should come again."

"Bring a light—it is growing dark," replied the countess, entering the sitting-room.

"I hope Your Highness will excuse it," said the girl. "Everything is still just as it was left after the funerals of Josepha and the child. Herr Freyer wouldn't allow me to clear anything away." She left the room to get a lamp. There lay the dry pine branches, there stood the crucifix with the candles, which had burned low in their sockets. *This* for weeks had been his sole companionship. Poor, forsaken one! cried a voice in the countess' heart, and a shudder ran through her limbs as she saw on the sofa a black pall left from Josepha's funeral. It seemed as if it were Josepha herself lying there, as if the black form must rise at her entrance and approach threateningly. Horror seized her, and she hurried out to meet the girl who was coming with a light. The steward's room was one story higher, adjoining her own apartments. She went up the stairs with an uncertain tread, leaving the girl below. She needed no witness for what she expected to find there.

She thrust the key into the lock with a trembling hand and opened the door. Sorrowful duty! Wherever she turned in this house of mourning, she was under the ban of her own guilt. Wherever she entered one of the empty rooms, it seemed as if whispering, wailing spirits separated and crept into the corners—to watch until the moment came when they could rush forth as an avenging army.

At her entrance the movement was communicated through all the boards of the old floor until it really seemed as if viewless feet were walking by her side. For a moment she stood still, holding her breath—she had never before noticed this effect of her own steps, she had never been here *alone*. Her

sleeping-room was beside her husband's—the door stood open
—he must have been in there to bid farewell before going
away. She moved hesitatingly a few steps forward and cast a
timid glance within. The two beds, standing side by side,
looked like two coffins. She felt as if she beheld her own
corpse lying there—the corpse of the former Countess Wildenau, Freyer's wife. The woman standing here now was a
different person—and her murderess! Yet she grieved for her
and still felt her griefs and her death-struggle. She hastily
closed and bolted the door—as if the dead woman within
might come out and call her to an account.

Then she turned her dragging steps toward Freyer's writing-desk, for that is always the tabernacle where a lonely soul
conceals its secrets. And—there lay a large envelope bearing
the address: "To the Countess Wildenau. To be opened
by her own hands!"

She placed the lamp on the table, and sat down to read.
She no longer dreaded the ghosts of her own acts—*he* was
with her and though he had raged yesterday in the madness
of his anguish—he would protect her!

She opened the envelope. Two papers fell into her hands.
Her marriage certificate and a paper in Freyer's writing.
The lamp burned unsteadily and smoked, or were her eyes
dim ? Now she no longer saw the mistakes in writing, now
she saw between the clumsy characters a noble, grieving soul
which had gazed at her yesterday from a pair of dark eyes—
for the last time! Clasping her hands over the sheet, she
leaned her head upon them like a penitent Magdalene upon
the gospel. It was to her also a gospel—of pain and love. It
ran as follows:

"COUNTESS:

"I bid you an affectionate farewell, and enclose the marriage certificate, that you may have no fear of my causing
you any annoyance by it—

"Everything else which I owe to your kindness I restore,
as I can make no farther use of it. I am sincerely sorry that
you were disappointed in me—I told you that I was not He
whom I personated, but a poor, plain man, but you would
not believe it, and made the experiment with me. It was a
great misfortune for both. For you can never be happy, on

account of the sin you wish to commit against me. I will pray God to release you from me—in a way which will spare you from taking this heavy sin upon you—but I have still one act of penance to perform toward my home, to which I have been faithless, that it may still forgive me in this life. I hear that the Passion Play cannot be performed in Ammergau next summer, because there is no Christus—that would be terrible for our poor parish! I will try whether I can help them out of the difficulty if they will receive me and not repulse me as befits the renegade" (Here the writing was blurred by tears) "Only wait, for the welfare of your own soul, until the performances are over, and I have done my duty to the community. Then God will be merciful and open a way for us all.

Your grateful

JOSEPH FREYER.

Postscript:—If it is possible, forgive me for all I did to offend you yesterday."

There, in brief, untutored words was depicted the martyrdom of a soul, which had passed through the school of suffering to the utmost perfection! The most eloquent, polished description of his feelings would have had less power to touch the countess' heart than these simple, trite expressions—she herself could not have explained why it was the helplessness of the uncultured man who had trusted to her generosity, which spoke from these lines with an unconscious reproach, which pierced deeper than any complaint. And she had no answer to this reproach, save the tears which now flowed constantly from her eyes.

Laying her head upon the page, she wept—at last wept.

She remained long in this attitude. A sorrowful peace surrounded her, nothing stirred within or without, the spirits seemed reconciled by what they now beheld. The dead Countess Wildenau in the next room had risen noiselessly, she was no longer there! She was flying far—far beyond the mountains—seeking—seeking the lost husband, the poor, innocent husband, who had resigned for her sake all that constitutes human happiness and human dignity, anxious for one thing only, her deliverance from what, in his childlike view of religion, he could not fail to consider a heavy, unforgivable sin! She was flying through a broad portal in the air—it was the rainbow formed of the tears of love shed by sundered human hearts for thousands of years. Even so looked the rainbow, which had arched above her head when she stood on the peak with the royal son of the mountains, high above the embers of the forest, through which he had borne her, ruling the flames. They had spared him—but *she* had had no pity —they had crouched at his feet like fiery lions before their tamer, but the woman for whom he had fought trampled on him. Yet above them arched the rainbow, the symbol of peace and reconcilation, and under *this* she had made the oath which she now intended to break. The dead Countess Wildenau, however, saw the gleaming bow again, and was soaring through it to her husband, for she had no farther knowledge of earthly things, she knew only the old, long denied, all-conquering love!

Suddenly the clock on the writing-table began to strike, the penitent dreamer started. It was striking nine. The clock was still going—he had wound it. It was a gift from her. He had left all her gifts, he wrote. That would be terrible. Surely he had not gone without any means? The key of the writing-table was in the lock. She opened the drawer. There lay all his papers, books, the rest of the housekeeping money, and accounts, all in the most conscientious order, and beside them—oh, that she must see it—a little purse containing his savings and a savings-bank book, which she herself had once jestingly pressed upon him. The little book was wrapped in paper, on which was written: "To keep the graves of my dear ones in Countess Wildenau's chapel."

"Oh, you great, noble heart, which I never understood!" sobbed the guilty woman, restoring the little volume to its place.

But she could not rest, she must search on and on, she must know whether he had left her as a beggar? Against the wall beside the writing-table, stood a costly old armoire, richly ornamented, which had seen many generations of the Prankenbergs come and pass away. Madeleine von Wildenau turned the lock with an effort—there hung all his clothing, just as he had received it from her or purchased it with his own wages; nothing was missing save the poor little coat, hat and cane, with which he had left Ammergau with the owner of a fortune numbering millions. He had wandered forth again as poor as he had come.

Sinking on her knees, she buried her face, overwhelmed with grief and shame, in her clasped hands.

" Freyer, Freyer, I did not want this—not this !" Now the long repressed grief which she had inflicted upon herself burst forth unrestrained. Here she could shriek it out; here no one heard her. "Oh, that you should leave me thus—unreconciled, without a farewell, with an aching heart—not even protected from want ! And I let you go without one kind word—I did not even return your last glance. Was it possible that I could do it ?"

The old Prankenberg lion on the coat of arms on the armoire had doubtless seen many mourners scan the garments whose owners rested under the sod—but no one of all the women of that failing race had wept so bitterly over the contents of the armoire—as this last of her name.

The candle had burned low in the socket, a star glinting through the torn clouds shone through the uncurtained windows. Beyond the forest the first flashes of spring lightning darted to and fro.

Madeleine von Wildenau rose and stood for a while in the middle of the room, pondering. What did she want here? She had nothing more to find in the empty house. The dead Countess Wildenau was once more sleeping in the adjoining room, and the living one no longer belonged to herself. Was it, could it be true, that she had thrust out the peaceful inmate of this house ? Thrust him forever from the modest home she had established for him ? "Husband, father of my child, where are you ? " No answer! He was no longer hers! He had risen from the humiliation she inflicted upon him, he had stripped off the robe of servitude, and gone forth, scorning her and all else—a poor but free man !

She must return to the slavery of her own guilt and of prosaic existence, while he went farther and farther away, like a vanishing star. She felt that her strength was failing, she must go, or she would sink dying in this place of woe—alone without aid or care.

She folded the marriage certificate and Freyer's letter together, and without another glance around the room—the ghost of her awakened conscience was stirring again, she took the dying candle and hurried down. The steps again creaked behind her, as though some one was following her downstairs. She had ordered the carriage at nine, it must have been waiting a long time. Her foot faltered at the door of the sitting-room, but she passed on—it was impossible for her to enter it again—she called—but the maid-servant had gone to her work in the stables—nothing save her own trembling voice echoed back through the passages. She went out. The carriage was standing at the side of the house. The rain had ceased, the forest was slumbering and all the creatures which animated it by day with it.

The countess locked the door. " Now interweave your boughs and shut it in !" she said to the briers and pines which stood closely around it. "Spread out your branches and compass it with an impenetrable hedge that no one may find it. The Sleeping Beauty who slumbers here—nothing must ever rouse ! "

CHAPTER XXX.

THE " WIESHERRLE."

HIGH above the rushing Wildbach, where the stream bursts through the crumbling rocks and in its fierce rush sends heavy stones grinding over one another—a man lay on the damp cliff which trembled under the shock of the falling masses of water. The rough precipices, dripping with spray, pressed close about him, shutting him into the cool, moss-grown ravine, through which no patch of blue sky was visible, no sunbeam stole.

Here the wanderer, deceived in everything, lay resting on his way home. With his head propped on his hand, he gazed steadfastly down into the swirl of the foaming, misty, ceaseless rush of the falling water! On the rock before him lay a small memorandum book, in which he was slowly writing sorrowful words, just as they welled from his soul—slowly and sluggishly, as the resin oozes from the gashed trees. Wherever a human heart receives a deep, fatal wound, the poetry latent in the blood of the people streams from the hurt. All our sorrowful old folk-songs are such drops of the heart's blood of the people. The son of a race of mountaineers who sung their griefs and joys was composing his own mournful wayfaring ballad for not one of those which he knew and cherished in his memory expressed the unutterable grief he experienced. He did not know how he wrote it—he was ignorant of rhyme and metre. When he finished, that is, when he had said all he felt, it seemed as though the song had flown to him, as the seed of some plant is blown upon a barren cliff, takes root, and grows there.

But now, after he had created the form of the verses, he first realized the full extent of his misery!

Hiding the little book in his pocket, he rose to follow the toilsome path he was seeking high among the mountains where there were only a few scattered homesteads, and he met no human being.

While Countess Wildenau in the deserted hunting-castle was weeping over the cast-off garments with which he had flung aside the form of a servant, the free man was striding over the heights, fanned by the night-breeze, lashed by the rain in his thin coat—free—but also free to be exposed to grief, to the elements—to hunger! Free—but so free that he had not even a roof beneath which to shelter his head within four protecting walls.

> " Both love and faith have fled for aye,
> Like chaff by wild winds swept away—
> Naught, naught is left me here below
> Save keen remorse and endless woe.
>
> " No home have I on the wide earth—
> A ragged beggar fare I forth,
> In midnight gloom, by tempests met,
> Broken my staff, my star has set.
>
> " With raiment tattered by the sleet,
> My brain scorched by the sun's fierce heat,
> My heart torn by a human hand,
> A shadow—I glide through the land.
>
> " Homeward I turn, white is my hair,
> Of love and faith my life is bare—
> Whoe'er beholds me makes the sign
> Of the cross—God save a fate like mine."

So the melancholy melody echoed through the darkness of
the night, from peak to peak along the road from the Griess
to Ammergau.   And wherever it sounded, the birds flew
startled from the trees deeper into the forest, the deer fled into
the thickets and listened, the child in the cradle started and
wept in its sleep.   The dogs in the lonely courtyards barked
loudly.

"That was no human voice, it was a shot deer or an owl"
—the peasants said to their trembling wives, listening for a
time to the ghostly, wailing notes dying faintly away till all
was still once more—and the spectre had passed.   But when
morning dawned and the time came when the matin bells
drove all evil spirits away the song, too, ceased, and only its
prophecy came true.   Whoever recognized in the emaciated
man, with hollow eyes and cheeks, the Christus-Freyer of
Ammergau, doubtless made the sign of the cross in terror, ex-
claiming: "Heaven preserve us!"   But the lighter it grew,
the farther he plunged into the forest.   He was ashamed to
be seen!   His gait grew more and more feeble, his garments
more shabby by his long walk in the rain and wind.

He still had a few pennies in his pocket—the exact sum
he possessed when he left Ammergau.   He was keeping them
for a night's lodging, which he must take once during the
twenty-four hours.   He could have reached Ammergau easily
by noon—but he did not want to enter it in broad day as a
ragged beggar.   So he rested by day and walked at night.

At a venerable old inn, the "Shield," on the road from
Steingaden to Ammergau, he asked one of the servants if he
might lie a few hours on the straw to rest.   The latter hesitated before granting permission—the man looked so doubtful.
At last he said: "Well, I won't refuse you, but see that you
carry nothing off when you go away from here."

Freyer made no reply.   The wrath which had made him
hurl the lackey from the countess' door, no longer surged
within him—now it was his home which was punishing him,
speaking to him in her rude accents—let her say what she
would, he accepted it as a son receives a reproof from a
mother.   He hung his drenched coat to dry in the sun, which
now shone warmly again, then slipped into the barn and lay
down on the hay.   A refreshing slumber embraced him, pov-

erty and humility took the sorrowing soul into their maternal
arms, as a poor man picks up the withered blossom the rich
one has carelessly flung aside, and carrying it home makes it
bloom again.

Rest, weary soul! You no longer need to stretch and dis-
tort the noble proportions of your existence to fit them to relations to which they were not born. You need be nothing
more than you are, a child of the people, suckled by the
sacred breast of nature and can always return there without
being ashamed of it. Poverty and lowliness extend their protecting mantle over you and hide you from the looks of scorn
and contempt which rend your heart.

A peaceful expression rested upon the sleeper's face, but
his breathing was deep and labored as if some powerful feeling was stirring his soul under the quiet repose of slumber and
from beneath his closed lids stole a tear.

During several hours the exhausted body lay between
sleeping and waking, unconscious grief and comfort.

Opposite, "on the Wies" fifteen minutes walk from the
Shield," a bell rang in the church where the pilgrims went.
There an ancient Christ " our Lord of the Wies," called simply "the Wiesherrle," carved from mouldering, painted wood,
was hung from the cross by chains which rattled when the
image was laughed at incredulously, and with real hair, which
constantly grew again when an impious hand cut it. At times
of special visitation it could sweat blood, and hundreds jour-
neyed to the " Wies," trustfully seeking the wonder-working
" Wiesherrle." It was a terrible image of suffering, and the
first sight of the scourged body and visage contorted by pain
caused an involuntary thrill of horror—increased by the black
beard and long hair, such as often grows in the graves of the
dead. The face stared fixedly at the beholder with its glassy
eyes, as if to say: " Do you believe in me?" The emaciated
body was so lifelike, that it might have been an embalmed
corpse placed erect. But the horror vanished when one
gazed for a while, for an expression of patience rested on the
uncanny face, the lashes of the fixed eyes began to quiver, the
image became instinct with life, the chains swayed slightly,
and the drops of blood again grew liquid. Why should they
not? The heart, which loves forever can also, to the eye of

23

faith, bleed forever. Hundreds of wax limbs and silver hearts, consecrated bones and other anomalies bore witness to past calamities where the Wiesherrle had lent its aid. But he could also be angry, as the rattling of his chains showed, and this gave him a somewhat spectral, demoniac aspect.

Under the protection of this strange image of Christ, whose power extended over the whole mountain plateau, the living image of Christ lay unconscious. Then the vesper-bells, ringing from the church, roused him. He hastily started up and, in doing so, struck against the block where the wood was split. A chain flung upon it fell. Freyer raised and held it a moment before replacing it on the block, thinking of the scourging in the Passion Play.

"Heavens, the Wiesherrle!" shrieked a terrified voice, and the door leading into the barn, which had been softly opened, was hurriedly shut.

"Father, father, come quick—the Wiesherrle is in the barn!"—screamed some one in deadly fright.

"Silly girl," Freyer heard a man say. "Are you crazy? What are you talking about?"

"Really, Father, on my soul; just go there. The Wiesherrle is standing in the middle of the hay. I saw him. By our Lord and the Holy Cross. Amen!"

Freyer heard the girl sink heavily on the bench by the stove. The father answered angrily: "Silly thing, silly thing!" and went to the door in his hob-nailed shoes. "Is any one in here?" he asked. But as Freyer approached, the peasant himself almost started back in terror: "Good Lord, who are you? Why do you startle folks so? Can't you speak?"

"I asked the man if I might rest there, and then I fell asleep."

"I don't see why you should be so lazy, turning night into day. Tramp on, and sleep off your drunkenness somewhere else! I want no miracles—and no Wiesherrle in my house."

"I'll pay for everything," said Freyer humbly, almost beseechingly, holding out his little stock of ready money, for he was overpowered with hunger and thirst.

"What do I care for your pennies!" growled the tavern keeper angrily, closing the door.

There stood the hapless man, in whom the girl's soul had recognized with awe the martyred Christ, but whom the rude peasant turned from his door as a vagrant—hungry and thirsty, worn almost unto death, and with a walk of five hours before him. He took his hat and his staff, hung his dry coat over his shoulder, and left the barn.

As he went out he heard the last notes of the vesper-bell, and felt a yearning to go to Him for whom he had been mistaken, it seemed as if He were calling in the echoing bells: " Come to me, I have comfort for you." He struck into the forest path that led to the Wiesherrle. The white walls of the church soon appeared and he stepped within, where the showy, antiquated style of the last century mingled with the crude notions of the mountaineers for and by whom it was built.

Skulls, skeletons of saints, chubby-cheeked cupids, cruel martyrdoms, and Arcadian shepherdesses, nude penitents and fiends dragging them down into the depths, lambs of heaven and dogs of hell were all in motley confusion! Above the chaotic medley arched on fantastic columns the huge dome with a gate of heaven painted in perspective, which, according to the beholder's standpoint rose or sank, was foreshortened or the opposite.

A wreath of lucernes beautifully ornamented, through which the blue sky peeped and swallows building their nests flew in and out, formed as it were the jewel in the architecture of the cornice. Even the eye of God was not lacking, a tarnished bit of mirror inserted above the pulpit in the centre of golden rays, and intended to flash when the sun shone on it.

And there in a glass shrine directly beneath all the tinsel rubbish, on the gilded carving of the high altar, the poor, plain little Wiesherrle hung in chains. The two, the wooden image of God, and the one of flesh and blood, confronted each other—the Christ of the Ammergau Play greeted the Christ of the Wies. It is true, they did resemble each other, like suffering and pain. Freyer knelt long before the Wiesherrle and what they confided to each other was heard only by the God in whose service and by whose power they wrought miracles—each in his own way.

" You are happy," said the Wiesherrle. " Happier than

I I Human hands created and faith animated me ; where that is lacking, I am a mere dead wooden puppet, only fit to be flung into the fire. But you were created by God, you live and breathe, can move and act—and highest of all—*suffer* like Him whom we represent. I envy you!"

"Yes!" cried Freyer; "You are right; *to suffer* like Christ is highest of all! My God, I thank Thee that I suffer."

This was the comfort the Wiesherrle had for his sorely tried brother. It was a simple thought, but it gave him strength to bear everything. It is always believed that a great grief requires a great consolation. This is not true, the poorer the man is, the more value the smallest gift has for him, and the more wretched he is—the smallest comfort! To the husbandman whose crops have been destroyed by hail, it would be no comfort to receive the gift of a blossom, which would bring rapture to the sultry attic chamber of a sick man.

In a great misfortune we often ask: "What gave the person strength to endure it?" It was nothing save these trivial comforts which only the unhappy know. The soul lamenting the loss of a loved one while many others are left is not comforted when the lifeless figure of a martyr preaches patience— but to the desolate one, who no longer has aught which speaks to him, the lifeless wooden image becomes a friend and its mute language a consolation.

Beside the altar stood an alms-box. The gifts for which it was intended were meant for repairs on the church and the preservation of the Wiesherrle, who sometimes needed a new cloth about his loins. Freyer flung into it the few coins which the innkeeper had disdained, because he looked like the Wiesherrle, now they should go to him. He felt as if he should need no more money all his life, as if the comfort he had here received raised him far above earthly need and care.

Twilight was gathering, the sun had sunk behind the blue peaks of the Pfrontner mountains, and now the hour struck— the sacred hour of the return home.

. Already he felt with joy the throbbing of the pulses of his home, a mysterious connection between this place and distant Ammergau. And he was right: Childish as was the representation of the divine ideal, it was, nevertheless, the rippling of one of those hidden springs of faith which blend in the

Passion Play, forming the great stream of belief which is to
supply a thirsting world. As on a barren height, amid tangled thickets, we often greet with delight the low murmur of
a hidden brook which in the valley below becomes the mighty
artery of our native soil, so the returning wanderer hurried on
longingly toward the mysterious spring which led him to the
mother's heart. But his knees trembled, human nature asserted its rights. He must eat or he would fall fainting. But
where could food be had ? The last pennies were in the alms-
box—he could not have taken them out again, even had he
wished it. There was no way save to ask some one—for
bread. He dragged himself wearily to the parsonage—he
would try there, the priest would be less startled by the
"Wiesherrle " than the peasant. Thrice he attempted to pull
the bell, but very gently. He fancied the whole world could
hear that he was ringing—to beg. Yet, if it did not sound,
no one would open the door. At last, with as much effort as
though he was pulling the bell-rope in the church steeple, he
rang. The bell echoed shrilly. The pastor's old cook appeared.

Freyer raised his hat. " Might I ask you for a piece of
bread ? " he murmured softly, and the tall figure seemed to
droop lower with every word.

The cook, who was never allowed to turn a beggar from
the door, eyed him a moment with mingled pity and anxiety.
" Directly," she answered, and went in search of something,
but prudently closed the door, leaving him outside as we do
with suspicious individuals. Freyer waited, hat in hand.
The evening breeze swept chill across the lofty mountain
plateau and blew his hair around his uncovered head. At last
the cook came, bringing him some soup and a bit of bread.
Freyer thanked her, and eat it ! When he had finished he
gave the little dish back to the woman—but his hand
trembled so that he almost let it fall and his brow was damp.
Then he thanked her again, but without raising his eyes, and
quietly pursued his way.

CHAPTER XXXI.

THE RETURN HOME.

THE "Wies" towered like an island from amid a grey sea of clouds. All the mountains of Trauchgau and Pfront, Allgau and Tyrol, which surround it like distant shores and cliffs, had vanished in the mist. The windows in the comfortable tavern were lighted and a fire was blazing on the hearth. One little lamp after another shone from the quiet farm-houses.

The lonely church now lay silent! Silent, too, was the Wiesherrle in his glass shrine, while the wayfarer pressed steadily down through the mist toward home and the cross! Freyer moved on more and more swiftly across the hill-sides and through the woods till he reached the path leading down the mountain to the "Halb-Ammer," which flowed at its base. Gradually he emerged from the strata of mist, and now a faint ray of moonlight fell upon his path.

Hour after hour he pursued his way. One after another the lights in the houses were extinguished. The world sank into slumber, and the villages were wrapped in silence.

In the churches only the ever-burning lamps still blazed, and he made them his resting-places.

The clock in the church steeple of Altenau struck twelve as he passed through. A belated tippler approached him with the reeling step of a drunkard, but started back when he saw his face, staring after him with dull bewildered eyes as if he beheld some spectre of the night.

"An image of horror I glide through the land!" Freyer murmured softly. To-night he did not sing his song. This evening his pain was soothed, his soul was preparing for another pæan—on the cross!

Now the little church of Kappel appeared before him on its green hill, like a pious sign-post pointing the way to Ammergau. But patches of snow still lingered amid the pale green of the Spring foliage, for it is late ere the Winter is conquered by the milder season and the keen wind swept down the broad highway, making the wayfarer's teeth chatter with cold. He felt that his vital warmth was nearly exhausted, he had walked two days with no hot food. For the soup at the parsonage that day was merely lukewarm—he stood still a moment, surely he had dreamed that! He could not have begged for bread ? Yes, it was even so. A tremor shook his limbs : Have you fallen so low ? He tried to button his thin coat—his fingers were stiff with cold. Ten years ago when he left Ammergau, it was midsummer—now winter still reigned on the heights. " Only let me not perish on the highway," he prayed, " only let me reach home."

It was now bright cold moonlight, all the outlines of the mountains stood forth distinctly, the familiar contours of the Ammergau peaks became more and more visible.

Now he stood on the Ammer bridge where what might be termed the suburb of Ammergau, the hamlet of Lower Ammergau, begins. The moon-lit river led the eye in a straight line to the centre of the Ammer valley—there lay the sacred mountains of his home—the vast side scenes of the most gigantic stage in the world, the Kofel with its cross, and the other peaks. Opposite on the left the quiet chapel of St. Gregory amid boundless meadows, beside the fall of the Leine, the Ammer's wilder sister. There he had watched his horses when a boy, down near the chapel where the blue gentians had garlanded his head when he flung himself on the grass, intoxicated by his own exuberant youth and abundance of life.

He extended his arms as if he would fain embrace the whole infinite scene : " Home, home, your lost son is returning—receive him. Do not fall, ye mountains, and bury the beloved valley ere I reach it ! "

One last effort, one short hour's walk. Hold out, wearied one, this one hour more !

The highway from Lower Ammergau stretched endlessly toward the goal. On the right was the forest, on the left the fields where grew thousands of meadow blossoms, the Eden of his childhood where a blue lake once lured him, so blue that he imagined it was reflecting a patch of the sky, but when he reached it, instead of water, he beheld a field of forget-me-nots !

Oh, memories of childhood—reconciling angel of the tortured soul! There stands the cross on the boundary with the thorny bush whence Christ's crown was cut.

"How will you fare, will the community receive you, admit you to the blissful union of home powers, if you sacrifice your heart's blood for it?" Freyer asked himself, and it seemed as if some cloud, some dark foreboding came between him and his home. "Well for him who no longer expects his reward from this world. What are men? They are all variable, variable and weak! Thou alone art the same. Thou who dost create the miracle from our midst— and thou, sacred soil of our ancestors, ye mountains from whose peaks blows the strengthening breath which animates our sublime work—it is not *human beings*, but ye who are home!

Now the goal was gained—he was there! Before him in the moonlight lay the Passion Theatre—the consecrated space where once for hours he was permitted to feel himself a God.

The poor, cast off man, deceived in all things, flung himself down, kissed the earth, and laid a handful of it on his head, as though it were the hand of a mother—while from his soul gushed like a song sung by his own weeping guardian angel,

> " Thy soil I kiss, beloved home,
>   Which erst my fathers' feet have trod,
> Where the good seed devoutly sown
>   Sprang forth at the command of God !
> Thy lap fain would I rest upon,
>   Though faithlessly from thee I fled
> Still thy chains draw thy wand'ring son
>   Oh ! mother, back where'er his feet may tread.
> And though no ray of light, no star,
>   Illumes the future—and its gloom,
> Thou wilt not grudge, after life's war,
>   A clod of earth upon my tomb."

He rested his head thus a long time on the cold earth, but he no longer felt it. It seemed as though the soul had consumed the last power of the exhausted body—and bursting its fetters blazed forth like an aureole. "Hosanna, hosanna!" rang through the air, and the earth trembled under the tramp of thousands. On they came in a long procession bearing palm-branches, the shades of the fathers—the old actors in the Passion Play from its commencement, and all who had lived and died for the cross since the time of Christ!

"Hosanna, hosanna to him who died on the cross. Many are called, but few chosen. But you belong to us!" sang the chorus of martyrs till the notes rang through earth and Heaven. "Hosanna, hosanna to him who suffers and bleeds for the sins of the world."

Freyer raised his head. The moon had gone behind a cloud, and white mists were gathering over the fields.

He rose, shivering with cold. His thin coat was damp with the night frost which had melted on his uncovered breast, and his feet were sore, for his shoes were worn out by the long walk.

He still fancied he could hear, far away in the infinite distance, the chorus of the Hosanna to the Crucified! And raising his arms to heaven, he cried: "Oh, my Redeemer and Master, so long as Thou dost need me to show the world Thy face—let me live—then take pity on me and let me die on the cross! Die for the sins of one, as Thou didst die for the sins of the world." He opened the door leading to the stage. There in the dim moonlight lay the old cross. Sobbing aloud, he embraced it, pressing to his breast the hard wood which had supported him and now, as of yore, was surrounded by the mysterious powers, which so strongly attracted him.

"Oh, had I been but faithful to thee," he lamented, "all the blessings of this world—even were it the greatest happiness, would not outweigh thee. Now I am thine—raise thyself with me and bear me upward, high above all earthly woe."

The clock in the church steeple struck three. He must still live and suffer, for he knew that no one could play the Christus as he did, because no one bore the Redeemer's image in his heart like him. But—could he go farther? His strength had failed, he felt it with burdened breast. He took up his hat and staff, and tottered out. Where should he go? To Ludwig Gross, the only person to whom he was not ashamed to show himself in his wretchedness.

for the first time he realized that he could scarcely
⋯ ⋯ ⋯ther. Yet it must be done, he could not lie there.

⋯ ⋯ by step he dragged himself in his torn shoes along
⋯ ⋯gh village street. When half way down he heard
⋯ ⋯ nd singing alternating with cries and laughter, echoing
⋯ ⋯ ⋯ tavern. It was a wedding, and they were preparing
⋯ ⋯ t the bride and groom home—he learned this from
⋯ ⋯ of some of the lads who came out. Was he really in
Ammergau ? His soul was yet thrilling with emotion at the
sight of the home for which he had so long yearned and now
—this contrast! Yet it was natural, they could not all devote themselves to their task with the same fervor. Yet it
doubly wounded the man who bore in his heart such a
solemn earnestness of conviction. He glided noiselessly
along in the shadow of the houses, that no one should see
him.

Did not the carousers notice that their Christ was passing
in beggar's garb ? Did they not feel the gaze bent on them
from the shadow through the lighted window, silently asking :
" Are these the descendants of those ancestors whose glorified spirits had just greeted the returning son of Ammergau ? "

The unhappy wanderer's step passed by unheard, and
now Freyer turned into the side street, where his friend's
house stood—the luckless house where his doom began.

It was not quite half-past three. The confused noise did
not reach the quiet street. The house, shaded by its broad,
projecting roof, lay as if wrapped in slumber. Except during
the passion Ludwig always slept in the room on the ground
floor, formerly occupied by the countess. Freyer tapped
lightly on the shutter, but his heart was beating so violently
that he could scarcely hear whether any one was moving
within.

If his friend should not be there, had gone away on a
journey, or moved—what should he do then ? He had had
no communication with him, and only heard once through
Josepha that old Andreas Gross was dead. He knocked
again. Ludwig was the only person whom he could trust—
if he had lost him, all would be over.

But no—there was a movement within—the well-known voice asked sleepily : " Who is there ? "

" Ludwig, open the window—it is I—Freyer ! " he called under his breath.

The shutters were flung back. " Freyer—is it possible ? Wait, Joseph, wait, I'll admit you." He heard his friend hurriedly dressing—two minutes after the door opened. Not a word was exchanged between the two men. Ludwig grasped Freyer's hand and drew him into the house. " Freyer—you—am I dreaming ? You here—what brings you ? I'll have a light directly." His hand trembled with excitement as he lighted a candle. Freyer stood timidly at the door. The room grew bright, the rays streamed full on Freyer. Ludwig started back in horror. " Merciful Heaven, how you look ! "

The friends long stood face to face, unable to utter a word, Freyer still holding his hat in his hand. Ludwig's keen eye glided over the emaciated form, the shabby coat, the torn shoes. "Freyer, Freyer, what has befallen you ? My poor friend, do you return to me *thus ?* " With unutterable grief he clasped the unfortunate man in his arms.

Freyer could scarcely speak, his tongue refused to obey his will. " If I could rest a little while," he faltered.

" Yes, come, come and lie down on my bed—I have slept as much as I wish. I shall not lie down again," replied Ludwig, trembling with mingled pity and alarm, as he drew off his friend's miserable rags as quickly as possible. Then leading him to his own bed, he gently pressed him down upon it. He would not weary the exhausted man with questions, he saw that Freyer was no longer master of himself. His condition told his friend enough.

" You—are—kind ! " stammered Freyer. " Oh, I have learned something in the outside world."

" What—what have you learned ? " asked Ludwig.

A strange smile flitted over Freyer's face : " *To beg.*"

His friend shuddered. " Don't talk any more now—you need rest ! " he said in a low, soothing tone, wrapping the chilled body in warm coverlets. But a flash of noble indignation sparkled in his eyes, and his pale lips could not restrain the words : " I will ask no questions—but whoever sent you home to us must answer for it to God."

The other did not hear, or if he did his thoughts were too confused to understand.

" Freyer ! Only tell me what I can do to strengthen you. I'll make a fire, and give you anything to eat that you would like."

" Whatever—you—have ! " Freyer gasped with much difficulty.

" May God help us—he is starving." Ludwig could scarcely control his tears. " Keep quiet—I'll come presently and bring you something ! " he said, hurrying out to get all the modest larder contained. He would not wake his sisters —this was no theme for feminine gossip. He soon prepared with his own hands a simple bread porridge into which he broke a couple of eggs, he had nothing else—but at least it was warm food. When he took it to his friend Frëyer had grown so weak that he could scarcely hold the spoon, but the nourishment evidently did him good.

" Now sleep ! " said Ludwig. " Day is dawning. I'll go down to the village and see if I can get you some boots and another coat."

A mute look of gratitude from Freyer rewarded the faithful care, then his eyes closed, and his friend gazed at him with deep melancholy.

CHAPTER XXXII.

TO THE VILLAGE.

THE burgomaster's house, with its elaborate fresco, " Christ before Pilate," still stood without any signs of life in the grey dawn. The burgomaster was asleep. He had been ill very frequently. It seemed as if the attack brought on by Freyer's flight had given him his death-blow, he had never rallied from it. And as his body could not recuperate, his mind could never regain its tone.

When Ludwig Gross' violent ring disturbed the morning silence of the house the burgomaster's wife opened the door with a face by no means expressive of pleasure. " My husband is still asleep ! " she said to the drawing-master.

"Yes, I cannot help it, you must wake him. I've important business!"

The anxious wife still demurred, but the burgomaster appeared at the top of the staircase. "What is it? I am always to be seen if there is anything urgent. Good morning; go into the sitting-room. I'll come directly."

Ludwig Gross entered the low-ceiled but cheerful apartment, where flowers bloomed in every window. Against the wall was the ancient glass cupboard, the show piece of furniture in every well-to-do Ammergau household, where were treasured the wife's bridal wreath and the husband's goblet, the wedding gifts—cups with gilt inscriptions: "In perpetual remembrance," which belonged to the wife and prizes won in shooting matches, or gifts from visitors to the Passion Play, the property of the husband. In the ivy-grown niche in the corner of the room was an ancient crucifix—below it a wooden bench with a table, on which lay writing materials. On the pier-table between the windows were a couple of images of saints, and a pile of play-bills of the rehearsals which the burgomaster was arranging. Against the opposite wall stood a four-legged piece of furniture covered with black leather, called "the sofa," and close by the huge tiled stove, behind which the burgomaster's wife had set the milk "to thicken." Near by was a wall-cupboard with a small writing-desk, and lastly a beautifully polished winding staircase which led through a hole in the ceiling directly into the sleeping-room, and was the seat of the family cat. This was the home of a great intellect, which reached far beyond these narrow bounds and to which the great epochs of the Passion Play were the only sphere in which it could really live, where it had a wide field for its talents and ambition—where it could find compensation for the ten years prose of petty, narrow circumstances. But the intervals of ten years were too long, and the elderly man was gradually losing the elasticity and enthusiasm which could bear him beyond the deprivations of a decade. He tried all sorts of ventures in order at least to escape the petty troubles of poverty, but they were unsuccessful and thereby he only became burdened the more. Thus in the strife with realism, constantly holding aloft the standard of the ideal, involved in inward and outward contradictions, the hapless man was wearing himself out—like most of the natives of Ammergau.

"Well, what is it?" he now asked, entering the room. "Sit down."

"Don't be vexed, but you know my husband must have his coffee, or he will be ill." The burgomaster's wife brought in the breakfast and set it on the table before him. "Don't let it get cold," she said warningly, then prudently retreated, even taking the cat with her, that the gentlemen might be entirely alone and undisturbed.

"Drink it, pray drink it," urged Ludwig, and waited until the burgomaster had finished his scanty breakfast; which was quickly done. "Well? What is it!" asked the latter, pushing his cup aside.

"I have news for you: Freyer is here!"

"Ah!" The burgomaster started, and an ominous flush crimsoned his face. His hand trembled nervously as he smoothed his hair, once so beautiful, now grey. "Freyer—! How did he get here?"

"1 don't know—the question died on my lips when I saw him."

"Why?"

"Oh, he is such a spectacle, ill, half starved—in rags, an *Ecce homo!* I thought my heart would break when I saw him."

"Aha—so Nemesis is here already."

"Oh! do not speak so. Such a Nemesis is too cruel! I do not know what has befallen him—I could ask no questions, but I do know that Freyer has done nothing which deserves such a punishment. You can have no idea of the man's condition. He is lying at home—unable to move a limb."

The burgomaster shrugged his shoulders. "What have I to do with it? You know that I never sympathize with self-created sorrows."

"You need not, only you must help me obtain some means of livelihood for the unfortunate man. He still has his share of the receipts of the last Passion Play. He was not present at the distribution, but he played the Christus from May until

August—to the best of my recollection his portion was between seven and eight hundred marks."

"Quite right. But as he had run away and moreover very generously bequeathed all his property to the poor—I could not suppose that I must save the sum for a rainy day, and that he would so soon be in the position of becoming a burden upon the community!"

"What did you do with the money?"

"Don't you know? I divided it with the rest."

Ludwig stamped his foot. "Oh, Heaven! that was my only hope! But he must have assistance, he has neither clothing nor shoes! I haven't a penny in the house except what we need for food. He cannot be seen in these garments, he would rather die. We cannot expose him to mockery—we must respect ourselves in him, he was the best Christus we ever had, and though the play was interrupted by him, we owe him a greater success and a larger revenue than we formerly obtained during a whole season. And, in return, should we allow him to go with empty hands—like the poet in Schiller's division of the earth, because he came too late?"

"Yes." The burgomaster twisted his moustache with his thin fingers: "I am sorry for him—but the thing is done and cannot be changed."

"It must be changed, the people must return the money!" cried the drawing-master vehemently.

The burgomaster looked at him with his keen eyes, half veiled by their drooping lids. "Ask them," he said calmly and coldly. "Go and get it—if it can be had."

Ludwig bit his lips. "Then something must be done by the parish."

"That requires an agreement of the whole parish."

"Call a meeting then."

"Hm, hm!" The burgomaster smiled: "That is no easy matter. What do you think the people will answer, if I say: 'Herr Freyer ran away from us, interrupted the performances, made us lose about 100,000 marks, discredited the Passion Play in our own eyes and those of the world, and asks in return the payment of 800 marks from the parish treasury?'"

Ludwig let his arms fall in hopeless despair. "Then I don't know what to do—I must support my helpless old sisters.

I cannot maintain him, too, or I would ask no one's aid. I think it should be a point of honor with us Ammergau people not to leave a member of the parish in the lurch, when he returns home poor and needy, especially a man like Freyer, whom we have more cause to thank than to reproach, say what you will. We are not a penal institution."

" No, nor an asylum."

"Well, we need be neither, but merely a community of free men, who should be solely ruled by the thought of love, but unfortunately have long ceased to be so."

The burgomaster leaned quietly back in his chair, the drawing-master became more and more heated, as the other remained cold.

"You always take refuge behind the parish, when you don't *wish* to do anything—but when you *desire* it, the parish never stands in your way!"

The burgomaster pressed his hand to his brow, as if thinking wearied him. He belonged to the class of men whose hearts are in their heads. If anything made his heart ache, it disturbed his brain too. He remained silent a long time while Ludwig paced up and down the room, trembling with excitement. At last, not without a touch of bitter humor, he said :

"I am well aware of that, you always say so whenever I do anything that does not suit you. I should like to see what would become of you, with your contradictory, impulsive artist nature, to-day 'Hosanna' and to-morrow 'Crucify Him,' if I did not maintain calmness and steadiness for you. If I, who bear the responsibility of acting, changed my opinions as quickly as you do and converted each of your momentary impulses into an act—I ought at least to possess the power to kill to-day, and to-morrow, when you repented, restore the person to life. Ten years ago, when Freyer left us in the lurch for the sake of a love affair, and dealt a blow to all we held sacred—you threw yourself into my arms and wept on my breast over the enormity of his deed—now—because I am not instantly touched by a few rags and tatters, and the woe-begone air of a penitent recovering from a moral debauch, you will weep on your friend's bosom over the harshness and want of feeling of the burgomaster! I'm used to it. I know you hotspurs."

He drew a pair of boots from under the stove. "There—

I am the owner of just two pairs of boots. You can take one to your protégé, that he may at least appear before me in a respectable fashion to discuss the matter! I don't do it at the cost of the parish, however. And I can give you an old coat too—I was going to send it to my Anton, but, no matter! Only I beg you not to tell him from whom the articles come, or he will hate me because I was in a situation to help *him*— instead of he *me*."

"Oh, how little you know him!" cried Ludwig.

The burgomaster smiled. "I know the Ammergau people—and he is one of them!"

"I thank you in his name," said Ludwig, instantly appeased.

"Yes, you see you thank me for that, yet it is the least important thing. This is merely a private act of charity which I might show any rascal I pitied. But when I, as burgomaster, rigidly guard the honor of Ammergau and consider whom I recommend to public sympathy, you reproach me for it! Before I call a parish meeting and answer for him officially, I must know whether he is worthy of it, and what his condition is." He again pressed his hand to his head. "Send him to me at the office—then we will see."

Ludwig held out his hand. "No offence, surely we know how we feel toward each other."

When the drawing-master had gone, the burgomaster drew a long breath and remained for some time absorbed in thought. Then he glanced at the clock, not to learn the hour but to ascertain whether the conversation had lasted long enough to account for his headache and exhaustion. The result did not seem to soothe him. "Where will this end?"

His wife looked in "Well, Father, what is it?"

The burgomaster took his hat. "Freyer is here!"

"Good Heavens!" She clasped her hands in amazement.

"Yes, it was a great excitement to me. Tell Anastasia, that she may not learn the news from strangers. She has long been resigned, but of course this will move her deeply! And above all, don't let anything be said about it in the shop, I don't want the tidings to get abroad in the village, at least through us. Farewell!"

The burgomaster's family enjoyed a small prerogative:

24

the salt monopoly, and a little provision store where the tire-less industry of the self-sacrificing wife collected a few groschen. "If I don't make something—who will?" she used to say, with a keen thrust at her husband's absence of economy. So the burgomaster did not mention his extrava-gance in connection with the boots and coat. He could not bear even just reproaches now. "A man was often compelled to exceed his means in a position like his"—but women did not understand that. Therefore, as usual, he fled from domestic lectures to the inaccessible regions of his office.

The burgomaster's sister no longer lived in the same house. As she grew older, she had moved into one near the church which she inherited from her mother, where she lived quietly alone.

"Yes, who's to run over to Stasi," lamented the burgo-master's wife, when we all have our hands full. As if she wouldn't hear it soon enough. He'll never marry her! Rosel, Rosel!

The burgomaster's youngest daughter, the predestined Mary of the future, came in from the shop.

"Run up to your aunt and tell her that Herr Freyer has come back, your father says so!"

"Will he play the Christus again?" asked the child.

"How do I know—your father didn't say! Perhaps so—they have no one. Oh dear, this Passion Play will be your father's death!"

The shop-bell, pleasantest of sounds to the anxious woman, rang—customers must not be kept waiting, even for a little package of coffee. She hurried into the shop, and Rosel to her aunt Stasi.

This was a good day to the burgomaster's worthy wife. The whole village bought something, in order to learn some-thing about the interesting event which the Gross sisters, of course, had told early in the morning. And, as the burgo-master's wife maintained absolute silence, what the people did not know they invented—and of course the worst and most improbable things. Ere noon the wildest rumors were in circulation, and parties had formed who disputed vehemently over them.

The burgomaster's wife was in the utmost distress. Everybody wanted information from her, and how easily she might let slip some incautious remark! In her task of keeping silence, she actually forgot that she really had nothing at all to conceal—because she knew nothing herself. Yet the fear of having said a word too much oppressed the conscientious woman so sorely that afterward, much to her husband's benefit, she was remarkably patient and spared him the usual reproach of not having thought of his wife and children, when she discovered that he had given away his boots and coat!—

Thus in the strange little village the loftiest and the lowliest things always go hand in hand. But the noble often succumbs to the petty, when it lacks the power to rise above it.

CHAPTER XXXIII.

RECEIVED AGAIN.

ALL through the morning the street where Ludwig's house stood was crowded with people. Toward noon a whisper ran through the throng: "He is coming!" and Freyer appeared. Many pressed forward curiously but shrank back again as Freyer drew near. "Good Heavens, how he looks!"

Freyer tottered past them, raising his hat in greeting, but spite of his modest bearing and simple garb he seemed to have become so aristocratic a gentleman, that no one ventured to accost him. Something emanating from him inspired reverence, as if—in the presence of the dead. He was dead—at least to the world. The people felt this and the gossip suddenly ceased—the parties formed in an envious or malicious spirit were reconciled.

"He won't live long!" This was the magic spell which soothed all contention. If he had any sin on his conscience, he would soon atone for it, if he had more money than the rest, he must soon "leave it behind," and if he desired to take a part he could not keep it long! Only the children who meanwhile had grown into tall lads and lasses ran trustfully to meet him, holding out their hands with the grace and charm peculiar to the Ammergau children. And because the grown people followed him, the little ones did the same. He stopped and talked with them, recognizing and calling by name each of the older ones, while their bright eyes gazed searchingly into his, as sunbeams pierce dark caverns. " Have you been ill, Herr Freyer ?"

" No, my dear children—or yes, as people may regard it, but I shall get well with you !" And, clasping half a dozen of the little hands in his, he walked on with them.

" Will you play the divine friend of children with us again ?" asked one of the larger girls beseechingly.

" When Christmas comes, we will all play it again !" A strange smile transfigured Freyer's features, and tears filled his eyes.

" Will you stay with us now ?" they asked.

" Yes !" It was only a single word, but the children felt that it was a vow, and the little band pressed closer and closer around him : " Yes, now you must never go away !"

Freyer lifted a little boy in his arms and hid his face on the child's breast : " No, *never, never* more !"

A solemn silence reigned for a moment. The grief of a pure heart is sacred, and a child's soul feels the sacredness. The little group passed quietly through the village, and the children formed a protecting guard around him, so that the grown people could not hurt him with curious questions. The children showed their parents that peace must dwell between him and them—for the Ammergau people knew that in their children dwelt the true spirit which they had lost to a greater or less degree in the struggle for existence. The *children* had adopted him—now he was again at home in Ammergau; no parish meeting was needed to give him the rights of citizenship.

The little procession reached the town-hall. Freyer put the child he was carrying on the ground—it did not want to leave him. The grown people feared him, but the children considered him their own property and were reluctant to give him up. Not until after long persuasion would they let him enter. As he ascended the familiar stairs his heart throbbed so violently that he was obliged to lean against the wall. A long breath, a few steps more—then a walk through the empty council room to the office, a low knock, the well-known " come in !"—and he stood before the burgomaster.

It is not the custom among the people of Ammergau to rise when receiving each other. "Good-morning!" said the burgomaster, keeping his seat as if to finish some pressing task—but really because he was struggling for composure: " Directly !"

Freyer remained standing at the door.

The burgomaster went on writing. A furtive glance surveyed the figure in his coat and shoes—but he did not raise his eyes to Freyer's face, the latter would have seen it. At last he gained sufficient composure to speak, and now feigned to be aware for the first time of the new-comer's identity. "Ah, Herr Freyer!" he said, and the eyes of the two men met. It was a sad sight to both.

The burgomaster, once so strong and stately, aged, shrunken, prematurely worn. Freyer an image of suffering which was almost startling.

"Herr Burgomaster, I do not know—whether I may still venture—"

" Pray take a chair, Herr Freyer," said the burgomaster.

Freyer did so, and sat down at some distance.

"You do not seem to have prospered very well," said the other, less to learn the truth than to commence conversation.

"You doubtless see that."

"Yes— —! I could have wished that matters had resulted differently!"

Both were silent, overpowered by emotion. At the end of a few minutes the burgomaster continued in a low tone: "I meant so well by you—it is a pity—!"

"Yes, you have *much* to forgive me, no one knows that better than I—but you will not reject a penitent man, if he wishes to make amends for the wrong."

The burgomaster rubbed his forehead: "I do not reject you, but—I have already told the drawing-master, I only regret that I can do nothing for you. You are not ill—I cannot support you from the fund for the sick and it will be difficult to accomplish anything with the parish."

"Oh, Herr Burgomaster, I never expected to be supported. Only, when I arrived yesterday I was so weary that I could explain nothing to Ludwig, otherwise he would surely have spared you and me the step which his great sympathy induced

him to take. The clothing with which you have helped me
out of embarrassment for the moment, I will gratefully accept
as *loaned*, but I hope to repay you later."

"Pray let us say no more about it!" answered the burgomaster, waving his hand.

"Yes! For it can only shame me if you generously bestow material aid—and yet cherish resentment against me in
your heart for the wrong I have done. What my sick soul
most needs is reconciliation with you and my home. And for
that I *can* ask."

"I am not implacable, Herr Freyer! You have done me
no personal wrong—you have merely injured the cause which
lies nearest to my heart of anything in the world. This is a
grief, which must be fought down, but for which I cannot hold
you responsible, though it cost me health and life. I feel no
personal rancor for what had no personal intention. If a man
flings a stone at the image of a saint and unintentionally
strikes me on the temple, I shall not make him responsible for
that—but for having aimed at something which was sacred to
others. *To punish* him for it I shall leave to a higher judge."

"Permit me to remain silent. You must regard the matter thus from your standpoint, and I can show you no better
one. The right of defense is denied me. Only I would fain
defend myself against the reproach that what is sacred to
others is not to me. Precisely because it is sacred to me—
perhaps more sacred than to others, I have sinned against it."

"That is a contradiction which I do not understand!"

"And I cannot explain!"

"Well, it is not my business to pry into your secrets and
judge your motives. I am not your confessor. I told you
that I left God to judge such things. My duty as burgomaster requires me to aid any member of the parish to the best of
my ability in matters pertaining to earning a livelihood. If
you will give me your confidence, I am ready to aid you with
advice and action. I don't know what you wish to do. You
gave your little property to our poor—do you wish to take it
back?"

"Oh, never, Herr Burgomaster, I never take back what I
give," replied Freyer.

"But you will then find it difficult, more difficult than

others, to support yourself," the burgomaster continued. "You went to the carving-school too late to earn your bread by wood-carving. You know no trade—you are too well educated to pursue more menial occupations, such as those of a day-laborer, street-sweeper, etc.—and you would be too proud to live at the expense of the parish, even if we could find a way of securing a maintenance for you. It is really very difficult, one does not know what to say. Perhaps a messenger's place might be had—the carrier from Linderhof has been ill a long time."

"Have no anxiety on that score, Herr Burgomaster. During my absence, I devoted my leisure time mainly to drawing and modelling. I also read a great deal, especially scientific works, so that I believe I could support myself by carving, if I keep my health. If that fails, I'll turn wood-cutter. The forest will be best for me. That gives me no anxiety."

The burgomaster again rubbed his forehead. "Perhaps if the indignation roused by your desertion has subsided, it may be possible to give you employment at the Passion Theatre as superintendent, assistant, or in the wardrobe room."

Freyer rose, a burning blush crimsoned his face, instantly followed by a deathlike pallor. "You are not in earnest, Herr Burgomaster—I—render menial service in the Passion—I? Then woe betide the home which turns her sons from her threshold with mockery and disgrace, when they seek her with the yearning and repentance of mature manhood."

Freyer covered his face with his hands, grief robbed him of speech.

The burgomaster gave him a moment's time to calm himself. "Yes, Herr Freyer, but tell me, do you expect, after all that has occurred, to be made the Christus?"

"What else should I expect? For what other purpose should *I* come here than to aid the community in need, for my dead cousin Josepha received a letter from one of our relatives here, stating that you had no Christus and did not know what to do. It seemed to me like a summons from Heaven and I knew at that moment where my place was allotted. Life had no farther value for me—one thought only sustained me, to be something to my *home*, to repair the injury I had done her, atone for the sin I had committed—and this time I should have accomplished it. I walked night and day, with one desire in my heart, one goal before my eyes, and now—to be rejected thus—oh, it is too much, it is the last blow!"

"Herr Freyer—I am extremely sorry, and can understand how it must wound you, yet you must see yourself that we cannot instantly give a man who voluntarily, not to say *wilfully*, deserted us and remained absent so long that he has become a stranger, the most important part in the Play when want forces him to again seek a livelihood in Ammergau."

"I am become a stranger because I remained absent ten years? May God forgive you, Herr Burgomaster. We must both render an account to Him of our fulfilment of His sacred mission—He will then decide which of us treasured His image more deeply in his heart—you here—or I in the world outside."

"That is very beautiful and sounds very noble—but, Herr Freyer, you *prove* nothing by your appeal to God, He is patient and the day which must bring this decision is, I hope, still far distant from you and myself!"

"It is perhaps nearer to me than you suppose, Herr Burgomaster!"

"Such phrases touch women, but not men, Herr Freyer!"

Freyer straightened himself like a bent bush which suddenly shakes off the snow that burdened it. "I have not desired to touch any one, my conscience is clear, and I do not need to appeal to your compassion. A person may be ill and feeble enough to long for sympathy, without intending to profit by it. I thought that I might let my heart speak, that I should be understood here. I was mistaken. It is not *I* who have become estranged from my home—home has grown alienated from me and you, as the ruling power in the community, who might mediate between us, sever the last bond which united me to it. Answer for it one day to Ammergau, if you expel those who would shed their heart's blood for you, and to whom the cause of the Passion Play is still an earnest one."

"Oh, Herr Freyer, it would be sad indeed if we were compelled to seek earnest supporters of our cause in the ranks of the deserters—who abandoned us from selfish motives."

"Herr Burgomaster!—"Freyer reflected a moment—it was

difficult to fathom what was passing in his mind—it seemed as if he were gathering strength from the inmost depths of his heart to answer this accusation. "It is a delicate matter to speak in allegories, where deeds are concerned—you began it out of courtesy to me—and I will continue from the same motive, though figurative language is not to my taste—we strike a mark in life without having aimed! But to keep to your simile: I have only deserted in my own person, if you choose to call it so, and have now voluntarily returned—But you, Herr Burgomaster, how have you guarded, in my absence, the fortress entrusted to your care?"

The burgomaster flushed crimson, but his composure remained unshaken: "Well?"

"You have opened your gates to the most dangerous foes, to everything which cannot fail to destroy the good old Ammergau customs; you have done everything to attract strangers and help Ammergau in a business way—it was well meant in the material sense—but not in the ideal one which you emphasize so rigidly in my case! The more you open Ammergau to the influences of the outside world, the more the simplicity, the piety, the temperance will vanish, without which no great work of faith like the Passion Play is possible. The world has a keen appreciation of truth—the world believes in us because we ourselves believe in it—as soon as we progress so far in civilization that it becomes a farce to our minds, we are lost, for then it will be a farce to the world also. You intend to secure in the Landrath the cutting of a road through the Ettal Mountain. That would be a great feat—one might say: 'Faith removes mountains,' for on account of the Passion Play consent would perhaps be granted, then your name, down to the latest times, would be mentioned in the history of Ammergau with gratitude and praise. But do you know what you will have done? You will have let down the drawbridge to the mortal foe of everything for which you battle, removed the wall which protected the individuality of Ammergau and amid all the changes of the times, the equalizing power of progress, has kept it that miracle of faith to which the world makes pilgrimages. For a time the world will come in still greater throngs by the easier road—but in a few decades it will no longer find the Ammergau it seeks—its

iv performing a puppet show with God, and
e withdrawn."
nd stood gazing into vacancy with folded

r watched him calmly a long time. " I
u quietly because your view of the matter
is the idea of an enthusiast, a character be-
d more rare in our prosaic times. But
ive it only a subjective value. According
st keep Ammergau, as a bit of the Middle
act with the outside world, rob it of every
ent of its industrial and material interests
, to prepare the unfortunate people, by
he worthy representatives of the Passion.
i ble if, instead of Burgomaster of Am-
d Master of an Order for the practice of
- nd Ammergau were a Trappist monas-
ster of a secular community, I must first
prosperity, and that this would produce
here is not, as yet, unfortunately, the
My task as chief magistrate of a place is
at, rich, and happy as possible, that is
the village and an indirect one to the
ave satisfied this can I consider the
av office—in my capacity as director of
but even there I have no authority to ex-
straint in the sense of your noble—but
tical view. You must have had bitter
yer, that you hold earthly blessings so
st not expect to convert simple-hearted
eir lives and their work, to these pessi-
e could serve our God only with a
must let a people, as well as a single
luality. I want to rear no hypocrites,
martyrdom on any one, in order to repre-
more naturally. Such things cannot be

son you need people who will do them
gh, thank Heaven, they still exist in
ot such an over supply that you need

flood will have submerged it, washed it away, and a new, prosperous, politic population will move upon the ruins of a vanished time and a buried tradition.

"Freyer!" The burgomaster was evidently moved: "You see the matter in too dark colors—we are still the old people of Ammergau and God will help us to remain so"

"No, you are so no longer. Already there are traces of a different, more practical view of life—of so-called progress. I read to-day at Ludwig's the play-bills of the practise theatre which you have established during the last ten years since the Passion Play! Herr Burgomaster, have you kept in view the seriousness of the mission of Ammergau when you made the actors of the Passion buffoons?"

"Freyer!" The burgomaster drew himself up haughtily.

"Well, Herr Burgomaster, have you performed no farces, or at least comic popular plays? Was the Carver of Ammergau—which for two years you had *publicly* performed on the consecrated ground of the Passion Theatre, adapted to keep the impression of the Passion Play in the souls of the people of Ammergau? No—the last tear of remembrance which might have lingered would be dried by the exuberant mirth, which once roused would only too willingly exchange the uncomfortable tiara for the lighter fool's cap! And you gave the world this spectacle, Herr Burgomaster, you showed the personators of the story of our Lord and Saviour's sufferings in this guise to the strangers, who came, still full of reverence, to see the altar—on which the sacred fire had smouldered into smoke! I know you will answer that you wished to give the people a little breathing space after the terrible earnestness of the Passion Play and, from your standpoint, this was prudent, for you will be the gainer if the community is cheerful under your rule. Happy people are more easily governed than grave, thoughtful ones! I admit that you have no other desire than to make the people happy according to your idea, and that your whole ambition is to leave Ammergau great and rich. But, Herr Burgomaster, you cannot harmonize the two objects of showing the world, with convincing truth, the sublime religion of pain and resignation, and living in ease and careless frivolity. The divine favor cannot be purchased without the sacrifice of pleasure and personal comfort, other-

wise we are merely performing a puppet show with God, and
His blessing will be withdrawn."

Freyer paused and stood gazing into vacancy with folded
arms.

The burgomaster watched him calmly a long time. " I
have listened to you quietly because your view of the matter
interested me. It is the idea of an enthusiast, a character becoming more and more rare in our prosaic times. But
pardon me—I can give it only a subjective value. According
to your theory, I must keep Ammergau, as a bit of the Middle
Ages, from any contact with the outside world, rob it of every
aid in the advancement of its industrial and material interests
in order, as it were, to prepare the unfortunate people, by
want and trouble, to be worthy representatives of the Passion.
This would be admirable if, instead of Burgomaster of Ammergau, I were Grand Master of an Order for the practice of
spiritual asceticism—and Ammergau were a Trappist monastery. But as burgomaster of a secular community, I must first
of all provide for its prosperity, and that this would produce
too much luxury there is not, as yet, unfortunately, the
slightest prospect! My task as chief magistrate of a place is
first to render it as great, rich, and happy as possible, that is
a direct obligation to the village and an indirect one to the
State. Not until I have satisfied *this* can I consider the
more ideal side of my office—in my capacity as director of
the Passion Play. But even there I have no authority to exercise any moral constraint in the sense of your noble—but
fanatical and unpractical view. You must have had bitter
experiences, Herr Freyer, that you hold earthly blessings so
cheap, and you must not expect to convert simple-hearted
people, who enjoy their lives and their work, to these pessimistic views, as if we could serve our God only with a
troubled mind. We must let a people, as well as a single
person, retain its individuality. I want to rear no hypocrites,
and I cannot force martyrdom on any one, in order to represent the Passion Play more naturally. Such things cannot be
enforced."

" For that very reason you need people who will do them
voluntarily! And though, thank Heaven, they still exist in
Ammergau, you have not such an over supply that you need

repel those who would fain increase the little band. Believe me, I have lived in closer communion with my home in the outside world than if I had remained here and been swayed by the various opposing streams of our brothers' active lives! Do you know where the idea of the Passion Play reveals itself in its full beauty? Not here in Ammergau—but in the world outside—as the gas does not give its light where it is prepared, but at a distance. Therefore, I think you ought not to measure a son of Ammergau's claim according to the time he has spent here, but according to the feeling he cherishes for Ammergau, and in this sense even *the stranger* may be a better representative of Ammergau than the natives of the village themselves."

"Yes, Freyer, you are right—but—*one* frank word deserves another. You have surprised and touched me—but although I am compelled to make many concessions to circumstances and the spirit of the times, which are in contradiction to my own views and involve me in conflicts with myself, of which you younger men probably have no idea—nothing in the world will induce me to be faithless to my principles in matters connected with the Passion. Forgive the harsh words, Freyer, but I must say it: Your actions do not agree with the principles you have just uttered, and you cannot make this contradiction appear plausible to any one. Who will credit the sincerity of your moral rigor after you have lived nine years in an equivocal relation with the lady with whom you left us? Freyer, a man who has done *that*—can no longer personate the Christ."

Freyer stood silent as a statue.

The burgomaster held out his hand—"You see that I cannot act otherwise; do you not? Rather let the Play die out utterly than a Christus on whom rests a stain. So long as you cannot vindicate yourself—"

Freyer drew himself proudly: "And that I will never do!"

"You must renounce it."

"Yes, I must renounce it. Farewell, Herr Burgomaster!"

Freyer bowed and left the room—he was paler than when he entered, but no sound betrayed the mortal anguish gnawing at his heart. The burgomaster, too, was painfully moved.

His poor head was burning—he was sorry for Freyer, but he could not do otherwise.

Just as Freyer reached the door, a man hurried in with a letter. Freyer recognized the large well-known chirography on the envelope as he passed—Countess Wildenau's handwriting. His brain reeled, and he was compelled to cling to the door post. The burgomaster noticed it. "Please sit down a moment, Herr Freyer—the letter is addressed to me, but will probably concern you."

The man retired. Freyer stood irresolute.

The burgomaster read the contents of the note at a glance, then handed it to Freyer.

"Thank you—I do not read letters which are not directed to me."

"Very well, then I must tell you. The Countess Wildenau, not having your address, requests me to take charge of a considerable sum of money which I am to invest for you in landed property or in stocks, according to my own judgment. You were not to hear of it until the gift had been legally attested. But I deem it my duty to inform you of this."

Freyer stood calmly before him, with a clear, steadfast gaze. "I cannot be forced to accept a gift if I do not desire it, can I?"

"Certainly not."

"Then please write to the countess that I can accept neither gifts nor any kind of assistance from—strangers, and that you, as well as I, will positively decline every attempt to show her generosity in this way."

"Freyer!" cried the burgomaster, "will you not some day repent the pride which rejects a fortune thus flung into your lap?"

"I am not proud—I begged my bread on my way here, Herr Burgomaster—and if there were no other means of livelihood, I would not be ashamed to accept the crust the poorest man would share with me—but from Countess Wildenau I will receive nothing—I would rather starve."

The burgomaster sprang from his chair and approached him. His gaunt figure was trembling with emotion, his weary eyes flashed with enthusiasm, he extended his arms: "Freyer

—now you belong to us once more—*now* you shall again play the Christus."

Silently, in unutterable, mournful happiness, Freyer sank upon the burgomaster's breast.

His home was appeased.

CHAPTER XXXIV.

AT DAISENBERGER'S GRAVE.

IT was high noon. The children were at school, the grown people had gone to their work. The village was silent and no one stopped Freyer as he hurried down the broad old "Aussergasse," as the main street of the place was called, with its painted houses, toward the graveyard and the church.

In the cemetery beside the church stands a simple monument with a bronze bust. An unlovely head with all sorts of lines, as if nature had intentionally given this soul an ugly husk, out of wrath that it was not to be hers, that she could not have as much power over it as over other dust-born mortals—for this soul belonged to Heaven, earth had no share in it. But no matter how nature strove to disfigure it, its pure beauty shone through the physical covering so radiantly that even mortal eyes perceived only the beauty and overlooked the ugliness.

This soul, which might also be called the soul of Ammergau, for it cherished the whole population of the village, lived for the people, gave them all and kept nothing for itself—this noble spirit, to whom the gratitude of the survivors, and they embraced the whole community, had created a monument, was Alois Daisenberger—the reformer of the Passion Play.

It is a peculiar phenomenon that the people of Ammergau, in contrast to all others, are grateful only for intellectual gifts while they punish physical benefits with scorn. It offends their pride to be compelled to accept such trifling donations and they cherish a suspicion that the donor may boast of his benefits. Whoever has not the self-denial to allay this suspicion by enduring all sorts of humiliations and affronts must not try to aid the Ammergau villagers. He who has done any

good deed has accomplished *nothing*—not until he has atoned
for it, as though it were something evil, does he lend it its
proper value and appease the offended pride of the recipient.
This was the case with Daisenberger. He bore with saintly
patience all the angularities and oddities of these strange characters—and they honored him as a saint for it. He had the
eye of genius for the natural talent, a heart for the sufferings,
appreciation of the intellectual grandeur of these people. And
he gave security for it—for no worldly honor, no bishopric
which was offered could lure him away. What was it that outweighed everything with which church and government desired
to honor him? Whoever stands in the quiet graveyard, fanned by the keen mountain air which brings from the village
stray notes of a requiem that is being practised, surrounded by
snow-clad mountain-peaks gazing dreamily down on the little
mound with its tiny cross, whoever gazes at the monument
with its massive head, looking down upon the village from
beneath a garland of fresh blue gentians, is overwhelmed by a
mournful suspicion that here is concealed a secret in which a
great intellect could find the satisfaction of its life! But it
seems as if the key rested in Daisenberger's grave.

To this grave Freyer hastened. The first errand of the returned personator of Christ was to his author! The solitary
grave lay forgotten by the world. It is a genuine work of faith
and love when the author vanishes in his creation and leaves
the honor to God. The whole world flocks to the Passion
Play—but no one thinks of him who created for it the form
which renders it available for the present time. It is the
"Oberammergau," not the "Daisenberger" Passion Play.

He gave to the people of Ammergau not only his life and
powers—but also that which a man is most loth to resign—his
fame. He was one to whom earth could neither give anything, nor take anything away. Therefore there were few who
visited his grave in the little Ammergau churchyard. The
grace and beauty of his grand and noble artist soul weave
viewless garlands for it.

Freyer knelt in mute devotion beside the grave and prayed,
not for himself, not even for him who was one of the host of
the blessed, but *to* him, that he might sanctify his people and
strengthen them with the sacred earnestness of their task.

The longer he gazed at the iron, yet gentle face, without see-ing any change in the familiar features, which had once smiled so kindly at him when he uttered for the first time the words expelling the money-changers from the temple—the greater became his grief, as if the soul of his people had died with Daisenberger, as if Ammergau were only a graveyard and he the sole mourner.

"Oh, great, noble soul, which had room for a world, and yet confined yourself to this narrow valley in order to create in it for us a world of love—here lies your unworthy Christus moistening with his tears the stone which no angel will roll away that we may touch your transfigured body and say, give us thy spirit!"

Then, as if the metal mouth from which he implored an answer spoke with a brazen tongue, a bell echoed solemnly on the air. It was twelve o'clock. What the voice said could not be clothed in words. It had exhorted him when, in bap-tism, he was received into the covenant of Him whom he was chosen to personate—it had consoled him when, a weeping boy, he followed his father's bier, it had threatened him when on Sunday with his schoolmates, he pulled too violently at the bell-rope, it had warned him when he had lingered high up on the peaks of the Kofel or Laaber searching for Alpine roses or, shouting exultantly, climbing after chamois. A smile flitted over his face as he thought of those days! And then—then that very bell had pealed resonantly, like a voice from another world, on the morning of the Passion, at the hour when he stood in the robes of the Christ behind the curtain with the others to repeat the Lord's Prayer before the performance—the lofty, fervent prayer that God would aid them, that all might go well "for His honor." And again it had rung solemnly and sweetly, when he saw the beautiful woman praying at dawn in the garden—to the imaginary God, which he was *not*. Then it seemed as if the bell burst—there was a shrill discord, a keen pang through brain and heart. Oh, memory—the past! Angel and fiend at once—why do you conjure up your visions before one dedicated to the cross and to death, why do you rouse the longing for what is irrevocably lost? Freyer, groan-ing aloud, rested his damp brow against the cold stone, and the bronze bust, as if in pity, dropped a blue gentian from its garland on the penitent's head with a light touch, like a kiss from spirit lips. He took it and placed it in his pocketbook beside the child's fair curl—the only thing left him of all his vanished happiness.

Then a hand was laid on his shoulder: " I thank you— that *this* was your first visit." The sexton stood before him: "I see that you have remained a true son of Ammergau. May God be with you!"

Freyer's tears fell as he grasped the extended hand. "Oh, noble blood of Daisenberger, thank you a thousand times. And you, true son of Ammergau—nephew of our dead guardian angel, tell me in his name, will you receive me again in your midst and in the sacred work?"

"I do not know what you have done and experienced," said the sexton, gazing at him with his large, loyal brown eyes. "I only saw you at a distance, praying beside my uncle's grave, and I thought that whoever did that could not be lost to us. By this dear grave, I give you my hand. Will you work with me, live, and if need be die for the sacred will of this dead man, for our great task, as he cherished it in his heart?"

" Yes and amen! "

" Then may God bless you."

The two men looked earnestly and loyally into each other's eyes, and their hands clasped across the consecrated mound, as though taking an oath.

Suddenly a woman, still beautiful though somewhat beyond youth, appeared, moving with dignified cordiality toward Freyer: "Good-day, Herr Freyer; do you remember me?" she said in a quiet, musical voice, holding out her hand.

"Mary!" cried Freyer, clasping it. "Anastasia, why should I not remember you? How do you do? But why do you call me Herr Freyer? Have we become strangers?"

"I thought I ought not to use the old form of speech, you have been away so long, and"—she paused an instant, looking at him with a pitying glance, as if to say : "And are so unhappy." For delicate natures respect misfortune more than rank and wealth, and the sufferer is sacred to them.

The sexton looked at the clock: " I must go, the vesper

service begins again at one o'clock. Farewell till we meet again. Are you coming to the gymnasium this evening?"

"Hardly—I am not very well. But we shall see each other soon. Are you married now? I have not asked—"

The sexton's face beamed with joy. "Yes, indeed, and well married. I have a good wife. You'll see her when you call on me."

"A good wife—you are a happy man!" said Freyer in a low tone.

"She has a great deal to do just now for the little one."

"Ah—you have a child, too!"

"And such a beautiful one!" added Anastasia. "A lovely little girl! She will be a Mary some day. But the sexton's wife is spoiling her, she hardly lets her out of her arms."

"A good mother—that must be beautiful!" said Freyer, with a strange expression, as if speaking in a dream. Then he pressed his friend's hand and turned to go.

"Will you not bid me good bye, too?" asked Anastasia. The sexton sadly made a sign behind Freyer's back, as if to say: "he has suffered sorely!" and went into his church.

Freyer turned quickly. "Yes, I forgot, my Mary. I am rude, am I not?"

"No—not rude—only unhappy!" said Anastasia, while a pitying look rested upon his emaciated face.

"Yes!" replied Freyer, lowering his lids as if he did not wish her to read in his eyes *how* unhappy. But she saw it nevertheless. For a time the couple stood beside Daisenberger's grave. "If *he* were only alive—he would know what would help you."

Freyer shook his head. "If Christ Himself should come from Heaven, He could not help me, at least except through my faith in Him."

"Joseph, will you not go home with me? Look down yonder, there is my house. It is very pretty; come with me. I shall consider it an honor if you will stop there!" She led the way. Freyer involuntarily followed, and they soon reached the little house.

"Then you no longer live with your brother, the burgomaster?"

"Oh, no! After I grew older I longed for rest and solitude, and at my sister-in-law's there is always so much bustle on account of the shop and the children—one hears so many painful things said—" She paused in embarrassment. Then opening the door into the little garden, they went to the rear of the house where they could sit on a bench undisturbed.

"What you heard was undoubtedly about me, and you could not endure it. You faithful soul—was not that the reason you left your relatives and lived alone?" said Freyer, seating himself. "Be frank—were you not obliged to hear many things against me, till you at last doubted your old schoolmate?"

"Yes—many evil things were said of you and the princess—but I never believed them. I do not know what happened, but whatever it was, *you* did nothing wrong."

"Mary, where did you obtain this confidence?"

"Why," she answered smiling, "surely I know my son—and what mother would distrust her *child?*"

Freyer was deeply moved: "Oh, you virgin mother. Marvel of Heaven, when in the outside world a mother abandoned her own child—here a child was maturing into a mother for me, a mother who would have compassion on the deserted one. Mary, pure maid-servant of God, how have I deserved this mercy?"

"I always gave you a mother's love, from the time we played together, and I have mourned for you as a mother all the nine years. But I believed in you and hoped that you would some day return and close your old mother's eyes and, though twenty years had passed, I should not have ceased to hope. I was right, and you have come! Ah! I would not let myself dream that I should ever play with you again in the Passion—ever hold my Christus in my arms and support his weary head when he is taken down from the cross. That happiness transcends every other joy! True, I am an old maid now, and I wonder that they should let me take the part again. I am thirty-nine, you know, rather old for the Mary, yet I think it will be more natural, for Mary, too, was old when Christ was crucified!"

" Thirty nine, and still unmarried—such a beautiful creature—how did that happen, Mary? "

She smiled : " Oh, I did not wish to marry any one.—I could not care for any one as I did for my Christus ! "

" Great Heaven, is this on my conscience too ?   A whole life wasted in silent hope, love, and fidelity to me—smiling and unreproachful !   This soul might have been mine, this flower bloomed for me in the quiet home valley, and I left it to wither while searing heart and brain in the outside world. Mary, I will not believe that you have lost your life for my sake—you are still so beautiful, you will yet love and be happy at some good man's side."

" Oh, no, what fancy have you taken into your head! That was over long ago," she answered gayly.   " I am a year older than you—too old for a woman.   Look, when the hair is grey, one no longer thinks of marrying."   And pushing back her thick brown hair from her temples, she showed beneath white locks—as white as snow !

" Oh, you have grown grey, perhaps for me—! " he said, deeply moved.

" Yes, maternal cares age one early."

He flung himself in the grass before her, unable to speak. She passed her hand gently over his bowed head : " Ah, if my poor son had only returned a happy man—how my heart would have rejoiced.   If you had brought back a dear wife from the city, I would have helped her, done the rough work to which she was not accustomed—and if you had had a child, how I would have watched and tended it !   If it had been a boy, we would have trained him to be the Christus— would we not ?   Then for twenty years he could have played it—your image."

Freyer started as though the words had pierced his inmost soul. She did not suspect it, and went on : " Then perhaps the Christus might have descended from child to grandchild in your family—that would have been beautiful."

He made no reply; a low sob escaped his breast.

" I have often imagined such things during the long years when I sat alone through the winter evenings !   But unfortunately it has not resulted so !   You return a poor lonely man —and silver threads are shining in *your* hair too.   When I look at them, I long to weep. What did those wicked strangers in the outside world do to you, my poor Joseph, that you are so pale and ill ? It seems as if they had crucified you and taken you down from the cross ere life had wholly departed; and now you could neither live nor die, but moved about like one half dead. I fancy I can see your secret wounds, your poor heart pierced by the spear! Oh, my suffering child, rest your head once more on the knee of her who would give her heart's blood for you ! " She gently drew his head down and placing one hand under it, like a soft cushion, lovingly stroked his forehead as if to wipe away the blood-stains of the crown of thorns, while tear after tear fell from her long lashes on her son—the son of a virgin mother.

Silence reigned around them—there was a rustling sound above their heads as if the wind was blowing through palms and cedars—a weeping willow spread its boughs above them, and from the churchyard wall the milkwort nodded a mute greeting from Golgotha.

CHAPTER XXXV.

THE WATCHWORD.

WHILE the lost son of Ammergau was quietly and sadly permitting the miracle of his home to produce its effect upon him, and rising from one revelation to another along the steep path which again led him to the cross, the countess was languishing in the oppressive atmosphere of the capital and its relations.

Three days had passed since the parting from Freyer, but she scarcely knew it ! She lived behind her closed curtains and in the evenings sat in the light of lamps subdued by opalescent shades, as if in a never-changing white night, in which there could be neither dusk nor dawn. And it was the same in her soul. Reason—cold, joyless reason, with its calm, monotonous light, now ruled her, she had exhausted all the forces of grief in those farewell hours. For grief, too, is a force which can be exhausted. and then the soul will rest in indifference. Everything was now the same to her. The sacrifice and the cost of the sacrifice. What did the world contain that was worth trouble and anxiety? Nothing! Everything she had hoped for on earth had proved false—false and treacherous. Life had kept its promise to her in nothing; there was no happiness, only he who had no desires was happy—a happiness no better than death! And she had not even reached that stage! She still wanted so many things: honor, power, beauty, and luxury, which only wealth procures—and therefore this also.

Now she flung herself into the arms of beauty—"seeking in it the divine" and the man who offered her his hand in aid would understand how to obtain for her, with taste and care, the last thing she expected from life—pleasure! Civilization had claimed her again, she was the woman of the century, a product of civilization! She desired nothing more. A marriage of convenience with a clever, aristocratic man, with whom she would become a patron of art and learning; a life of amusement and pleasurable occupation she now regarded as the normal one, and the only one to be desired.

While Freyer, among his own people, was returning to primitiveness and simplicity, she was constantly departing farther from it, repelled and terrified by the phenomena with which Nature, battling for her eternal rights, confronted her. For Nature is a tender mother only to him who deals honestly with her—woe betide him who would trifle with her—she shows him her terrible earnestness.

"Only despise reason and learning, the highest powers of mankind!" How often the Mephistopheles within her soul had jeeringly cried. Yes, he was right—she was punished for having despised and misunderstood the value of the work of civilization at which mankind had toiled for years. She would atone for it. She had turned in a circle, the wheel had almost crushed her, but at least she was glad to have reached the same spot whence she started ten years ago. At least so she believed!

In this mood the duke found her on his return from Prankenberg.

"Good news, the danger is over! The old pastor was prudent enough to die with the secret!" he cried, radiant with joy, as he entered.

"Nothing was to be found! There is nothing in the church record! The Wildenaus have no proof and can do nothing unless Herr Freyer plays us a trick with the marriage certificate—"

"That anxiety is needless!" replied the countess, taking from her writing-table the little package containing Freyer's farewell note, the marriage certificate, and the account-book. "There, read it."

Her face wore a strange expression as she handed it to him, a look as if she were accusing him of having tempted her to murder an innocent person. She was pale and there was something hostile, reproachful, in her attitude.

The duke glanced through the papers. "This is strange," he said very gravely: "Is the man so great—or so small?"

"So great!" she murmured under her breath.

"Hm! I should not have expected it of him. Is this no farce? Has he really gone?"

"Yes! And here is something else." She gave him the burgomaster's letter: "This is the answer I received to-day to my offer to provide for Freyer's future."

"If this is really greatness—then—" the prince drew a long breath as if he could not find the right word: "Then—I don't know whether we have done right."

The countess felt as if a thunderbolt had struck her. "*You* say that—*you?*"

The duke rose and paced up and down the room. "I always tell the truth. If this man was capable of such an act —then—I reproach myself, for he deserved better treatment than to be flung overboard in this way, and we have incurred a great responsibility."

"Good Heavens, and you say this now, when it is too late!" groaned the unhappy woman.

"Be calm. The fault is *mine*—not yours. I will assume the whole responsibility—but it oppresses me the more heavily because, ever since I went to Prankenberg, I have been haunted by the question whether this was really necessary? My object was first of all to save you. In this respect I have nothing for which to reproach myself. But I overestimated

your danger and undervalued Freyer. I did not know him—
now that I do my motive dissolves into nothing."

He cast another glance at Freyer's farewell note and shook
his head: "It is hard to understand! What must it have
cost thus at one blow to resign everything that was dear, give
up without conditions the papers which at least would have
made him a rich man—and all without one complaint, without
any boastfulness, simply, naturally! Madeleine, it is over-
whelming—it is *shameful* to us."

The countess covered her face. Both remained silent a
long time.

The duke still gazed at the letter. Then, resting his head
on his hand and looking fixedly into vacancy, he said: "There
is a constraining power about this man, which draws us all into
its spell and compels us not to fall behind him in generosity.
But—how is this to be done? He cannot be reached by ordinary means. I am beginning now to understand *what* bound
you to him, and unfortunately I must admit that, with the
knowledge, my guilt increases. My justification lay only in
the misunderstanding of what now forces itself upon me as an
undeniable fact—that Freyer was not so unworthy of you,
Madeleine, as I believed!" He read the inscription on the little
bank book: "To keep the graves of my dear ones!" and was
silent for a time as if something choked his utterance: "How
he must have suffered—! When I think how *I* love you, though
you have never been mine—and he once called you his—resigned you and went away, with death in his heart! Oh, you
women! Madeleine, how could you do this in cold blood? If
it had been for love of me—but that illusion vanished long
ago."

" Condemned—condemned by you!" moaned the countess
in terror.

" I do not condemn you, Madeleine, I only marvel that you
could do it, if you knew the man as he is."

" I did not know him in this guise," said the countess
proudly. "But—I will not be less honest than you, Duke, I am
not sure that I could have done it, had I known him as I do
now."

The duke passed his handkerchief across his brow, which

was already somewhat bald. " One thing is certain—we owe the man some reparation. Something must be done."

"What shall we do? He will refuse anything we offer—though it were myself. That is evident from the burgomaster's letter." She closed her eyes to keep back the tears. "All is vain—he can never forgive me."

"No, he certainly cannot do that. But the man is worthy of having us fulfill the only wish he has expressed to you—"

"And that is?"

"To defer our marriage until the first anguish of his grief has had time to pass away."

The countess drew a long breath, as if relieved of a heavy burden: "Duke, that is generous and noble!"

"If you had been legally wedded and were obliged to be legally divorced, we could not be united in less than a year. Let us show the poor man the honor of regarding him as your lawfully wedded husband and pay him the same consideration as if he were. That is all we can do for him at present, and I shall make it a point of honor to atone, by this sacrifice, in some degree for the heavy responsibility which is undeniably mine and which, as an honest man, I neither can nor desire to conceal from myself."

He went to her and held out his hand. "I see by your radiant eyes, Countess, that this does not cost you the sacrifice which it does me—I will not pretend to be more unselfish than I am, for I hope by means of it to gain in your esteem what I lose in happiness by this time of delay!"

He kissed her hand with a sorrowful expression which she had never seen in him before. "Permit me to take leave of you for to-day, I have an engagement with Prince Hohenheim. To-morrow we will discuss the matter farther. *Bon soir!*"

The countess was alone. An engagement with Prince Hohenheim! When had an engagement with any one taken precedence—of her? Duke Emil was using pretexts. She could not deceive herself, he was—not really cold, but chilled. What a terrible reproach to her! What neither time, nor any of her great or trivial errors had accomplished, what had not happened even when she preferred a poor low-born man to the rich noble—occurred now, when she rejected the former—for the latter.

Many a person does not realize the strength of his own moral power, and how it will baffle the most crafty calculation. Every tragical result of a sin is merely the vengeance of these moral forces, which the criminal had undervalued when he planned the deed. This was the case with the duke. He had advised a breach with Freyer—advised it with the unselfish intention of saving her, but when the countess followed his advice and he saw by Freyer's conduct *what* a heart she had broken, he could not instantly love the woman who had been cruel enough to do an act which he could not pardon himself for having counselled.

Madeleine Wildenau suspected this, though not to its full extent. The duke was far too chivalrous to think for a moment of breaking his plighted troth, or letting her believe that he repented it. But the delay which he proposed as an atonement to the man whom they had injured, said enough. Must *all* abandon her—every bridge on which she stepped break? Had she lost by her act even the man of whom she was sure—surer than of anything else in the world! How terrible then this deed must have been! Madeleine von Wildenau blushed for herself.

Yet as there are certain traits in feminine nature which are the last a woman gives up, she now hated Freyer, hated him from a spirit of contradiction to the duke, who espoused his cause. And as the feminine nature desires above all things else that which is denied, she now longed to bind the duke again because she felt the danger of losing him. The fugitive must be stopped—the sport might perhaps lend her charmless, wretched life a certain interest. An unsatisfactory one, it is true, for even if she won him again—what then? What would she have in him? Could he be anything more to her than a pleasant companion who would restore her lost power and position? She glanced at her mirror—it showed her a woman of thirty-eight, rouged to seem ten years younger—but beneath this rouge were haggard cheeks. She could not conceal from herself that art would not suffice much longer—she had faded —her life was drawing toward evening, age spared no one! But—when she no longer possessed youth and beauty, when the time came that only the moral value of existence remained, what would she have then? To what could she look back—in what find satisfaction, peace? Society? It was always the

same, with its good and evil qualities. To one who entered
into an ethical relation with it, it contained besides its apparent
superficiality boundless treasures and resources. " The snow
is hard enough to bear " people say in the mountains when, in
the early Spring, the loose masses have melted into a firm crust.
Thus, under the various streams, now cold, now warm, the surface of society melts and forms that smooth icy rind of form
over which the light-foot glides carelessly, unconscious that
beneath the thin surface are hidden depths in which the philosopher and psychologist find material enough for the study of a
whole life. But when everything which could serve the purposes of amusement was exhausted, the countess' interest in
society also failed. Once before she had felt a loathing for it,
when she was younger than now—how would it be when she
was an old woman? The arts? Already their spell had been
broken and she had fled to Nature, because she could no
longer believe in their beautiful lies.

The sciences? They were least suited to afford pleasure !
Had she not grown so weary of her amateur toying with their
serious investigations that she fled, longing for a revelation, to
the childish miracles of Oberammergau? Aye—she was again,
after the lapse of ten years, standing in the selfsame spot,
seeking her God as in the days when she fancied she had
found His footprints. The trace proved delusive, and must
she now begin again where ten years before she ended in
weariness and discontent? Must she, who imagined that she
had embraced the true essence, return to searching, doubting?
No, the flower cannot go back into the closed bud ; the feeling which caused the disappointment impelled onward to
truth ! Love for God had once unfolded, and though the object proved deceptive—the *feeling* was true, and struggled to
find its goal as persistently as the flower seeks the sun after it
has long vanished behind clouds. But had she missed her
way because she thought she had reached the *goal* too *soon ?*
She had followed the trace no longer, but left it in anger—
discouragement, at the first disappointment ! What if the path
which led her to Ammergau was the *right* one ? And the
guide along it *had* been sent by God ? What if she had
turned from the path because it was too long and toilsome,
rejected the guide because he did not instantly bring God

near to her impatient heart, and she must henceforth wander aimlessly without consolation or hope ? And when the day of final settlement came, what imperishable goods would she possess ? When the hour arrived which no mortal can escape, what could aid her in the last terror, save the consciousness of dwelling in the love of God, of going out of love to love— out of longing to fulfillment ? She had rejected love, she had turned back in the path of longing and contented herself with earthly joys—and when she left the world she would have nothing, for the soul which does not seek, will not find! A life which has not fulfilled its moral task is not *finished*, only *broken off*, death to it is merely *destruction*, not *completion*.

The miserable woman flung herself down before the mirror which showed her the transitoriness of everything earthly and, for the first time in her life, looked the last question in the face and read no answer save—despair.

" Help my weakness, oh God !" she pleaded. " Help me upward to Thee. Show me the way—send me an angel, or write Thy will on the border of the clouds, work a miracle, oh Lord, for a despairing soul !" Thus she awaited the announcement of the divine will in flaming characters and angel tongues —and did not notice that a poor little banished household sprite was standing beside her, gazing beseechingly at her with tearful eyes because it had the word which would aid her, the watchword which she could find nowhere—only a simple phrase : *the fulfillment of duty !* Yet because it was as simple and unassuming as the genius which brought it, it remained unheeded by the proud, vain woman who, in her arrogance, spite of the humilations she had endured, imagined that her salvation needed a messenger from Heaven of apocalyptic form and power.

CHAPTER XXXVI.

MEMORIES.

AMID conflicts such as those just described, the countess lived, passing from one stage of development to another and unconsciously growing older—mentally maturing. Several weeks had now passed since her parting with Freyer, but the apathy with which, from that hour, she had regarded all external things still remained. She left the duke to arrange the affair with the Wildenaus, which, a short time ago, she had considered of sufficient importance to sacrifice Freyer. She admired the duke's tact and cleverness, but it seemed as if he were not acting for her but for some other person.

When he brought the news that the Wildenaus, owing to the obstinacy of the witness Martin, had given up their plan of a legal prosecution on the ground of Josepha's deposition, and were ready for an amicable settlement—she did not rejoice over anything save the old servant's fidelity; everything else she accepted as a just recompense of fate in return for an *unwarrantably* high price she had paid.

She was not annoyed because obliged to pay those whom she had injured a sum so large as considerably to lessen her income. She did not care for the result; her father was now a dying man and the vast sums he had used were again at her disposal. After all—what did it matter? If she married the duke in a year, she would be obliged to give up the whole property! But—need she marry him, if the Wildenaus could prove nothing against her? She sank into a dull reverie. But when the duke mentioned the cousins' desire for the little hunting-castle, life suddenly woke in her again. "Never, never!" she cried, while a burning blush crimsoned her face: "Rather all my possessions than that!" A flood of tears suddenly dissolved her unnatural torpor.

"But, dearest Madeleine, you will never live there again!" said the duke consolingly.

"No—neither I nor any living mortal will enter it again; but, Duke—must I say it? There sleeps my child; there sleeps the dream of my heart—it is the mausoleum of my love! No, leave me that—no stranger's foot must desecrate it! I will do anything, will give the Wildenaus twice, thrice as much; they may choose any of my estates—only not that one, and even if I marry you, when I must resign everything, I will ask you to buy it from my cousins, and you will not refuse my first request?"

The prince gazed at her long and earnestly; for the first time a ray of the old love shone in his eyes. "Do you know that I have never seen you so beautiful as at this moment?

Now your own soul looks out from your eyes! Now I absolve you from everything. Forgive me—I was mistaken in you, but this impulse teaches me that you are still yourself. It does me good!"

"Oh, Duke! There is little merit, when the living was not allowed his rightful place—to secure it to the dead!"

"Well, it is at least an act of atonement. Madeleine, there cannot be more joy in Heaven over the sinner who repents than I felt just now at your words. Yes, my poor friend, you shall keep the scene of your happiness and your grief untouched—I will assure you of it, and will arrange it with the Wildenaus."

"Duke! Oh, you are the best, the noblest of men!" she exclaimed, smiling through her tears: "Do you know that I love you as I never did before? I thought it perfectly natural that you could not love me as you saw me during those days. I felt it, though you did not intend to let me see it."

She had not meant to assume it, but these words expressed the charming artlessness which had formerly rendered her so irresistible, and the longer the duke had missed it, the less he was armed against the spell.

"Madeleine!" he held out his arms—and she—did she know how it happened? Was it gratitude, the wish to make at least *one* person happy? She threw herself on his breast—for the first time he held her in his embrace. Surely she was his betrothed bride! But she had not thought of what happened now. The duke's lips sought hers—she could not resist like a girl of sixteen, he would have considered it foolish coquetry. So she was forced to submit.

"*Honi soit qui mal y pense !*" he murmured, kissing her brow, her hair—and her lips. But when she felt his lips press hers, it suddenly seemed as though some one was saying close beside her: "*You !*" It was the word Freyer always uttered when he embraced her, as though he knew of nothing better or higher than that one word, in which he expressed the whole strength of his emotion! "You—you!" echoed constantly in her ears with that sweet, wild fervor which seemed to threaten: "the next instant you will be consumed in my ardor." Again he stood before her with his dark flaming eyes and the overwhelming earnestness of a mighty passion, which shadowed his pale brow as the approaching thunder-storm clouded the snow-clad peaks of his mountains. And she compared it with the light, easy tenderness, the " *honi soi qui mal y pense*" of the trained squire of dames who was pressing his first kiss upon her lips—and she loathed the stranger. She released herself with a sudden movement, approached the window and looked out. As she gazed, she fancied she saw the dark figure of the deserted one, illumined by the crimson glare of the forest conflagration, holding out his hand with a divinely royal gesture to raise and shelter her on his breast. Once more she beheld him gaze calmly down at the charred timber and heard him say smiling: "The wood was mine."

Then—then she beheld in the distant East a sultry room, shaded by gay awnings, surrounded by rustling palm-trees, palm-trees, which drew their sustenance from the soil on which the Redeemer's blood once flowed. He sat beside the bed of the mother of a new-born child, whispering sweet, earnest words—and the mother was she herself, the babe was his.

Then she beheld this same man kneeling by the coffin of a child, the rigid, death-white face buried under his raven locks. It was the child born on the consecrated soil of the burning East, which she had left to pine in the cold breath of the Western winter. She withdrew from it the mother-heart, in which the tender plant of the South might have gained warmth. She had left that father's child to die.

Yet he did not complain; uttered no reproach—he remained silent.

She saw him become more and more solitary and silent. The manly beauty wasted, his strength failed—at last she saw him noiselessly cross the carpeted floor of this very room and close the door behind him never to return! No, no, it could not be—all that had happened was false—nothing was true save that he was the father of her child, her husband, and no one else could ever be that, even though she was separated from him for ever.

"Duke!" she cried, imploringly. "Leave me to myself. I do not understand my own feelings—I feel as if arraigned before the judgment seat of God. Let me take counsel with my own heart—forgive me I am a variable, capricious

woman—one mood to-day and another to-morrow; have patience with me, I entreat you."

The duke looked gravely at her, and answered, nodding:
" I understand—or rather—I am afraid to understand !"

" Duke, I am not suited to marry. Let the elderly woman
go her way alone—I believe I can never again be happy.
I long only for rest and solitude."

"You need rest and composure. I will give you time
and wait your decision, which can now be absolutely untrammelled, since your business affairs are settled and the peril is
over."

" Do not be angry with me. Duke—and do not misunderstand me—oh Heaven—you might think that I had only given
my promise in the dread of poverty and disgrace and now that
the peril was past, repented."

The duke hesitated a moment. Then he said in a low,
firm tone : " Surely you know that I am the man of sober
reason, who is surprised by nothing. ' *Tout comprendre c'est
tout pardonner.*' So act without regard to me, as your own
feeling dictates." He held out his hand : "There was a time
when I seriously believed that we might be happy together.
That is now past—you will destroy no illusion, if you assert
the contrary."

" Perhaps not even a sincere desire of the heart ?" replied
the countess, smiling.

The duke became deeply earnest. "That suggestion is
out of place here.—Am I to wound you from gallantry and increase the measure of your self-reproaches by showing you
that I suffer ? Or tell a falsehood to lessen your responsibility ? We will let all that rest. If you want me, send for me.
Meanwhile, as your faithful attorney, I will arrange the matter of the hunting castle."

" Duke—how petty I am in your presence—how noble
you are !"

" That is saying far too much, Countess! I am content, if
you can bear me witness that at least I have not made myself
ridiculous." He left the room—cold, courteous, stoical as ever!

Madeleine von Wildenau hurried to the window and flung
it open. " Pour in, light and air, mighty consolers—ah, now
I breathe, I live again !"

Once more she could freely show her face, had no occasion to conceal herself. The danger of a "scandal" was over, thanks to the lack of proof. She need no longer shun the Wildenaus—old Martin was faithful and her husband, the most dangerous witness, had gone, disappeared. Now she had nothing more to dread; she was free, mistress of her fortune, mistress of her will, she breathed once more as if new-born.

Liberty, yes, *this* was happiness. She believed that she had found it at last! And she would enjoy it. She need not reproach herself for breaking her troth to the prince, he had told her so—if thereby she could appease the avenging spirits of her deed to Freyer, they must have the sacrifice! True, to be reigning duchess of a country was a lofty position; but—could she purchase it at the cost of being the wife of a man whom she did not love? Why not? Was she a child ?—a foolish girl ? A crown was at stake—and should she allow sentimental scruples to force her to sacrifice it to the memory of an irrevocably lost happiness?

She shook her head, as if she wanted to shake off a bandage. She was ill from the long days spent in darkness and confinement like a criminal. That was the cause of these whims. Up and out into the open air, where she would again find healthy blood and healthy thoughts.

She rang the bell, a new servant appeared.

"My arrival can now be announced. Tell Martin to bring the carriage round, I will go to drive."

"Very well, Your Highness."

She seemed to have escaped from a ban. She had never known liberty. Until she married the Count von Wildenau she had been under the control of a governess. Then, in her marriage with the self-willed old man she was a slave, and she had scarcely been a widow ere she forged new fetters for herself. Now, for the first time, she could taste liberty. The decision was not pressing. The cool stoic who had waited so long would not lose patience at the last moment —so she could still do what she would.

So the heart, struggling against the unloved husband, deceived the ambitious, calculating reason which aspired to a crown.

26

The carriage drove up. It was delightful to hear a pair
of spirited horses stamping before a handsome equipage, to
be assisted to enter by a liveried servant and to be able to
say: "This is yours once more!" The only shadow which
disturbed her was that on Martin's face, a shadow resting
there since she had last visited her castle of the Sleeping
Beauty. She well knew for whom the old man was grieving.
It was a perpetual reproach and she avoided talking with
him, from a certain sense of diffidence. She could justify
herself to the keen intelligence of the duke—to the simplicity
of this plain man she could not; she felt it.

It was a delightful May evening. A sea of warm air and
spring perfumes surrounded her, and crowds thronged the
streets, enjoying the evening, after their toilsome work, as if
they had just waked from their winter sleep. On the corners
groups paused before huge placards which they eagerly
studied, one pushing another away. What could it be?

Then old Martin, as if intentionally, drove close to the
sidewalk, where the people stood in line out to the street before those posters. There was a little movement in the
throng; people turned to look at the splendid equipage, thus
leaving the placard exposed. The countess read it—the
blood congealed in her veins—there, in large letters, stood
the words: " Oberammergau Passion Play." What did it
mean? She leaned back in the carriage, feeling as if she
must shriek aloud with homesickness, with agonized longing
for those vanished days of a great blissful delusion! Again
she beheld the marvellous play. Again the divine sufferer
appeared to the world—the mere name on that wretched
placard was already exerting its spell, for the pedestrians,
pausing on their errands, stopped before it by hundreds, as if
they had never read the words " Passion Play " before! And
the man who helped create this miracle, to which a world was
again devoutly pilgrimaging, had been clasped in her arms—
had loved her, been loyally devoted to her, to her alone, and
she had disdained him! Now he was again bringing the salvation of the divine word and miracle—she alone was shut out,
she had forfeited it by her own fault. She was—as in his
wonderful gift of divination he had once said—one of the
foolish virgins who had burned her oil, and now the heavenly

bridegroom was coming, but she stood alone in the darkness while the others were revelling at the banquet.

The rattle of wheels and the trampling of the crowds about her were deafening, and it was fortunate, for, in the confused uproar, the cry which escaped the tortured heart of the proud lady in the coroneted carriage died away unheard. Lilacs and roses—why do you send forth so intoxicating a fragrance, why do you still bloom? Can you have the heart to smile at a world in which there is such anguish? But lilacs, roses, and a beautiful May-sun laughed on, the world was devoutly preparing for the great pilgrimage to Oberammergau. She only was exiled, and returned to her stone palace, alone, hopeless—with infinite desolation in her heart.

A note from the duke awaited her. He took his leave for a few weeks, in order to give her time to understand her own heart clearly. Now she was utterly alone.

CHAPTER XXXVII.

THE MEASURE IS FULL.

From that day the countess showed an unwonted degree of interest in the newspapers. The first question when she waked in the morning was for the papers. But the maid noticed that she opened only the pages containing the reports from Oberammergau.

"Your Highness seems to be very much interested in the Passion Play," the woman ventured to remark.

The countess blushed, and her "yes" was so curt and repellent that the maid was alarmed at her own presumption.

One thing, however, was certain—her mistress, after reading these reports, always looked pale and worn.

And in truth the unhappy woman, while reading the descriptions of this year's performances, felt as if she were drinking a cup of wormwood drop by drop. Freyer's name was echoing throughout the world. Not only did the daily press occupy itself with him—but grave men, æsthetes of high rank, found his acting so interesting that they wrote pamphlets about it and made it the subject of scientific treatises. The countess read them all. Freyer was described as the type in which art, nature, and religion joined hands in the utmost harmony! "As he himself stands above the laws of theatrical routine, he raises us far above what we term stage effect, as it were into a loftier sphere. He does not act—he *is* the Christ! The power of his glance, the spirituality of the whole figure, and an indefinable spell of the noblest sorrow which pervades his whole person, are things which cannot be counterfeited, which are no play, but truth. We believe what he says, because we feel that this man's soul does not belong to this world, that its own individual life has entered into his part. Because he thinks, feels, and lives not as Joseph Freyer, but as the Christus—is the source of the impression which borders upon the supernatural."

Madeleine von Wildenau had just read these words, which cut her to the heart. Ah, when strangers—critics—men said such things—surely she had no cause to be ashamed. Who would reproach her, a weak, enthusiastic woman, for yielding to this spell? Surely no one—rather she would be blamed for not having arrested the charm, for having, with a profane hand, destroyed the marvel that approached her, favoring her above the thousands who gazed at it in devout reverence!

She leaned her head on her hand and gazed mournfully out of the window at which she sat. They had now been playing six weeks in Oberammergau. It was June. The gardens of the opposite palace were in their fullest leafage; and the birds singing in the trees lured her out. Her eyes followed a little swallow flying toward the mountains. "Oh, mountain air and blue gentians—earthly Paradise!" she sighed! What was she doing here in the hot city when all were flying to the mountains, she saw no society, and the duke had gone away. She, too, ought to have left long before. But where should she go? She could not visit Oberammergau, and she cared for no other spot—it seemed as though the whole world contained no other place of abode than this one village with its gay little houses and low windows—as if in all the world there were no mountains, and no mountain air save in Ammergau. A few burning tears ran down her cheeks. Doubtless there was mountain air, there were mountain peaks higher, more beautiful than in Ammergau, but nowhere else could be found the same capacity for enjoying the magnificence of nature! Everywhere there is a church, a religion, but nowhere so religious an atmosphere as there.

"Oh, my lost Paradise, my soul greets you with all the anguish of the exiled mother of my sex and my sin!" she sighed.

And yet, what was Eve's sin to hers? Eve at least atoned in love and faith with the man whom she tempted to sin. Therefore God could forgive her and send to the race which sprung from her fall a messenger of reconciliation. Eve was a wife and a mother. But she, what was she? Not even that! She had abandoned her husband and lived in splendor and luxury while he grieved alone. She had given him only one child, and even to that had acted no mother's part, and finally had thrust him out into poverty and sorrow, and led a life of wealth and leisure, while he earned his bread by the sweat of his brow. No, the mother of sin was a martyr compared to her, a martyr to the nature which *she* denied, and therefore she was shut out from the bond of peace and pity which Eve's atonement secured.

Some one knocked. The countess started from her reverie. The servant announced that His Highness' nurses had sent for her; they thought death was near.

" I will come at once!" she answered.

The prince lived near the Wildenau Palace, and she reached him in a few minutes.

The sick man's mind was clearer than it had been for several months. The watery effusions in the brain which had clouded his consciousness had been temporarily absorbed, and he could control his thoughts. For the first time he held out his hand to his daughter: "Are you there, my child?"

It touched her strangely, and she knelt by his side. "Yes, father!"

He stroked her hair with a kindly, though dull expression: "Are you well?"

" In body, yes papa! I thank you."

" Are you happy?"

The countess, who had never in her life perceived any token of paternal affection in his manner, was deeply moved by this first sign of affection in the hour of parting. She strove to find some soothing reply which would not be false and yet satisfy his feeble reasoning powers; but he had again forgotten the question.

" Are you married? " he asked again, as if he had been absent a long time, and saw his daughter to-day for the first time.

The nurses withdrew into the next room.

The father and daughter were alone. Meantime his memory seemed to be following some clue.

" Where is your husband? "

"Which one? " asked the countess, greatly agitated. " Wildenau? "

" No, no—the—the other one ; let him come ! " He put out his hand gropingly, as if he expected some one to clasp it : " Say farewell—"

" Father," sobbed the countess, laying the seeking hand gently back on the coverlet. " He cannot bid you farewell, he is not here ! "

" Why not ? I should have been glad to see him—son-in-law—grandson—no one here ? "

" Father—poor father !" The countess could say no more. Laying her head on the side of her father's bed, she wept bitterly.

" Hm, hm ! " murmured the invalid, and a glance of intelligence suddenly flashed from his dull eyes at his daughter. " My child, are you weeping ?" He reflected a short time, then his mind seemed to grow clear again.

"Oh, yes. No one must know ! Foolish weaknesses ! Tell him I sincerely ask his pardon; he must forgive me. Prejudiced, old—! I am very sorry. Can't you send for him ? "

"Oh, papa, I would gladly bring him, but it is too late—he has gone away ! "

"Ah ! then I shall not see him again. I am near my end."

The countess could not speak, but pressed her lips to her father's cold hand.

" Don't grieve; you will lose nothing in me; be happy. I spent a great deal of money for you—women, gaming, dinners, what value are they all ? "   He made a gesture of loathing : " What are they now ? "

A chill ran through his veins, and his breath grew short and labored.   "I'm curious to see how it looks up there!" He pondered for a time.   "If you knew of any sensible pastor, you might send for him; such men often *do* know something."

" Certainly, father ! "

The countess hurried into the next room and ordered a priest to be sent for to give extreme unction.

" You wish to confess and take the communion too, do you not, papa ? "

" Why yes; one doesn't wish to take the old rubbish when starting on the great journey. We don't carry our soiled linen with us when we travel. I have much on my conscience, Magdalena—my child—most of all, sins committed against you! Don't bear your foolish old father ill-will for it."

"No, father, I swear it by the memory of this hour ! "

"And your husband "—he shook his head—"he is not here; it's a pity !"

Then he said no more but lay quietly, absorbed in his own thoughts, till the priest came.

Madeleine withdrew during the confession. What was passing in her mind during that hour she herself could not understand. She only knew that her father's inquiry in his dying hour for his despised, disowned son-in-law was the keenest reproach which had been addressed to her.

The sacred ceremony was over, and the priest had left the house.

The sick man lay with a calm, pleasant expression on his face, which had never rested there before. Madeleine sat down by the bed and took his hand; he gratefully returned her gentle pressure.

" How do you feel, dear father? " she asked gently.

" Very comfortable, dear child."

" Have you made your peace with God ? "

" I hope so, my child! So far as He will be gracious to an old sinner like me."   He raised his eyes with an earnest,

trustful look, then a long—agonizing death struggle came on.
But he held his daughter's hand firmly in his own, and she
spent the whole night at his bedside without stirring, resolute
and faithful—the first fulfillment of duty in her whole life.

The struggle continued until the next noon ere the daughter could close her father's eyes. A number of pressing business matters were now to be arranged, which detained her
in the house of mourning until the evening, and made her
sorely miss her thoughtful friend, the duke. At last, at nine
o'clock, she returned to her palace, wearied almost unto
death.

The footman handed her a card: "The gentleman has
been here twice to-day and wished to see Your Highness on
very urgent business. He was going to leave by the last
train, but decided to stay in order to see you. He will try
again after nine o'clock—"

The countess carried the card to the gas jet and read:
"Ludwig Gross, drawing-teacher." Her hand trembled so
violently that she almost dropped it. "When the gentleman
comes, admit him!" She was obliged to cling to the balus-
trade as she went upstairs, she was so giddy. Scarcely had
she reached her boudoir when she heard the lower bell ring
—then footsteps, a familiar voice—some one knocked as he
had done ten years ago in the Gross House; but the man
whom he then brought, nothing would ever bring again.

She did not speak, her voice failed, but she opened the
door herself—Ludwig Gross stood before her. Both gazed
at each other a long time in silence. Both were struggling
for composure and for words, and from the cheeks of both
every drop of blood had vanished. The countess held out
her hand, but he did not seem to see it. She pointed to a
chair, and said in a hollow tone: "Sit down," at the same
time sinking upon a divan opposite.

"I will not disturb you long, Your Highness!" Ludwig
answered, seating himself a long distance off.

"If you disturbed me, I should not have received you."

Ludwig felt the reproof conveyed in the words for the
hostility of his manner, but he could not help it.

"Perhaps Your Highness remembers a certain Freyer?"

"Herr Gross, that question is an insult · but I admit that,

from your standpoint, you have a right to ask it. At any rate, Freyer did not commission you to do so."

"No, Countess, for he does not know that I am here ; if he did, he would have prevented it. I beg your pardon, if I perform my mission somewhat clumsily! I know it is unseemly to meddle with relations of which one is ignorant, for Freyer's reserve allowed me no insight into these. But here there is danger in delay, and where a human life is at stake, every other consideration must be silent. I have never been able to learn any particulars from Freyer. I only know that he was away nine years, as it was rumored, with you, and that he returned a beggar!"

"That, Herr Gross, is no fault of mine."

"Not that, Countess, but it must be *your* fault alone which has caused relations so unnatural that Freyer was ashamed to accept from you even the well-earned payment for his labor."

"You are right there, Herr Gross."

"And that would be the least, Countess, but he has returned, not only a beggar, but a lost man."

"Ludwig!"

"Yes, Countess. That is the reason I determined, after consulting with the burgomaster, to come here and talk with you, if you will allow it."

"Speak, for Heaven's sake; what has befallen him?"

"Freyer is ill, Countess."

"But, how can that be? He is acting the Christus every week and delighting the world?"

"Yes, that is just it! He acts, as a candle burns down while it shines—it is no longer the phosphorescence of genius, it is a light which feeds on his own life and consumes it."

"Merciful God!"

"And he *wishes* to die—that is unmistakable—that is why it is so hard to aid him. He will heed no counsel, follow no advice of the physician, do nothing which might benefit him. Now matters have gone so far that the doctor told us yesterday he might fall dead upon the stage at any hour—and we ought not to allow him to go on playing! But he cannot be prevented. He desires nothing more than death."

"What is the matter?" asked the pale lips of the countess.

"A severe case of heart disease, Countess, which might be arrested for several years by means of careful nursing, perfect rest, and strengthening food ; but he has no means to obtain the better nourishment his condition requires, because he is too proud to be a burden on any one, and he lacks the ease of mind necessary to relieve his heart. Nursing is out of the question—he occupies, having given his own home to the poor when he left Ammergau, as you know, a miserable, damp room in a wretched tavern, just outside the village, and wanders about the mountains day and night. Of course speedy death is inevitable—hastened, moreover, by the exertions demanded by his part."

Ludwig Gross rose. " I do not know how you estimate the value of a poor man's life, Countess," he said bitterly— " I have merely done my duty by informing you of my friend's condition. The rest I must leave to you."

" Great Heaven! What shall I do! He rejects everything I offer. Perhaps you do not know that I gave him a fortune and he refused it."

Ludwig Gross fixed an annihilating glance upon her. "If you know no other way of rendering aid here save by *money* —I have nothing more to say."

He bowed slightly and left the room without waiting for an answer.

"Ludwig!" she called: " Hear me !"

He had gone—he was right—did she deserve anything better? No—no! She stood in the middle of the room a moment as if dazed. Her heart throbbed almost to bursting. "Has it gone so far! I have left the man from whose lips I drew the last breath of life to starve and languish. I allowed the heart on which I have so often rested to pine within dark, gloomy walls, bleed and break in silent suffering. Murderess, did you hear it? He is lost, through your sin! Oh, God, where is the crime which I have not committed—where is there a more miserable creature? I have murdered the most innocent, misunderstood the noblest, repulsed the most faithful, abused the most sacred, and for what?" She sank prostrate. The measure was full—was running over.—The angel with the cup of wormwood had overtaken her, as Freyer had prophesied and was holding to her lips the bitter chalice of her own guilt, which she must drain, drop by drop. But now this guilt had matured, grown to its full size, and stood before her, grinning at her with the jeer of madness.

"Wings—oh, God, lend me wings!, While I am doubting and despairing here—it may be too late—the terrible thing may have happened—he may have died, unreconciled, with the awful reproach in his heart! Wings, wings, oh God!" She started up and flew to the bell with the speed of thought.

"Send for the head-groom at once!"

Then she hurried into the chamber, where the maid was arranging her garments for the night. "Pack as quickly as possible whatever I shall need for a journey of two or three days—or weeks—I don't know myself."

"Evening or street costumes?" asked the maid, startled by her mistress' appearance.

"Street dresses!"

Meantime the head-groom had come. She hastened into the boudoir: "Have relays of horses saddled and sent forward at once—it is after ten o'clock—there is no train to Weilheim—but I must reach Oberammergau to-night! Martin is to drive, send on four relays—I will give you four hours start—the men must be off within ten minutes—I will go at two o'clock—I shall arrive there at seven."

"Your Excellency, that is scarcely possible"—the man ventured to say.

"I did not ask whether it was possible—I told you that it *must* be done, if it kills all my horses. Quick, rouse the whole stable—every one must help. I shall wait at the window until I see the men ride away."

The man bowed silently, he knew that opposition was futile, but he muttered under his breath: "To ruin six of her best horses in one night—just for the sake of that man in Ammergau, she ought to be put under guardianship."

The courtyard was instantly astir, men were shouting and running to and fro. The stable-doors were thrown open, lanterns flashed hither and thither, the trampling and neighing of horses were heard, the noise and haste seemed as if the wild huntsman was setting off on his terrible ride through the starless night.

The countess stood, watch in hand, at the lighted window, and the figure of their mistress above spurred every one to the utmost haste. In a few minutes the horses for the relays were saddled and the grooms rode out of the court-yard.

"The victoria with the pair of blacks must be ready at two," the head-groom said to old Martin. "You must keep a sharp look-out—I don't see how you will manage—those fiery creatures in that light carriage."

The countess heard it at the window, but she paid no heed. If only she could fly there with the light carriage, the fiery horses, as her heart desired. Forward—was her only thought.

"Must I go, too?" asked the maid, pale with fright.

"No, I shall need no one." The countess now shut the windows and went to her writing-desk, for there was much to be done within the few short hours. Her father's funeral—sending the announcements—all these things must now be entrusted to others and a representative must be found among the relatives to fill her own place. She assigned as a pretext the necessity of taking a short journey for a day or two, adding that she did not yet know whether she could return in time for the funeral of the prince. Her pen fairly flew over the paper, and she finally wrote a brief note to the duke, in which she told him nothing except her father's death. The four hours slipped rapidly away, and as the clock struck two the victoria drove to the door.

The countess was already standing there. The lamps at the entrance shone brightly, but even brighter was old Martin's face, as he curbed the spirited animals with a firm hand.

"To Ammergau, Martin!" said the countess significantly, as she entered the equipage.

"Hi! But I'll drive now!" cried the old man, joyously, not suspecting the sorrowful state of affairs, and off dashed the steeds as though spurred by their mistress' fears—while guilt and remorse accompanied her with the heavy flight of destiny.

CHAPTER XXXVIII.

ON THE WAY TO THE CROSS.

IT was Sunday. Again the throngs surged around the Passion Theatre, more devout, more numerous than ever.

Slowly, as if his feet could scarcely support him, a tall figure, strangely like one who no longer belongs to the number of the living, tottered through the crowd to the door of the dressing-room, while all reverently made way for him, yet every one perceived that it must be the Christus! Whoever met his eye shuddered as if the incarnation of woe had passed, as if he had seen the face of the god of sorrow.

Eight o'clock had struck, the cannon had announced the commencement of the play, the waiting throng pressed in, crowding each other, and the doors were closed.

Outside of the theatre it was silent and empty. The carriages had driven away. The people who could get no tickets had dispersed. Only the venders of photographs and eatables still sat in their booths, listening idly and sleepily to the notes of the music, which came in subdued tones through the board partition.

Suddenly the ground trembled slightly under the wheels of a carriage driven at furious speed. A pair of horses covered with foam appeared in the distance—in a few seconds a dusty victoria stopped before the Passion Theatre.

" St, st!" said one of the box-tenders, appearing at the top of the stairs and hurrying down to prevent farther disturbance.

" Can I get a ticket ?" asked the lady in the carriage.

" I am very sorry—but unfortunately every seat is filled."

" Oh, Heaven! I lost an hour—one of the horses met with an accident, I have driven all night—I beg you—I *must* get in !"

The box-tender shrugged his shoulders. " Unfortunately it is impossible !" he said with an offensively lofty manner.

"I am not accustomed to find anything which I desire impossible, so far as it depends upon human beings to fulfill it," she answered haughtily. " I will pay any price, no matter whether it is a thousand marks, more or less—if you will get me even the poorest seat within the walls."

"It is not a question of price!" was the smiling answer. "If we had the smallest space, we could have disposed of it a hundred times over to-day."

"Then take me on the stage."

"Oh, it is no use to speak of that—no matter who might come—no one is allowed there."

"Then announce me to the burgomaster—I will give you my card."

"I am very sorry, but I have no admittance to the stage during the performance. In the long intermission at twelve o'clock you might be announced, but not before."

The countess' heart throbbed faster and faster. She could hear the notes of the music, she fancied she could distinguish the different voices, yet she was not permitted to enter. Now came the shouts of "Hosanna!"—yes, distinctly—that was the entry into Jerusalem, those were the exulting throngs who attended him. If she could only look through a chink—! Now, now it was still—then a voice—oh! she would recognize those tones among thousands. A draught of air bore them to her through the cracks in the walls. Yes, that was he; a tremor ran through every limb—he was speaking.

The world hung on his lips, joy was in every eye, comfort in every heart—within was salvation and she must stand without and could not go to her own husband. But he was not her husband, that had been her own wish. Now it was granted!

The "foolish virgin" outside the door burst into tears like a child.

The man who had just refused her request so coldly, pitied her: "If I only knew how to help you, I would do so gladly," he said thoughtfully. "I'll tell you! If it is so important come during the intermission, but on *foot*, without attracting attention, to the rear entrance of the stage—then I'll try to smuggle you in, even if it is only into the passage for the chorus!"

"Oh, sir, I thank you!" said the countess with the look which a lost soul might give to the angel who opened the gates of Paradise.

"I will be there punctually at twelve. Don't you think I

might speak to Herr Freyer during the intermission?" she asked timidly.

A smile of sorrowful pity flitted over the man's face. "Oh, he speaks to no one. We are rejoiced every time that he is able to get through the performance."

"Alas! is he so ill?"

"Yes," replied the man in a tone very low as if he feared the very air might hear, "very ill."

Then he went up the stairs again to his post.

"Where shall we drive now?" asked Martin.

The countess was obliged to reflect a short time ere she answered. "I think it would be best—to try to find a lodging somewhere—" she said hesitatingly, still listening to the sounds from the theatre to learn what was passing within, what scene they were playing—who was speaking? "Drive slowly, Martin—" she begged. She was in no hurry now: "Stop!" she called as Martin started; she had just heard a voice that sounded like *his!* Martin made the horses move very slowly as he drove on. Thus, at the most tardy pace, they passed around the Passion Theatre and then in the opposite direction toward the village. At the exit from the square an official notification was posted: "No Monday performances will be given hereafter; Herr Freyer's health will not permit him to play two days in succession."

The countess pressed her clasped hands upon her quivering heart. "Bear it—it must be borne—it is your own fault, now suffer!"

A stranger in a private carriage, who was looking for lodgings on the day everybody else was going away, was a welcome apparition in the village. At every house to which she drove the occupants who remained in it hastened to welcome her, but none of the rooms pleased her. For a moment she thought of going to the drawing-master's, but there also the quarters were too low and narrow—and she could not deceive herself, the tie between her and Ludwig Gross was sundered—he could not forgive what she had done to his friend; she avoided him as though he were her judge. And besides—she wanted quiet rooms, where an invalid could rest, and these were not easy to find now.

At last she discovered them. A plain house, surrounded

by foliage, in a secluded street, which had only two rooms
on the ground floor, where they could live wholly unseen and
unheard. They were plain apartments, but the ceilings were
not too low, and the sunbeams shone through the chinks of
the green shutters with a warm, yet subdued light. A peaceful, cheerful shelter.

She hired them for an indefinite time, and quickly made
an agreement with the elderly woman to whom they belonged. There was a little kitchen also, and the woman was
willing to do the cooking. So for the next few days at least
she had a comfortable home, and now would to Heaven that
she might not occupy it in despair.

"Well, now Your Highness is nicely settled," said old
Martin, when the housewife opened the shutters, and he
glanced down from his box into the pretty room: "I should
like such a little home myself."

The countess ordered the luggage to be brought in.

"Where shall I put up, Your Highness?"

"Go to the old post-house, Martin!"

"Shan't I take you to the Passion Theatre?"

"No, you heard that I must walk there." Martin shook
his head – this seemed to him almost too humiliating to his
proud mistress. But he did not venture to make any comment, and drove off, pondering over his own thoughts.

It was nine o'clock. Three hours before the long intermission. What might not happen during that time? Could
she wait, would not anxiety kill her or rob her of her senses?
But nothing could be done, she *must* wait. She could not
hasten the hour on which depended life and death, deliverance or doom.—The nocturnal ride, the fright occasioned by
the fiery horses which had upset the carriage and forced her
to walk to the next relay and thus lose a precious hour, her
agitation beside her father's sick bed, now asserted themselves, and she lay down on one of the neat white beds in
the room and used the time to rest and recover her strength
a little. She was only a feeble woman, and the valiant spirit
which had so long created its own law and battled for it,
was too powerful for a woman's feeble frame. It was fortunate that she was compelled to take this rest, or she would
have succumbed. A restless slumber took possession of her

at intervals, from which she started to look at the clock and mournfully convince herself that not more than five minutes had elapsed.

The old woman brought in a cup of coffee, which she pressed upon her. No food had passed her lips since the day before, and the warm drink somewhat revived her. But the rapid throbbing of her heart soon prevented her remaining in bed, and rising, she busied herself a little in unpacking—the first time in her life that she had ever performed such work. She remembered how she had wept ten years ago in the Gross house, because she was left without a maid.

At last the time of torture was over. The clock struck quarter to twelve. She put on her hat, though it was still far too early, but she could not bear to stay in the room. She wished at least to be near the theatre. When she reached the door her breath failed, and she was obliged to stop and calm herself. Then, summoning all her courage, she raised her eyes to Heaven, and murmuring: "In God's name," went to meet the terrible uncertainty.

Now she repented that she did not use the carriage—she could scarcely move. It seemed at every step as if she were sinking into the earth instead of advancing, as if she should never reach the goal, as if the road stretched longer and longer before her. A burning noonday sun blazed down upon her head, the perspiration stood on her forehead and her lips were parched, her feet were swollen and lame from the night-watch at her father's bedside and the exhausting journey which had followed it. At last, with much effort, she reached the theatre. The first part of the performance was just over—throngs of people were pouring out of the sultry atmosphere into the open air and hurrying to get their dinners. But every face wore a look of the deepest emotion and sorrow—on every lip was the one word: "Freyer!" The countess stole through the throngs like a criminal, holding her sunshade lower and drawing her veil more closely over her face. Only let her escape recognition now, avoid meeting any one who would speak to her—this was her mortal dread. If she could only render herself invisible! With the utmost exertion she forced her way through, and now she

27

could at least take breath after the stifling pressure. But
everything around her was now so bare, she was so exposed as
she crossed the broad open space—she felt as though she
were the target for every curious eye among the spectators.
She clenched her teeth in her embarrassment—it was fairly
running the gauntlet. She could no longer think or feel anything except a desire that the earth would swallow her. At
last, tottering, trembling, almost overcome by heat and haste,
she reached the welcome shade on the northern side of the
theatre and stopped, this was her goal. Leaning against the
wall, she half concealed herself behind a post at the door.
Women carrying baskets passed her; they were admitted because they were bringing their husbands' food. They glanced
curiously at the dusty stranger leaning wearily behind the
door. "Who can she be? Somebody who isn't quite right,
that's certain!" The tortured woman read this query on every
face. Here, too, she was in a pillory. Oh, power and rank
—before the wooden fence surrounding the great drama of
Christian thought, you crumble and are nothing save what
you are in and through love!

The Countess Wildenau waited humbly at the door of the
Passion Theatre until the compassionate box-opener should
come to admit her.

How long she stood there she did not know. Burning
drops fell from brow and eyes, but she endured it like a suffering penitent. This was *her* way to the cross.

The clock struck one. The flood was surging back from
the village: "Oh, God, save me!" she prayed, trembling;
her agony had reached its height. But now the man could
not come until everyone was seated.

And Freyer, what was he doing in his dressing-room,
which she knew he never left during an intermission? Was
he resting or eating some strengthening food? Probably one
of the women who passed had taken him something? She
envied the poor women with their baskets because they were
permitted to do their duty.

Then—she scarcely dared to believe it—the box-opener
came running out.

"I've kept you waiting a long time, haven't I? But every
one has had his hands full. Now come quick!"

He slipped stealthily forward, beckoning to her to follow, and led her through by-ways and dark corners, often concealing her with his own person when anyone approached. The signal for raising the curtain was given just as they reached a hidden corner in the proscenium, where the chorus entered. "Sit down there on the stool," he whispered. "You can't see much, it is true, but you can hear everything. It's not a good place, yet it's better than nothing."

"Certainly!" replied the countess, breathlessly; she could not see, coming from the bright sunshine into the dusky space; she sank half fainting on the stool to which he pointed; she was on the stage of the Passion, near Freyer! True, she said to herself, that he must not be permitted to suspect it, lest he should be unable to finish his task; but at least she was near him—her fate was approaching its fulfillment.

"You have done me a priceless service; I thank you." She pressed a bank note into the man's hand.

"No, no; I did it gladly," he answered, noiselessly retreating.

The exhausted woman closed her eyes and rested a few minutes from the torture she had endured. The chorus entered, and opened the drama again, a tableau followed, then the High Priest and Annas appeared in the balcony of his house, Judas soon entered, but everything passed before her like a dream. She could not see what was occurring on her side of the stage.

Thus lost in thought, she leaned back in her dark corner, forgetting the present in what the next hours would bring, failing to hear even the hosannas. But now a voice startled her from her torpor.—"I spake openly to the world; I ever taught in the synagogue and in the temple—"

Merciful Heaven, it was he! She could not see him, the side scenes concealed him; but what a feeling! His voice, which had so often spoken to her words of love, entreaty, warning, lastly of wrath and despair—without heed from her, without waking an echo in her cold heart, now pealed like an angel's message into the dark corner where she sat concealed like a lost soul that had forfeited the sight of the Redeemer! She listened eagerly to the marvellous tones of the words no longer addressed to her' while the speaker's face remained concealed—the face on which, in mortal dread, she might have read the runes engraved by pain, and learned whether they meant life or death ? And yet, at least she was near him ; so near that she thought he must hear the throbbing of her own heart.

"Bear patiently ; do not disturb him in his sacred fulfill-ment of duty.   It will soon be over!"

The play seemed endlessly long to her impatient heart. Christ was dragged from trial to trial.   The mockery, the scourging, the condemnation—the tortured woman shared them all with him as she had done the first time, but to-day it was like a blind person.   She had not yet succeeded in seeing him, he always stood so that she could never catch a glimpse of his face.   Would he hold out? She fancied that his voice grew weaker hour by hour.   And she dared not tend him, dared not offer him any strengthening drink, dared not wipe the moisture from his brow.   She heard the audi-ence weeping and sobbing—the scene of bearing the cross was at hand !

The sky had darkened, and heavy sultry clouds hung low, forming natural soffits to the open front stage, as if Heaven desired to conceal it from the curious gods, that they might not see what was passing to-day.

Mary and John—the women of Jerusalem and Simon of Cyrene assembled, waiting in anxious suspense for the com-ing of the Christ.   Anastasia was again personating Mary, the countess instantly recognized her pure, clear tones, and the meeting in the fields ten years before came back to her mind—not without a throb of jealous emotion.   Now a move-ment among the audience announced the approach of the procession—of the cross ! This time the actors came from the opposite direction and upon the front stage.   Every vein in her body was throbbing, her brain whirled, she struggled to maintain her composure; at last she was to see him for the first time !

" It is he, oh God !—it is my son ! " cried Mary.   Christ stepped upon the stage, laden with the cross.   It was acting no longer, it was reality.

His feet could scarcely support him under the burden, panting for breath, he dragged himself to the proscenium.

The countess uttered a low cry of alarm; she fancied that she was looking into the eyes of a dying man, so ghastly was his appearance. But he had heard the exclamation and, raising his head, looked at her, his emaciated face quivered —he tottered, fell—he *was obliged* to fall; it was in his part.

The countess shuddered—it was too natural!

"He can go no farther," said the executioner. "Here, strengthen yourself." The captain handed him the flask, but he did not take it. "You won't drink? Then drive him forward "

The executioners shook him roughly, but Freyer did not stir—he *ought* not to move yet.

Simon of Cyrene took the cross on his shoulders, and now the Christ should have risen, but he still lay prostrate. The cue was given—repeated—a pause followed—a few of the calmer ones began to improvise, the man who was personating the executioner stooped and shook him, another tried to raise him—in vain. An uneasy movement ran through the audience—the actors gathered around and gazed at him. "He is dead! It has come upon us!" ran in accents of horror from lip to lip.

An indescribable confusion followed. The audience rose tumultuously from the seats. Caiaphas, the burgomaster, ordered in a low tone: "To the central stage—every one! Quick—and then drop the curtain!" But no one heard him: He bent over the senseless figure. "It is only an attack of faintness," he called to the audience, but the excitement could no longer be allayed—all were pressing across the orchestra to the stage.

The countess could bear it no longer—rank and station, the thousands of curious eyes to which she would expose herself were all forgotten—there is a cosmopolitanism which unites mortals in a common brotherhood more closely than anything else—a mutual sorrow.

"Freyer, Freyer!" she shrieked in tones that thrilled every nerve of the bystanders: "Do not die—oh, do not die!" Rushing upon the stage, she threw herself on her knees beside the unconscious form.

"Ladies and gentlemen—I must beg you to clear the stage "—shouted Caiaphas to the throng, and turning to the

countess, whom he recognized, added: "Countess Wildenau
—I can permit no stranger to enter, I *must* beg you to withdraw."

She drew herself up to her full height, composed and
lofty—an indescribable dignity pervaded her whole bearing:
"I have a right to be here—I am his wife!"

CHAPTER XXXIX.

STATIONS OF SORROW.

"I am his wife!" Heaven and earth have heard it. She
had conquered. The tremendous deed, fear of which had led
her to the verge of crime—love had now done in a *single* moment without conflict or delay. There was joy in heaven and
on earth over the penitent sinner! And all the viewless powers
which watch the way to the cross, wherever any human being
treads it; all the angels, the guardian spirits of the now interrupted Play hastened to aid the new Magdalene, that she
might climb the Mount of Calvary to the Hill of Golgotha.
And as if the heavenly hosts were rushing down to accompany
this bearer of the cross a gust of wind suddenly swept through
the open space across the stage and over the audience, and the
palms rustled in the breeze, the palaces of Jerusalem tottered,
and the painted curtains swayed in the air. This one gust of
wind had rent the threatening clouds so that the sun sent
down a slanting brilliant ray like the dawn of light when chaos
began to disappear!

A light rain which, in the golden streaks, glittered like
dusty pearls fell, settling the dust and dispelling the sultriness of the parched earth.

Silence had fallen upon the people on the stage and in
the audience, and as a scorched flower thirstily expands to
the cooling dew, the sick man's lips parted and eagerly inhaled the damp, refreshing air.

"Oh—he lives!" said the countess in a tone as sweet as
any mother ever murmured at the bedside of a child whom
she had believed dead, any bride on the breast of her wounded
lover.

" He lives, oh, he lives!" all the spectators repeated.

Meanwhile the physician had come and examined the sufferer, who had been placed on a couch formed of cloaks and shawls: " It is a severe attack of heart disease. The patient must be taken to better lodgings than he has hitherto occupied. This condition needs the most careful nursing to avoid the danger. I have repeatedly called attention to it, but always in vain."

" It will be different now, Doctor!" said the countess. " I have already secured rooms, and beg to be allowed to move him there."

" The Countess !" she suddenly heard a voice exclaim behind her—and when she glanced around, Ludwig Gross stood before her in speechless amazement.

" Can it be ? I have just arrived by the train from Munich —but I did not see—"

" I suppose so—I drove here last night. But do not call me Countess any longer, Herr Gross—my name is Magdalena Freyer." The drawing-master made no reply, but knelt beside the sick man, who was beginning to breathe faintly and bent over him a long time: " If only it is not too late !" he muttered bitterly, still unappeased.

The burgomaster approached the countess and held out his hand, gazing into her eyes with deep emotion. "Such an act can never be too late. Even if it can no longer benefit the individual, it is still a contribution to the moral treasure of the world," he said consolingly.

" I thank you. You are very kind !" she answered, tears springing to her eyes.

A litter had now been obtained and the physician ordered the sufferer to be lifted gently and laid upon it: " We will first take him to the dressing-room, and give him some food before carrying him home."

The countess had mentioned the street: " It is some little distance to the house."

The command was obeyed and the litter was carried to the dressing-room. The friends followed with the countess. On the way a woman timidly joined her and gazed at her with large, sparkling eyes: " I don't know whether you remember me? I only wanted to tell you how glad I am that you are here? Oh, how well he has deserved it!"

"Mary!" said the countess, shamed and overpowered by the charm of this most unselfish soul, clasping both her hands: "Mary—Mother of God!" And her head sank on her companion's virgin breast. Anastasia passed her arm affectionately around her and supported her as they moved on.

"Yes, we two must hold together, like Mary and Magdalene! We will aid each other—it is very hard, but our two saints had no easier lot   And if I can help in any way—" They had reached the dressing-room, the group paused, the countess pressed Anastasia's hand: "Yes, we will hold together, Mary!" Then she hastened to her husband's side— but the doctor motioned to her to keep at a distance that the sudden sight of her might not harm the sick man when he recovered his consciousness. He felt his pulse: "Scarcely fifty beats—I must give an injection of ether."

He drew the little apparatus from his pocket, thrust the needle into Freyer's arm and injected a little of the stimulating fluid. The bystanders awaited the result in breathless suspense: "Bring wine, eggs, bouillon, anything you can get —only something strong, which will increase the action of the heart."

The drawing-master hurried off. The pastor, who had just heard of the occurrence, now entered: "Is the sacrament to be administered ?" he asked.

"No, there is no fear of so speedy an end," the physician answered. "Rest is the most imperative necessity." The burgomaster led the pastor to the countess: "This is Herr Freyer's wife, who has just publicly acknowledged her marriage," he said in a low tone: "Countess Wildenau!"

"Ah, ah—these are certainly remarkable events. Well, I can only hope that God will reward such love," the priest replied with delicate tact: "You have made a great sacrifice, Countess."

"Oh, if you knew—" she paused. "Hark—he is recovering his consciousness!" She clasped her hands and bent forward to listen—"may God help us now."

"How do you feel, Herr Freyer?" asked the doctor.

"Tolerably well, Doctor! Are you weeping, Mary? Did

I frighten you ?" He beckoned to her and she hastened to his side.

The countess' eyes grew dim as he whispered something to Anastasia.

This was the torture of the damned—Mary might be near him, his first glance, his first words were hers, while she, his wife, stood banished, at a distance! And she had made him suffer this torture for years—without compassion. "Oh, God, Thou art just, and Thy scales weigh exactly!" But the all-wise Father does not only punish—He also shows mercy.

"Where is she ?" Anastasia repeated his words in a clear, joyous tone: "You thought you saw her in the passage through which the chorus passed. Oh, you must have been mistaken!" she added at a sign from the physician.

"Yes, you are right, how could she be there—it is impossible."

The countess tried to move forward, but the physician authoritatively stopped her.

The burgomaster gently approached him. "My dear Freyer—what could I do for you, have you no wish ?"

"Nothing except to die! I would willingly have played until the end of the performances—for your sake—but I am content."

The drawing-master brought in the food which the physician had ordered.

The latter went to him with a glass of champagne. "Drink this, Herr Freyer; it will do you good, and then you can eat something."

But the sick man did not touch the glass: "Oh, no, I will take nothing more."

"Why not ? You must eat something, or you will not recover."

"I cannot."

"Certainly you can."

"Very well, I *will* not."

"Freyer," cried Ludwig beseechingly, "don't be obstinate —what fancy have you taken into your head ?" And he again vainly offered the strengthening draught.

"Shall I live if I drink it ?" asked Freyer.

"Certainly."

"Then I will not take it."

"Not even if I entreat you, Freyer?" asked the burgo-master.

"Oh, do not torture me—do not force me to live longer!" pleaded Freyer with a heart-rending expression. "If you knew what I have suffered—you would not grudge the release which God now sends me! I have vowed to be faithful to my duty until death—did I not, sexton, on Daisenberger's grave? I have held out as long as I could—now let me die quietly."

"Oh, my friend!" said the sexton, "must we lose you?" The strong man was weeping like a child. "Live for *us*, if not for yourself."

"No, sexton, if God calls me, I must not linger—for I have still another duty. I have *lived* for you—I must *die* for another."

"But, Herr Freyer!" said the pastor kindly, "suppose that this other person should not be benefitted by your death?"

Freyer looked as if he did not understand him.

"If this other of whom you speak—had come—to nurse and stay with you?" the pastor continued.

Freyer raised himself a little—a blissful presentiment flitted over his face like the coming of dawn.

"Suppose that your eyes did *not* deceive you?" the burgo-master now added gently.

"Am I not dreaming—was it true—was it possible?"

"If you don't excite yourself and will keep perfectly calm," said the physician, "I will bring—your wife!"

"My — wife? You are driving me mad. I have no wife."

"No wife—you have *no wife?*" cried a voice as if from the depths of an ocean of love and anguish, as the unhappy woman who had forced her own husband to disown her, sank sobbing before him.

A cry—"my dove!" and his head drooped on her breast.

A breathless silence pervaded the room. Every one's hands were clasped in silent prayer. No one knew whether the moment was fraught with life or death.

But it was to bring life—for the Christus must not die on the way to the cross, and Mary Magdalene must still climb to its foot—the last, steepest portion—that her destiny might be fulfilled.

The husband and wife were whispering together. The others modestly drew back.

"And you wish to die? It was not enough that you vanished from my life like a shadow—you wish to go out of the world also?" she sobbed. "Do you believe that I could then find rest on earth or in Heaven?"

"Oh, dear one, I am happy. Let me die—I have prayed for it always! God has mercifully granted it. When I am out of the world you will be a widow, and can marry another without committing a sin."

"Oh, Heaven—Joseph! I will marry no other—I love no one save you."

He smiled mournfully: "You love me now because I am dying—had I lived, you would have gone onward in the path of sin—and been lost. No, my child, I must die, that you may learn, by my little sacrifice, to understand the great atonement of Christ. I must sacrifice myself for you, as Christ sacrificed himself for the sins of mankind."

"Oh, that is not needed. God has taken the will for the deed, and given it the same power. Your lofty, patient suffering has conquered me. You need not die. I mistook you for what you were not—a God, and did not perceive what you *were*. Now I do know it. Forgive my folly. To save me you need be nothing save a man—a genuine, noble, lovable man, as you are—then no God will be required."

"Do you believe that?" Freyer looked at her with a divine expression: "Do you believe you could be content with a *mortal man?* No, my child, the same disappointment would follow as before. The flame that blazes within your soul does not feed upon earthly matter. You need a God, and your great heart will not rest until you have found Him. Therefore be comforted: The false Christ will vanish and the true one will rise from His grave."

"No, do not wrong me so, do not die, let me not atone for my sin to the dead, but to the living! Oh, do not be cruel—do not punish me so harshly. You are silent! You are growing paler still! Ah, you will go and leave me standing *alone* half way along the road, unable either to move forward or back! Joseph, I have broken every bond with the duke, have cast aside everything which separated us—have become a poor, helpless woman, and you will abandon me—now, when I have given you my whole existence, when I am nothing but your wife."

Freyer raised himself.

"Give me the wine—now I long to live." A universal movement of delight ran through the group of friends, and the countess held the foaming cup to his lips and supported his head with one hand, that he might drink. Then she gave him a little food and arranged him in a more comfortable position. "Come, let your wife nurse you!" she said so tenderly that all the listeners were touched. Then she laid a cooling bandage on his brow. "Ah, that does me good!" he said, but his eyes rested steadily on hers and he seemed to be alluding to something other than the external remedies, though these quickly produced their effect. His breathing gradually became more regular, his eyes closed, weakness asserted itself, but he slept soundly and quietly.

The physician withdrew to soothe the strangers waiting outside by an encouraging report. Only Freyer's friends and the pastor remained. The countess rose from beside the sleeper's couch and stretched her arms towards Heaven: "Lend him to me, Merciful God! I have forfeited my right to him—I say it in the presence of all these witnesses—but be merciful and lend him to me long enough for me to atone for my sin—that I may not be doomed to the torture of eternal remorse!" She spoke in a low tone in order not to rouse the slumberer, but in a voice which could be distinctly heard by the others. Her hands were clasped convulsively, her eyes were raised as if to pierce to the presence of God—her noble bearing expressed the energy of despair, striving with eternity for the space of a moment.

"Oh, God—oh, God, leave him with me! Hold back Thy avenging hand—grant a respite. Omnipotent One, first witness my atonement—first try whether I may not be saved by mercy! Friends, friends, pray with me!"

She clasped their hands as if imploring help. Her strength was failing. Trembling, she sank beside Ludwig, and pressed her forehead, bedewed with cold perspiration, against his arm.

All bared their heads and prayed in a low tone. Madeleine's breast heaved in mortal anguish and, almost stifled by her suppressed tears, she could only falter, half unconsciously: "Have pity upon us!"

Meanwhile the doctor had made all necessary preparations and was waiting for the patient to wake in order to remove him to his home.

The murmured prayers had ceased and the friends gathered silently around the bed. The countess again knelt beside the invalid, clasping him in a gentle embrace. Her tears were now checked lest she might disturb him, but they continued to flow in her heart. Her lips rested on his hand in a long kiss—the hand which had once supported and guided her now lay pale and thin on the coverlet, as if it would never more have strength to clasp hers with a loving pressure.

"Are you weeping, dear wife?"

That voice! She raised her head, but could not meet the eyes which gazed at her so tenderly. Dared *she*, the condemned one, enjoy the bliss of that look? No, never! And, without raising an eyelash, she hid her guilty brow with unutterable tenderness upon his breast. The feeble hand was raised and gently stroked her cheek, touching it as lightly as a withered leaf.

"Do not weep!" he whispered with the voice of a consoling angel: "Be calm—God is good, He will be merciful to us also."

Oh, trumpet of the Judgment Day, what is thy blare to the sinner, compared to the gentle words of pardoning love from a wounded breast?

The countess was overpowered by the mild, merciful judgment.—

A living lane had formed in front of the theatre. He was to be carried home, rumor said, and the people were waiting in a dense throng to see him. At last a movement ran through the ranks. "He is coming! Is he alive? Yes, they say he is!"

Slowly and carefully the men bore out the litter on which he lay, pale and motionless as a dead man. The pastor walked on one side, and on the other, steadying his head, the

countess. She could scarcely walk, but she did not avert her
eyes from him.

As on the way to Golgotha. low sobs greeted the little
procession.   " Oh, dear, poor fellow! Ah, just one look, one
touch of the hand," the people pleaded.   " Wait just one
moment."

As if by a single impulse the bearers halted and the people pressed forward with throbbing hearts, modestly, reverently touching the hanging coverlet, and gazing at him with
tearful eyes full of unutterable grief.

The countess, with a beautiful impulse of humanity, gently
drew his hand from under the wraps and held it to the sorrowing spectators who had waited so long, that they might kiss
it—and every one who could get near enough eagerly drank
from the proffered beaker of love.   Grateful eyes followed the
countess and she felt their benediction with the joy of the
saints when God lends their acts the power of divine grace.
She was now a beggar, yet never before had she been rich
enough to bestow such alms: "Yes, kiss his hand—he deserves it!" she whispered, and her eyes beamed with a love
which was not of this earth, yet which blended *her*, the world,
and everything it contained into a single, vast, fraternal community!

Freyer smiled at her—and now she bore the sweet, tender
gaze, for she felt as if a time might come when she would
again deserve it.

At last they reached the pretty quiet house where she had
that morning hired lodgings for him and herself.   Mourning
love had followed him to the spot, the throng had increased
so that the bearers could scarcely get in with the litter. " Farewell—poor sufferer, may God be with you," fell from every
lip as he was borne in and the door closed behind him.

The spacious room on the lower floor received the invalid.
The landlady had hurriedly prepared the bed and he was laid
in it.   As the soft pillows arranged by careful hands yielded
to the weary form, and his wife bent over him, supporting his
head on her arm—he glanced joyously around the circle, unable to think or say anything except: " Oh, how comfortable
I am ! " They turned away to hide their emotion.

The countess laid her head on the pillow beside him, no longer restraining her tears, and murmuring in his ear: "Angel, you modest, forgiving, loving angel!" She was silent —forcing herself to repress the language of her heart, for the cry of her remorse might disturb the feeble invalid. Yet he felt what moved her, he had always read her inmost soul so long as she loved him—not until strangers came between them did he fail to comprehend her. Now he felt what she must suffer in her remorse and pitied her torture, he thought only of how he might console her. But this moved her more than all the reproaches he had a right to make, for the greater, the more noble his nature revealed itself to be the greater her guilt became!

The friends were to take turns in helping the countess watch the invalid through the night, and now left him. The doctor said that there was no immediate danger and went away to get more medicines. When all had gone, she knelt beside the bed and said softly, "Now I am yours! I do not ask whether you will forgive me, for I see that you have already done so—I ask only whether you will again take the condemned, sin-laden woman to your heart? In my deed to-day I chose the fate of poverty. I can offer you nothing more in worldly wealth, I can only provide you with a simple home, work for you, nurse you, and atone by lifelong love and fidelity for the wrong I have done you. Will you be content with that?"

Freyer drew her toward him with all his feeble strength. Tears of unutterable happiness were trickling down his cheeks. "I thank Thee, God, Thou has given her to me to-day for the first time! Come, my wife—place your fate trustfully in God's hands and your dear heart in mine, and all will be well. He will be merciful and suffer me to live a few years that I may work for you, not you for me. Oh, blissful words, work for my wife, they make me well again. And now, while we are alone, the first sacred kiss of conjugal love!"

He tried to raise his head, but she pressed it with gentle violence back upon the pillow. "No, you must keep perfectly quiet. Imagine that you are a marble statue—and let me kiss you. Remain cold and let all the fervor of a repentant, loving heart pour itself upon you." She stooped and touched his pale mouth gently, almost timidly, with her quivering lips.

"Oh, that was again an angel's kiss!" he murmured, clasping his hands over the head bowed in penitent humility.

CHAPTER XL.

NEAR THE GOAL.

FROM that hour Magdalena Freyer never left her husband's bedside. Though friends came in turn to share the night-watches, she remained with them. After a few days the doctor said that unless an attack of weakness supervened, the danger was over for the present, though he did not conceal from her that the disease was incurable. She clasped her hands and answered: "I will consider every day that I am permitted to keep him a boon, and submissively accept what God sends."

After that time she always showed her husband a smiling face, and he—perfectly aware of his condition—practiced the same loving deception toward her. Thus they continued to live in the salutary school of the most rigid self-control—she, bearing with dignity a sad fate for which she herself was to blame—he in the happiness of that passive heroism of Christianity, which goes with a smile to meet death for others! An atmosphere of cheerfulness surrounded this sick-bed, which can be understood only by one who has watched for months beside the couch of incurable disease, and felt the gratitude with which every delay of the catastrophe, every apparent improvement is greeted—the quiet delight afforded by every little relief given the beloved sufferer, every smile which shows us he feels somewhat easier.

This cup of anguish the penitent woman now drained to the dregs. True, a friendly genius always stood beside it to comfort her: the hope that, though not fully recovered, he might still be spared to her. "How many thousands who have heart disease, with care and nursing live to grow old." This thought sustained her. Yet the ceaseless anxiety and sleepless nights exhausted her strength. Her cheeks grew hollow, dark circles surrounded her eyes, but she did not heed it.

"I still please my husband!" she said smiling, in reply to all entreaties to spare herself on account of her altered appearance.

"My dove!" Freyer said one evening, when Ludwig came for the night-watch: "Now I must show a husband's authority and command you to take some rest, you cannot go on in this way."

"Oh! never mind me—if I should die for you, what would it matter? Would it not be a just atonement?"

"No—that would be no atonement," he said tenderly, pushing back the light fringe of curls that shaded her brow, as if he wished to read her thoughts on it: "My child, you must *live* for me—that is your atonement. Do you think you would do anything good if you expiated your fault by death and said: 'There you have my life for yours, now we are quits, you have no farther claim upon me!' Would that be love, my dove?"

He drew her gently toward him: "Or would you prefer that we should be quits *thus*, and that I should desire no other expiation from you than your death?" She threw her arms around him, clasping him in a closer and closer embrace. There was no need of speech, the happy, blissful throbbing of her heart gave sufficient answer. He kissed her on the forehead: "Now sleep, beloved wife and rest—do it for my sake, that I may have a fresh, happy wife!"

She rose as obediently as a child, but it was hard for her, and she nodded longingly from the door as if a boundless, hopeless distance already divided them.

"Ludwig!" said Freyer, gazing after her in delight: "Ludwig, *is* this love?"

"Yes, by Heaven!" replied his friend, deeply moved: "Happy man, I would bear all your sorrows—for one hour like this!"

"Have you now forgiven what she did to me?"

"Yes, from my very soul!"

"Magdalena," cried Freyer. "Come in again—you must know it before you sleep—Ludwig is reconciled to you."

"Ludwig," said the countess: "my strict, noble friend, I thank you."

Leading him to the invalid, she placed their hands together. "Now we are again united, and everything is just as it was ten years ago—only I have become a different person, and a new and higher life is beginning for me."

She pressed a kiss upon the brow of her husband and friend, as if to seal a vow, then left them alone.

"Oh, Ludwig, if I could see you so happy!"

"Do not be troubled—whoever has experienced this hour with you, needs nothing for himself," he answered, an expression of the loftiest, most unselfish joy on his pallid face.

The countess, before retiring, sent for Martin who was still in Oberammergau, awaiting her orders, and went out into the garden that Freyer might not hear them talking in the next room. "Martin," she said with quiet dignity, though there was a slight tremor in her voice, "it is time for me to give some thought to worldly matters. During the last few days I could do nothing but devote myself to the sick bed. Drive home, my good Martin, and give the carriage and horses to the Wildenaus. Tell them what has happened, if they do not yet know it, I cannot write now. Meanwhile, you faithful old servant, tell them to take all I have—my jewels, my palace, my whole private fortune. Only I should like—for the sake of my sick husband—to have them leave me, for humanity's sake, enough to get him what he needs for his recovery!" here her voice failed.

"Countess—"

"Oh, don't call me that!"

"Yes—for the countess will always be what she is, even as Herr Freyer's wife! I only wanted to say, Your Highness, that I wouldn't do that. If I were you, I wouldn't give *them* a single kind word. I'll take back the carriage and horses and say that they can have everything which belongs to you. But I won't beg for my Countess! I think it would be less disgrace if you should condescend to accept something from a plain man like myself, who would consider it an honor and whom you needn't thank! I—" he laughed awkwardly: "I only want to say, if you won't take offence—that I bargained for a little house to-day. But I did it in your name, so that

Your Highness needn't be ashamed to live with me! I haven't any kith and kin and—and it will belong to you."

" Martin, Martin!" the proud woman humbly bent her head. " Be it so! You shall help me, if all else abandons me. I will accept it as a loan from you. I can paint—I will try to earn something, perhaps from one of the fashion journals, to which I have always subscribed. The maid once told me I might earn my living by it—it was a prophecy! So I can, God willing, repay you at some future day."

" Oh, we won't talk about that!" cried Martin joyously, kissing the countess' hands.

" If I may have a little room under the roof for myself— we'll call it the interest. And I have something to spare besides, for—you must eat, too."

The countess covered her face with her trembling hands.

" Now I'll drive home and in Your Highness' name throw carriage, horses, and all the rest of the rubbish at the Wildenaus' feet—then I'll come back and bring something nice for our invalid which can't be had here — and my livery, for Sundays and holidays, so that we can make a good appearance! And I'll look after the garden and house, and—do whatever else you need. Oh, I've never been so happy in my life!"

He left her, and the countess stood gazing after him a long time, deeply shamed by the simple fidelity of the old man, who wished to wear her livery and be her servant, while he was really her benefactor: In truth—high or low—human nature is common to all. Martin returned: " Doesn't Your Highness wish to bid farewell to the horses? Shan't I drive past, or will it make you feel too badly?"

" Beautiful creatures," a tone of melancholy echoed in her voice as she spoke: " No, Martin, I don't want to see them again."

" Yes, yes—!" Martin had understood her, and pitied her more than for anything else, for it seemed to him the hardest of sacrifices to part with such beautiful horses.

The countess remained alone in the little garden. The stars were shining above her head. She thought of the diamond stars which she had once flung to Freyer in false atonement, to place in the dead child's coffin—if she had

them now to use their value to support her sick husband—
that would be the fitting atonement.

"Only do not let *him* starve, oh, God! If I were forced to
see him starve! Oh, God!—spare me that, if it can be!"
she prayed, her eyes uplifted with anxious care to the glittering star-strewn vault.

"How is he?" a woman's figure suddenly emerged from
the shadow at her side. ·

"Oh, Mary—Anastasia!"

"How is he?"

"Better, I think! He was very cheerful this evening!—"

"And you, Frau Freyer—how is it with you? It is hard, is
it not? There are things to which we must become accustomed."

"Yes."

"I can understand. But do not lose confidence—God is
always with us. And—I will pray to the Virgin Mary, whom
I have so often personated! But if there is need of anything
where *human power* can aid, I may help, may I not?"

"Mary—angel, be my teacher—sister!"

"No, *mother!*" said Anastasia smiling: "For if Freyer
is my son, you must be my daughter. Oh, you two poor
hearts, I am and shall now remain your mother, Mary!"

"Mother Mary!"—the countess repeated, and the two
women held each other in a loving embrace.— —

The week was drawing to a close, and the burgomaster
was now obliged to consider the question of the distribution
of parts. He found the patient out of bed and wearing a
very cheerful, hopeful expression.

"I don't know, Herr Freyer, whether I can venture to
discuss my important business with you," he began timidly.

"Oh—I understand—you wish to know when I can play
again? Next Sunday."

"You are not in earnest?" said the burgomaster, almost
startled.

"Not in earnest? Herr Burgomaster, what would be the
value of all my oaths, if I should now retreat like a coward?
Do you think I would break my word to you a second time,
so long as I had breath in my body?"

"Certainly not, so long as it is in your power to hold out.

But this time you *cannot !* Ask the doctor—he will not allow it so soon."

" Am I to ask *him*, when the question concerns the most sacred duty ? I will consult him about my life—but my duties are more than my life. Only thus can I atone for the old sin which ten years ago made me a renegade."

" And you say this now—when you are so happy ? "

" Herr Burgomaster," replied Freyer with lofty serenity: " A man who has once been so happy and so miserable as I, learns to view life from a different standpoint! No joy enraptures, no misfortune terrifies him. Everything to which we give these names is fluctuating, and only *one* happiness is certain: to do one's duty—until death ! "

" Herr Freyer! That is a noble thought, but if your wife should hear it—would she agree ? "

" Surely, for she thinks as I do—if she did not, we should never have been united—she would never have cast aside wealth, rank, power, and all worldly advantages to live with me in exile. Do you believe she did so for any earthly cause ? She thinks so—but I know better: The cross allured her— as it does all who come in contact with it."

" What are you saying about the cross ? " asked the countess, entering the room: " Good-morning, Friend Bur-gomaster ! "

" My wife ! He will not believe that you would permit me to play the Christus again—even should it cost my life ? "

The countess turned pale with terror. " Oh, Heaven, are you thinking of doing so ? "

" Yes "—replied the burgomaster: " He will not be dis-suaded from it ! "

" Joseph ! " said the countess mournfully: " Will you in-flict this grief upon me—now, when you have scarcely re-covered ? "

" I assure you that I have played the Christus when I felt far worse than I do now—thanks to your self-sacrificing care, dear wife."

Tears filled the countess' eyes, and she remained silent.

" My dove, do we not understand each other ? "

" Yes "—she said after a long, silent struggle: " Do it, my beloved husband—give yourself to God, as I resign you to

Him. He has only loaned you to me, I dare not keep you from Him, if He desires to show Himself again to the world in your form! I will cherish and tend and watch over you, that you may endure it! And when you are taken down from the cross, I will rub your strained limbs and bedew your burning brow with the tears of all the sorrows Mary and Magdalene suffered for the Crucified One, and—when you have rested and again raise your eyes to mine with a smile, I will rest your head upon my breast in the blissful feeling that you are no God Who will ascend to Heaven—but a man, a tender, beloved man, and—*my own*. Oh, God cannot destroy such happiness, and if He does, He will only draw you to Himself, that I may therefore long the more fervently for you, for Him, Who is the source of *all* love—then—" her voice was stifled by tears as she laid her head on his breast—"then your wife will not murmur, but wait silently and patiently till she can follow you." Leaning on his breast, she wept softly, clasping him in her arms that he might not be torn from her.

"Dear wife," he answered gently, and the wonderfully musical voice trembled with the most sacred emotion, "we will accept whatever God sends—loyal to the cross—you and I, beloved, high-hearted woman! Do not weep, my dove! Being loyal to the cross does not mean only to be patient—it means also to be strong! Does not the soldier go bravely to death for an earthly king, and should not I joyfully peril my life for my *God?*"

"Yes, my husband you are right, I will be strong. Go, then, holy warrior, into the battle for the ideal and put yourself at the disposal of your brave fellow combatants!" She slowly withdrew her arms from his neck as if taking a long, reluctant farewell.

The burgomaster resolutely approached. "We people of Ammergau must bow to this sacred zeal. This is indeed a grandeur which conquers death! Whoever sees this effect of our modest Play on souls like yours cannot be mistaken in believing that the power which works such miracles does not emanate from men, and must proceed from a God. But as He is a God of love, He will not accept your sacrifice. Freyer must not take the part which might cost him his life.

We will find a Christus elsewhere and thus manage for this time."

Freyer fixed his eyes mournfully on the ground. " Now the crown has indeed fallen from my head! God has no longer accepted me—I am shut out from the sacred work ! "

The burgomaster placed his wife in his arms : " Let it be your task now to guard this soul and lead it to its destination —this, too, is a sacred work ! "

" Yes, and amen ! " said Freyer.

* *

The ex-countess and the former God, both divested of their temporary dignity, verified his words, attaining in humility true dignity ! Freyer rallied under the care of his beloved wife, and they used the respite allotted to them by leading a life filled with labor, sacrifice, and gratitude toward God.

" You ask me, dear friend," the countess wrote a year later to the Duke of Barnheim, " whether you can assist me in any way ? I thank you for the loyal friendship, but must decline the noble offer. Contentment does not depend upon what we have, but what we need, and I have that, for my wants are few. This is because I have obtained blessings, which formerly I never possessed and which render me independent of everything else. Much as God has taken from me, He has bestowed in exchange three precious gifts : contempt for the vanities of the world, appreciation of the little pleasures of life, and recognition of the real worth of human beings. I am not even so poor as you imagine. My faithful old Martin, who will never leave me, helped me out of the first necessity. Afterwards the Wildenaus' were induced to give up my private property, jewels, dresses, and works of art, and their value proved sufficient to pay Martin for the little house he had purchased for me and to establish for my husband a small shop for the sale of wood-carving, so that he need not be dependent upon others. When he works industriously—which he is only too anxious to do at the cost of his delicate health—we can live without anxiety, though, of course, very simply. I know how many of my former acquaintances would shudder at the thought of such a prosaic existence! To them I would say that I have learned not to seek poetry in life, but to place it there. Yes, tell the mocking world that Countess Wildenau lives by her husband's labor and is not ashamed of it! My friend! To throw away a fortune for love of a woman is nothing—but to toil year in and year out, with tireless fidelity and sacrifice, to earn a wife's daily bread in the sweat of one's brow, *is* something! Do you know what it is to a woman to owe her life daily to her beloved husband? An indescribable happiness! You, my friend, would have bestowed a principality upon me, and I should have accepted it as my rightful tribute, without owing you any special gratitude—but the hand which *toils* for me I kiss every evening with a thrill of grateful reverence.

"So do not grieve for me! Wed the lovable and charming Princess Amalie of whom you wrote, and should you ever came with your young wife into the vicinity of the little house surrounded by rustling firs, under the shadow of the Kofel, I should be cordially glad to welcome you.

"Farewell! May you be as happy, my noble friend, as you deserve, and leave to me my poverty and my *wealth*. You see that the phantom has become reality—the ideal is attained. "Your old friend "MAGDALENA FREYER."

When the duke received this letter his valet saw him, for the first time in his life, weep bitterly.

CONCLUSION.

FROM ILLUSION TO TRUTH.

For ten years God granted the loving wife her husband's life, it seemed as if he had entirely recovered. At last the day came when He required it again. For the third time the community offered Freyer the part of the Christus. He was still a handsome man, and spite of his forty-eight years, as slender as a youth, while his spiritual expression, chaste and lofty— rendered him more than ever an ideal representative of Christ. God bestowed upon him the full cup of the perfection of his destiny, and it was completed as he had longed. Not on a sickbed, succumbing to lingering disease—but high on the cross, as victor over pain and death. God had granted him the grace of at last completing the task—he had held out this time until the final performance—then, when they took him down from the cross for the last time under the falling leaves, amid the first snow of the late autumn—he did not wake again. On the cross the noble heart had ceased to beat, he had entered into the peace of Him Whom he personated—passed from illusion to truth—from the *copy* to the *prototype*.

Never did mortal die a happier death, never did a more beautiful smile of contentment rest upon the face of a corpse.

"It is finished! You have done in your way what your model did in His, you have sealed the sacred lesson of love by your death, my husband!" said the pallid woman who pressed the last kiss upon his lips.

The semblance had become reality, and Mary Magdalene was weeping beside her Redeemer's corpse.

On the third day after the crucifixion, when the true Christ had risen, Freyer was borne to his grave.

But, like the phœnix from its ashes, on that day the real Christ rose from the humble sepulchre for the penitent.

"When wilt thou appear to me in the spring garden, Redeeming Love?" she had once asked. Now she was—in the autumn garden—beside the grave of all happiness.

When the coffin had been lowered and the pall-bearers approached the worn, drooping widow, the burgomaster asked: "Where do you intend to live now, Madame?"

"Where, except in Ammergau, here—where his foot has marked for me the path to God? Oh, my Gethsemane!"

"But," said the pastor, "will you exile yourself forever in this quiet village? Do you not wish to return to your own circle and the world of culture? You have surely atoned sufficiently."

"Atoned? No, your Reverence, not atoned, for the *highest happiness* is no atonement—expiation is beginning *now*." She turned toward the Christ which hung on the wall of the church, not far from the grave, and extending her arms toward it murmured: "Now I have *nothing* save *Thee!* Thou hast conquered —idea of Christianity, thy power is eternal!"— — — —

The cloud of tears hung heavily over Ammergau, falling from time to time in damp showers.

Evening had closed in.   Through the lighted windows of the ground floor of a little house, surrounded by rustling pines, two women were visible, Mary and Magdalena.   The latter was kneeling before the "Mother" whose clasped hands were laid upon her head in comfort and benediction.

The lamps in the low-roofed houses of the village were gradually lighted.   The peasants again sat in their ragged blouses on the carvers' benches, toiling, sacrificing, and bearing their lot of poverty and humility, proud in the consciousness that every ten years there will be a return of the moment which strips off the yoke and lays the purple on their shoulders, the moment when in their midst the miracle is again performed which spreads victoriously throughout a penitent world—the moment which brings to weary, despairing humanity peace and atonement—*on the cross.*

THE END.

www.ingramcontent.com/pod-product-compliance
Lightning Source LLC
Chambersburg PA
CBHW022019110726
47901CB00006B/1591